1—142

On the Job

On the Job

Fiction About Work by
Contemporary American Writers

Edited and with an Introduction by
William O'Rourke

Vintage Books
A Division of Random House, New York

VINTAGE BOOKS EDITION, March 1977
First Edition
Copyright © 1972, 1977 by William O'Rourke

"Works and Ways" Copyright © 1977 by Alan Goldfein.
Reprinted by permission of the author.

Library of Congress Cataloging in Publication Data
Main entry under title:

On the job.

1. American fiction—20th century. 2. Work—
Fiction. I. O'Rourke, William.
PZ1.05864   [PS648.W63]   813'.5'080355   76–62487
ISBN 0–394–72083–0

Manufactured in the United States of America

Grateful acknowledgment is made to the following for permission to reprint
previously published material:

Black Sparrow Press (Santa Barbara, Ca.): Selection from pages 9–32 of *Post
Office* by Charles Bukowski. Copyright © 1974 by Charles Bukowski.

Coward, McCann & Geoghegan, Inc.: Selection from pages 45–54 of *Dickie's
List* by Ann Birstein. Copyright © 1973 by Ann Birstein.

John Cushman Associates, Inc.: "Widow Water" by Frederick Busch. Copyright
© 1974 by Frederick Busch. First published in The *Paris Review*, #59, 1974.

Doubleday & Company, Inc.: "I Am Not Luis Beech-Nut" by Rosellen Brown.
Reprinted from *Street Games* by Rosellen Brown. Copyright © 1974 by Rosellen
Brown.

Farrar, Straus & Giroux, Inc.: Selection from pages 119–128 of *Max Jamison* by
Wilfred Sheed. Copyright © 1970 by Wilfred Sheed; also, "The Death of Me"
from *Idiots First* by Bernard Malamud. Copyright © 1963 by Bernard Malamud.

Harcourt Brace Jovanovich, Inc.: Selection from pages 57–63 of *The Pawnbroker* by Edward Lewis Wallant. Copyright © 1961 by Edward Lewis Wallant.

Harper & Row Publishers, Inc.: Selection from pages 74–82 of *Turkey Hash* by
Craig Nova. Copyright © 1972 by Craig Nova; also, Chapter 9 (pages 107–116)

For my parents

(How could mere toil align thy choiring strings!)

—Hart Crane, "To Brooklyn Bridge"

☆☆☆ Editor's Note

On the Job is an anthology that presents the way we work in America as seen through the eyes of some of our foremost contemporary fiction writers. It is not a historical study of work in modern fiction (nor is it about the "Working Class" as defined by sociologists). I have searched, but have not discovered that such a study exists; I would be gratified if this volume served as an impetus to an investigation of work in American fiction. (The Introduction is meant to supply a few prefatory remarks on the subject.)

The stories collected here are all of high literary merit, and the criterion for inclusion—beyond that—was that each of them, regardless of its ultimate intent, detail what it is like to work in America: from laboring through the professions. The selection is not meant to be definitive, but representative. I have tried to vary location as much as occupation to give as complete a portrait as possible. The order of placement is for the reader who will read from first to last, and my intention is to amplify each story by its position rather than to diminish it.

Even though this is a "theme" anthology, it remains for me a quite personal selection. I have attempted to keep the stories (or contained sections of longer works) from within the last twelve years; a good many are quite recent (there are now more to choose from, for reasons alluded to in the Introduction). An editor, no matter how conscientious, is always aware that something good can be missed. There are tour de force examples of American work literature over the decades for the curious reader to discover or rediscover, from the "Custom House" section of Hawthorne's *The Scarlet Letter* to Herbert Selby, Jr.'s "The

Strike" from *Last Exit to Brooklyn,* from Rebecca Harding Davis' *Life in the Iron Mills* to Agnes Smedley's *Daughter of Earth.* Other diverse examples are: the coffin building in Faulkner's *As I Lay Dying;* Saul Bellow's *Looking for Mr. Green;* Jack Kerouac's *October in the Railroad Earth;* and Fred Exley's *A Fan's Notes.*

I have avoided, though not entirely, stories found in other collections. And any story that seems to deviate from the raison d'être of this anthology has—you can assume—my permission to do so.

W.O.

☆☆☆ Editor's Acknowledgments

The poet Alan Dugan planted the seed for this collection in 1971, when he remarked to me that he enjoyed reading stories about work but that there weren't many of them, since so few American writers worked. I began to wonder about that and this anthology is the result. I would like to thank Edward Zuckerman for helping the project begin its journey to print and my colleagues at Rutgers University for their advice, especially Professors Marsha McCreadie, Heyward Ehrlich and H. Bruce Franklin. In addition, the following offered helpful suggestions on questions that arose out of this task: Joan Silber, Mary Jarrett, Dr. William G. Bartholome, Elizabeth Tingom, Alexandra Mezey, David Black, Jean Boudin, Harry Lewis, Louise Bernikow, Irini Spanidou.

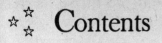

Contents

☆ ☆ ☆ Introduction

Contemporary American literature resists categories (though the Linnaeuses of the academy still find them). We live in an age of entirely retrieved history, so we are surrounded by all preceding forms. A decade ago the term avant-garde, though jejune, meant something. Today the vanguard does not necessarily have any divisions behind it; as we are aware of all forms, so all forms are employed. Our literature has lost its sense of time: sons precede fathers, prophets announce the coming of those just gone, others exit before they enter.

It is conjecture when any graph of development is plotted and we turn, perhaps mistakenly, into cultural astronomers, predicting the return of comets (styles, movements) and exploding supernovas (deaths of forms). Yet it is clear that realistic social fiction, though never entirely displaced, is now forcing itself again to the forefront and for reasons that I will sketch.

One cause is our society's changing and challenging views about work. Work is possibly literature's oldest subject (and though all such claims are essentially fatuous, the importance here is that it *can* be claimed). No examination of work in modern fiction has ever been undertaken as an end in itself (though working will be discussed indirectly in studies of the "Laboring Class"[1]). If fiction encompasses life, it will include

---

[1] One rare document that pertains is *The Worker in American Fiction: an Annotated Bibliography*, by Virginia Prestridge. Champaign, Ill., 1954. The Introduction states: ". . . we have compiled this list with the hope that from these books the reader may gain insight into various phases of the labor movement." Work, as a subject in fiction, has not been discussed by literary critics. Ms. Prestridge's bibliography was published by the Institute of Labor & Industrial Relations. It has 159 titles, ending at 1954, and it would be valuable to anyone contemplating a study of work in American fiction.

work, yet what is the center of that life? Western man's attitudes about work have shifted no more rapidly than the crust of earth he lives upon.[2] The most recent taboo to have been violated is not sex, nor even death, but work. And because work is tied to the rawest facts of survival, it still evokes modesty in those who seem to possess none.[3]

The post Second World War period of reconstruction and the resultant "baby-boom" led to a romance with the youth-culture which flourished in the sixties and is now rapidly fading (as indeed, those young are aging); that population bell-curve had created new growth markets that have peaked. Students[4] and youth are being jilted and this country has rekindled its affair with the Worker—not coincidently just as great numbers of the baby-boom era have finally entered the civilian work force. This transformation (from student to worker) has, in part, forced the current reexamination, for it has helped produce a new light-blue collar class which is searching for fresh definitions of work.

The contemporary fiction writer presents a sorry economic triptych; s/he comes from wealth; s/he becomes dry-docked in some slip of the academy; or s/he struggles. We are not talking about great numbers. A current directory boasts of 800 living American fiction writers;[5] perhaps another 800 have escaped their scrutiny. We live in a country of 200,000,000; not quite .001 percent—no mind, they comfort themselves the competition is as small as it is. Writing creatively has never been a fully sanctioned occupation in this country; as Nelson Algren has remarked, "Here you get to be a writer when there's absolutely nothing else you can do." Those who are capable may try their hand at journalism, or will fall into one of the allied professions: public relations, advertising, publishing. Many have careers of

[2] For a brief survey, see the entry "Work" in the *Dictionary of the History of Ideas*, edited by Philip P. Wiener. Charles Scribner's Sons, N.Y., 1973, Vol. IV, pp. 530–535.

[3] See the preface to *Making It*, by Norman Podhoretz. Random House, N.Y., 1967, pp. xi-xvii. Also *Working*, by Louis "Studs" Terkel. Pantheon, N.Y., 1974. The bibliography of recent nonfiction on work is extensive and growing.

[4] At the close of 1960, according to the U.S. Office of Education, there were 3,215,544 Americans enrolled in institutions of higher learning; by 1971 there were 8,948,000. That unprecedented increase (it had not even doubled from 1919 to 1960, much less tripled within a decade) has had a profound impact.

[5] A Directory of American Fiction Writers, Poets & Writers, Inc., N.Y., 1976.

"odd" jobs. The work of writers is writing, but indeed, they have other employment. The writer as both worker and artist has brought about an attempted resolution of an ancient conflict. Contemplation and manual labor have been in opposition since antiquity.[6] But this conflict is momentarily resolved when fiction writers write about working: a compelling synthesis comes nearest to realization. It is stoop-labor in the Goldsmithean sense: the dichotomy has been conquered. Parnassus has installed a time-clock.

Writing about work requires a realistic style, which is, at once, the form most readily attempted and the one most difficult to perfect. Whatever literary mode happens to be in fashion, realistic narrative perseveres, for it may not be the crest of the wave but it is the water from whence it is drawn. The cant of the hour is that nonfiction has taken on the techniques of fiction, whereas, of course, it is the reverse that has always been true. Modern fiction and journalism spring from the same matrix (the journal, the diary, the epistle, spiced by the novella, fabliau, fable) and very few American writers of quality have not written both.

Periods of literature, to those who seek to name them, present little problem, until the classifiers are met with dividing the smallest portion, their own time. Distance often masquerades as perspective and time shores events with structure unearned. The querulous labels of Naturalism, Social Realism, Proletarian Literature[7] tried to channel wild streams. The philosopher-novelist, so abundant in European tradition, is largely absent in our own. In the twentieth century philosophy gave way to politics. Between World Wars fiction writers participated in rancorous, divisive social movements, and literary styles became forever identified with partisan issues.

It was Ben Jonson's remark that Shakespeare knew little Latin and less Greek, and today it can be said that writers know little physics and less astro-chemistry. In literature what often seems to disappear may just be overlooked, and the experimentalist who

[6] In Plato's *Gorgias* (512c) Socrates and Callicles banter, in the most modern of prejudices, about the horror Callicles would feel if his daughter wanted to marry a worker. *The Collected Dialogues of Plato*, edited by Edith Hamilton and Huntington Cairns, Princeton University Press, Princeton, N.J., 1971, p. 294. Aristotle's (384–322 B.C.) master and slave became Marx's (1818–1883) boss and worker.
[7] See the late Josephine Herbst's discussion of these labels in *Proletarian Writers of the Thirties,* edited by David Madden. Southern Illinois University Press, Carbondale, Ill., 1968, pp. xvi-xvii.

took the spotlight during the sixties is more akin to the medieval alchemist or physic who brought more imagination to his work than learning. The two cultures,[8] often remarked upon during that time, saw a generation of writers retreat from the world of twentieth-century science and industry (for the nineteenth-century world which seemed comprehensible to the naturalist was over and the Atomic Age, at its inception, seemed comprehensible not at all[9]). Experimental writing (with scant historic content) was inadvertently encouraged by an academy fixated on New Criticism, which treats the text directly, forgoing any social or biographical inquiry. This textual myopia, though in many ways corrective, gained wide acceptance, in part, because it served as a socially prudent respite for a country entering a Cold War, retrenching from the damage of a hot one, and tired of the insistent demands for change decades of prewar social fiction had called for. This retreat produced a literature of social alienation,[10] which spawned a hydra of subheadings: black humor, post-modernism, neo-fabulism.

Yet the deep concerns of realistic social fiction, seeing the world as it is and reproducing it so it is immediately recognizable, continued. The semi-serious discussions of the death of the novel during the sixties were sessions of dressing straw men: fiction is still read, escapist fiction, the pseudo-naturalistic potboilers where "how the other half lives" (or rather, the other one percent) can be vicariously enacted. (Though these books never provide the keys needed to enter those kingdoms.) Between high mountains of trash there runs a clear small stream, neglected because it produces no roar.[11] Since the Popular Culture is self-regenerative,

[8] From C. P. Snow's pamphlet (which was addressed to an English situation: an upper-class humanistic establishment versus a lower-class scientific one). In this country it signified a split between the humanist and the scientist. See Susan Sontag's remarks in *Against Interpretation*. Dell Publishing Co., N.Y., 1969, p. 295.

[9] See the Introduction to *The Beat Generation and the Angry Young Men*, edited by Gene Feldman and Max Gartenberg. The Citadel Press, N.Y., 1958, pp. 11–12.

[10] Even though the "old time lag between America and Europe" (in Alfred Kazin's words) may be over, what crystallized in literature in Europe between the First and Second World Wars did not take hold completely in our country till the interim between World War II and the Vietnam war. For a discussion of the former, see *Realism in Our Time*, by Georg Lukács. Harper & Row, N.Y., 1964.

[11] Though 40,000 books are published annually, the number of first novels remains the same: between 90–120 a year. *Library Journal* has been keeping count for the last fifteen years; the figure is constant and includes science fiction, detective/mystery novels. This number points to the deterioration of serious fiction's power to affect the culture.

serious fiction has little effect on it (though the opposite is not true).

Writers find it difficult to combat the technological arts. A book is now the rare dry shelter found during the media storm. During the last two decades the experimental competition by writers with film, television and recordings forced fiction to its nether end: that which the camera or recorder cannot say. A literature *in extremis* flourished. "Real life" was left to the camera and nonfiction. Escapist fictions (fantasy, gothic, mystery, western, adventure) prosper, creating worlds that do not require confirmation because the novel as sensory artifact has become suspect.

American fiction decamped after the Second World War from the regiment of social activism (it had, after all, been reluctantly conscripted). Serious fiction had become almost entirely personal; in the sixties the confessional mode triumphed in fiction, poetry and journalism, which, after a period of hypocrisy and excess—the writer needing something to confess—is not unexpected. But confessional literature brings along its own chaperone (as often famous debauchees take on a religious mentor late in life): realistic writing. And when confessional literature begins to flag (as it has now), it turns from the merely private to the public, and social concerns are reintroduced. When anything scandalous can be repeated or alleged, when any impropriety can be reported, the only incident with any weight is the one that actually occurred. Nonfiction has thrived over serious fiction simply because it boasts that it can be trusted. Nonfiction is an awkward way to say it is the truth. An unfortunate legacy of anti-realistic fiction is that it has robbed the genre of the power of belief that accompanies verisimilitude. Fiction long ago lost its moral force (though writers are returning to the church of realism in hopes of restoring it to grace). Eighteenth-century novels were passed off as "discovered" journals or diaries; fiction again needs the imprimatur of a nonfictional source.

The stories collected here are not examples of a backlash, but of the evolution I have outlined. Their authors have inherited, besides a native realistic tradition, the developments of our modern era (they have traveled through the dark woods of self); and though their stories about work are examples of social fiction, their voices remain, for the most part, private rather than partisan. It is not my intention to explain how each of them views work; as lawyers say, the documents speak for themselves. This collection is not a capstone, but a cornerstone; it is to announce new attitudes, not recapitulate them.

There will be more work fiction to come because work is in the crucible of our attention and its elements are separating, changing before our eyes. It is the familiar made strange, and our fiction writers recognize the difference.

William O'Rourke

July 4, 1976
New York City

On the Job

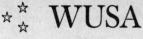

WUSA

from *A Hall of Mirrors*

by Robert Stone

With the Sunday morning sun in his face, Rheinhardt walked along Canal Street, hunching his shoulders now and then to air the armpits of his suit jacket. It was eight o'clock. In mid-street, the traffic islands were empty and simmering, brown wasted palm fronds hung dead-still over the gleaming trolley rails. Atop the Cotton Exchange buildings, carillons began "A Mighty Fortress Is Our God"; in the deep shade of the downtown side a party of Negro churchwomen walked sanctified under black umbrellas.

At the corner of Burgundy Street, he followed humming traffic signals across the deserted street and stood for a while before the unlit display windows of Torneille's Department Store. The glass front doors were locked when he tried them. Walking slowly he went around to the delivery ramps on Burgundy and saw a uniformed guard at the far end of the block, who was standing just out of the sun reading the morning's funny papers. Above the guard, mounted on the metal railing of a fire escape was a large sign showing a white eagle rampant over a starred and striped shield and a microphone from which radiated variously red, white and blue thunderbolts. Printed beneath it in white capital letters was:

WUSA—The Voice of an American's America
—The Truth Shall Make You Free

Rheinhardt showed his appointment slip and followed the guard to a small hot room of the service entrance that was hung

ROBERT STONE (b. 1937) is the author of *A Hall of Mirrors* (1966) and *Dog Soldiers* (1974).

with canvas fenders and time clock machines. On the service elevator button which the guard pressed, was another placard with the WUSA call letters and a small black arrow pointing upward. The elevator came, operated by a large dark man in a neat blue business suit—the rented guard went out to finish the comics, and Rheinhardt rode to the top floor between stacked wooden crates and coils of electrical wire.

Rheinhardt came out of the elevator into a room crowded with workmen and equipment. There was a litter of excelsior on the floor; at the rear where a row of splintering inventory shelves were still standing, they had taken out a section of wall to show a labyrinth of colored wire.

He walked across the hall and on to a raised platform leading to the next room. A group of men in shirtsleeves were drinking coffee on the far side of a newly taped-in glass pane; Rheinhardt found a door and went in—from nearby he heard the clatter of wire service tickers. He nodded amiably to the coffee drinkers and stopped a blond girl in a seersucker suit who was speeding by with a wicker basket of stationery.

"Mr. Noonan," Rheinhardt asked her, "where is he?"

The girl flipped a limp tanned wrist toward another door and smiled at him.

"God knows."

One of the men in shirtsleeves set his cup down and came over. "Looking for Noonan?"

"Right." Rheinhardt said.

The man went to the door and called out. "Jack!"

"Wha?" someone said.

"A man."

Jack Noonan came out holding a yellow sheaf of wire copy. He was a fairly young man who bore, with some self-consciousness, the traces of theatrical good looks. His temples were graying impressively; his features were clean lined, a trifle drawn. He had rather dull and vaguely malevolent blue eyes. He glanced at Rheinhardt, handed the page of copy to the shirt-sleeved man with a cool imperious gesture and smiled comfortably.

"Hi," he said.

"Hi," Rheinhardt said. "I heard something the other day about you boys filling out a staff."

"Yah," Jack Noonan said. "Right. Definitely."

"I thought I could help you with that."

"Are you an announcer?"

"I usually work in a musical format," Rheinhardt said. "I mean I have been. But I can work up news breaks too—I can work from wire copy and I can deliver pitches and I can work the pitches over if they need it."

Jack Noonan nodded tolerantly, still smiling.

"You sound like a pretty powerful package."

"I worked a lot of small stations. You get to keep your hand in."

"Uh huh," Noonan said. "This isn't a small station."

"No," Rheinhardt said.

"Where did you work last?"

"DCKO. In Orangeburg."

"Orangeburg where?"

"South Carolina."

Jack Noonan fixed his dull smile on the points of Rheinhardt's freshly shined Italian shoes.

"That must be small," he said.

"500 kilowatts. About 500."

"Uh huh."

Looking suddenly disinterested, Noonan took the wire copy back from the man who had been holding it and exchanged a smile with him.

"Waal, goodbuddy," he told Rheinhardt humorously, "unlike your average station, see, WUSA is a well planned out business operation. Most of the time a station starts out without knowing what the hell it wants to do, or who it wants to do what. But here, see, we know pretty much exactly."

"You mean it isn't amateur night." Rheinhardt said.

"No," Jack Noonan said, "it isn't amateur night." He took a handkerchief from the breast pocket of his jacket and ran it over the film of sweat across his high forehead. "But—as it stands right now we have the deal of a lifetime for the right personnel. As it stands right now just about anyone can walk off the street and show us what he can do. And we'll watch him awhile, see, but we can't exactly give him all our time and sympathetic understanding."

"What would you like to see?" Rheinhardt said.

"I think I'd like to see if you're really such a heavy caliber utility man. For example I'd like to see you hit those tickers back there and take off enough for a real swinging five minute news spot—hard delivery, something to turn people on to what's happening. And then I'd like to hear you tape and deliver it."

"OK," Rheinhardt said.

"Crazy," Jack Noonan said. "The ticks are right through that door. I'll give you twenty minutes to make up five minutes worth and if you make it I'll get you an engineer."

"Who listens to it?"

"Me." Jack Noonan said. "I do."

"Are you the hiring man?"

"Well," Noonan said, smiling, "if you really skull me, see, then I'll run it up to Mr. Bingamon."

Rheinhardt started through the door to the teletype room.

"Good luck," Jack Noonan said.

"You know," Rheinhardt said, looking back at him, "it's funny . . . I mean when you say five minutes of news to turn the people on with. I don't think I ever hear of much call for swinging news."

"Nah," Noonan said. "There isn't much. But, see, here there is."

"You must expect people to listen to it."

"Oh, we do," Noonan said cheerfully. "It's something new with us."

Rheinhardt went on into the soundproofed cacophony of the ticker room; through a large glass window at the left wall he could see down to the elevator lobby where the pushing and toting was still going on. There were seven tickers in the room, all of them running—stopping and starting in fits, a steady clacking counterpoint measured with the periodic urgent ring of the line bell. Beside the window were a desk and chair with a glue pot, a sharpened blue pencil and a pair of scissors.

Rheinhardt hung his jacket across the back of the chair and went over to the row of spikes above the machines. He took four or five items from the international wire and worked them over briefly—there were no specials, it was not much of a day. Khrushchev and Castro had said nasty things and Johnson had said something more or less unintelligible. Someone had shot at De Gaulle's chauffeur. A Boeing 747 had blown up and fallen into the Quadalaquivir. In Indo-China the defense of civilization was proceeding.

Setting the international to one side, he took down a few strips from the statewide wire; this would be where the meat was hung. It consisted mainly of local bits assembled by the city service office, the State House wire from Baton Rouge and whatever gleanings the service's editor in the rest of the country thought would be useful to Southern subscribers. Most of them were race items in one sense or another.

He went down the line with the pencil in his hand, drawing small blue F clefs in the right margin.

What kind of a day has it been in the heartland?

In open weekend session the Legislature's Un-American Activities Committee approved a motion introduced by a young comer, twenty-one-year-old Representative Jimmy "Dimples" Snipe of Hotckkiss. Representative Snipe's motion called for the issuance of a subpoena to one Morris Lictheim of New Orleans, curator of the Touro Collection of Contemporary Art. "Dimples" told his colleagues how he and his bride, on a cultural visit to the city, had stopped by the collection and found it the work of obscene madmen from beginning to end. This collection, he had learned, was state supported; the honest yeomanry of the state were bled dry to pander the diseased taste of a volatile and subversive city rabble. His suspicions aroused, "Dimples" had unearthed Lictheim as the man in charge; delving further he had examined the man's application papers and found them a tissue of lies. For example, Morris Lictheim had entered his country of origin as Austria, when documented research proved that the city and province of his birth had been an integral part of Poland since 1918, the year following the Bolshevik rising. Supporting his motion with colored slides of the exhibit taken by his wife, Representative Snipe reminded a hushed and sober chamber that Poland was a Communist slave nation, bordering extensively on Russia itself. They would see about this Lictheim.

Four sixteen year olds burned to death in an overturned Pontiac on U.S. Highway 90: a little farther down the road three strawberry pickers fell out of a contractor's speeding truck—one dead.

At a ceremony, during which he presented a trophy to the

winner of the Emoryville Stock Car Tournament, Judge Horace
St. Saens of Bracque Parish, a candidate for governor, explained
that his reference to Negroes as burrhead gorillas and nun-raping
Congolese did not indicate that he hated their race or any race.
Damp-eyed, he spoke of his love for so many old and faithful
souls, how the very sight of these old and faithful souls brought a
lump to his throat. At the conclusion of the address, an old and
faithful soul was released upon the platform to shake the judge's
hand as the crowd burst spontaneously into Dixie. All present
were amused at the epilogue, when the youthful trophy winner
revealed himself as an unlicensed fifteen-year-old girl.

Before a chili parlor in the oil town of Houma a man with an
urge to kill encountered a man with a premonition of death and
cut his throat after a brief chase.

In Shreveport, the local newspaper announced its sponsorship
of a quick-draw contest with cap pistols as a feature of the
annual rodeo; the contest open to all white adults.

There followed a digest of the week's segregation protests
including a number of militant statements by Negro leaders that
was marked for attention by Southern subscribers. People were
being locked up in McComb and Jackson; there was a march in
Birmingham, a boycott in Montgomery, a little street rough stuff
in Memphis and New Bern, North Carolina. In Mobile, a Baptist
minister pointed out that it was legally impossible for a colored
man to get his feet wet in the Gulf of Mexico for some six
hundred miles, unless he contrived to fall off a shrimp boat. A
Negro citizen of Biloxi then horrified weekend bathers by darting
past desperate policemen and immersing himself to the neck—the
beach was closed. The subsequent evening by the moonlight was
punctuated with exchanges of small arms fire on the edge of the
Negro district.

Next came a few carefully worded declarations of intention
from the attorney general's office and the statement, by a big city
Negro congressman to his constituents, that "the White Man was
on the run"—both put on the line for the clients in Dixie.

But an obliging editor in New York had provided the *pièce de
résistance*—a bad one, a big bad one, a real chiller diller for the
folks down home.

A minister's wife from Tulsa on a solitary search for the

Rockefeller Memorial Church had been rousted in the 116th Street I.N.D. station by the traditional six foot spade, backed to the wall, cut, although not badly, and raped. New York had served it up with all the trimmings.

Rheinhardt read it over, whistling softly through his teeth.

WUSA would use that one, Rheinhardt thought. It was a red, white and blue thunderbolt if ever there was one. He marked it, leaving in all the side effects—the unfortunate lady's reflections, the shock and horror of kith and kin in godly Tulsa, the works.

Armed with scissors and paste-pot he went back up and took from the top, made some sharp one-liners out of the international stuff with a premium on Castro, stuffed the middle with the first or last paragraphs of the assembled racial routines and a sprinkling of the jazzier neutral items. The piece closed with a reverent thirty seconds on the lady from Tulsa and a harmless Pete Smith style comedy accident that happened to a man in Venice fixing his roof.

That would be it—five minutes. And what did it look like?

Reading it through again, Rheinhardt felt a curious chill about the edges of his spinal column. How could it be so easy? The rhythm of instinct—that must be it; you didn't even have to think about it particularly and there it was ready to press, five minutes of sheer eagles and lightning. The cumulative effect of it was really something to read. And to hear, Rheinhardt thought, something to hear—all five minutes of it. WUSA—The Truth Shall Make You Free.

Where did you learn to do that? he asked himself.

He put his jacket on and gathered the paste-ups; the girl in seersucker came to clear the machines.

"Have fun," she told him.

Jack Noonan was outside, walking up and down with a program sheet.

"OK," Rheinhardt said.

"Fine," Noonan said, reopening his smile. "I was giving up on you."

"Where's the engineer?"

"Irving," Jack Noonan called, still smiling at Rheinhardt.

One of the men in shirt sleeves, a tall young man with thin uncombed red hair and horn-rimmed glasses came over to them.

"Irv, baby, this man's gonna read to us. Want to get him taped?"

"C'mon," Irving said.

They went down a flight of cement stairs and into an empty studio on the floor below. Bits of heavy brown wrapping paper was still lying about the floor; the equipment was new and sparkling.

"There's your mike," Irving said pointing to a gleaming turn table unit.

Rheinhardt sat down and looked the copy over again. Irving went into the control booth to turn on his machines.

"What is it? Five minutes?"

"Right," Rheinhardt said.

"Say something."

"Double Yew Yew Ess A," Rheinhardt said. "The Voice of an American's America."

Irving smiled bemusedly behind the glass.

"WUSA," the machine came back, "The voice of an American's America. . . ."

"Breathy," Irving said.

"What?"

"Breathy," Irving said. "You know—with breath?"

Rheinhardt looked up. "Oh, I'll try to get some palate in there."

"That's the way," Irving said, and made little clicking sounds with his tongue and palate. "Lots palate."

"You want me to start right in?"

"Take your time. Pick up any time after I give you the marker." Both he and Rheinhardt turned to the wall clock. Irving waved a hand toward the floor.

"Anytime."

"Double Yew Yew Ess A," Rheinhardt began . . . "WUSA Insider's report . . . Havana."

It ran a shade under five minutes. Irving closed the switches and came out of the booth.

"So," he said. "A lot happened."

"A little of this and a little of that," Rheinhardt said.

"OK. You know the way up? Go tell Jack I got it if he wants to hear it."

"Thanks."

"Anytime," Irving said. "You want to hear it?"

"No," Rheinhardt said. "Maybe later."

Rheinhardt went up the stairs and found Jack Noonan and the girl taking coffee at the ticker room desk.

"Ready?" Noonan asked him.

"Yeah," Rheinhardt said. "He has it."

"Good, good. Just have a seat somewhere. Marge," he said to the girl, "get him a magazine."

"I want to hear too," the girl said.

The two of them went toward the stairway.

Rheinhardt sat down on the desk and spent the next five minutes or so, reading an article on creativity in the Ladies' Home Journal. When he had finished that, he noticed that he was still holding the sheaf of copy he had prepared for the broadcast. He crumpled it and tossed it on the floor, then read the letters to the editor and the movie reviews. Neither Noonan or the girl appeared to be coming back.

He stood up and went over to the window to watch them haul equipment off the elevator, smoking one cigarette and then another. The shirt-sleeved men were still standing around, doing nothing in particular, paying no attention to him.

About twenty minutes after he had gone out, Jack Noonan came back in, alone.

He looked at Rheinhardt and shrugged.

"Ever met M. T. Bingamon?"

"No," Rheinhardt said.

"He'd like to see you."

"Is he going to hear the tape?"

"He's heard it," Jack Noonan said. "C'mon."

There were three large empty storerooms beyond the teletype enclosure with more splintering shelves and bits of tissue paper wadded in the corners. The air conditioners were not working there; they were airless and dead hot, carrying a faint presence of cheap cloth, moldering wood and discarded lunches. Above the largest, the center room, ran a strangely ornate balustrade that circled past some twenty small circular windows which had been sealed with opaque yellow paint so that the fierce sunlight outside filtered through to charge the railing and the upper part of the room with ocher light.

Jack Noonan walked ahead fanning himself with the ticker copy.

"Mad, huh," he asked Rheinhardt as they went. "Like a crazy roller-skating rink."

"Lots of room," Rheinhardt said, blinking up at the yellow ceiling.

"That's why we're moving," Noonan told him. "Y'see, it used to be piled full of beds. The story is that old Claude Torneille started out up here with two rooms, see. In one he had a shop that turned out cheap caskets for niggers and the other he kept full of beds that he sold to the cathouses in Storeyville. He sold them on time before anybody else did that and he was good buddies with the cops. Whenever they staged one of their raids, the old man would come along to repossess the beds and sell them over again somewhere else. He did that like hundreds of times. Then he got rich and respectable and pretty soon he owned the whole building right down to the street."

"He must have been a great old man," Rheinhardt said.

"Yeah, he had something going for him," Jack Noonan said. "Imagine thinking that up."

At the end of the last room, they went through a finished maple door marked Keep Out and into an air-conditioned room where a number of middle-aged women were working over thick loose-leaf folders.

Rheinhardt followed Jack Noonan through to another door. "Mailing lists," Noonan said over his shoulder. "They put a couple of grand into collecting them and a couple of grand more into public opinion research. How many stations you ever hear of doing that?"

The last room was an office with wood panelling and a set of French windows overlooking motionless Canal Street. The walls were hung with maps of the city and lithographed sea engagements from the War of 1812. Behind the dark antique desk was a panel hung with autographed photos of golfers and polo players, enlargements of grazing African wildlife, of a handsome graying man in safari gear with a speckled band across his slouch hat— Bingamon himself. There were a great many movie faces—some stylized, publicity shots, and some posed in informal groups with Bingamon. All were autographed and inscribed with sentiments;

they gave the room the air of a celebrity barbershop or a theatrical delicatessen.

Bingamon had come in immediately behind them; when they turned from the desk he was halfway across the room, one hand adjusting his horn-rimmed spectacles, the other outstretched in greeting. "Hi, Jack," he was saying.

"Bing," Jack Noonan said, "this is Mr. Rheinhardt."

Rheinhardt had already shaken the outstretched hand, but this done he experienced some iittle difficulty in getting loose, so that as Jack Noonan walked out of the room he found himself standing in the center of the carpet holding hands with Matthew J. Bingamon.

"Have a seat, Mr. Rheinhardt," Bingamon said, turning him loose.

Rheinhardt sat down on a leather chair beside the desk and watched him. He was a particularly big man. He wore no jacket and his quiet striped tie was loosened at the collar of a short-sleeved button-down shirt. There was nothing of age about him though his hair was gray, nearly white. His face was clear—tight and tanned. He was not, as far as Rheinhardt could see, what one would call a Hollywood type. He looked nothing at all like a grasping factor. His whole appearance and manner had a perfect balance between easily carried urban elegance and an outdoor muscularity compressed with good-natured reluctance into city clothes. He had, Rheinhardt considered, a singular and formidable cool.

"I heard your tape, Rheinhardt," Matthew Bingamon said. "I liked it pretty well."

"Good," Rheinhardt said. "Good."

"It was very selective and it was very well delivered."

Rheinhardt lit a cigarette and nodded modestly.

"Thank you," he said.

"You seem to have come by a good sound constitutional grounding. That's something of a rarity in a young man."

Rheinhardt settled back with a look of polite interest. He was beginning to get the pain in his back again.

"Well, I've worked a good deal with news . . ."

Bingamon laughed pleasantly. "You never picked it up at radio stations. You'll have to tell me a lot more about yourself one of these times. And you'll get a chance to because I believe I liked your tape well enough to hire you."

"Fine," Rheinhardt said. "Fine."

"I don't think from what I heard," Bingamon said, whipping off his glasses with the same razor-sharp gesture he had used before, "that we could have any misunderstanding about why you're being taken on—but just in case, I'll tell you exactly why. When I listened to that spot I was able to see a picture. A part of a pattern. If I had listened to any other five minute straight news broadcast on any other station it would have been obscured, wouldn't it? But because you see it, you made me see it."

"The pattern," Rheinhardt said. "Yes."

"Well the news, so called, is a very important part of what we're trying to do with WUSA. Because there *is* a pattern. But it's hard, Rheinhardt, it's very hard to get across. Every honest man in this country feels it—and not only in the South—but everywhere in the country. They feel it, they pick up a trace of it here and there. But there are other people whose business it is to keep that pattern obscured. From our point of view these people are the enemy."

"Right," Rheinhardt said. "Right."

"People can't see because they don't have the orientation, isn't that right? And a lot of what we're trying to do is to give them that orientation."

"Certainly," Rheinhardt said eagerly.

"Well you realize that, I'm sure," Bingamon said, standing up. "You'd have to realize that or you wouldn't have been able to make up the sort of copy I just listened to."

"Aha," Rheinhardt said.

"Well all right then, Mr. Rheinhardt." Rheinhardt rose from his chair. "You could be quite a find for the station. I really like your delivery. You've got that kind of voice—you make things sound right important when you say them."

"Well," Rheinhardt said, starting for the door, "of course they're important things."

"Sure," Bingamon said. "Sure they are. I can't think of anything to hold you back with us, Rheinhardt. Except maybe one thing."

"What's that?" Rheinhardt asked smiling.

"Well you could think I was a damn fool. That'd hold you back some."

Rheinhardt watched him. The man's face was sheer *bonhomie*. "Why would I think that?"

Bingamon laughed and dismissed his own words with a shrug.

"Well I don't mean that exactly. I mean you might underestimate the seriousness of what we're trying to do. If you did, you know . . . you'd be all wrong for us."

"It's important work," Rheinhardt said. "Certainly I realized that." He swallowed, easing the dryness in his throat. "I take it very seriously."

"Good," Matthew Bingamon said. "If I'm wrong I'm giving myself time to find out. I always do."

They stood looking at one another in the center of the room.

"Yes," Rheinhardt said, for no reason.

"You're hired for the time being," Matthew Bingamon said, sliding open a cabinet. "Are you a drinking man?"

He took a bottle of Southern Comfort and two glasses from a cabinet. "Would you join me?"

Rheinhardt looked at the bottle and at Bingamon.

"Too early for me," he said with great force.

"Really," Bingamon said. "I'm having one."

"Oh all right," Rheinhardt said. "Thank you. A short one."

He watched Bingamon fill the two liquor glasses and carefully accepted the drink, raised it and swallowed it.

When it was down he knew it had been a mistake. After the first warm relaxation he felt the sudden careening of his brain, the dives; standing a foot from Bingamon with the glass in his hand, the foolish smile still on his face, he was plunging headlong into the dives, the whirling breathless curves that led, always to the lights—he could see them down at the bottom, flashing yellow and red. He had to get out now, he told himself. He had to get out.

Bingamon stood watching him, his own glass still untouched.

"You look a little peaked, Mr. Rheinhardt. I'm sorry if I pressed you too hard. I guess you really aren't used to it."

"No," Rheinhardt said. "I don't use it a great deal."

"Can you come in Tuesday?"

"What?" Rheinhardt said.

"Tuesday." Bingamon repeated. "Come in Tuesday afternoon at three o'clock. I've got you in mind for about a three A.M. musical slot—late night stuff at first. I want you to tape a few of them Tuesday afternoon. With news, naturally."

"OK," Rheinhardt said. "Tuesday at three."

"Your salary, which you've been too polite to ask about, is ninety a week. I don't pay a lot to start, Rheinhardt, I don't believe in it. But I do believe that you have to pay for quality in anything so I'll tell you now you can make a hell of a lot more if you keep me with you."

"Good," Rheinhardt said, starting out again.

"Would you like some cash now?"

"Oh," Rheinhardt said. "Well, all right."

"The banks are closed of course and my cashiers aren't here. You won't consider it demeaning if I pay you out of my pocket?" He took five twenties from a simple tin box on the desk and put them in Rheinhardt's hand. " 'Cause hell, that's where it comes from anyway. It's symbolic, everybody that works for me has got to have some sort of personal relationship with me. I don't believe in the impersonal business organization. Especially in this business."

Rheinhardt put the bills in his wallet and took Bingamon's hand again.

"Mr. Bingamon," he said, "it's been a pleasure meeting you, sir."

"Mr. Rheinhardt," Bingamon said without the faintest irony, "it's been a pleasure meeting *you,* sir."

Rheinhardt went out, past the women at their mailing lists and down a long flight of back stairs. He had to stop once, in order to come to terms with the number of steps and the manner of their arrangement; it seemed there were a great many concentrated in too narrow a shaft. Coming out on the street, he found it difficult to take the sun.

☆☆☆ I Am Not Luis Beech-Nut

by Rosellen Brown

How long it take you to go all around the world? A day and a half something like that? A day and a half I get up, drink this Bustelo down with grit in the bottom, dirt, and I tell Adela get another sleeve for the coffee, this little flannel for the cup, this one is stinking by now and have a hole. I'm looking at the Bustelo bag, the yellow always look so old and faded, and in my mind I got to learn these things, it's true it say "TOSTADO Y ENVASADO POR BUSTELO COFFEE ROASTING CO. (Div. of Beech-Nut, Inc.)." Son of a bitch. "Tostado y Molido Para El Gusto Hispano"—y el Profit Americano. Like me. Their little fertilizer, manure, what you call it, for their flower gardens, beauty roses. Little shit, this Luis, and all day long George Street, Leon Street, going by the store so fast you think I'm selling the plague in here two for a dollar.

No, I was saying what I do while the world going round, and I could go with it—if I was Luis Beech-Nut. I drink this shit down, wipe my mouth, push my mustache out flat, scatter the crumbs for the birds, buckle up my belt that I keep loose for breakfast, and goodby, seven days a week. The girls, some of them are up, Enery go on sleeping, she'll be sleeping when the last day of the great world come, and I go on. Adela come later, all the help she bring me. Whatever a woman is good for might be between the sheets she wash—Adela will do, I'm not a man who force a woman to be *una puta,* you know—but this one of mine, she is mostly a maker of girl children to embarrass me. Not one boy in that lot, just all these babies with those little bottoms that are

ROSELLEN BROWN (b. 1939) is the author of a collection of stories, *Street Games* (1974), and a novel, *The Autobiography of My Mother* (1976).

always cloved like the devil's feet. I checked each time I had one of them alone the first time, put my hands in the diaper, hoping for a mistake, something to get hold of, but the only sticks in this family, Jesús, are this one of mine and the one that prop the kitchen window open in the summer!

And then after making herself round with kids in front before, and behind after, she is a first-class maker of mistakes at the store. The adding machine is like some mystery, it could be a rocket ship, she stand there with her fingers on the controls, they could be her feet in shoes, not graceful, and smile her little smile looking so scared, and drive away the customers right into the arms of Anthony and his thieves' market up there. So I tell her to scrub the counter while I go up to the money, eleven cents for one can of tomato sauce—tell me what can you do with one can?—and she polish and shine, that metal edge on the counter is like a mirror, till she deserve a genie popping out of it, and say: Lady, what you wish? I don't know about her but my wish is two dozen ladies coming in to do the whole week's shopping one after another, they say No More Supermarkets, Never, with their big squeaky carts parked over there in the corner. Asking for staples first, economy size, and then all the stupid little things that last sucker, *coño,* had to go and order. What for? Capers? How many capers you think I sell in a week? Chili yes, *cumino,* but what is this other stuff here. This lemon-pepper, marjoram, coriander? This was never any Gristedes, not even the old days. No wonder that old Jew sold out.

So. This morning. I have seen the old McTave lady who buy Alka-Seltzer so often she going to take off her roof some morning and never stop, fly out to sea. Seventy-three cents, plus tax on the Alka-Seltzer. Fontaine over there come get himself an electric-green toothbrush. He brush in the dark? Then from across the intersection, long distance, that slut, that nigger girl who hustle for the *tecato,* what she come for? Adela watch me with her eyes little when she twitch her ass at me, but it's O.K., I don't like women that are built like tweezers. I swear to the Virgin Mary, she heap up a little pile and give me her business dimple: one box kitchen matches, one small can Hormel corned beef hash, panty-hose on sale, cloud-mist, two for $1.07, and a pack of gum. The matches go for his habit, the stockings go for hers, the dog eat the corned beef, I bet you, and they all split the gum. What else I got to do here but think?

I rearranged everything on the shelves twice already, I'm trying ways to get your eye when you walk in—if nobody's around I pretend to come in the door and what hit me? Campbell's Pork and Beans. O.K., now what would go good with it to put by its right hand? You got to strain yourself to do this, what they call good retailing practices. Bread and butter pickles. I try that for a day. The label's getting this dust that stick, damp dust, I'm afraid to go see what the basement doing to me, but I can't dust it off and I can't wash it. At the door when I'm pretending to come on in smiling, pocket full of change and no holes in it, the cod stink and the whole place have such dust flying in on the light it could be a barnyard back home with a cockfight going on.

I don't know. Eight years' work at Cappy's Market, two months here, my Grand Opening banners are still out there looking like a lord's funeral, and that Jew that bought me all that coriander went to where? Palm Springs? Palm Beach? Someplace warm, a little closer to my Bayamón, no seven-day-a-week night-mares, and gave it all to Luis instead, and after my last breakfast of steamed shit they going to bury me under the concrete out back if things don't shake out better soon. I can add, my machine can add if my wife stay off it, but all I get to add is OUTGOING, cash, credit. Everything else is *subtracción*.

I take a candle home. Adela will say shame but she be the first to help me light it. The candles are selling better because what's her name, that Hortensia, old Negri, down George corner of Smith, dropped dead a couple weeks ago with a goiter as big as that mailman's pouch out there. So her Botánica is shut up behind a ripped old black shade. How could she die, and scream-ing, they said, like a saint sent to hell by mistake, with all the herbs and candles and little sacks of cures right there? Well, she died sure as she lived, sitting there in that old couch popping springs, telling people how to change Jesus's mind or get their mans back, his wandering ass back in their bed, if you'll pardon me. She brought luck with the horses, luck with the *boleta*. Tony Aguilar said it was rat-shit but she did him a good turn, he won three hundred dollars the day before her goiter choked her. Luck with women who couldn't bear—not so much luck with the ones who bore stones they didn't want to carry, I can promise you that—but she died.

And I got her business. The nearest spirit woman now, it make you think, is a bus ride, thirty-five cents, or that blind woman up State Street who only do bad spells, death, or make sworn enemies disappear. And the nearest *bodega* that gots candles is a good solid walk. Nobody want to go a block rain or shine these days, you notice? We getting like the suburbs, only with rats and no parking. Anthony's little shelf shits but he don't need that business, when he sell one out, say St. Michael, it stay out till the person who need it fall down dead or go broke. Can they sue him for lousy inventory? So there's the PEACEFUL HOME candle, and the MONEY DRAWING that has to say (ALLEGED) in small letters we all so honest now, while Beech-Nut take all the money away in a wheelbarrow anyhow. SAFE CROSSING sell in going-home season, the 7 AFRICAN POWERS so-so, the WORK candle, all the saints, and the black ones with no words and a cat hissing with his back arched way up.

Maybe somebody gots one burning for me. Hey that's a good idea. Trying to get me on the welfares. Two packs of cigarettes. Adela sell them and what can she mess up? She forget the matches. The blond bitch come on back in and ask for them making these little lips to tell us she's pissed off for the ten extra steps. I hold out a handful and she take two. The cat bring a mouse up the cellar stairs and drop it splat right in front of the bread rack. Stiff already. Some kid, Widdoes his name is, come over from the Projects, and I hate it but I tell him go home and tell your mama no, no more credit, not till I get that page full of hot dog dinners paid back here. Enough. It's enough this place eat up my bank account, do they mean to pull my hairs out one by one?

I went home last night, my Enery, my first best daughter I had when I was nineteen and had the best still in me, she is waiting to ask a question. What, dear? I got a problem, from school. What, you got in some trouble? No. She is almost blond, bless her, we call her Blanqui, I don't know where she get that but she always like a movie starlet with that wavy hair that give off lights like a three-way bulb. No, I mean some homework, I don't know what to do with it. She bring her notebook that's fat with doodlings of girls with all their noses pointed up. It say on the blue line:

LIST 5 REASONS BEHIND MAN'S DESIRE TO ESCAP
THIS WORLD.

This is for what class?

She don't remember that, only she going to have to answer it
somehow. I say, what you think, Dolly? My name for this beautiful girl. Blanqui, you can do this.

Well, love? Maybe sometimes love goes wrong? She is thinking
of her soldier who took her little silver ring off to Vietnam and
she worry will they let him wear it? They took all his hair away,
maybe they get his ring too. She going to get married when he
come back (if, I say, but never to her) and he get his army pay
and then her sweet cherry she been saving, and her babysitting
bank account too, and don't laugh, one of these days I wake up
and see it bigger than mine. All those half-babies of hers get to
wait a little longer where it's warm inside her while the other half
run away from flying bullets.

Yes, I say. Love.

And there's always war.

War. Sure, war.

She bite her finger-knuckle thinking. Maybe they're afraid to
die. I tell her write that. That's good. They can't escape but they
want to if they could. She print it out slowly and carefully. Her
writing go both ways, left, right, and straight up. That's three.
Sickness, that's not the same as dying. *Sí.* Write it. Pain and
sickness, you could say. Sometime it take forever just to die.

Now she is out of griefs. Imagine that, to be seventeen. Enery,
mi vida, I say, and I take her hands. Enery, think hard.

She make big eyes at me, looking into mine. Little stranger
who already outgrew all the Spanish she ever want to know, who
is so smart in the dress department, and polished fingernails, and
pants. *Muchacha,* money. You ever heard of money? *El dinero?*
What make the whole world go around? And is killing your
father? (I don't say that. Why make her wounds for me to bleed
from?) She looking a little disappointed—oh that—but she still
need one more or she get a bad grade, so she write in MONY and
smile and slam her book closed, gone already halfway down the
stairs to meet her friends. I watch them from the window going
around to the church to play or up to Livingston, Fulton, the
stores to spend her baby-sitting money? To go put her little nose.
that don't turn up like her pictures, right against the dusty win-

dow at the *joyería,* she make eyes at this ring, fifty-eight carats or fifty-eight facets or what, she want her boy to buy her so bad she pay half herself. Why? I'm smart now. So they can get married and be in hock already on their wedding night to a man who hack up stones and sell the chips and dust? Then to the furniture man? then everything, and sure to be a baby hatching by the time the sun come up. I don't want her eyes wet but once in a while I see a bullet keeping him there forever, a nice boy, decent, but so she remember the best of him, what they planned, not what the whole world gots planned for them.

Three times I left Adela or she left me, one time she had a good cut across her eye that left a scar, once a slash I won't say where, with a Gem, the usual thing. The first time Enery was just walking, then a couple more times, don't ask me why I went, why I came back like a tomcat bleeding between the legs. I feel like I grow up since then, or I don't care about some things as much as others no more. I mind my business. I only want to say, I wish my Enery could stay just like she is this minute, no matter what she doing: bending over to tie her shoe that's in style right up to the second, this year lacing shoes, like they always going out hiking, last year platforms, they up on the third floor just walking down the block, laughing, her teeth so perfect and white like baby teeth, and her skirt pulling up in back over these strong legs Adela never had with her tree-stumps. Looking like a girl who can go home to a comfortable bed and no sisters in it, no men, no tears in it, not real tears she bleed from her womb, or her little breasts like milk. No standing on line at the prison door with packages, no running to the hospital, Jesús, no doing foul things standing up in the stair wells like her father done. *Mi Blanquita,* who give me one more reason not to close the gates to this beat-down store for the last time and run someplace before the creditors come up behind me with blackjacks.

But. One more thing to tell about Rojas Spanish Favorites. It should have been born a pool hall. The one robbery don't matter much, it was only an insult because I knew this *maricón* who come bouncing in here with his finger poking in his pocket like a hard-on, he called it a *gun.* "Hey, spic, I got a *gun* here. No tricks." Was he on the late show? O.K., you know what he went home with, back down to Baltic Street where he live with his mama? Eleven dollars, one check I wasn't so sure was worth a piss against the wall, two unopen packages, one dimes, one pennies—see, I let him take it all out of the money box himself. He'd of killed me if I gave him that and say that's all. He had to come *see*. So he shovel it into his pocket, he still fierce, his cheeks going, his eyes bugged, and he can't smile or laugh at the little turds I get to call my profit. His profit now! Can't spare a smile. I can't even make change, man—these big executive bastards, whatever they are, they come in on the way home from the subway with their tens, their twenties for a pack of Larks, a quart of milk and I get wiped out, no change, I got to let them go. Right out of the net up to Anthony's or do without milk. So this bandit, he can't let up and laugh because we both getting the same pitchfork shook at both of us, he just go clomp, clomp, out, no more gun, and slam the door I keep propped open to be inviting. The bells jangle and I laugh till these giant tears come out and wash the scared shitless sweat right off my face. And you know what I'm thinking—just the luck, Luis, you could get your head blown off for eleven bucks too. For eleven cents.

But what I start to say. The only real trouble I had in here besides cream going bad and the offers on the box top expiring before some kid get his hands on them, and me drying up like 120 pounds of salt cod?—it was a time about a week ago some *chulo,* this pimp, come walking in here. Yeah, I'm remembering when I used to look at shoes like that, and suits—good I didn't see his car, the pain used to get me in the groin like a bite with all the teeth closed, when I was younger. As soon as I saw him I knew he had big trouble in his fist. He was a wop who tried some Spanish on me. But I didn't like that, I shook it off and asked him in English what he want. I felt, I tell you, like a whore some customer was trying to kiss, you know? Just close the door behind you and get the fucking over with. What you want, *amigo?* Some fruit juice, what you got? Tomato, prune, orange, orange-grapefruit, some of it's in the refrigerator, nice and cool. And, let's see, maybe a small bottle of grape. Right. Welch's. The best. Got any pineapple? All out. Sorry. Just sold the last can. (Adela took it home yesterday to drink herself. I got to watch that.) So he take this midget grapefruit juice and look all around, slow. Oh, and spaghetti-o's. For lunch, he tell me. What, he going to open the can with his teeth?

So this dago pimp talk a little. About how much noise and dirt the bus make, where does it go? George Street, this is a major thoroughfare? I laugh. Yeah, everybody go by so fast they can't stop themself. But they wave when they go by. No really. *Sí*, really. You want a good burial plot? I'm trying to discourage him, get him to not notice me. More, nonsense, this bubble-gum talk. I want to ask him what's the point. I mean, he don't want to buy me out. He walk around on the balls of his fifty-buck shoes while little Luz Pacheco buy a dime worth of candy penny by penny, thinking hard. I wasn't so sure I'd live long enough to hear what he want. Finally. I could guess. A little trouble with Anthony up there, the bodega where everything hot except for the grocery business. He didn't say that but it's clear. Something he wasn't doing that they wanted. Did I ever put a little money down on a number? *Ay,* who doesn't? What would I think of using this place for, you know, a drop? I could use a little business, no? And maybe a little consideration, one kind or another? Something nice to keep the warm juices flowing? This was a man not much bigger than me but broad in the shoulders, broad maybe only with a shoulder holster, how do you know? What do I see? Blood, of course—Anthony's, mine, Adela in the middle of some cross fire, the traffic ticket cops dropping their books and coming in with their guns out. Also I see myself wearing some shirts I like, maybe, not this worn-out dishrag because I won't keep more than rent and lights and school clothes for the kids out, all the rest of nothing stay in inventory. I want to go home and go to sleep, that's all. I'm young but not that young. People I know go around wishing they could make this kind of connections and I'm just standing here. But it's not the dirty part that scaring me, breaking the law, I mean we a people who gots our own law, the law down Court Street don't do much for me, give it all to the men with their feet up on their shiny desk. The part that scare me is all the rest. This connection put your clean face right up against an asshole that never get wiped. You know? Like you get involved you disappear down this long tunnel, who know where you come out, or how. And you can't call nobody for help, who you call?

See, I never was strong about much, just hung on. I just say this, I say so much already. All my life I got this little problem with women. With myself, I mean. I can get it up, no trouble, I always can, first thing, long before I see the bull's-eye in front of me, but only once. Can't hit a double, you could say, a triple, go all the bases, a grand slam. One time at a time. O.K.? No complaints. Well, this is it, the store. My one time. This is it for the rest of my whole life, and I admitted the first week when I totaled up it's a lousy lay, too—numb. Nothing. Is this what I been saving all these years for? Going without? But you never want it to stop, do you, anyway? You don't want to be all done with it and no more coming.

So I told him O.K. Fine. We get the guarantees straightened out, I say no hot goods in here, I don't want nobody's ripped-off televisions, no drugs, nothing like that. Sure, *amigo*. He pat my back. I'm not wearing his kind of sharkskin. We shake hands. Whose guarantees? These *chulos,* they can move around, go where they want, get out when the wind change, and here I am with my banners and my light bill and yesterday's potato salad. Luis Beech-Nut, he could sweep these bastards out with his broom, throw the cat at them, call the cops, say no blood on my floor, you listening, unless it's yours.

But I got to say maybe they'll be some new faces in here with their quarters, new friends, new half-dollars with some new president on them. Maybe I should have asked for time to think but I got this feeling they don't do that kind of business. Pay now, think later. Well, I don't got to make it gangster paradise in here, I can keep the place alive like Anthony never did, still selling two-year-old Ivory Snow that look like a car came in his window and ran over the box. If he don't come down here and kill me first.

So here I am. A couple more sales, they saying it take time, all the time take time. I'm taking my pail and go put suds in the water, wash down the sidewalk, the least I can do. Otherwise it all pile up out there and I see enough dust inside all day. George Street, you and your hurry, you looked so good to me when I came to see this place. Back and forth like the ocean tides, all these well-dressed people who look like they eat good, smoke a lot, drink a six-pack every night, and this corner is a little pebble sticking up in the tide. How was I supposed to know nothing stop here? Nothing except the cars for the stop sign, not even a mailbox, a trash can, nothing. I got a sign out there that say NO PARKING, M-F, 7-11, 4-7. Big shit. Listen to Luis, goddamn. Goddamn, I'm cutting the price of milk today. Two cents, running a risk. *Mira!* Will you come in now?

☆☆☆ Works and Ways

by Alan Goldfein

Recently I sublet my Greenwich Village apartment, flew to Berkeley, and worked in a hippie candle factory. I had been living in New York for a half-dozen years, writing, drinking at writers' bars, playing basketball with Little Italy kids, black kids, playing flute in Washington Square Park and small clubs, shooting pool with Puerto Ricans up on La Quatorze—Fourteenth Street. In New York one may not see much nature, but he covers a lot of culture territory just going round the block. This was why I'd stayed. I loved New York, its raw nation-mixed intelligence; but after a time I felt like a teacher trapped in a world perpetually apple-cheeked: drinkers got married, or quit (drinking and/or writing), black and Puerto Rican jocks, my pals, went into social work. On flute, playing Coltrane from his melodic "pre-consciousness" days, I lost an audience. My stories grew quixotic. Never much of a fan of the contemporary antiseptic—transcendence and blank-faced bliss—always a sucker for ethnicity, I decided "Go where the other world is new." I left the "melting pot" I loved and went West. Broke.

Buddy of Berkeley; I stayed with him. I'd known the guy since high school, where he'd been a do-er. A major Do-er: debater, editor, seeker of office every time you turned your head. In those days—the fifties—Buddy wore sports coats to class every day. Glen plaids, charcoals, cords, corduroys, natural gabardines. Rep ties knotted tight into his neck, squeezing his Adam's apple out as if he were perpetually about to go "Gulp"; his shoes were Scotch-grain cordovan. Buddy's rep tie flew like a banner over his

ALAN GOLDFEIN (b. 1940) is the author of *Heads: A Metafictional History of Western Civilization, 1762–1975* (1973).

shoulder, his coattails flapped officiously as he strutted to the assembly podium, crisp as Katharine Hepburn in an office suit, a Candidate! He hovered over our school seal—winged, Latin-mottoed—eyes certain as a saint. Here was a youth in tune with the ideals of his age: "motivated" and "self starting . . ." He went to MIT, then Columbia, then Berkeley. Like everybody, Buddy became a radical; like few, a Physicist. Like everybody, he jettisoned sports coats and gave them to Saint Vincent's and Goodwill; as with some, a headband took the rep tie's place—he marched, he preached, he read *Das Kapital*—but like few, like very, very few, Buddy never carried into a new ideal the frustration, the enmity of the old. Childlike, yes—perhaps always scholastic—but with the most exquisite aspect of the ingénue: an energy aesthetic in its honesty. Physics, impersonal yet grand (ah, transcendent!), was the perfect home for him. Some adults kindle in us all the sometime urge to emulate the child.

Now, however, Buddy had given up physics—at least the academic sort—and he made candles, at the CosmiColor Candle Factory. He'd been doing it already for two years, and had proudly sent some of his prized creations back East, where they burned on mantels in Soho lofts, glowed on bookcases in Greenwich Village apartments, and generally splashed our narrow walls with West Coast easy life reproach. Buddy made mushroom candles, large, patchworked, veneered and sparkling; minis in various colors and floral designs. He was paid as a pieceworker, came and left the factory as he pleased, took off weeks when he was in the mood, and went hiking in Yosemite or gambling in Reno. He could make, he claimed, upwards of fifty dollars a day, if he knuckled down.

First morning, sleepless, I watched the sun illumine a distant toyish San Francisco, glistening in its surrounding hills, as if they formed the palm of a giant protective hand. It was January, and warm. Back East, tenement radiators would be steaming and clanging. I slid open the ranch-style window, smelled honeysuckle, and for a moment the world that surrounded me was the same one I tasted as a child. Honeysuckle is the most nostalgic aroma I have ever known.

"Awwwww-*rahhhhhhht!*" Buddy, from his bedroom. The West Coast idiom popular this year. Back East, no one over ten years old bellowed "Awwwww-rahhhhhhht." Back East, all California phrases sound phony, innocent and concocted—arrogant in a sneaky back-door way.

"Awwwww-*rahhhhhhht!*" I replied.

Last night we had dredged the past, each man's laughter deep, long, and though genuine, dodging present time. It was understandable.

I went to make coffee, while Buddy showered and sang (some Indian risey-shiney *raga,* joyous to him, a metabolic corkscrew for me). Two mugs, I discovered, sat waiting, dressed in oblique light and shade. And they were measured already—instant coffee, honey, cream. I knew Buddy had not yet been into the kitchen, so he must have spooned out the condiments the night before— skulking, mince-stepped as a housekeeper. Incredible! Oriental order meets native pragmatist . . . Or Jewish motherhood.

"Pour when it gurgles," Buddy yelled.

"Gurgles?"

"Don't wait till it pops." Then, through the hissing of the shower, he said something that sounded like "Bana-wana-sana," and kept repeating it. Obviously he'd incorporated into his *raga* a *mantram* of his own. Very innovative, I thought. Occidentally shortcut.

"Boiling bums the flavor out." A truth of a very low order for a Physicist, but he chanted it rhythmic, baritone.

Over Buddy's prefab coffee, we stared quizzical at each other's older faces. Our smiles charged the air with talklessness, they swallowed up the mugs. Buddy's hair was mostly gray now, coiling and receded; boundary lines trailed from the corners of his eyes to the edges of his mouth, as if demarcating areas where expression was allowed play. His eyes seemed larger than before. Pitch, red-rimmed. Crazy, sympathetic eyes. Einsteinian.

Buddy fixed and packed his lunch while I watched. Alfalfa sprouts and avocado, on nine grain . . . I resolved to work on my "Awwwww-rahhhhhhht."

The old working-class part of Berkeley, near the waterfront. The CosmiColor Candle Factory is a white stucco one-story building that sits between a mayonnaise plant and a bakery. (Jokes are told about candle sandwiches, unfunny health-food jokes.) All are white, one-story and stucco. They were built before World War Two, before the West became an alternative state of mind, so they are blocklike and unselfconscious, no different from the rows of small prewar factories and shops that back onto railroad sidings in the East . . . Inside, a dozen workers sat making candles. They were all T-shirted and in Levis, and most had long hair tied behind in buns and tails and knots. They were young. Kids. Much younger than Buddy and myself . . . Like hangers-on round Washington Square Park, without ethnicity.

"Brubeck," Buddy said. His teeth chomped up, churlish, under his top lip, in the fashion of Elliot Gould.

Twin speakers were perched atop high wrought-iron shelves, like sentinels. They were candle-cluttered, as if they'd sprouted shoots of wax. They belted piano, alto, like counterset alarms.

"Brubeck," I said. I repeated myself, to show I valued communication: "Brubeck."

"Shit," said Buddy. "We don't play Muzak here. It's a Coop."

I didn't see anybody tap feet; I didn't even get the connection between jazz and coop-ery. But Buddy was distilling his patented naïf wonder look. If you don't slack your jaw and stretch your brows like apocalypse, you feel like a creep . . . Back East, among "ethnics" such slack could cause you pain.

"Oh wow, a *coop!*" I said. I earned a Buddy nod.

We stood near the center of the workroom, candles in cartons all about us. Large foot-high mushrooms with thick stems and billowing tops; spheroids streaked with blue green red yellow orange veneers, wobbly and warped, rainbows melted down— mini mushrooms, two inches high, phallicly erect and blunt. The paraffin was strong, like incense on medieval dust, watering my eyes; I blinked a lot.

"You'll get used to that," Buddy said. His eyes were rabbit-red.

I watched the kids; they looked rugged, boy or girl. Hiking, mountain climbing, depressing accelerators all day on freeways. Sex wasn't overwhelmingly distinguishable. Palms and fingers obeyed interior pace, heads bent solemn, as in prayer. The candles might be icons.

A machine started up in the back room, clattering; a hum rose through the floor.

"Brubeck," I said, nodding, lost for words.

"Good for your *mandala*," said my pal.

"I hope jazz comes back," I said.

Buddy regarded me as if he didn't understand.

We stood still some moments, beached among the colors, kids and paraffin. I blinked some, troubling my eyes with a finger. I saw brothers lost, split by the continent.

"We haven't made a profit clear yet," Buddy said.

He watched my eyes, then led me between a Raleigh ten-speed and a German shepherd, both at their owners' feet. The dog's snout held casual on crossed paws. It looked like a dull sexless dog; maybe it was doing doga yoga, or maybe it had smoked too much dope.

"You get the Cook's tour," Buddy said. "Then we hit the wax." We walked into the back room of the hippie factory.

A thick black potbellied machine lay sideways on its thorax, grinding out wax. It had tentacles reaching long and sensual. The hippies, solemn and tentative as sycophants, relieved the spider squid (as I saw it) of its burden: thin long shiny tubes, each a different kaleidoscope. The kids, light and delicate in sneakers— wet nurses!—bathed the tubes with chamois cloths, and then placed them in hoppers of lukewarm water. On the other side of the hoppers, other kids—T-shirted, Levi'd, solemn—lifted the dried tubes and began cutting them. Their faces showed respect for ritual, while their motions resembled some Betty Crocker slicing cookie dough. As each tube was lifted, I could see patterns at their ends; each slice produced what would be a mushroom top.

"Extrusion," Buddy announced. He beamed at the squid as if he'd fathered it.

"Come again?" I said. People don't just say certain words out loud and then not connect them up to any more words. I don't care if West Coast people have mastered the art of slimming down sentences to slender oriental threads.

"Ex*tru*sion," a hippie said, without looking up from caressing his tube. Pedagogical.

"Oh, ex*tru*sion," I acknowledged.

"This is the only candle lab in the country, in the *world,* where extrusion is going on."

"Does the FBI know about this?"

Buddy, unamused, looked like a Physicist again: full face drawn distinct and dramatic. I was sure he had a hand in invention here. He explained the process, saying *candle lab* a few times—which struck me incredible—he touched down on every word ever used in *The Whole Earth Catalog,* the books of Buckminster Fuller and Alan Watts. Buddy said "organic" about twelve times, and I began nodding; by the time he started working over jobs like molecular change and synergy, my nod turned involuntary. Brubeck had faded long into the distance and Bob Dylan was being extremely strident, in that way of his which you know is damn artificial, so perfectly artificially less artificial than anyone else—the great trick of his artifice . . . "so they flow," Buddy droned, "like polyhedra, into essential cosmic shapes." And the machine, about which he was droning, clattered and the floor vibrated like a penny-arcade massage.

Dylan, meantime, lamented the quote railroading of Hurricane Carter.

Factorial eyes, I saw, took Dylan serious, more serious than Brubeck, who was good for their *mandalas.* But Buddy stood yet lost in the synergy of extrusion, his eyes rattling some mechanic-spirit syntax . . . He made one hundred fifty mini mushrooms that day, as I sat by, learning, making a crooked mini now and then. He got fifteen cents apiece; the coop, not yet "clear," sold them for a buck.

"You ought to form Local One, Wickers and Dippers," I said.

"New York humor." He grunted this. "I'm part damn owner. Anyway, you slowed me up."

"You're one fast cat," I said.

"Dude," Buddy said. "Cat's old East Coast talk." His fast hands moved without observation, nor did he look at me . . . His linguistics were more interesting than his synergy.

Buddy's patio in the Berkeley hills. Buddy rolled a joint, diligent over the papers as a watchmaker. His eyes were still rodent-red, lids swollen. This seemed permanent.

"Hurts my thumbs," Buddy said. "Making minis in the day, rolling *j's* at night." He sealed the papers with his tongue.

San Francisco's lights danced in the fading sunset, which hung over the city like a beautiful, spreading, ohGod, *mushroom*. My thumbs were burning too. I drank while Buddy smoked. Jack Daniel's cooled my thumb.

"Is this *it* for you?" I asked.

He took a deep, proclamatory draw; it lit up his face.

"It's a rotten job," I said. "Buddy, this is a rotten job you got."

He laughed. "You think my brain's gone to mush, don't you? Ground up, stewed out, fodder for the pigs."

"That's swill—fodder's for horses—but yeah."

"Yeah."

"How about we just settle on extruded?"

He stood up and hovered over me, giving out a cacklish laugh. It grew cool as the sunset died. An orange rim was now left, rising from the hills on the ocean side; a fire burning evenly. The Trans-America building—pyramidical—looked dusty, old as desert land. A sunset meant finality in the West, while in New York you knew Pittsburgh yet had light.

Buddy threw his right hand at my face; I flinched, tossing up a blocking left, and spilled some drink.

"Relax, Mister New York uptight. I just wanted to show you my pulse." He laid his wrist in my palm, giggling, and I sat holding it, embarrassed.

"That's a pulse, all right."

"Count it, asshole. Count it."

It was slow: fifty-four.

"Some pulse, huh."

"One of the best I've ever felt."

Buddy laughed. He withdrew his arm and laughed, and the hills rocked like the factory floor. He laughed like he didn't take himself serious, but wanted, wanted earnestly, others to mark that fact. He kept standing over me too. With his lousy fifty-four pulse, big breaths pumping up his laugh.

Finally he made a gesture. He leaned back, half stumbling, as if he would crash into his patio railing, spill over, ricochet to the bottom of the hills. He bounced off the railing like a boxer, spreading his arms, explaining, "I did physics, and nobody knew I was alive. I talked calculus, Pythagoras, Euclid, bridging them, and people ran for the fire escapes. I couldn't walk into a lousy room. I had things to *tell* people, and they'd hear my voice on the phone and hang up . . . I called *you* once, joker, and said I wanted to shoot the breeze—I'll never forget this—and you said, okay, hurry up . . ."

I smiled at my cleverness. He didn't.

"You ever tell the eternal verities to a dial tone, pal?"

I didn't say yes or no.

"I got a lot of headaches holding the eternal verities in. Now I make candles and everybody burns them in the night." He spread his arm again, paternal: Moses-Heatonian. "Look down there. Look!"

There are, indeed, many lights in Berkeley.

"I could make a thousand minis in a day," Buddy said.

"That's a lot of alfalfa sprouts."

"The minis are a yoga," Buddy said. He toked, and a flash funnel lit his nose and eyes.

"Hindu bullshit social science," I said. "In the West it's called gestalt." I drank, biting ice, my ears full of the crush of ice, my eyes full of his lean silver crazy face.

"Mini yoga," Buddy said.

The trick to mushroom making of the mini variety is your thumb. You take a top—a patchwork or floral or kaleidoscope (there are bucketsful, cut flat and round by the extruders)—and you attach it firmly to a stem about two inches long, which you have cut from twenty-inch strips of wax and veneer. You must make sure stems and tops have been heated to the optimum consistency—malleable yet firm—or your thumb will fail at attachment. The procedure is as follows: (1) Drop stems and tops into a cauldron of bubbling water (allowing your fingers don't drop in with them); (2) wait one half-hour, during which you may (a) read the paper (one of the Berkeley underground jobs; not *The Chronicle,* certainly not Hearst's *Examiner* and most definitely not a dirty magazine; (b) be West Coast "lay back" and "mellow"—i.e., go into the side room equipped with fridge, couches, speakers and gargoylish minis and maxis (the Candle Hall of Fame), and "lay back," "mellowly." Records and tapes are stacked: jazz, jazz rock, folk, folk rock, folk jazz rock jazz folk. And Bach. It is best to be very relaxed during this interim, for you are on piecework, and it is disturbing to be reminded that while your tops boil you aren't making one red cent.

Buddy sat by his desk, reading an underground paper, Patti Tanya Hearst's face—that wide-jowled unimaginative face—stretched across its front. Buddy's mouth was pulled into a grin as undiscriminating as Patti's. I went into the lounge.

A girl sat cross-legged on a couch and played chords on guitar. Lugubrious. She was thick through the shoulders, and bowed, as if she'd backpacked one too many times. The prickly taste of marijuana floated in the room.

I nodded to the girl, but she sat sunk in her guitar, its edge pressing a definitory slope into the bicep of her stroking arm.

More lugubrious chords: "The Waiting for Your Wax to Boil Blues?"

I got a brainstorm:

"Awwwww-*rahhhhhhht!*" Grinning.

"No it ain't," she said. "I know what's all right, and what I was doing isn't all right." She lay the guitar at her feet. Her breasts were large, they hovered sacklike in her T-shirt as she bent. She was probably in her late teens. *"Man,"* she said.

"That was exasperation, right?—that 'man.' "

"That wasn't ex-uh-zasperation." She said it like it was a music style, or a song. "I was ex*peri*menting, if you wanna know. What it sounded like to me, it don't sound like to you, because you're listening for plain music stuff. What I was doing was all right, but you didn't think it was all right, but you said it was, because you don't really know . . . But I said it *wasn't* all right just because I knew you were shitting—even though I knew it was."

Back to mini yoga. (3) Extract extruded stems and tops from the boiling cauldron (making sure, again, your fingers don't intrude); (4) store the tops in the small makeshift oven beneath your desk, while cutting the stems; (5) deposit stems in oven, to keep them warm as you work.

Now comes the craftsmanship. Taking one stem in the left hand, and one top in the right (unless you're a southpaw), you attach, centering the top on the stem, so there will be no undue over- or under-lapping of the mushroom's head—which would result in a reject, and no fifteen cents. Attachment requires considerable tensile strength of the thumb, combined with a calloused insensitivity, for these materials are still very resistant to a lot of pushing around. Not to mention hot. (Here is where Buddy developed his Chandler's Thumb; I drew a blister right away.) One turns the stem clockwise, and rapidly, while pressing down heavily on the top, around the edges of its design, at the same time taking precious care to press up with the wrist of the left (stem) hand, which results (or *ought* to) in the neat meshing of said stem and top, and, with further pressing and spinning, the gradual formation of a convex mushroom shape, the center of its parabolic peak coming out, like magic, in the center of the psychedelic design. (You hope.)

Simple enough. And at this stage you have your basic mini. All that remains for one to earn one half the price of a cup of coffee is to smooth it out so there are no fingerprints or lumps; then, centering again, cathetering it with what Buddy affectionately called the "jabber" (a straight thin piece of wire that could puncture your more vulnerable spots), inserting the wick down through the incision (urethra?) and soldering wax to wick. Presto! And people waste *years* learning *kundalini* yoga.

I tried. All week long I tried. Jumping up from my desk, above my little oven, rushing to the hopper where the extruders deposited stems, hopping to the baskets where the tops were kept, boiling, cutting, attaching, pressing, spinning, catheterizing, wicking, dipping into water. Fifteen cents! . . . More rapidly next time. My heart raced. I felt my pulse arterial in my neck—it wasn't fifty-four. I looked at others, especially the young girls, caressing their mushrooms and spheroids, sensual and undisturbed. Oh, I'm *weird,* I thought; sublimation, not extrusion, turns me on. I try to drop out and I can't even drop! I am just a New York guy . . . My legs grew tight, ropes pulling up from the small of my back, knotted at the calfs. I heard no music either. Buddy beat me, mini-making, roughly fifteen to one. Plus, mine were tilted and off center, the products of labor that had no essential relation to motions that were me . . . I longed for accents, gutter grime, mean hostile depraved predatory unbeatific realistic faces, profiles stamped with origins: East Coast poverty and pool. Distantly I realized my yearning was phantasmagoric, even vengeful. Each day, yet, the yen grew stronger, as the realization too. I wanted to hurt someone.

"These are the worst minis in history," a kid finally said. He was fiddling with his hair, angelically hauteur. "I'm quality control this week. I can't pass this shit." He leaned over me, and I threw my eyes at him, instead of fists, because, being West Coast, he seemed in healthy shape; still I wanted, badly, to tap the aggressive in the pacific—as Patti, Panthers, Manson, Hell's Angels—in one instant I understood California violence in its fierce Inquisitional rectitude: religious hards against religious softs—a Thirty Years' War out here. New York was not religious any more.

"The factory system makes people dumb!" I cried. "*Marx* said that. Adam Smith said that. Studs Terkel, Sinclair, Mike Gold, six trillion sociologists. But you never heard of them, kid, because you're dumb. Dumb! Confucius probably said it too!" I felt better, a bit Loyolaish.

"This ain't the factory system," Buddy said. "Don't pull that fey on us. *We* understand what's going on. We feel close to it. We *made* this place. We know every twist and stall and turn. We *love* it. We've *all* been quality control."

"Yeah, it's all *one*, right?" I was ironic.

"It's just 'the factory system' to *you*."

"*You're* dumb," the haughty angel to me.

"He's not dumb," said Buddy. "He knows things. He thinks he gave them up. He doesn't know he's already learned here too."

Buddy sounded cuckoo as that guitar girl.

I jogged to the lounge, mumbling about West Coast literacy, syntax and sacerdotal style.

I lay back (not mellowly). Music played. Occasionally someone came in to check on me, eat alfalfa sprouts, avocados, smoke dope. They checked me out of the corners of their eyes. I could hear them thinking: "If he's so smart, how come he's with us? Not analyzing or writing or editing, like they do in New York?" . . . Out the speakers on the shelf, between the gargoyle creatures of the Candle Hall of Fame, through my recollections, came Jean Pierre Rampal, the world's greatest flute virtuoso, trying to make jazz. He had real American ax-men behind him, but it was riveting—skilled dead routine riveting—on brocade. Rotten. Factorial.

"He shouldn't have given up classicism," I said.

A Chandler Humanist screwed me above his stash of edible-smokable greens. "He didn't give nothing up." The Humanist sneered angelically.

That winter, then, I worked. As challenge, first, no longer with the desire to "join up," to reject the Atlantic Coast. I boiled, twisted, pressed, catheterized with a vengeance. On breaks, while others smoke-a-doped, I read (de Grazia, *Of Time, Work and Leisure;* Mills on alienation; Arendt: *homo faber* verses *laborans;* Weber-Tawney on religion and industry, anthropology), brandishing the titles—for show, for assertion, reprisal, *and* interest. I got so—out of the pure zeal, not of conversion, but enmity and sheer intellectual self-righteousness—I could make, myself, one hundred fifty minis a day, I could fabricate mushrooms without straining, thinking, looking (I showed off, eyes closed), I could hike, after work, up the Berkeley hills (as little fatigued as Buddy), amid wildflowers, grass bleached and rhythmic as wheat, blueberry junipers; laurel thickets secreting my way as if I were a pioneer. I hurled myself into West Coast beauty—studying, memorizing, picturing, *taking-in*—with the conviction of, no Congregationalist, a Conquistador . . . I reproduced daily work efforts—even—some nights in my sleep (as I had once done with fares as a New York hackie), and awoke expecting pay. I worked until April, when it would be warmer in my hometown. When I left, Buddy said, "Yoga."

"Competition," I replied. "I've been slaving, not like an Aquarian, but an immigrant."

He smiled a Sophist-idiot grin.

On a bench in Washington Square Park, now spring. I am playing flute, and by accident I produce a vaguely familiar chord. Lately I've not been shooting pool so much, or playing basketball; more content to watch the intensity of the adversaries—the infinity of bitchings, elbows, forearms, pushing, leaps, wondrous, yet horrid, antagonism; it will follow these kids into their professions. No, I've not indulged. Yet my prose, more naturalistic, more romantic perhaps, remains a New York style. I close my eyes and listen to that chord, then repeat it. Rampal . . . Across from me Ohio buckeyes burst, pink-orange, dancing in the breeze, before the scallops of an ocher church, Roman Byzantine. Sycamore buttonballs dodge the accent helter-skelter of junkies, cops, dealers, joggers, kids, tourists, immigrants: New York! . . . More notes return from the Berkeley factory. They're richer (to me), more comprehended in this town.

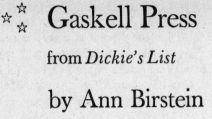

Gaskell Press

from *Dickie's List*

by Ann Birstein

The offices of Gaskell Press were not exactly modern, especially compared to the ones at Harcourt, Brace or Random House, or even, for that matter, Ed Gaskell's summer place out at Greenwich. But of course that was part of its charm and character: the small, quality publishing house, occupying not some new architect's dark glass tower but just a suite of elderly offices in a building not far from the Forty-second Street Library. Which also had trouble keeping its doors open these days, Dickie realized, looking down at the notation on his calendar of a ten o'clock appointment with Sophie Katz. Norma, his secretary, had just reminded him of it again, which wasn't necessary—Norma was just a great reminder-of—and also brought in the folder that now lay open on his desk on a great messy heap of other papers. He picked up the carbon copy of the letter on top: "To my mind, Miss Katz is very close to writing a truly successful book. If she would care to come in and discuss the matter, I would be delighted to talk to her in greater detail. . . ." He glanced at the blank space where his signature had been on the original and then looked out the window, consoling himself with the view. It was high and misty, a crisscrossing of gray stone rooftops along Fifth Avenue, and a lot better than what those young editors on Third Avenue were looking at, what with the low fluorescent ceilings and corrugated partitions and blank walls. Maybe in trying to replace Aaron Lasch, whom Ed Gaskell just hadn't been able to stand, they should advertise "windowed offices," like the "windowed kitchens" in the apartment ads in the *Times*.

ANN BIRSTEIN (b. 1927) is the author of *Summer Situations* (1972) and *Dickie's List* (1973), among other books.

The telephone on his desk began to ring, and after stalling a moment, he told Norma to have Miss Katz take a seat and he would be right out. He had always made a point of being courteous to his authors, present and prospective, and he certainly had no desire to keep Sophie Katz waiting just to impress her with his own importance. Nevertheless, as he started down the hall, having taken one more look out the window, it seemed to Dickie that it was getting more and more difficult to deal with writers lately, novelists especially (in spite of Lancelot Hale's oft-repeated thesis on the necessary madness of poets). Look at Hershel Meyers, once the sweetest nicest guy in the world, now an impossible egomaniac. That sock in the jaw, accidental or not, hadn't been funny, though Sandra kept insisting it never hurt at all. Physically. Spiritually, almost a week later she was still rubbing her jaw and talking about the actual experience of violence. Where the hell did she think she lived anyway? A look at the news from Vietnam, a walk to the IRT, though she refused to take the subway anymore, would have told her more about violence than she needed to know. Should he have socked Hershel back? That didn't seem right either. No, it was a lot easier on the nerves and frankly more civilized to deal with academicians, even the poets, even such surly types as George Auerbach, who fancied himself a literary lion at dinner parties but was an absolute lamb when it came to questions of contracts. Though even here you could never tell in advance. For example, a year ago, when they had accepted that first novel by Gertrude Dienst, then unknown, except that she had just been divorced from a famous husband whose pseudo-Freudian interpretation of history she was reputed to have written, they had all feared the worst. A terrifying young woman, tall, dark, oily-skinned, with a very strong dyke potential. But in no time at all, Gert had graduated from intense first novelist to all-around femme de lettres, and now there wasn't a party you could go to where Gertrude wasn't always accompanied by that very Jewish-looking nephew with the dark olive complexion, even darker and more olive than his aunt's, and the long sideburns that could have passed for forelocks. Practically a living illustration for Eli Mandel's new coffee table (he had almost thought Christmas) book, *Jews of the Old Country.*

"Miss Katz?" Dickie said, pausing in the doorway of the

reception room and addressing his question toward the woman who was nervously investigating the glass case of new books.

There was a loud clearing of throat and a squeak that could possibly be interpreted to mean, "Mr. Baxter." Dickie smiled and, with a courteous wave, indicated that perhaps Miss Katz would be good enough to precede him back down the hall. He went behind with a sinking heart. This was no good old Gert Dienst. Whatever Sophie Katz was, she would remain permanently, which happened to be, as that one quick glance at her had revealed, wet-eyed, eager, middle-aged, probably glandular, and, as this longer view of her back confirmed, endowed with long lank graying blond hair whose stray locks snaked their way into the collar of her navy blue raincoat.

"Sorry—this way," Dickie murmured as they collided at the corner of the corridor. He opened the door to his office and then the two of them regarded each other dubiously.

"Won't you sit down?" Dickie said.

"I'd *love* to. Where?"

"Where?" Dickie repeated and then, adding "Oh, here," indicated a small couch in the cluttered corner by his own bookshelves. He watched her sink down with her collar crowding her ears, returned to his desk, realized that she was sitting too far away, beckoned her to the chair facing him, and finally helped her off with her coat. It did not surprise him that neither of them knew where to put it and, also, that a slightly rancid odor hovered about the person of Miss Katz, as of old perfume impregnated at the dry cleaners or, actually, almost an animal smell of acute nervousness. Suddenly Dickie pitied the woman, always a bad policy, and hoped more than ever that the interview could be accomplished quickly.

"Miss Katz—" he began, resuming his seat and leaning forward on his elbows.

"*Yes?*"

Dear god, why did the woman have to speak in italics?

"We feel, *I* feel—" now he was doing it "—that you are very close to writing a—"

"Truly successful book," Sophie Katz finished for him.

Dickie surreptitiously glanced under his arm. Had she been reading the carbon copy of his letter upside down?

"A truly successful book," Dickie agreed. "However . . . it's awfully good of you to come in, by the way. I'm glad you were willing to discuss it."

Sophie Katz nodded, impatient of the ceremony, and fixed him intently with her large, protuberant, red-rimmed eyes. "Where do you think it goes sour, Mr. Baxter?"

"Sour?" Dickie said. "Well, that's the thing. What I mean is that, well, look, I think what you have here is a first-rate tragedy of innocence for about one-third through of this novel. The influence of *Joseph Andrews* is great, by the way. I recognize your use of it and think it's terrific."

"I've never read *Joseph Andrews.*"

"Haven't you?" Dickie said, with a surprised, interested inclination of his head. "Maybe you should. It's damn good. Very reminiscent of your work. Or should I say, vice-versa—?" He laughed, waiting vainly for Miss Katz to join him, then cleared his throat. "Fielding."

"I know. I'm crazy about *Tom Jones,*" Miss Katz volunteered.

"Are you really?"

"Oh, yes."

"Well, then I think you'd like *Joseph Andrews* too."

"Oh, I'm sure."

"Yes," Dickie said.

Miss Katz fixed him again with her bulgy, anxious eyes. "You say one-third. Why do you stop just at that point?"

Dickie took a deep breath. "Because, well, you see, I think her fall comes too early on. Before we're sufficiently clued in on the topography of this book. The reader's confused. He's not sufficiently clued in to the background. Now, if there were some way you could postpone her commitment, tantalize the reader a bit. . . . Otherwise, you see, she trips but—"

"Doesn't fall."

"—stoops, but—"

"Doesn't conquer," Sophie Katz finished for him. He didn't bother to lift his arm again. She knew the letter by heart.

"Yes, exactly," Dickie said.

"But how would you change it?"

There was a silence that Dickie let prolong itself. He looked down at his entwined fingers, then out the window in the general direction of the Forty-second Street Library—turnstiles for the general public?—then back at Miss Katz, who had kept staring at him with those tremulously eager, protruding eyes. She was even older than he had first thought. Her skin, a chalky white, sagged on either side of her chin, reflecting the yellow of a double string of amber beads. Little planes of gray showed under the straight blond hair at her temples.

"Shift the seduction scene," Dickie said.

Miss Katz blinked and gulped hard, as if she had just swallowed a marble.

"Shift it?"

"That's right," Dickie said.

"But that's a major change."

"That's right," Dickie said.

"But where would I shift it *to?"*

"Well, I don't have the text right at hand," Dickie said, and continued quickly before Miss Katz had time to finish rummaging through what looked like a child's plaid schoolbag. "But, just roughly, mind you, I'd say certainly west of page 150."

"But that means—"

"Figuring out what to do with the reader until the two of them climb into bed together. Right—" Dickie smiled. "But I think, in fact I'm sure, that much of the material that you now have coming in afterward can be interwoven with the stuff that comes before. This way, you see, you'll be able to carry the reader's interest right along through all the complicated exposition— much of which can be cut, by the way—instead of losing it two-thirds of the way through."

The telephone rang.

"It would require eliminating an awful lot of Lester," Miss Katz said dubiously.

"Well, yes, maybe—" Dickie said and told Norma not to put through any calls for about ten more minutes.

"On the other hand, of course," Miss Katz said, screwing up her face in overagonized concentration, "it might *just* give the love affair itself a deeper meaning."

"It might," Dickie said, excusing himself. Chicago? Well, in that case, could Norma please find out who was calling?

"I mean, *per esempio,* coming at the end, the seduction scene might come as a less dramatic but more natural climax, couldn't it? Forgive the pun. I mean, giving Nolan's refusal to marry her a double edge to the affair. Mightn't it?"

"Well, that hadn't occurred to me, but yes, I suppose so," Dickie said, cupping his hand over the receiver for a moment. George Auerbach? Then would Norma please explain he was in conference and would call back later?

"Sorry," Dickie said.

". . . And then, when the brother's letter arrives, the fact that she literally can't read it, wouldn't invite any top-heavy symbolism. We could skip right over to the wife's bedroom."

"Terrific," Dickie said, more disappointed about the call than he should have been. "Marvelous idea."

"And then, when Mona—" Miss Katz's eager chin sagged down again into the region of the amber beads. "No," she said, sighing, "it won't work."

"Oh? Why not?"

"Because the brother isn't there anymore."

"How about using Stephanie to get him back?"

"Stephanie? Because she's seen him at the party? You mean, she could ask him to take her home, something like that?"

"Well, unless," Dickie said, "you'd prefer not to—"

"Oh, no! You're absolutely *right!*" Miss Katz said excitedly. "God, yes, it's *perfect!* I mean, you've suggested all kinds of possibilities to me. My mind's agog with them, absolutely *awhirl.*"

"I'm glad," Dickie said.

"Well, I'm not sure *I* am," Miss Katz said, with a laugh that reminded Dickie of a line from Fitzgerald, ". . . *the stiff, tinny drip of a banjo.* . . ." She cocked her head coquettishly. "It would be an enormous job, you know. Like breaking a bone and setting it again."

"I guess it would," Dickie said.

"Could you help me with it? Could you give me advice as we go along?"

"I don't see why not," Dickie said. "Look, let me read it again. Let me go over it very carefully."

"Oh, good! I will too. I have my own Xerox."

"I won't make any marks," Dickie said. "What I do is put in these little slips of paper."

"How long will it take you?" Miss Katz said.

"Well, actually, I'm a little pressed right now," Dickie said, "but give me a week, a solid week, and I'll call you. Okay?"

He stood up, as did Miss Katz, rising from the wreckage of her raincoat, a middle-aged parody of a shipwrecked Venus.

"I can't tell you how *happy* I am about all this," Miss Katz said. "How terribly excited. I'm terribly, terribly grateful to you for all your suggestions."

"Well, it would be a fun book to publish," Dickie said, holding out her coat at arm's length. It turned out to be a cape. How did you help a woman on with one of those things anyway? "A lot of books you do are drags. But this would definitely be a fun book."

The faint warm nervous aroma suffused the atmosphere between them again. Miss Katz swiveled her head and gave him a frightened look, like a rabbit about to be trapped in its own bag.

"Look, Mr. Baxter," she said, before Dickie could quite complete the anxious business of draping the heavy navy felt over her shoulders, "I'd better explain that much as I want to work with you, and happy a connection as I feel it would be, I'm afraid I simply couldn't embark on such a venture, that is, I literally couldn't afford to commit myself to a major revision of this kind—"

"Without a similar commitment from us," Dickie said. "Sure, that makes sense."

"Can you give me one?"

"Not right now," Dickie said, after a slight hesitation. "But let me read it again. And if my opinion of it holds, which I'm pretty sure it will, by the way, then there'll be plenty of time to discuss—"

"But is your opinion enough?"

"I could hardly function as an editor if it weren't," Dickie said, smiling.

"Yes, I understand that," Miss Katz said worriedly. "But I've had some experience . . . I know of firms where—"

"Right," Dickie agreed, hoping that if he put her at her ease, he could end the interview that much sooner. "Technically, what you're suggesting is absolutely justified. I have a boss and my boss has a veto I can't override. That's technically." He smiled. "Untechnically, Ed Gaskell hasn't used his veto in the twelve years I've been here. Okay?"

"I only meant—"

"No, please don't apologize," Dickie said, ushering her down the hall again and out past the switchboard to the bank of elevators. "You've got an absolutely legitimate concern there, and if I were in your place I'd ask the same questions. In fact, I'm glad I've had this chance to—ah, here's one going down."

"You'll call me?" Miss Katz said, halfway into the elevator.

"Absolutely."

"Then I'll be waiting!" Miss Katz cried, right before the door slid to and swallowed her up. "Oh—and *thank* you!"

"Thank *you*," Dickie said, waiting there civilly for a moment. He turned and started back to the office. In her glass cubicle, Norma rolled her eyes in exaggerated sympathy, and he shrugged and smiled. In fact, the interview had not only taken less time than he had feared, he was more excited by the book than he had let the author know. He would mention it again to Ralph Gorella when they had a drink later—why did Sandra dislike the man so much?—since if *Hindsight* took a piece, however small, it would grease the wheels all around. The thought of drinks made him mentally run down the rest of the day before then. Lunch with Carol Curtis at La Rochefoucauld, an interview with a prospective young editor at three, and then, well, what about Hershel? Ed had said something about wanting to see him. He started toward Ed's office and changed his mind, not particularly anxious to hover over Ed's desk just then, sharing honors with the silver-framed photograph of Felicity and the unused onyx ashtrays. Maybe he'd give Sandra a call, tell her he had just seen Sophie Katz and that she had absolutely nothing to worry about. But when, laughing, he dialed his home number, the desultory voice of the maid answered instead. Or should one call Orvietta a maid? The term "cleaning lady" seemed to be in better order these days, also "housekeeper." "Mother's helper" in this case was out of the question on account of the helper being about twice as old and fat as the mother. Funny that there really always was some slight nagging anxiety about the subject, though, in fact, Orvietta herself called herself the maid. Anyway, whatever she was, she told him Mrs. Baxter was out and hung up. Which was just as well, because now that Dickie thought about it, it hadn't been such a hot joke about Sophie after all.

The Interrogation of the Prisoner Bung by Mister Hawkins and Sergeant Tree

by David Huddle

The land in these provinces to the south of the capital city is so flat it would be possible to ride a bicycle from one end of this district to the other and to pedal only occasionally. The narrow highway passes over kilometers and kilometers of rice fields, laid out square and separated by slender green lines of grassy paddy-dikes and by irrigation ditches filled with bad water. The villages are far apart and small. Around them are clustered the little pockets of huts, the hamlets where the rice farmers live. The village that serves as the capital of this district is just large enough to have a proper marketplace. Close to the police compound, a detachment of Americans has set up its tents. These are lumps of new green canvas, and they sit on a concrete, French-built tennis court, long abandoned, not far from a large lily pond where women come in the morning to wash clothes and where policemen of the compound and their children come to swim and bathe in the late afternoon.

The door of a room to the rear of the District Police Headquarters is cracked for light and air. Outside noises—chickens quarreling, children playing, the mellow grunting of the pigs owned by the Police Chief—these reach the ears of the three men inside the quiet room. The room is not a cell; it is more like a small bedroom.

The American is nervous and fully awake, but he forces himself to yawn and sips at his coffee. In front of him are his papers, the report forms, yellow notepaper, two pencils and a ball-point pen. Across the table from the American is Sergeant Tree, a

DAVID HUDDLE (b. 1942) is the author of *A Dream with No Stump Roots in It: Stories* (1975).

young man who was noticed by the government of his country and taken from his studies to be sent to interpreter's school. Sergeant Tree has a pleasant and healthy face. He is accustomed to smiling, especially in the presence of Americans, who are, it happens, quite fond of him. Sergeant Tree knows that he has an admirable position working with Mister Hawkins; several of his unlucky classmates from interpreter's school serve nearer the shooting.

The prisoner, Bung, squats in the far corner of the room, his back at the intersection of the cool concrete walls. Bung is a large man for an Asian, but he is squatted down close to the floor. He was given a cigarette by the American when he was first brought into the room, but has finished smoking and holds the white filter inside his fist. Bung is not tied, nor restrained, but he squats perfectly still, his bare feet laid out flat and large on the floor. His hair, cut by his wife, is cropped short and uneven; his skin is dark, leathery, and there is a bruise below one of his shoulder blades. He looks only at the floor, and he wonders what he will do with the tip of the cigarette when the interrogation begins. He suspects that he ought to eat it now so that it will not be discovered later.

From the large barracks room on the other side of the building comes laughter and loud talking, the policemen changing shifts. Sergeant Tree smiles at these sounds. Some of the younger policemen are his friends. Hawkins, the American, does not seem to have heard. He is trying to think about sex, and he cannot concentrate.

"Ask the prisoner what his name is."

"What is your name?"

The prisoner reports that his name is Bung. The language startles Hawkins. He does not understand this language, except the first ten numbers of counting, and the words for yes and no. With Sergeant Tree helping him with the spelling, Hawkins enters the name into the proper blank.

"Ask the prisoner where he lives."

"Where do you live?"

The prisoner wails a string of language. He begins to weep as he speaks, and he goes on like this, swelling up the small room with the sound of his voice until he sees a warning twitch of the interpreter's hand. He stops immediately, as though corked. One of the Police Chief's pigs is snuffling over the ground just outside the door, rooting for scraps of food.

"What did he say?"

"He says that he is classed as a poor farmer, that he lives in the hamlet near where the soldiers found him, and that he has not seen his wife and his children for four days now and they do not know where he is.

"He says that he is not one of the enemy, although he has seen the enemy many times this year in his hamlet and in the village near his hamlet. He says that he was forced to give rice to the enemy on two different occasions, once at night, and another time during the day, and that he gave rice to the enemy only because they would have shot him if he had not.

"He says that he does not know the names of any of these men. He says that one of the men asked him to join them and to go with them, but that he told this man that he could not join them and go with them because he was poor and because his wife and his children would not be able to live without him to work for them to feed them. He says that the enemy men laughed at him when he said this but that they did not make him go with them when they left his house.

"He says that two days after the night the enemy came and took rice from him, the soldiers came to him in the field where he was working and made him walk with them for many kilometers, and made him climb into the back of a large truck, and put a cloth over his eyes, so that he did not see where the truck carried him and did not know where he was until he was put with some other people in a pen. He says these other people also had been brought in trucks to this place. He says that one of the soldiers hit him in the back with a weapon, because he was afraid at first to climb into the truck.

"He says that he does not have any money, but that he has ten kilos of rice hidden beneath the floor of the kitchen of his house. He says that he would make us the gift of this rice if we would let him go back to his wife and his children."

When he has finished his translation of the prisoner's speech, Sergeant Tree smiles at Mister Hawkins. Hawkins feels that he ought to write something down. He moves the pencil to a corner of the paper and writes down his service number, his Social Security number, the telephone number of his girl friend in Silver

Spring, Maryland, and the amount of money he has saved in his allotment account.

"Ask the prisoner in what year he was born."

Hawkins has decided to end the interrogation of this prisoner as quickly as he can. If there is enough time left, he will find an excuse for Sergeant Tree and himself to drive the jeep into the village.

"In what year were you born?"

The prisoner tells the year of his birth.

"Ask the prisoner in what place he was born."

"In what place were you born?"

The prisoner tells the place of his birth.

"Ask the prisoner the name of his wife."

"What is the name of your wife?"

Bung gives the name of his wife.

"Ask the prisoner the names of his parents."

"What are the names of your parents?"

Bung tells the names.

"Ask the prisoner the names of his children."

"What are the names of your children?"

The American takes down these things on the form, painstakingly, with help in the spelling from the interpreter, who has become bored with this. Hawkins fills all the blank spaces on the front of the form. Later, he will add his summary of the interrogation in the space provided on the back.

"Ask the prisoner the name of his hamlet chief."

"What is the name of your hamlet chief?"

The prisoner tells this name, and Hawkins takes it down on the notepaper. Hawkins has been trained to ask these questions. If a prisoner gives one incorrect name, then all names given may be incorrect, all information secured unreliable.

Bung tells the name of his village chief, and the American takes it down. Hawkins tears off this sheet of notepaper and gives it to Sergeant Tree. He asks the interpreter to take this paper to the Police Chief to check if these are the correct names. Sergeant Tree does not like to deal with the Police Chief because the Police Chief treats him as if he were a farmer. But he leaves the room in the manner of someone engaged in important business. Bung continues to stare at the floor, afraid the American will kill him now that they are in this room together, alone.

Hawkins is again trying to think about sex. Again, he is finding it difficult to concentrate. He cannot choose between thinking about sex with his girl friend Suzanne or with a plump girl who works in a souvenir shop in the village. The soft grunting of the pig outside catches his ear, and he finds that he is thinking of having sex with the pig. He takes another sheet of notepaper and begins calculating the number of days he has left to remain in Asia. The number turns out to be one hundred and thirty-three. This distresses him because the last time he calculated the number it was one hundred and thirty-five. He decides to think about food. He thinks of an omelet. He would like to have an omelet. His eyelids begin to close as he considers all the things that he likes to eat: an omelet, chocolate pie, macaroni, cookies, cheeseburgers, black-cherry Jell-O. He has a sudden vivid image of Suzanne's stomach, the path of downy hair to her navel. He stretches the muscles in his legs, and settles into concentration.

The clamor of chickens distracts him. Sergeant Tree has caused this noise by throwing a rock on his way back. The Police Chief refused to speak with him and required him to conduct his business with the secretary, whereas this secretary gloated over the indignity to Sergeant Tree, made many unnecessary delays and complications before letting the interpreter have a copy of the list of hamlet chiefs and village chiefs in the district.

Sergeant Tree enters the room, goes directly to the prisoner, with the toe of his boot kicks the prisoner on the shinbone. The boot hitting bone makes a wooden sound. Hawkins jerks up in his chair, but before he quite understands the situation, Sergeant Tree has shut the door to the small room and has kicked the prisoner's other shinbone. Bung responds with a grunt and holds his shins with his hands, drawing himself tighter into the corner.

"Wait!" The American stands up to restrain Sergeant Tree, but this is not necessary. Sergeant Tree has passed by the prisoner now and has gone to stand at his own side of the table. From underneath his uniform shirt he takes a rubber club, which he has borrowed from one of his policeman friends. He slaps the club on the table.

"He lies!" Sergeant Tree says this with as much evil as he can force into his voice.

"Hold on now. Let's check this out." Hawkins' sense of justice has been touched. He regards the prisoner as a clumsy, hulking sort, obviously not bright, but clearly honest.

"The Police Chief says that he lies!" Sergeant Tree announces. He shows Hawkins the paper listing the names of the hamlet chiefs and the village chiefs. With the door shut, the light in the small room is very dim, and it is difficult to locate the names on the list. Hawkins is disturbed by the darkness, is uncomfortable being so intimately together with two men. The breath of the interpreter has something sweetish to it. It occurs to Hawkins that now, since the prisoner has lied to them, there will probably not be enough time after the interrogation to take the jeep and drive into the village. This vexes him. He decides there must be something unhealthy in the diet of these people, something that causes this sweet-smelling breath.

Hawkins finds it almost impossible to read the columns of handwriting. He is confused. Sergeant Tree must show him the places on the list where the names of the prisoner's hamlet chief and village chief are written. They agree the prisoner has given them incorrect names, though Hawkins is not certain of it. He wishes these things were less complicated, and he dreads what he knows must follow. He thinks regretfully of what could have happened if the prisoner had given the correct names: the interrogation would have ended quickly, the prisoner released; he and Sergeant Tree could have driven into the village in the jeep, wearing their sunglasses, with the cool wind whipping past them, dust billowing around the jeep, shoeshine boys shrieking, the girl in the souvenir shop going with him into the back room for a time.

Sergeant Tree goes to the prisoner, kneels on the floor beside him, and takes Bung's face between his hands. Tenderly, he draws the prisoner's head close to his own, and asks, almost absentmindedly, "Are you one of the enemy?"

"No."

All this strikes Hawkins as vaguely comic, someone saying, "I love you," in a high-school play.

Sergeant Tree spits in the face of the prisoner and then jams the prisoner's head back against the wall. Sergeant Tree stands up quickly, jerks the police club from the table, and starts beating the prisoner with random blows. Bung stays squatted down and covers his head with both arms. He makes a shrill noise.

Hawkins has seen this before in other interrogations. He listens closely, trying to hear everything: little shrieks coming from Sergeant Tree's throat, the chunking sound the rubber club makes. The American recognizes a kind of rightness in this, like the final slapping together of the bellies of a man and a woman.

Sergeant Tree stops. He stands, legs apart, facing the prisoner, his back to Hawkins. Bung keeps his squatting position, his arms crossed over his head.

The door scratches and opens just wide enough to let in a policeman friend of Sergeant Tree's, a skinny, rotten-toothed man, and a small boy. Hawkins has seen this boy and the policeman before. The two of them smile at the American and at Sergeant Tree, whom they admire for his education and for having achieved such an excellent position. Hawkins starts to send them back out, but decides to let them stay. He does not like to be discourteous to Asians.

Sergeant Tree acknowledges the presence of his friend and the boy. He sets the club on the table and removes his uniform shirt and the white T-shirt beneath it. His chest is powerful, but hairless. He catches Bung by the ears and jerks upward until the prisoner stands. Sergeant Tree is much shorter than the prisoner, and this he finds an advantage.

Hawkins notices that the muscles in Sergeant Tree's buttocks are clenched tight, and he admires this, finds it attractive. He has in his mind Suzanne. They are sitting in the back seat of the Oldsmobile. She has removed her stockings and garter belt, and now she slides the panties down from her hips, down her legs, off one foot, keeping them dangling on one ankle, ready to be pulled up quickly in case someone comes to the car and catches them. Hawkins has perfect concentration. He sees her panties glow.

Sergeant Tree tears away the prisoner's shirt, first from one side of his chest and then the other. Bung's mouth sags open now, as though he were about to drool.

The boy clutches at the sleeve of the policeman to whisper in his ear. The policeman giggles. They hush when the American glances at them. Hawkins is furious because they have distracted him. He decides that there is no privacy to be had in the entire country.

"Sergeant Tree, send these people out of here, please."

Sergeant Tree gives no sign that he has heard what Hawkins

has said. He is poising himself to begin. Letting out a heaving grunt, Sergeant Tree chops with the police club, catching the prisoner directly in the center of the forehead. A flame begins in Bung's brain; he is conscious of a fire, blazing, blinding him. He feels the club touch him twice more, once at his ribs and once at his forearm.

"Are you the enemy?" Sergeant Tree screams.

The policeman and the boy squat beside each other near the door. They whisper to each other as they watch Sergeant Tree settle into the steady, methodical beating. Occasionally he pauses to ask the question again, but he gets no answer.

From a certain height, Hawkins can see what is happening is profoundly sensible. He sees how deeply he loves these men in this room and how he respects them for the things they are doing. The knowledge rises in him, pushes to reveal itself. He stands up from his chair, virtually at attention.

A loud, hard smack swings the door wide open, and the room is filled with light. The Police Chief stands in the doorway, dressed in a crisp, white shirt, his rimless glasses sparkling. He is a fat man in the way that a good merchant might be fat—solid, confident, commanding. He stands with his hands on his hips, an authority in all matters. The policeman and the boy nod respectfully. The Police Chief walks to the table and picks up the list of hamlet chiefs and village chiefs. He examines this, and then he takes from his shirt pocket another paper, which is also a list of hamlet chiefs and village chiefs. He carries both lists to Sergeant Tree, who is kneeling in front of the prisoner. He shows Sergeant Tree the mistake he has made in getting a list that is out of date. He places the new list in Sergeant Tree's free hand, and then he takes the rubber club from Sergeant Tree's other hand and slaps it down across the top of Sergeant Tree's head. The Police Chief leaves the room, passing before the American, the policeman, the boy, not speaking nor looking other than to the direction of the door.

It is late afternoon and the rain has come. Hawkins stands inside his tent, looking through the open flap. He likes to look out across the old tennis court at the big lily pond. He has been fond of water since he learned to water-ski. If the rain stops before dark, he will go out to join the policemen and the children who swim and bathe in the lily pond.

Walking out on the highway, with one kilometer still to go before he comes to the village, is Sergeant Tree. He is alone, the highway behind him and in front of him as far as he can see and nothing else around him but rain and the fields of wet, green rice. His head hurts and his arms are weary from the load of rice he carries. When he returned the prisoner to his hamlet, the man's wife made such a fuss Sergeant Tree had to shout at her to make her shut up, and then, while he was inside the prisoner's hut conducting the final arrangements for the prisoner's release, the rain came, and his policeman friends in the jeep left him to manage alone.

The ten kilos of rice he carries are heavy for him, and he would put this load down and leave it, except that he plans to sell the rice and add the money to what he has been saving to buy a .45-caliber pistol like the one Mister Hawkins carries at his hip. Sergeant Tree tries to think about how well received he will be in California because he speaks the American language so well, and how it is likely that he will marry a rich American girl with very large breasts.

The prisoner Bung is delighted by the rain. It brought his children inside the hut, and the sounds of their fighting with each other make him happy. His wife came to him and touched him. The rice is cooking, and in a half hour his cousin will come, bringing with him the leader and two other members of Bung's squad. They will not be happy that half of their rice was taken by the interpreter to pay the American, but it will not be a disaster for them. The squad leader will be proud of Bung for gathering the information that he has—for he has memorized the guard routines at the police headquarters and at the old French area where the Americans are staying. He has watched all the comings and goings at these places, and he has marked out in his mind the best avenues of approach, the best escape routes, and the best places to set up ambush. Also, he has discovered a way that they can lie in wait and kill the Police Chief. It will occur at the place where the Police Chief goes to urinate every morning at a certain time. Bung has much information inside his head, and he believes he will be praised by the members of his squad. It is even possible that he will receive a commendation from someone very high.

His wife brings the rifle that was hidden, and Bung sets to

cleaning it, savoring the smell of the rice his wife places before him and of the American oil he uses on the weapon. He particularly enjoys taking the weapon apart and putting it together again. He is very fast at this.

☆ ☆
☆
Timmy

by Richard Elman

Mrs. Golden's children rarely visited her. She didn't mind, although she told them that she did. Edgar, her husband, was like the children; he was always busy with one thing or another, and that Mrs. Golden didn't care for any of his activities wasn't necessarily his fault. Edgar was a fine provider, an energetic, active sort of man who had gotten quite far rather early in life and thought he should still be going somewhere. The only trouble was his wife hadn't cared to make the trip with him. She had liked it much better in her comfortable home. Bitterly, once, Mrs. Golden had accused Edgar of inspiring the children's neglect for her, but even as she spoke she saw this wasn't so. She knew her husband would have liked the kids to spend more time with their mother if only to relieve him of some of the burden.

Not that you could honestly call Lilly Golden a ball-and-chain; she was far too meek, long-suffering, devoted, and was considered by most strangers to be a good wife. Although she and her husband rarely saw each other (except at breakfast), or spent time with each other (except on those combination business-trip vacations which Edgar liked to take), they knew deeply that their marriage was inextricable in the same way that some dreams make one aware that one is dreaming. If Lilly happened to be awake at night when Edgar would come home from one of his trade banquets or dinner meetings, she would register the proper notes of protest and solicitude at being awakened while always

RICHARD ELMAN (b. 1934) has published six novels, including *An Education in Blood* (1971); *Fredi & Shirl & The Kids* (1972); and a number of nonfiction books.

making sure to ask him questions about his day. Drowsy, bored, yet somehow strengthened by her husband's return, Lilly would lie back and listen to Edgar thump about in the darkness while he undressed, proud that she had sustained the loneliness once again. Shuddering when the covers were rolled back, or when Edgar brushed against her with a gross caress, she had schooled herself never to move away. Pretending sleep, she would wait until he had dozed off, and then she would get up, would walk out into the parlor, and stare blankly at the evening paper for an hour or so.

During the day Lilly found that being alone was an exhausting chore. Then she tried hard to be "self-sufficient" in response to Edgar's constant declarations that he was not going to live forever, but as she was not a club woman and did not like to window shop in Manhattan or to go to museums or matinees, the hours dragged. Her three sons, their wives, and the grandchildren might have kept her company, but the daughters-in-law frightened Lilly; the sons were now businessmen themselves; and she knew enough not to want to interfere in the raising of their children. Consequently, her main companion had to be Timmy.

Timmy was about the same age as her mistress and she had been with the Goldens as a day worker ever since the children were infants. The two women got along well. Boisterously, each entertained the other without ever being mean or condescending; with Timmy in the house, Lilly did not need to feel so shut in. From 9 A.M. to 5 P.M. on Mondays, Wednesdays, and Fridays, the two women carried on a running kaffee klatsch and pajama party. At times they giggled together like schoolgirls; at other times Timmy called her mistress "ma'am" and "honey" and never Lilly, but that was merely a convention; they talked to one another like old friends.

Timmy was a tall, heavy-set colored woman who had once been slim and pretty. She had a brazen stare and the skin along her arms and shoulders had a smooth, deep brown luster. Only her high cheekbones and her long delicate eyelashes gave an indication of her former voluptuousness. Otherwise, in her tattered stocking-cap, with her sleeves rolled up above her crinkled elbows, she gave off a perfume of starch and bleaching fluid and affected a plodding, goonish sloppiness in comparison with which Lilly Golden looked withered, skimpy, almost unformed—a frail, not quite blond woman with narrow hips and shoulders, whose large blue, staring eyes seemed so much brighter than her habitually drab, printed bathrobes. Placed alongside Timmy, Lilly could not help but look meager indeed.

Yet she would spend hours in the kitchen with the colored woman, gossiping, or smoking cigarettes, or just watching those big soft shoulders and strong arms plod through the ironing. "How's your sister these days?" Lilly might ask. ". . . You know the one I mean . . . the one who needs insulin . . . don't you remember? I gave you the money . . ."

"Oh, that one," Timmy would say with a good-natured smile, "that one that has the diabetes," signifying that she had been caught in an earlier lie or an exaggeration. Hurriedly then, as she creaked back and forth against the ironing board, Timmy would find a way to change the subject, or she would begin a long dissertation on the family's squalid condition in far-away Pine Ridge, Georgia. She would squeal, "That reminds me," and then would throw Lilly completely off the scent by quickly narrating one harrowing New York adventure, followed by a second one, in the process of which the names of dozens of exotic gin mills, movie theaters, barbecues, and hotels might be summoned up as evidence. Tying her bathrobe tightly about her waist, Lilly would sit cross-legged on the kitchen stool, a shrewd inquisitor. She could always tell when Timmy was lying, but she never cared to catch her up and make her stammer; she preferred to hide her secret glee behind the terry-cloth lapels of her robe.

Because Timmy had never married, to Lilly's knowledge, the first question every Monday would invariably be: "How was your weekend? How did the boys treat you?"

Then Timmy's thick, tinted lips would break into a rare frown. "Missus Goldenhoney," she would say, wiping a hand along her bandana, "sometimes I think them men creatures oughtn't to be allowed to carry on the way they do."

What followed then would be a salty discourse concocted half of Bessie Smith and half of Mary Worth. Timmy's escapades with the men of Harlem or Bedford-Stuyvesant had not ceased at the menopause. They always seemed to begin with her stepping out with one man, losing track of him, then running into a second, an even older friend. But, despite the inept plotting, the years had taught Timmy to color such improbable yarns to Lilly's satisfac-

tion with numerous strandlike asides and great quantities of a
dark rhetoric of the streets that permitted her to invent infinite
epithets with which to allude to the act of love, or to such actions
as dancing, boozing, or even singing in a church choir. All these
experiences breathed life when Timmy told them, and the result
was that Mrs. Golden might frown, or sigh, or make little clucking noises of disapproval with her tongue, but she would find
herself muttering, "Ah yes," and, "Go ahead," and "Then what
happened?"

Even over lunch, the colored maid's lusty monologue might
continue. If Timmy was too busy with her housework, Mrs.
Golden would prepare the sandwiches and brew tea. Then they
would sit down opposite each other. Later, if it was a nice day,
Mrs. Golden might get dressed to do her shopping. Otherwise,
she would order by telephone and they would spend the afternoon in more talk, with Lilly following Timmy about the house
to issue the kinds of instructions which after twenty years were
no longer necessary.

Usually, then, the two women would talk in a confidential way
about the Golden family. In the master bedroom, Mrs. G would
pitch in with the moving and lifting of heavy objects as she
related what a busy man her husband was; one at a time, through
her sons' deserted lairs, she would discuss what eventually should
be done with the various pieces of sporting equipment, books,
records, and souvenirs that still lay around on the tops of night
tables and bureaus, catching dust; or she would show the maid
the newest snapshots of her grandchildren, or tell her dry, un-
interesting stories of their latest antics. In the face of all this,
Timmy played her role convincingly; she was polite without
ceasing for a minute to attend to her chores. She made no secret
of the fact that she didn't like any of the other Goldens. "Them,"
she called the children, and Lilly no longer winced when she
heard the word. She was much too pleased that she could have
this intimacy with Timmy and she never felt that she was permit-
ting the girl liberties. When Edgar asked if she had paid "the
schwartsa," she did not rebuke him, for she knew the name was
important to him for his image of himself, but she almost never
used such a word herself, and if she did she crossed her fingers.
The fact was that when her maid had left the house Lilly Golden
thought only about her next visit.

That is why, when Edgar died suddenly in his sleep of a heart attack, Timmy was the first person she wanted to come and be with her.

The children lined up solidly against that idea. On the morning of the funeral, when the maid was out of earshot in the kitchen, they argued that Lilly could afford a real companion, a college girl or another widowed lady like herself, not just a colored maid. They also suggested that Mrs. Golden sell the house and move into an apartment nearer the city. When Lilly raised her voice in protest, her eldest son puffed out his cheeks just like Edgar, and declared: "Mother, please. We know you're still upset."

It rained for the funeral, and the cold, dreary affair went off according to a precise timetable. There were the usual number of staged and unstaged outbursts; there was even a moment of genuine pathos for Lilly when the coffin was lowered into the grave and she found that she could not release the pocket of dirt that had been thrust into her hands. Afterward, she and the children returned to the old house for a cold luncheon prepared by Timmy, but Lilly retired as soon thereafter as possible, and when, early the next morning, the children returned for a visit along with two of Edgar's brothers, the assistant rabbi, and the family lawyer, Lilly greeted them by announcing her plans with dry eyes.

She would keep the big house and ask Timmy to sleep in. She did not want to go away on a trip; she did not think it would be fair to live in White Plains with her eldest son; she did not want her sister in Minneapolis to come and stay with her awhile. "We never got along when Edgar was alive. Why should we now?" Lilly asked. "Besides," she added, "Flora has no sense of humor and Timmy does." She preferred Timmy, or to be left alone, if need be, for she wanted time to think. Patiently, Lilly explained that just so long as she had someone to do the heavy cleaning and cook for her occasional guests, she would be happy, but her second son, Robert, exclaimed: "Honestly, Mamma, it sounds so impractical."

Lilly didn't deny that it was. "That's the way I want it . . . and I can afford it," she simply said.

"Besides," she smiled vaguely again, as if her colorless smile and her colorless voice were conspiring together, "I won't be lonely. There's TV and the telephone and a great big world outside."

"But Mother . . ."

Lilly held up her hand to demand silence. "If all else fails, I'll have my memories," she said.

This sentiment took everybody by surprise. The three sons thought: "She means memories of us." The daughters-in-law smiled guiltily together. "Jesus," went the astonished lawyer, and even Edgar's brothers mused: "Memories of him. The old girl liked him after all. God help her."

Then, because none of the sons had wanted Lilly to move in with them in the first place, one by one they relented and it was agreed that she was to do as she pleased, as long as the situation was manageable, if she would release some of the money from the estate to compensate the younger Goldens for the valuable property on which the house stood.

Wearily, Lilly agreed. It was small blackmail for her freedom, she thought, as she signed all the necessary papers, kissed her children, and made them promise to visit her often with the little ones. Then the lawyer had to go and Edgar's brothers sat around coughing, whispering, and glancing at condolence cards, before they, too, departed.

On the very next morning, Timmy came to work late as usual, but Mrs. Golden didn't make her intentions known to the girl on that day or the next, for she was still too busy receiving visitors, and when the last of these had departed, she preferred to remain alone in her room. It was not that Lilly felt timid. On the contrary, she felt sure that Timmy would be more comfortable in that large suite of rooms in her attic than in some Harlem tenement, and she had promised herself not to impose any restrictions on the maid. If she didn't make the invitation right away, it was because she wanted to endure her isolation for just a little while longer; for the moment, it gave her a kind of joy.

Ever since that morning when she had opened her eyes to find Edgar dead alongside her, Lilly had hardly a moment to make her peace with that part of her life that began and ended with Edgar. To be finally alone was like waking from a bad dream to be assured by somebody you wanted to trust that the dream had been a fact and now the real dream was to start; and when she looked down into Edgar's rude, cold eyes for the last time, Lilly wondered if it weren't all hallucination. How else had she ever been tamed by such a man? Death had twisted Edgar's lips and blanched his cheeks, turning his expression sullen and pathetic. How then had he managed to frighten her so in their former life together? When she was alone she pondered this question as she meandered about the big house in her peignoir, going from room to room, throwing out letters, magazines, and papers without discrimination, save for the fact that she touched everything that had once been Edgar's with a faintly pleasurable sense of dread.

For nearly two weeks she lived that way. Timmy was given a vacation with pay; for a few days the phone was lifted off its cradle; and she told her family not to worry and not to try and see her for awhile. Getting up when she pleased and going to sleep when she pleased, Lilly Golden drew the shades about her, threw away the stacks of black-edged cards without acknowledging them or the wreaths and flowers from her late husband's Gentile friends, and lived for the most part on coffee and on the baskets of fruits and sweets that kept arriving. She wandered through the house, her eyes glancing from the television set to the sliver of daylight beneath the drawn shades, or to the ancient sepia photos of her husband and the babies that were on the mantel, and while she made preparations for her new mode of life, she was not stirred to thoughts of Timmy. But on the Monday of the third week after Edgar's death, the maid returned.

It was a warm, springish day in late March when Lilly woke up quite late in the morning from a dream about New Orleans, where she had spent her honeymoon, to find that the shades had been raised and that the sun was streaming across her face brightly. At first, she was alarmed by all the sunshine and the ringing stillness to the air, until she detected Timmy's familiar whistle coming from downstairs in the kitchen. Then she looked up and noticed that the television was still lit from the night before with tiny incandescent specks, although it made no noise now save for a low, steady, shushing sound. Lilly jumped out of bed. She rushed to the machine and flicked the switch. Slipping into her robe, she hurried out of the room and down the hall to wash her face and comb her hair in the bathroom. Presently, she was hurrying again toward the stairway when she stopped herself short, cinched the belt on her robe once more, and began to walk downstairs slowly into the kitchen.

The first thing she saw was Timmy's broad bent back. "Good morning," she called to the girl, who had already set up her ironing board and was going over the last of Edgar's shirts.

Between puffs of steam, Timmy lifted her head gracefully. "I got your juice ready," she announced, without yet looking around.

Lilly's glance went to the counter near the sink, where Timmy had placed a setting for breakfast. There was light toast in the salver and the percolator stood on the stove, warmed by a smudge of blue flame. On the ironing board, alongside Timmy's elbow, a cold cup of coffee stood.

"Why, that's very sweet of you," Lilly said, trying still to get the girl to turn around. She went toward the counter.

"Maybe you should give the juice a stirring," Timmy suggested.

"Yes, I will . . . of course," murmured Lilly, glancing sideways as she walked past and noticing Timmy's bright green pinafore and the new pink bandana that held her straight hair in place against her head. At the counter she spun around and met the girl full face. She had expected a smile but was greeted with a stare and a slow look of irony around the corners of the mouth. "You look well," Lilly said.

Timmy nodded: "Uh huh."

"Very well indeed," Lilly added. As she downed her juice with a quick toss of the head, she heard the iron sizzle against the shirt front. Then Mrs. Golden walked to the stove and poured herself some coffee. Lighting a cigarette, she sat down on the kitchen stool, simultaneously kicking her bright gingham slippers off her feet and curling her white toes around the chrome stool support, to watch Timmy glide over the shirt front and to sip her coffee.

"Well?" she asked.

And again: "Well?"

But the maid was reluctant to start a conversation, so Lilly finally had to add: "Well, how was your vacation?"

Timmy pretended to frown. "Trouble," she mumbled, "nothing but trouble, expense, and aggravation."

Lilly's heart began to pound. Then, aloud, she heard Timmy add: "Didn't even get to Pine Ridge. Didn't get nowhere. Stayed home most of the time with Bill and watched teevee. Well, you know," she explained rather archly, as if an explanation was in order, ". . . Bill . . . he's my new fella . . . he don't like to go nowheres . . ."

"Oh?"

Timmy's body heaved. She dipped the ends of her fingers under the dripping sink and sprinkled the area around the blue ESG monogram on Mr. Golden's shirt. Tiny currents of steam shot out when she placed the hot iron over the monogram. "God damn Bill," she mumbled grouchily.

"Men are like that sometimes," Lilly said, trying to console her.

"Oh, but I didn't mean," Timmy started to say, before succumbing to a giggle. Then she smirked: "You said it, sister. You're lucky to be done with all that. Maybe Jewish men are different . . ."

"No." Lilly shook her head. Then she decided to be bold. "I didn't know you had a new man," she said. "Tell me about him. What's his full name? What is he like? What does he do?"

The smile faded from Timmy's lips. "Name's Bill," she replied, folding Edgar's shirt and reaching down into her wicker basket for another damp white bundle. "Bill don't do nothing much," she added with a grunt.

"Oh, Timmy. I'm sorry," said Lilly again. The expression had been formed without her choosing it. She had expected more from Timmy—a story, a ribald explanation of Bill's do-nothing attitude—but that was no reason for her to be sorry, and when the maid remained silent as she wrung out the shirt between her pudgy, dark pink hands, she wished she could recall the phrase. "He don't do nothing . . . that one," she heard Timmy say, almost belligerently, bending low over the plane of the board now so that her ample bosoms were pendant behind the pinafore, and when she saw her reach for the hot iron again, Lilly suddenly blurted: "Timmy . . ."

The maid looked up.

". . . I don't know whether it's necessary for you to do Mr. Golden's shirts with such care now," Lilly said.

Timmy's smooth forehead was dense with perspiration and her hand was clutching the iron. "No, ma'am? she asked, incredulously.

"No," Lilly announced, gaining courage. "As a matter of fact, there's a lot of Mr. Golden's stuff lying around that we ought to organize and throw away. I tried to do some things when you were gone, but I didn't know where to begin or what to do with certain items. There's all his suits, for instance. Some are like new. My husband was quite a dandy, you know. Maybe your Bill can use them?"

"No, ma'am. Not Bill," the maid spoke loudly and sternly. She stared hard at Lilly as if delivering a prepared lecture. "Bill wouldn't like no hand-me-downs . . ."

Lilly's throat went dry: "I see . . ."

Turning away, she tried to close her eyes, to shut the incident from her thoughts, to dissociate herself from this second blunder. She realized she might have offended her old friend by offering a dead man's clothes to her new lover. Negroes, she knew, were apt to be superstitious. But she had meant no offense. She swore she hadn't. She had only thought that Bill might want to make use of such nice clothes. Walking barefoot to the stove to pour herself a second cup of coffee, Lilly could feel Timmy's eyes upon the back of her neck, and she was aware of a strong, cheap perfume. "Ma'am?" she heard. Spinning around so that she spilled some of the coffee into the saucer, Lilly saw the maid staring down at the wilted monogram on the damp white shirt.

She whispered. "Yes?"

"Ma'am," Timmy's lips moved again.

"Yes," she replied.

"Maybe you don't understand what I meant . . ."

"Oh, never mind," Lilly interrupted.

"But Mrs. Goldenhoney . . ."

"Timmy, I think I understand and I certainly didn't mean to offend your Bill; however, I do think we ought to try and dispose of these things, come what may."

She waited patiently for the colored woman to agree with her, but when not another word was said, Lilly lit a fresh cigarette from the still-smoldering butt end and began to speak again in a hoarse, croaking voice. "Timmy," she asked then, "along these lines . . . what would you say . . . how would you like a full-time job?"

Timmy gave no sign that she had understood. She brushed the sweat off her forehead and again started to lift the iron.

"Didn't you hear what I asked you?" Lilly's throat began to hurt. "Do you understand what I mean?"

The maid breathed heavily. "I heard you and I understan' and I was thinkin' about it . . ."

"Well . . . what do you think?"

"Well, now, Mrs. Goldenhoney, I think that's darn nice of you, but, ma'am"—she smiled—"you see, I don't know's if Bill would like that idea . . ."

"But he can sleep in with you. What is there not to like about it?"

"Oh . . . you know." The maid turned shy.

Lilly could no longer contain her curiosity. More than ever before, she felt that she did not know and that Timmy was not trying to understand what she had offered her. "Do you always do what this Bill likes you to do?" she asked sharply. Then: "Why him and not the others?"

Timmy mimicked shock. Her mouth fell open. "Because Bill . . . he ain't like any of the others," she said, and when Lilly didn't let on that she had understood, Timmy added: "I mean he's different . . . treats me good. Them others . . . they don't give a good goddamn for old Timmy . . . all except Bill. . . . He's serious with me. Now do you understan'?"

She paused to see if her message had been understood before adding, with another curious heave of her shoulders: "Matter of fact . . . Bill, he say he don' want me to work here at all no more. He say I could do much better in a factory. But I keeps telling him about you and how you needed me now that the Mister is passed away and he say okay . . . okay, maybe you should stay on awhile, Timmy, until she is straightened out with the estate and can move in with her folks . . ."

The maid's voice trailed off as she saw Mrs. Golden clap her hands over her burning ears. Then it rose again for a moment, but Lilly clearly was no longer listening. The dullest of headaches was coming on her and she had already begun to reply in an uncanny echo of a voice: "That's very understanding of Bill. Thank you, Timmy. Bill is very understanding and you are being too kind . . . but . . . I hadn't planned to move in with my *folks* ever . . ."

Timmy interrupted: "Mrs. Golden, you oughtn't to talk that way . . ."

"Why not? Lilly cried. *"Don't you understand that I don't like them any better than you do?"*

The maid did not answer. She merely shook her head as a further warning to Lilly before turning away to resume her ironing. And Lilly, wanting to beg her now to stop, became strident: "Why are you treating me like this? You're lying again, aren't you? You nigger . . ."

But in the middle of that last sentence, a sudden surge of humiliation went through her. The extent of her own impudence became unbearable as she perceived that Timmy would never have considered such an arrangement even if there had been no Bill. Then Lilly felt terribly meager and embarrassed in the presence of the stout, complacent colored woman. She pushed aside her stool and walked to the doorway. But spite got the better of her once again. Turning, she announced: "I am going upstairs to dress. Then I am going shopping. When you get a chance I want you to clean out Mr. Golden's closet. Keep anything you think Bill will like. I'm sure he can't be that particular."

"Uh huh."

That special grunting sound of the maid's pierced Lilly's being, draining the spite from her so that—for a moment—she stared at the stolid figure bent low over the ironing board with a quiet tenderness, but when she tried to imagine Timmy once more as she had in her fantasies, her eyes filled with tears and she had to flee upstairs.

Twenty minutes later a hot bath had revived her sufficiently to allow her to dress and stand fully clothed for the street on the top landing. As she went down the stairs, Lilly heard Timmy vacuuming and humming to herself in the living room. She said nothing to the maid as she rushed out onto the front steps, but when she returned from the supermarket and the bank an hour and a half later, still wide-eyed from the unaccustomed glare of day, Timmy had fled. The old house was deserted once more. The shutters banged; the floors rang with her footsteps; and there was not even a note left behind, although Timmy had not taken any of her uniforms and had carefully placed Edgar's shirts on the bed above her pillow.

That evening Mrs. Golden could not sleep. As she lay in the darkness of her room with her eyes open she imagined as if in a dream that Timmy had been caught in a tenement fire and was dying of burns. Rushing to the hospital by taxi, she knew that she would offer to forgive the maid, but when she was ushered into the dingy, tiled hospital room she saw Edgar's naked white body lying on the bed.

She cried out.

Early the next morning a man called on the telephone.

Timmy was taking a job in a factory, he said. She was not going to do housework anymore. Whatever was still owed, Mrs. Golden could send care of Bill Dawson at Post Office Box E 120, Bronx 11, N.Y.

"Did you write that number down?" the man asked.

Sprawled across her bed, Lilly Golden swallowed painfully as she assured the man that she had copied the address.

"Timmy says it comes to twenty-nine dollars and seventy-five cents for three days plus carfare and for you to send a money order, not a check," the man said then.

"All right," went Lilly, before realizing that she had something more to say, a message to give. She added: "I hope Timmy will be happy and that she will forgive me for what I said. I was sorry that she had to leave so abruptly."

But when she heard the dial tone break in she knew that Timmy's boyfriend had already hung up.

The Oklahoma
and Western

by Speer Morgan

You can't get visible in New York, and San Francisco just doesn't cut it anymore, so you serve time in this junkyard. I live here now so I won't have to in the future. At first you think, Jesus, what a circus. As you walk to the studio on Sunset Boulevard, doorways mutter to you, "Hey man, I can fix your mouth, your nose, your arm. . . ." Hands reach out and grab you. "Give me five bucks, Daddy. My old lady needs a glass eye." A fifteen-year-old walks by in drag with the latest hairstyle—burned down to his scalp. At the corner, a pale man with sloping shoulders gives you a manifesto: "The Right to Be Dying Humans." You pass signs: INSTITUTE OF ORAL SEX/SHEER EROTIC EDUCATION/DEGREES GIVEN. Across the street: WRESTLE NUDE WOMEN/THE REAL THING. As you approach the studio, sirens begin to wail across the city. It's summer, no rain, and each day the sun rises to poison. It's setting now, somewhere over the ocean, the gauzy, whitened eye of a dead fish.

But you get used to it. You join the sideshow. The other day, in the supermarket, my own little girl started a big fight with me. In this place they open meat, bread, pickles, mustard, and make sandwiches right in the store. A guy with a poor boy was watching us. The argument was nothing new—we'd been having it off and on for weeks—but it was a new twist, because this time Katie had decided to resolve it by exposing me to the public. She got that damn squinched-up look on her face and said, "Daddy, you smoke narcotics. I've told you it's bad for you, and now I'm

SPEER MORGAN (b. 1946) is the author of *Frog Gig and Other Stories* (1976).

going to tell everybody in the store." She immediately started pulling people on the arm, saying, "That man over there, my daddy, smokes narcotics. That man over there, my daddy, smokes narcotics," which aroused only minimal interest from anybody except the guy with the sandwich, who had hair down to his elbows and a luminous glaze in his eye. He came over to me and said, "Hey, Brother, haven't you found Jesus yet? You'll never o.d. on him." And I had to stand in front of the meat counter arguing with him that I don't smoke marijuana, dammit, it's bad for my ambition, I just smoke tobacco, and I can't help it if Jesus wouldn't like that either.

I was telling him the truth. I smoke nothing but air and Tareytons now. Pharmaceuticals and coke, of course, people are always giving them to me. I seldom buy the stuff. If you've got talent and something going, they'll feed it to you like a queen bee. At the big parties, it's kind of a thing, you know, when somebody takes you off into a bedroom and says, "Shut the door." *Snuff, snuff.* "You know, Freud did it for seven years," somebody always says, "and Hitler . . . a-a-aCHOO!" Before the circle breaks, you'll all be standing there with that metal taste down to your stomachs and a kind of pleasant new freeway with no cars on it leading from your sinuses up through two hundred miles of brain out the top of your skulls, and energy pouring down your throats, down your shoulders and arms like ice water, and maybe for just a second you glance around at each other, and there's a brotherhood, a softness, anyway, before you all grow back your alligator hides and rattlesnake neckties.

I got started in music up in San Francisco in the good old days, I was up there for three years trying to make a band out of a bunch of bums. Then I wrote some stuff for a famous group up in Mendocino—famous on one song—but they were already losing it, acting senile except for maybe five minutes a day, when all their chemicals flowed smoothly together. Now they're all dead, divorced, burned out, and sued. They had one song just one, that was beautiful, and when I catch myself singing it, my hands start to sweat. Back when I wrote for them, they drank pure carrot juice for breakfast, made from Scandinavian carrots in a $1200 juicer, and then began a rigorous day of fifteen or twenty joints apiece, all prerolled in a king-size silver cigar box with a cameo of Batista on the lid, all the white stuff they could find, and assorted pills to take the edge from Ups, give the Downs a little gusto, and invest the Just Rights with full-bodied pleasure. All in all, it was a relaxing kind of San Francisco suicide, performed amid the finest recording and speaker equipment available, turned up so loud that the ranch house, and the green hill itself, shook. I'd give them a song; they'd get it down after a few tries, and then listen quietly to the tape, their heads all bowed in priestly contemplation, while the speakers battered us like an aspirin commercial.

I went to work for a rock 'n' roll magazine in San Francisco, writing reviews—I'm literate, too, or at least used to be—but most of the people I knew then have since been fired or quit. That magazine is a tomb with a bunch of good-looking, ambitious mummies walking around in it. The offices are like going back to your hometown grade school after fifteen years of growing up. Yes sir, real exciting there at the journalistic heart of R & R, lots of sound, fury, smoke, dope, deals, and wheels—the Wizard of Oz behind his little curtain operating the boom-boom gadgets. There's one guy now who keeps the place from falling apart, and he's got a cork up his ass, like a Wall Street accountant. He's mildly dudish, leathery rich hip, he tells jokes like he never expects people to laugh at them, and he's as dependable as a cow. He clunks around the offices in expensive boots, eyeing people like a Presbyterian minister in a home for unwed mothers, keeping it together, keeping psychosis below organization level and meeting stomach-grinding deadlines, dishing out the hippest sludge in the business with excruciating regularity. A decent straw boss, but a lousy job of work.

San Francisco would not do, so I did gather my household together and move southward to the Pit, where the winds blow shrouds of desert sand and internal combustion over our house, covering everything, sifting through the windows and dusting even the keys of my closed piano. From this place, thirty miles in every direction but the sea, houses elbow each other for room, muttering to themselves, gossipless, and there is no rain to wash the soot from their itching skins, or the shit from their yards. When I work at night in this living room, my possum, pet from back home, stays up with me. He appears in one corner, then another, staring clear rings through the room. I got him on a visit back home last summer. He has a pink nose, an ugly dead-skin tail that he drags behind him, and very dark eyes, and sometimes when I'm working late at night, he winks at me. Katie gets up in the middle of some nights. Not that the noise bothers her; she could sleep with a guitar plugged in her ear. She just enjoys the company of Possum and me, busy at our appointed labors. Sometimes she holds the animal down for staring contests. She puts her nose right up to his and tells him how much he stinks. And she hassles me about Hollywood, how she wants to be an actress and all. She claims that all her friends are famous but she isn't. I tell her, all in due time, but of course that just irritates her.

We're from Oklahoma. There's railroad blood in us. My grandfather, who mostly raised me, was a mechanic for the railroad for forty-one years, and his father was cut into three pieces by a night train outside Atoka, before Indian Territory had become Oklahoma. I have a tintype miniature of Great-Grandfather, taken when he was a young man: his eyes unambiguous and clear as murder, a practical joker's half smile curled against his face. In the early days, he made big money near Whitefield, cutting black walnut for gun stocks and furniture, and when the trees ran out, he went to work for the railroads, which had been spreading for years across the territory of the Five Civilized Tribes in official reparation for their part in the Civil War. Great-Grandfather was a crew boss to start with, and soon higher. He had a good job and family. Then one night, in 1893, he got drunk and walked six or seven miles down a spur line with a coal oil signal lamp, and for no reason anybody could figure, stood in the track and tried to stop a train—in country, Grandfather used to say, where you flat didn't interfere with an engine unless you had something pretty big to do it with.

Ghostly rail, jack me up and feather me down, make me rich and famous so I can leave this Pit. Rich and famous—and I really will be. Does that tick you off? Kind of like the other side of Lennon's primal scream, ain't it: *I don't believe in Beatles.* That was more outrageous than all the rest. Only I haven't made it yet. Not quite. I'm on the way, though, and not even scared anymore. The crossties are laid, the rails in place. Sometimes I sit up like this and waste time making lists, writing notes and strategies and titles to hits. A good title is half the trip, as you know, like the name of a group. "The Ozark Mountain Daredevils"—those guys have got it made with that name. They could beat on a washtub and sell records. I write eighty to a hundred titles in a night, smoke forty cigarettes, and love myself to death. I mess with my guitar, and sometimes, a good many times, I light up and howl. Kris and Katie are used to it. They could sleep through a Stones concert. The possum slopes around and keeps me company through the night, and we get along just fine. I bought him for three-fifty from a shy Choctaw kid at a filling station not far from Atoka.

Possums aren't too smart, but they have good instincts. Once some big people were over here listening to new stuff, and he crawled up the side of the chair and sat on my shoulder while I sang. His claws were like razors, but I didn't let on, because I knew that sight was better than a full-length hype on my fascinating Okie background. A coarse ball of bristly fur on four delicate pink feet that walk separately and with creepy smoothness, as if out of some night forest where children walk in dreams, and those sloe, depthless eyes looking at nothing in particular—a galvanic image, if I do say so myself, perched there on my shoulder, as I plucked and sang for the hotshots.

People have tried to call me "Possum," but I won't let them—too familiar. You've got to pick up every stitch.

I used to be a thief: drove all over eastern Oklahoma in my '55 Ford, singing along with WNOE and stealing money out of pop boxes outside filling stations and stores. By myself, with a decent set of keys. I made fifty bucks every working night. I was a hood, I guess. I bit a guy's ear off once, which is another thing they like to hear about out here. I told that story to the president of a record company once, and he offered me my first contract. That was in New York. I had sent him a tape, and he called back and asked me to come up. "I like the cuts," he said. "Fantastic lyrics, but you're going to need good production. And I want to see if you have charisma." I was asleep, kind of—he had awakened me with the call—and I said, "You don't have to fly me to New York to find that out. I can tell you over the phone. I have charisma. I got it out my ass." He flew me up anyway, and somehow we got around to biting the guy's ear off back in Oklahoma, and that was when he offered me the contract. This wasn't any cheese-faced promo man, but the president of what was then the biggest label in the business. I told him maybe. Everybody back here said I was out of my mind, that I should suck up that contract like a popsicle. But I was lucky I didn't. He got fired six months later over a payola scandal, and I ended up with a better contract here.

My label is the biggest in R & R now. The president is twenty-nine years old, and he's made a million dollars for every one of them. He's a criminal, but I kind of like him. He likes me okay, too, but if he didn't think I'd make him some money, he'd have his secretary cut my nuts off. I went to see him a year ago to talk about an advance, a modest forty-three hundred dollars to be exact, and he said, "Goddammit, people are always asking me for money. You people think I'm a vending machine of some kind? Write him a check, Jane. How much did you say?" I told him I didn't want a single stinking cent of his money, and started to walk out, but he leaned over his desk and said, "Yes, you do. You want it now," and he pounded his desk, *thunk,* "and you'll want it again," *thunk,* "and again, and again," *THUNK,* "AND AGAIN!"

He was right. Sometimes he can be real friendly. He once told me the key to our relationship. We were at a topless organic bar, where executives go to drink apple juice and make fun of tits. "Look," he said, "there's one thing you have to do for me. Just one thing. You have to make yourself indispensable. You can cuss me, you can make outrageous demands, you can fool with my secretary, and as long as I need you enough, I'll take it. That's it, Baby."

He works twenty hours a day, makes an endless number of telephone calls, a hundred thousand words, every one of them designed to make money. He pays a hundred and sixty dollars a week to talk to a psychiatrist, and he uses no drugs except prescribed downers to get to sleep. When they ran low on record vinyl because of the oil embargo, he fired almost half of the nontechnical employees and every unestablished artist in the company except me. I'm the only gamble on the label now.

Before that, he held my first record up for fifteen months, and I learned pretty quickly that the key isn't exactly what he said. The key is to make the demands and cuss him now if I have to, to show him every way he looks that I could give a damn whether he keeps me or not, and with all the slouch I can muster. It takes a painted face to attract that bastard and keep his attention, because he lives somewhere out there in a pure blizzard of money. Reaching him takes everything you've got and just a little bit more. You have to tickle, move and surprise him, amaze him with your crudeness, wit, subtlety. And when he talks back you listen carefully, because a machine in the back of his head is arranging those words to conjure the maximum amount of dollars. You can always trust him if you know that.

It's not I who makes me indispensable, but his idea of me. He didn't spend a red cent promoting my first album—no telephone calls, no tour, no gimmicks, no coke to the big stations. He just put the album on the market and waited for it to sink. But I've got friends and a telephone myself. The reviews were decent, but not hot. They were mostly impressed by my backup people—one of Lennon's old drummers, two of the biggest women in town, and a bunch of others who wouldn't even take money for helping me, most of them, because they could have wiped their feet on me and they knew it. They like me.

Because I'm pretty elegant as Okie stars go: I have a possum, a wife with Indian blood, and a mind like a giant Wurlitzer jukebox with water bubbling up the sides in five colors, a whole show to fill the room with sound and light. I can make your pulse rise. Imitations? I sing early Dylan better than Dylan. I can sound like guitars, drums, and horns with just my mouth. The musicians love that most of all, because in the studio I can show them a song part fast. I can make your favorite singer, the one with the full crystal voice, sing for me alone, and desire me for a closer friend. Not that she'd eyed me that way quite yet, but when she does, I'll just have to make her desire me more. After all, I'm a married man with an eleven-year-old kid. I'll sing. I'll snort, I'll swim in the nude with her, but I won't get close enough to let her hate me. Business aside, I wouldn't want that to happen anyway. She's nice. At the studio she sometimes works with all the lights out, and just a candle on her piano. She does cast that spell of sorrow and lost innocence. She's not engineered. And she's a regular cannibal at business. She learned long ago that in this place you're either a mere head or a hunter, and the mere heads lose every way. She drives her own Rolls, no chauffeur.

I still drive a Dodge Dart, which makes me kind of quaint around here, but then again that's why they still love me, because I'm a down-home boy who's got it but ain't made it yet. After you're up there, they suck your blood and wait for you to make mistakes, or to kill yourself, like most of the ones who don't turn into zombies at thirty-five—like Dylan, if he hadn't broken his neck and walked out of the hospital believing in the Old Testament.

When were we innocent? In the sixties? Back in the holy days, when the best group in San Francisco made it without one singles hit? When they hung out on their farm, smoking dope grown specially for them by a contractor in Mexico, obeying their leader like Stalin, shooting their thirty-aught-sixes and automatic pistols for entertainment, and giving that endless train of sweethearts a free ride on the roller coaster of quick fame? Or Janis Joplin, who never claimed to be looking for anything but the ultimate spasm, hurting for her audiences like someone much older, her mind a bed of snakes, and her life a mess to obliterate, singing her throat raw, boogying loose at full tilt for a hit sweeter than the needle? Or Jimi Hendrix, dominating his guitar at Monterey Pop with "Wild Thing," playing it upside down and backwards, as if there was something just ever so nicely obscene about the way he used his instrument to death—tamed, broke, pissed on it with lighter fluid and brought it to flames, the band still going behind him as he hunched and sneered over its destruction and yet still loved it, feedback from the flames growling, barking through the speakers like a live thing in agony, and then falling to silence, ending the song in ashes, wistful disgust.

Innocent? Was I innocent driving my '55 Ford through the hills of eastern Oklahoma, singing along with WNOE and looking for pop boxes to break into? I guess I wasn't. When you get married at sixteen, and have a kid a month later, it's hard to stay innocent. I wasn't just a juvenile delinquent, but a married man, a thief, and I was lucky I didn't get sent to McAlester. But that's a whole different story. Kris is a quarter Cherokee, and she hung in there pretty tough. We smashed lamps on the floor, knocked holes in walls, and chased each other around with knives. One time we were driving somewhere, and she kicked me in the leg so hard that I had to stop the car. I tried to strangle her, and would have done it, too, if a blood vein hadn't burst like red lightning across her eye at the same instant she cracked me breathless in the ribs. More than once, I hated Kris enough to dream of poison, and I could hate little Katie just as much. Alone with her, I would sometimes let her squall in dirty diapers to get back at her for being born. I would squall back, mocking her in the futile wish that she could feel my spite. I was a bad father. I still am. Very unprofessional. But she's alive, as pretty as her momma and twice as mean, going to a fancy Hollywood school, and our family will stay together unless one of us dies. Even back then, I knew we had to stay together no matter what, no matter if our duplex became a prison of outrage. And I drove away from that house every night, through the quiet hills in my skin of steel, dreaming of fortune in the light of my radio, learning to sing with Elvis and Fats and a dozen dozen others whom I remember to this moment better than any house or room.

Katie is eleven now, and we're only twenty-seven, which will be nice in a few years. You've got to be ignorant to have kids, just like you've got to be ignorant to get married, or be a star. If you understand all the implications of it, you'll never do it. I have friends now approaching thirty who still don't have a kid, and their ideas about families are getting more and more complicated. By the time they have them, their heads will be worn out and gray worrying about it. The first step is ignorance, ambition itself is ignorance, and without it nothing gets done.

Kris and I get along better now. She's into speed a little bit, and pretty well off my back about L.A. Speed is her trip—strictly pharmaceutical, though, none of that homemade crap, and with a time-release downer that makes eight hours as smooth as glass. She never takes more than one at a time. Bad? Hell yes, it's bad. They even made a bad movie about it a few years ago. It can kill you. But L.A. will kill you faster, and we're in a race to beat it. I take a lot of stuff myself, like I said before, but once I get out of here with a reputation, and buy some land back east, I'll be independent of the scene, the ten thousand bloodsuckers and their drugs, and able to work at sessions in Nashville or anywhere. That sounds idealistic, doesn't it, but watch me.

I spend hours making calls and waiting for people, just waiting for technicians, promo men, musicians, everybody, to make up their minds about things. With a lot of them, you learn to act totally insane. It's the only way to get their attention. You exaggerate, you call them names: "You *stupid* son of a bitch, that's *not* what I want." You'd be surprised at how often that works. If you're not ready, though, I mean on top of the situation, they'll hype you out the door. How do you get ready day after scorching, rainless, smog-itching day? You take what you have to, you paw and snort, you put on your crazy face and come at the bastards like Atilla the Hun.

Maybe that's just my way of doing it. But that's what we're here for, isn't it? Here, in this midnight ball on the San Andreas Fault, where we work in masquerade, in windowless studios, passing around a prophylactic heavy as a cow's udder—part of someone's tax return converted to powder—breathing it for thirty-six hours until our nerves are white and brittle and we are working like blind masters to get down harmonies that will make you feel so good; in this Fat Tuesday, where leather coats, hands covered with jade rings, pants stitched by psychotic fags with heavy reputations, blouses clinging wetly to prodigal skin, where English cars guaranteed for life, cedar sauna baths, and all the rest stand perfected in George Washington's shrewd gaze, saying yes, we're making it, mother, but watch out, we're outlaws, savages, we're ugly or too beautiful to care, we can't be trusted, our faces are cut free, our moves agile as silver-eyed wolves, and if we suffer, it's from too much of every wish.

And can you lose it in the factory of dreams? I worry about that sometimes. But no, I'm up and coming in the Year of Our Lord 1974, and when you hear my music, you'll love what you think I am. You and the teenies both, because not even a genius can get off the ground now without the teenies and their billion-dollar hunger for hits under three minutes with good titles and catchy choruses. But you, too, will love me, because I'm already smuggling art across in my lyrics, producing to hit but writing to last.

Kris is my best ear. I sing and watch her face. She always says it's good, fantastic, but I can tell by her expression when it's really money sound, especially those Cherokee eyes, which never lie unless she's peaking out on something, at which times she likes everything—my songs, the sound of the washing machine, a pallid sunset against the kitchen window. . . . Me, I like less and less out there, the ten thousand bloodsuckers and their impediments, one after another, and I'm learning to cut through them like butter.

Last year I went to a lot of Hollywood parties and hung around with stars. I even went to see a Beatle once. He was slouched down in a lounge chair almost horizontally, and had a tired look on his face. When I was introduced, he waved bleakly and murmured, "Aello. I'm a Bea-le." I was walking the ceiling on a couple of weeks of speed, and talked a lot. I got worked up telling him my theory about *A Hard Day's Night,* a real theoretical oration that must have lasted twenty or twenty-five minutes, criticism as well as praise. He just sat there, looking at me steadily with a weak smile, occasionally agreeing. When I finally got through, he said with surprising vigor, but somehow like a college professor feigning interest in a book report, "I want you to know that I quite agree with what you've said. Quite agree." Then he slid from his chair, levitated himself, hobbled across the room like his legs were asleep, bumped into a glass table, turned profile to me, and said thoughtfully, still in a friendly tone, but vaguely troubled, "Kind of like the Jap stock market . . . ain't we? . . ."

Then there was the time the famous sex starlet patted me on the privates. My former manager took me over to visit her. He's only a couple of years older than I, went to Harvard, writes western and horror movies, and talks constantly about sex. He insisted that I take my possum. He acted like we were going to some kind of private showing, which, in a way, it turned out to be. At the front door, she was raw to the waist, wearing a bikini bottom and nursing a baby. She said, "Hi, this is Baby, maybe God, we're not sure yet." So I introduced my possum as Possum, maybe Elephant, he ain't fully grown yet. Ho-ho. Ahem. Her nose was red, and she had the sniffles from doing coke. It was in a Chinese sugar bowl on the living room table, along with a couple of rolled, pinned bills to snort it through, a one and a hundred. She explained that the sugar bowl had come from one of Chairman Mao's factories, and she offered us some coke. It was sweet, without too much speed, the kind that lays you back for a while before the edge comes on. She put the top back on the sugar bowl and nursed her baby. I told her I hoped Baby made it to God, but wouldn't it be kind of strange when she got older and you were sitting at dinner. Pass the green beans, please, God. Or when she got to be a teen-ager and you made her do the chores. Take the garbage out, God. She sniffled and smiled at me across space, like I had just spoken a sublime mantra. Her face reminded me of 1968, San Francisco, only rich and famous, and Baby suckled her most noisily.

I sat for a while trying to think of something to talk about besides the possum, which was hard to do with all this maternal ecstasy filling the room, here on the very bosom that the workers of America, the tired and weary workers, the impatient teen-agers, and yes, even the frustrated executives and their pickled wives, have spent millions to see on the screen. I told her that back where I came from, people in the hills still thought there was something evil about possums, being ratty looking and nocturnal and all, and there was a superstition that the male possum had a forked penis which he stuck into the female's nose to inseminate her. Her eyes got real big and interested, so I talked on about the possum's thirteen-day gestation period, the shortest of any mammal, and how the infants crawl out of the uterus on their own, hardly more than worms of scum, but with good front claws to hang onto momma's nipples—thirteen nipples, twelve in a horseshoe shape with one in the middle—safe there in the pouch until they grow into strong little possums. She didn't believe me, and I explained that possums were related to kangaroos, they were both marsupials, the lowest form of mammal. She was still incredulous. Finally she gave me her baby to hold and got out an encyclopedia to look it up. It impressed the hell out of her when she discovered that it was true. She sat down beside me on the couch, her face strangely lit up and glowing. "That's *really* amazing. The *lowest* form!"

I was getting nervous. She's a blonde, so unlike Kris, and you know how that can be. She leaned over and played with Baby in my lap without taking her back, and I really started getting uptight. My manager leered at us from across the room, and Possum had ceased exploring the rug and wandered beneath a chair. His scaly tail stuck out, I could smell the milk on her breasts as she leaned over me—the kind of odor, I must admit, that could make an old rock 'n' roll rooster clear his throat and cockadoodledoo once more. Pretty soon, it seemed like I had to keep that baby over my lap. Of course then she took her back, and I lost it entirely, went hot in the face and stared down, like a true Okie, with my mouth open, at my pants, which were standing up like the Washington Monument. I said something stupid, an attempted joke which I have since forgotten. Then she did it. She reached down, patted my pants gently three times and said, "That's okay. It's organic."

When we left the house, my manager split into a grin. "Need some crutches?" I told him to shut up. In his Porsche, he choked out laughing, glancing at me back and forth like he always does. "You know the word on her. Her own agent's been talking all over town that she's had it. Sixty thousand dollars on coke last year, and five or six visits to the crackerbox. She blew a bunch of tests. . . ." We whined down through the hills in second gear, and I drifted away from what else he said. Railed to the ears, I floated out of soft white powderland toward jagged mineral peakland, and, yes, I was weirded out, because the actress had not been kidding, not Mae Westing me, but stupidly serious with her assurance and vague smile, distant in all her famous flesh and snowy as the ghost on a busted TV.

The energy in me was bitter. Business flashed into my mind, and I had the not unusual urge to go somewhere and eat the bloodsuckers alive, pull them apart with my teeth if necessary, to get them moving on my record, which had then been rusting for nine months. But my stomach heaved with thick, automatic laughter, like a drunkard's vomit, and in a funny way, I didn't give a damn. Possum blinked once slowly, putting his claws through my shirt to grasp on through the curves, and I held him against me.

I don't cultivate stars anymore. I won't even go to a Dylan party. I've missed two of those, and five years ago, I would have stood myself up against a wall and riddled myself with hot slugs for missing a chance to observe Dylan get into a taxi at fifty yards. I know something now, I'm smarter than Dylan, can sing better and write better lyrics. So I have to keep it together. The burden of genius, you know—it's hard on your nerves. I stay home at night working, watching these earthquake-cracked walls and Possum sniffing through the rooms on his silent, businesslike rounds. I've written three songs in the last week, and one of them is very good, I'd almost say classic. The company has an acetate with ten cuts on it, including six potential singles. It's in New York now. They have to agree with L.A. on what to make a hit out of, because nowadays it takes even more money and favors from both coasts to get a single out there, and without a single, no album sales. For a while, people believed in music enough to advertise it by word of mouth, and the new FM stations played whole albums, and shucked the cream puff entirely. That sold good music. Now FM is back to commercial, mostly canned, tapes complete with DJs and music from L.A., New York, Philadelphia. But I don't care, I'm making my music, it's good and getting better, and not long from now I'll be off the ground. The vampires are moving faster for me now.

I usually go to bed before sunrise so I don't have to see it, but yesterday Katie got up early and came in while I was still working. "Daddy," she whined, like a sleepy baby, and grabbed onto my arm. I sang her a new song about railroads, the railroad blood in our own past, the continental line that tied this country together and webbed it with steel, and her great-great-grandfather, drunk one night and cut to pieces on a spur of the Oklahoma and Western. I sang of him walking through the cool night and counting oak rails for miles, lost to who knows what purpose, like a boy at play; behind a face, though, that could never look boyish, but, like any man's face eighty years ago, was bitten by need, and drunk, as he dangled the signal lantern down the track. I sang of the mystery of him standing his ground and swaying the lantern in a ruby arc for the potbellied iron he must have known wouldn't stop, and the dim white eye bearing down on him in a fury of steam. I sang it to her in that moment before day when the nighttime has dried, and she rubbed her eyes and listened to some of it before going into the bathroom. I went to the door and sang the rest to her, and when she finally came back out, she was awake and acting haughty. I asked her how she liked it.

Instead of answering, she said, "I want to make ads. All the other kids at school get to. There's a stupid boy in the *fourth* grade who makes them for Nabisco. Every time I look, *he's* on TV. Will you get me a good agent?"

"Agent? What do you want to sell—gasoline? Foundation garments? You don't even have your breasts yet. You can't get an agent till you have them."

"No, silly. Shampoo or something. Maybe Pepsi. I'm better looking than that boy for sure. Get me an agent."

Muttering, I wandered back into the living room, where day now threatened through the curtains. "You're catching on, Baby." I played a few chords of "Oklahoma and Western," but my guitar had gone to sleep in my hands.

The Place

by Edith Konecky

The Place was what we always called my father's place of business which occupied the entire twelfth floor of a skyscraper on Seventh Avenue and Fortieth Street. I hated going there but sometimes it was unavoidable. Now that I was getting so tall it was even more unavoidable than usual as my father had decided that I could begin wearing his garments instead of imposing on his friend Iving Walkowitz, who made Dolly Dimple Preteen Frocks. I had hated going there, too, but my mother insisted that I had to try things on to make sure they were becoming. Becoming what, I always asked. My father's garments were certainly not becoming. They were designed for wealthy matrons and cost a lot of money and came in sizes all the way up to obese. No matter how carefully these dresses were fitted to me, I always felt like a freak in them as they were designed to have bosoms in the tops and hips in the bottoms, items I was unable to supply.

The chief reason I hated going there, though, was that it was the one place where I entirely lost any connection with the person I thought I was and became someone totally different, the boss's daughter, a complete stranger to me, an indentity I bumbled around in feeling inadequate, graceless, tongue-tied, and false. How I envied David, whose knickers came to him in a cardboard box. It was one dumb conversation after another with people who treated me as though I were her royal highness, a princess with a pea-sized brain.

"GOLD-MODES, MAX GOLDMAN, INC.," were the first

EDITH KONECKY (b. 1922) is the author of *Allegra Maud Goldman* (1976); her stories have appeared in *Kenyon Review, Esquire,* and *The Massachusetts Review.*

words to greet you when you stepped off the elevator, though there had already been a conversation with Joe, the elevator starter. Directly above these words behind a sliding-glass partition, wedged between switchboard and typewriter, was the carefully coifed head of Millie Brodsky, receptionist, deliverer of the next words:

"Well, will you look who's here. How nice to see your fresh young face, dearie."

"Glunk," I said, trying to decide whether to enter left to the showroom or right to the shipping room. I opted for left in the hope of fewer conversations. The showroom was a big plush blue and gray room with partitioned cubicles where buyers could sit behind little glass-topped tables writing orders while models waltzed before them parading the current line and salesmen hovered, buttering them up and touting the wares. No customers today. Just Mr. Feldman and Mr. Cohen, two of the salesmen, swapping the usual dirty stories.

"Good day, Madam," Feldman said, rearranging his crotch. "What can I sell you today?"

"Glunk," I said, not breaking my stride. Through a draped opening into the models' brightly-lit cave, all mirrors at one end, racks down the other on which hung the demonstration goods. Three models, Marlene, Charlotte, and Laverne, sitting in their underwear smoking cigarettes and drinking coffee out of soggy containers, watching themselves in the mirror through glazed eyes.

"Glunk," they said to me and "Glunk," I replied.

Into the office, a dreary place full of arithmetic. Bookkeepers making entries in ledgers, making out payrolls, making deposits. Secretaries typing letters saying, "Re: your order #359685 we regret that we are unable to supply our model #0058B, size 18, of which you ordered three (3) in champagne and are therefore substituting the sauterne, a popular shade. Please let us know if this is acceptable or if you would prefer the liebfraumilch."

Off this beehive, my father's office, a narrow, windowless, no-nonsense chamber with a big leather sofa and an even bigger desk, a coat tree sprouting his hat, overcoat, suit jacket, umbrella, his rubbers neatly toed-in at the roots. I peer in. My father is going over some sketches of the up-coming line with the designer, Gus Quinzanero. Both men are in their shirtsleeves, but there the similarity ends. My father's shirts are always white, often white on white (a man who can't get enough white in his shirts, a conservative dresser), the knot of his tie loosened. Gus Quinzanero's shirt is blush-hued, his impeccable flannel trousers are held high by broad scarlet suspenders with pictures of the king, queen, and jack running up and down them.

"Crap," my father is saying. "The same warmed-over crap. Cancel that one."

"You're a real bitch today, Max," the designer says amiably. "But so what else is new?" He is the only one of my father's 150 employees allowed to talk to him that way. My mother says this is because he can go almost anywhere tomorrow and get as good a job or better and what's worse could go into business for himself and compete with my father.

My father looks up as I slide quietly into a corner of the sofa. His face rarely lights up at the sight of me; if it changes at all it is to sour even further.

"I'm busy now," he says. "Can't you see I'm busy?"

I go into the factory, first to the cutting room where the cutters, important men, are slicing around patterns, through layers of costly fabrics. One false move and *disaster*. There is another huge room where the operators sit going blind over their whirring-machines and several smaller rooms for patternmakers, drapers, pressers, and etc. The factory people are mainly foreign born, Italian and Jewish, and it is they who treat me with such sub-servience and respect that if I were not too busy gagging I would leap onto a table and cry, "Workers of the world unite. Break the chains that bind you!" With a nod to Melanie. Though according to my father, they are already solidly united and between the crooked unions and the gangster truckers and the Mafia land-lords, he is being squeezed like a blackhead out of his own business that he built with the honest manly sweat of his brow in order to give employment and livelihood to all these people who would otherwise be starving and lying around in gutters with festering sores on their eyes, to say nothing of leprosy and cholera.

"Your father makes his wealth off the backs of the honest poor," said Melanie when she learned he was a Capitalist, an employer. "Every mouthful you eat is carved from the flesh of some simple, honest, upright, noble, exploited workingman coughing his lungs out in an unsanitary shop. For shame."

Though to be perfectly honest it was not an unsanitary place and the only people I ever actually saw sweating there were my father and the pressers, and pressers would sweat anywhere, as would my father.

I am waiting for my mother who is going to select my wardrobe for the coming season. She will go through the tens in the stockroom and select what she thinks is becoming, and then Sophie, the seamstress, will appear with pins in her mouth and her hands full of chalk and rulers and together they will decide on the necessary adjustments. Meanwhile, I have nothing to do. I forage around, looking for treasures to swipe. I collect scraps of material off the cutting-room floor and stuff them into a bag. These I will take home and, in a month or two, I will throw them away as I can never think of anything to do with them. While I am browsing among the cuttings I hear my father, finished now with Gus, screaming at Agnes Mortadella. Agnes' bailiwick is a cage at one end of the cutting room. Inside the cage are shelves filled with boxes of buttons and belt buckles. This is the trimming department, and Agnes, a short stocky woman with a nervous mouth and intense eyes, is in charge of all the trimmings, a responsible position. My father is yelling at her now about some buttons.

"They break, fa chrissake. They break right in their fingers. How the hell do you expect them to sew them on, fa chrissake, they're made of matzos."

"I'm sorry, Mr. Goldman, I'll take care of it."

"Who the hell sold you these lousy buttons?"

"I'll look it up, Mr. Goldman."

"Don't you know? You're supposed to know these things, what the hell do you think I'm paying you for?"

"Here it is, Mr. Goldman, it's Superior-Rivkin. I'll call them right now."

"Goddamn sons of bitches, tell them we sew on the buttons, fa chrissake, not crackers. Don't you feel the goddamn buttons before you buy them?"

"I can't feel all the buttons, Mr. Goldman, be reasonable."

"Don't stand there and tell me to be reasonable, fa chrissake, I'll throw you right out in the street where you came from."

By this time Agnes Mortadella was crying hard enough to make my father feel better so he stormed off to some greener pasture. I sidled up to Agnes' cage.

"Oh, hello, Allegra," she said, blowing her nose.

"Why don't you quit?" I said. "How can you let anyone talk to you that way?"

She was on the telephone. "Just a minute," she said to me. "Hello, Superior-Rivkin? Let me talk to Bernie." She put her hand over the mouthpiece, waiting. "Your father can kiss my ass on Forty-second Street. Hello, Bernie, you shit. That lot number WJZ127936. No, not that one. Yeah, those. Oh, you know about it, whadderyou some kind of jokers up there? You better haul your ass right over here. Not four o'clock, right now, or I'll throw the whole entire order back at you and good-bye Superior-Rivkin where Gold-Modes is concerned." She banged the two halves of the phone back together.

"Now, what were you saying, darling?"

"Why do you stand for it? Why don't you work for someone else? There must be lots of jobs for someone of your caliber."

She gave me a long look while she chewed her underlip.

"They're all the same," she said. "You think any of them are any better? You know how long I'm working for your father? Since the day he went into business. I was only fourteen. I lied. The way I was built I could get away with it."

"I don't understand it," I said. "I *have* to put up with him. I *can't* quit. But you."

"Oh, he's all right, your father," she said. "That's just the way he is. But fair's fair, he's someone you can count on."

"What do you mean?"

"He's as good as his word. He's an honest, dependable man."

She really liked my father. It was beyond all understanding, though I strained.

"You know what he makes me feel?" she said. "Safe. My own old man was much worse. He used to chain me to the bed so I wouldn't go out and screw with boys. After him, your father's a saint."

My mother appeared then so I took my leave of Agnes and

went back to the models' room where we got down to business. Forewarned, I was wearing a clean, practically new slip but oh how I hated to stand there in it between selections with all sorts of people, including Cohen and Feldman, walking through. No privacy and everyone a kibitzer.

"That looks very nice on you," my mother said. "Don't you think that looks nice, Allegra?" I glanced into the mirror and made a face. "Well, do you like it or don't you? You're the one who's going to have to wear it." What was there to like about a dress? Or to choose between one and another? Either it had buttons down the front or it didn't; it had a collar or it hadn't; the collar was pointed or round. No choice when it came to sleeves as all Gold-Mode frocks, except in summer, had bracelet-length sleeves, very flattering to skinny arms and bony wrists.

Sophie, who was kneeling on the floor at my hem, said through the pins in her mouth, "That's *her* color. Look how it makes those eyes look."

"It's a little too long in the front," my mother said.

"I'm fixing. Don't worry, it'll be perfect."

"Stand up straight," my mother said.

My father, passing through, glanced at me with genuine displeasure and, not pausing, said *"Shlump."*

"Shoulders back, stomach in. Like this," Marlene said, coming out of her coma and actually getting up off her chair to demonstrate standing.

"Gorgeous," Feldman said on his way to the toilet. "Next year she can come and model for us."

"It isn't right up here," my mother said to Sophie, pointing at my chest where the dress, as always, sagged dispiritedly.

"We'll put darts," Sophie said, sticking in pins. "I'll tell you what you should do, Allegra darling, just in the meantime till they grow in. Wear a brassiere and stuff it with socks."

"Glunk," I said.

"I mean it. You'd be surprised how many women do it."

"Fa chrissake," I said.

"How do you like this nice polka dot, Allegra? It has a nice little bolero jacket. It'll cover up your chest."

"How the hell many dresses are you getting her, fa chrissake?" my father said, passing through now in the opposite direction. "Where the hell is she going in all those dresses, on a cruise?"

"Yeah? Where the hell am I going?" I said.

"All what dresses?" my mother said. "Two, so far."

"You know what that number sells for?" my father said of the polka dot with the little bolero. "Forty-nine fifty wholesale. That's a hundred-dollar number in Bonwit's."

"I don't even want it," I said.

"Never mind," my mother said for my father's benefit. "Your cousin Sonia never walks out of here with less than eight dresses at a time. You're certainly entitled to two, the boss's daughter."

"I have a headache."

"You want some aspirin, darling?" Sophie said. "I have some aspirin right by my machine."

"Walk away, Allegra. Let me see how that looks walking."

I did my cripple's walk.

"Allegra! Walk properly."

I did my regular walk. My father, slashing through the room again in time to observe this, said, "Can't she learn to walk like a human being?" Once again Marlene tore her eyes from her reflection and rose to her feet, this time to give lessons in walking.

"Like this, dear heart. Make believe you've got a book on your head. Wait, I'll go find an actual book and you can try it," she said, vanishing gracefully.

"She's at the awkward age," my mother said to anyone present who happened to need that information.

"I've got a splitting headache," I whimpered. Socks on my chest, books on my head, what next?

"Little Cuban heels, that's the ticket," Feldman said on his way back from the toilet. "That number don't look so hot with saddle shoes."

"Where's Cohen?" I said. "We're waiting for his comments."

"Oh, look at this smart little spectator sport, Allegra," said my mother. "It's just the thing."

"Not one single goddamn book in this entire place," Marlene reappeared to say. "Nothing but phone books and ledgers and they're too heavy."

"Thanks anyway," I said, "but we're finished walking."

"Try this on, Allegra," my mother said. "It's adorable, even though it isn't your size."

"We'll put darts," Sophie said.

"I can't get out of this one," I said. "It's pinned to my slip. Maybe to my flesh. I think I have to throw up."

"Stop that nonsense, Allegra," my mother said while Sophie unpinned me from the little polka-dot number. "It's all in your head."

"It is?" I said, and a moment later it was out of my head and all over the cute little bolero.

John Henry's Home
by John McCluskey

In the longest moment of his life, John Henry Moore
stared down the barrel of a shotgun and reached slowly for the
toothpick in the corner of his mouth. The cigarette in his other
hand was burning down to the filter and he let his aching fingers
drop it, checking any sudden move. He watched the eyes of the
man holding the gun and, finding no mercy, looked to the man's
screaming wife.

"Don't kill him, Lou! Don't kill him!"

He cursed his luck, his life that flashed by like a doomed
comet, and that first weekend after he had returned to the world.
He had lied to himself about what was possible at home, lied
about how easy things would be. He had looked too long at the
reflection of the present and he had called that good. He held his
breath, hoping to ease the strain on his kidneys, and looked again
at the open lips of the barrel, down its blueblack length to the
man's nervous fingers . . .

He had closed the closet door, straightened the full-length
mirror hanging against its back, and studied his front. He had
dragged on his cigarette and watched the smoke ooze evilly from
his nostrils. The pose had dictated some kind of badassed movie
detective or mackman. He had pulled his slacks up, then frowned
at the tightness through the crotch and things. Most other dudes
home from the war were underweight. Like Mitchell, John Henry
was good sized when he came home and going strong now on his
mother's cooking. He had already put on five pounds in his first
week home. The added weight didn't look too bad except that

JOHN McCLUSKEY (b. 1945) is the author of *Look What They Done to My
Song* (1974).

women seemed to prefer their men looking like skinny sissies these days. It wasn't that way when he left. Tight pants and shirts and high heel shoes. It isn't how much or how little you have that counts, he knew. It's how you use it. He had grinned at himself, patted his belly, and left.

The barbershop was four blocks away and John Henry, as cool as he wanted to be, took them slowly. After all, there was the brightness of the day to consider. It was early March, though it looked more like October and touch football time for the old-timers and fake high school stars in the park. His second night home, Alice and Jody had thrown a welcome-home party for him and, drunk, he had promised to get together with the fellows for a game. Of course, he knew that the game would be forgotten in the morning. The party had been one of the few events in his life when more than two people in a room seemed happy to see him, listen to him, touch him. He had liked the feeling, despite the war, despite everything. He was not hard enough to shut out everything like Tony, his Army buddy, now riding shotgun for a Detroit gangster. Tony had sent a photo of himself posing against a silver-grey Rolls-Royce. Nor was John Henry soft enough to retire like Mitchell at the age of twenty-three. He'd look for himself somewhere in between. Here, back in the world.

He pushed into the barbershop and waved at RoughHouse and Irwin, the barbers. Then he nodded at faces vaguely remembered and at others, younger, he didn't remember at all. Little jitterbugs were shooting up like weeds. Like that Bobbie who was a basketball star now. John Henry had seen him on the street once and had teased him about playing marbles and wearing a Davy Crockett hat. Grabbing an old magazine, John Henry took a seat and pretended to read.

RoughHouse finishing a tale and giving a razor-line at the same time. "Some crackers too dumb to be white. They deserve to catch hell . . ."

Then Rough dragged out stories of hants and fools. John Henry did not look up. He hoped they wouldn't start on him, wouldn't ask about the war and whether he had killed a man, whether it was true the Blacks and whites were shooting at one another and calling such murders accidents. Did the Cong really take it easy on the brothers when they sneaked into camps and cut throats? Did they really seek out the white-only bars as

targets for grenades? Huh, was it like that for true? John Henry
wanted to be left alone with the memories of his war. His burned
arm was reminder enough.

Still the room grew smaller. RoughHouse, dipper in the business of all, cleared his throat. "John Henry, I'm sho glad you
here 'cause maybe you can straighten out something I was trying
to tell that hardheaded Jew-Don awhile ago. He claim he fought
the Japanese in the Second World War. I fought in Korea myself.
I was trying to tell him that the Japs were smaller and had bigger
heads than the Koreans. He come tellin me that the Japs is the
biggest, then the Vietnamese, then the Koreans."

"Well, Rough, I've never seen a Korean," John Henry said. "I
saw a few Japanese in California but that wasn't close up."
Yellow men among the snows, wave on wave through the jungles.
One was a wave, as precise as a scorpion.

They leaned back in their seats when John Henry couldn't
deliver the decisive word. RoughHouse started again. "I know
one thing, though. They can fight their asses off, can't they? I
mean, hell, I was in the Philippines and saw them coming and
coming."

"What did you do then, RoughHouse?" some joker asked.

"I kept shooting and praying. Yeah, buddy, that was me all
right. Look here, y'all. I cut Mitchell's hair last week and he
come talking about they would cool it on brothers over there.
You believe that mess? War is war and niggas always get caught
in the middle of it and after it's over we get booted out of the
army with some funky papers."

Then the war stories were strung together on the knotted
thread of memory. Certain that he had to give them something,
Roscoe shared a story told him by a buddy. He'd tell it early so
they wouldn't keep bothering him. His own story he would tell
some other time.

"Yeah, that war things is never always cool. I had to drive a
jeep miles down a road that had been closed off for a while
because of heavy shelling. So I drove out of camp for about a
mile when I met this white boy with a rifle. I told him where I
had to go and asked him whether the road up ahead had been
opened yet. He said yes that everything was OK, so I took off,
and had that old jeep hummin. All I had was a big pistol on my
hip, you understand. It was kind of nice that day, about like

today but a lot warmer, so I settled back to enjoy the drive. I was weaving around them big holes in the road where the shells had hit, all between the trees and stuff on the road. That drive was the only peaceful time I had all the time I was over there. Anyway, I'm doing it all the way in and when I get near the village there's another sentry, a brother. He looked at me like his eyes were going to pop. 'Where you come from?' he asked me. When I told him he sat down on the ground and started laughing like crazy. 'Man, that road been closed,' he said. 'You coulda had your head blown off. Them Viet Cong must have thought you was one crazy blood driving through there like that and they was probably laughin so hard they let you through.' I almost peed on myself behind that. I started thinkin of that soldier at the other end who let me through so I finished my business in that town and went back down that road. When I got to the other end, I found the guy and whipped him 'til he roped like okra."

The barbers stopped their clippers to rest against their chairs, laughing. When that died down they saw John Henry's stolid expression and started again. A belly-holding, thigh-slapping laughter, a welcome-home laughter that rumbled up from collective pasts. John Henry, never the athlete, never the smartest, slow with the girls, slow with the dozens, was ever swift with the jokes. Could beat One-Eyed Tommie when it came to stories. John Henry, that crazy John Henry, was home.

"What you plan on doing now that you're home, John Henry?" You couldn't beat RoughHouse for directness.

"I don't know yet. Right now I'm just gonna let Uncle Sam's pay support me." Then he pulled up his sleeve and showed the ugly scars of napalm. An accidental drop near his platoon. Fire-jelly from the sky, from one of their own nervous pilots. "Uncle Sam owe me something, don't he?" Waiting customers leaned closer for a better look and frowned at the ugly scars.

"I hear the mill is hiring," Irwin said.

"I ain't in no hurry for the mill, man," he said. He had to watch it: most of the men in the barbershop owed their thin bank accounts, their mortgages, their past bail bonds, doctor bills, and their children's first years in college to the steel mill. "Like I say, I'm still thinking. I'm behind by four years and I ain't gone catch up working for no hillbilly in a mill. You can bet on that."

RoughHouse noticed John Henry's eyes rolling up and the vacant stare. Another world was where he was now. Though the customers agreed within themselves about the mill, they didn't like his saying it. After all they were beyond choices now. Loans had to be repaid. RoughHouse stropped his razor again, humming in the quiet. It was always a long way home and John Henry wasn't there yet. Might never make it back. Rough knew so many who could never make it back.

"Y'all read the other day about Ali talkin about he could have whipped Joe Louis and Joe Frazier in a telephone booth, blindfolded and with one arm tied around his back . . . ?"

Smoke. A smoke no more harmful to the lungs than the dust-filled smoke at the mill where men like his father and two brothers breathed it and brought it back up with phlegm. Mill men were tough enough to work in the smoke for forty years and accept cheap watches for their struggle, men who would later die coughing on front porches or in bed, smoke never ever gone. John Henry dealt in a smoke that would keep the slicker men happy, could have them wrestling the bulls of the universe, could have them riding and leaning on falling stars as easily as they could in big cars. Just a gentle thing, this smoke.

Square it, John Henry. Ease a little pain, man. It started the very next day with a couple of nickel bags as a gift from an ex-soldier in the next town, a gift to John Henry, to the town. Two of his sidekicks, Tucker & Art, would go for it. They've been to the big city, they know what's happening.

"Man, this some righteous shit, John Henry . . ."

Noon was midnight and burning moon caught them in Tucker's car parked in front of the pool hall. They were on the Strip—a pool hall, grocery store, laundromat, bar and an abandoned printer's office—a block that had struggled to life while John Henry was away. Yokel cops cruising by, trying to scowl. Art blew smoke at them. Hip Art with no front teeth and the runny eyes.

"Simple dudes never heard of marijuana, let alone know what it smell like."

Dance strange and funky—butt bumping dances under this moon, town. Come on out, saditty couples living behind venetian blinds and hating the town and what your mirrors throw back. Did you hear what foxy Jeanette said about smoke opening her up and bringing her love down as if strange fingers tripped along the insides of her thighs? She would even buy John Henry a suit behind that pleasure. Come, dance. Not his fault the war-gods have died with the thunder and now the angels of pleasure had slipped on it.

John Henry moved from his home to a small apartment and later went to the mill. A front, though. He saw death there, slow, his. But young workers came to him and begged. At lunch-time he cooled them out with dollar joints, rolled tight as toothpicks. A few of the older, steadier workers drifted toward his corner of the plant. They were used to gin or scotch all night and slightly bored with it. He'd help them make it through the hard nights of their days.

Good news had traveled fast there. He was called into the office of one of the top men. The executive's face was pocked and puffed by alcohol. Grinning, he had pumped John Henry's hand and reached the point quickly. He had heard of John Henry around the plant (tomming spies, everywhere!) and wanted to know whether John Henry could help him. Of course, a small raise and protection would be given in exchange. They had shaken hands, John Henry laughing the rest of the day in the plant. He had figured the man as he had figured most of the executives at that plant: aging Christians aching to wear dungarees & sandals, to grow a beard, to stroke the behinds of their secretaries. He would be middleman to their heavens, too.

But if smoke could get your moving, the White Horse could get you there extra swift. That was how his soldier friend had described it. John Henry saw himself catching up with high school classmates who owned homes now. He saw the streets of his town paved with twenty dollar bills. Saw money in the faces of the young kids standing on the corners. It would be so easy, so quick. But he hesitated.

"Look, man. This heavy stuff is new for me. You been doing it up here ever since you came back from the war so you know what's what. I mean, for one thing you dealing in a big town. My town so tiny you can hear a fly fart."

"Don't worry, man, I'm just turning you on to something slick, that's all. It's not like a life-time thing. You think I want to spend my life pushing to jive chumps? I'm into bigger stuff. I got a brain, John Henry, and I'm gonna use it for the bigger things, know what I mean? Uncle Sam will be sorry he ever cut this pretty nigga loose with some messed up discharge papers. And I know you, John Henry. I know you didn't suck mud in a stupid-assed war for three years just to come home and knock your brains out in a steel mill. Tell me anything, man, but don't tell me that!"

How much heart, John Henry, how much heart you got? Be so bad you roll grass in ten dollar bills. He drove back to town to stay on top of things. To think.

He had run into Mitchell many times. God-fearing Mitchell who had a bad leg from the war. He had tried to share smoke with Mitchell but go nowhere. Mitchell worked in the post office and had married within four weeks after returning home. During John Henry's first month back, they stood one another a round of drinks in Roscoe's Place, early evening before the crowd.

"How's married life, Mitch?" John Henry usually began.

"It's cool with me, John Henry. You know me, man. I never was into a whole lot of running and stuff."

"Yeah, you and Jackie been tight, too, going way way back. Look like the post office ain't hurting you none either."

Mitchell laughed, stroked his goatee. He was shorter than John Henry, neat, always and forever a neat man. John Henry had concluded that Mitchell went to battle pressed clean. "You the one to talk. If I had your hand to play, I wouldn't have a worry in this world."

"Mitch, you seen bighead George Pendergrast? Somebody said he's teaching college in Cincinnati. They say he's got him a nice pad down there."

"No, man, I never see him. He comes home for a minute to see his people then—zoom!—he's back in Cincinnati. That dude ain't got no time for this place. I guess he's doing OK, though. Remember Billie Barnes? He tried out for the Detroit Lions, you know. He didn't make it so they say he kind of drifted out West. He didn't have anything to be ashamed of, if you ask me. Ain't too many from this town ever done much of anything except raise a lot of hell. Well, anyway, he's changed his name to Billy Africa and he's out in Colorado trying to start the revolution. Yeah, they say he's cutting hands off of dope pushers, too."

Mitchell coughed. He did not want that to slip. It had started as a joke, probably.

"Billy always was half-crazy," John Henry said, squirming. "Whatever happened to Daniel White? That cat was always quiet, but he could beat all of us drinking gin."

Mitchell laughed, slapping his chest. "John Henry, Daniel is way out in Los Angeles. I hear he's got a good job, too. They say the last time he was home he was pushing a deuce-and-a-quarter. Which must be a lie because we both know that wasn't his style. I can just see his stiffnecked self trying to be cool."

"You never know, Mitch. You never know how anybody's going to change." He had asked himself how Mitchell could be so blind. All their friends gone, living well, and the two of them sitting in a funky bar. And Mitchell has the nerve to laugh at their new ways. He's probably so confused he doesn't know whether to hate me or love me for what I'm doing.

"Why don't you drop over some time, John Henry?" Mitchell asked. "Bring one of your ladies and we'll play some whist or something."

John Henry nodded, wondering how many things Mitch could have been. College, maybe, a hellified basketball player. Might have made a dynamite lawyer; Mitchell always was smart. But he said he didn't want that now. Maybe he wasn't up to the strain of getting it. Maybe the war left him with only one ambition: to rest in peace. But John Henry would never go out that way. After making up lost ground, he'd start a business in another town and push on to the top. They'd remember him in this town. He'd visit home once a year and prowl the streets in a new car. Yes, they'd remember.

"What about you, John Henry? You thinking of staying here for awhile?"

"Not if I can help it. I'll be out of here before it turns warm again. Watch. You know I never was too crazy about this place, even though it is home."

Mitchell smiled and they finished their beers. They'd get together again, soon. They were as serious with that promise as buddies growing apart could ever be. John Henry had decided to do what he knew he would do all along. At the end of the summer he paraded the White Horse through town. At home they found this creature beautiful. They quietly lost their minds at the sight of it, taking turns to mount. They wanted its flesh, wanted to suck its veins, wanted its power. Instant friends offered their services now, wanted to walk in the shadow of John Henry. He paused on street corners to show off weird greens or way-out red outfits. But all the folk he touched, even the one or two who might have loved him, turned to stone.

That summer Bobbie played basketball in the shadow of the Horse. In the fall he would be a junior in high school and would start for the varsity. Knew he would start, though he had quit the junior varsity last winter because he couldn't get along with that team's coach. The coach had pronounced the sentence and benched him many times: Bobbie Powers is not a team player, Bobbie Powers has a bad attitude. A new year and a few new moves like the spinning jump shot and he'd be back out front again. No one worried. The coach needed a winning team to keep his job. He was no fool.

So Bobbie sharpened his moves that summer and when not playing he hung out with Chico, Cool Chico, his only real buddy. But one buddy is enough to turn you around. He shot up with Chico on a simple dare. Bobbie would try anything once, or twice.

On a hot afternoon in August, Bobbie fell out of a car at a highway rest stop twenty miles north of Cincinnati. Turning grey and dying. The needle was an ugly exclamation point to the vein. Chico vomited, cried and beat his fists on the hood of the car, while the sleepy-eyed truck drivers at the stop kept their distance. Miles away a few boys were playing ball on the hot court. The weaker players, minds steamed by dreams of superstardom, stood in the shade and waited their turn, making the myth of Bad Bobbie.

As Bobbie lay dying, John Henry and Tucker were making connections in New York. It was Tucker who had given Chico the phone number of the Cincinnati pusher. Nose running, Chico had been impatient and did not want to wait until they would get back from New York.

When John Henry and Tucker returned to town, they went directly to John Henry's apartment. A few minutes later Jeanette burst in to bring breathless news of Bobbie's death.

"A couple cops were around yesterday, asking questions," she said. "But I don't think they found out anything. Still they must know something on you, John Henry. Somebody must have told them something!"

Tucker was standing, shaking his head. "I told that stupid-assed Chico to hold off, but he kept pushing and pushing for the address. Did the boy O.D. or what, Jeanette?"

"I don't know, I don't know," she said. "O.D., poison, whatever. All I know is that he's dead."

In the silence they watched John Henry. He felt their eyes, knew their questions, and looked off. They had nothing to do with Bobbie's death. Directly, at least. It's too bad the boy died like that, a helluva shame, but they were clean. Then he lit a cigarette and announced, "Let's go to the park, Jeanette, we'll drop you off at your place, OK?"

By the time he and Tucker reached the park, John Henry had decided that the sale of the new batch would be his last at home. He'd leave, maybe go in with his friend in Dayton. Yes, he'd leave.

"I come back from the war to make money, not to go to jail," he said as they parked.

Tucker nodded. "But big money and risking jail go together."

They headed for the basketball court and John Henry watched the players for awhile. They were clowning around, all of them. None of them could ever be as smooth as Bobbie with the ball. John Henry told the players that they were sloppy, but they ignored him.

When a few more fellows showed up, Tucker got a nickel tonk game going. They were gathered on a picnic table in the shade. John Henry was grinning over his hand when he saw a car swerve to a stop across the street. A short squat man in work clothes rushed from the car. The basketball players saw the shotgun first and scattered. The card players froze. They were older and knew the danger of sudden movement. It was in the man's eyes, that danger. The man walked slowly to John Henry and aimed the gun at his chest. They had watched one another for long seconds before John Henry heard his breath slowly coming out . . .

"You chickenshit bastard! You're the one who killed my son."

And from behind the man the wife screamed and screamed again, reaching out to him, and John Henry's life in the town was no longer something bright and definite as a path leading upward, but as futile as aimless steps across a desert. He saw sand quaking, saw only his hand above it to show the world that someone had gone down slow. He controlled so little anymore.

"I was out of town when it happened. I just heard about it a few minutes ago. I've never sold your son anything."

"Don't lie to me or I'll blow your ass to Kingdom Come! You didn't have to sell it and I'll get that Chico and that punk in Cincinnati. But you the one brought the dope in this town. Because of you my son will be buried tomorrow. Before you came there wasn't no shit like this. They never should have let you out. You should have died in the war!"

The man was shaking his head wildly, one of his fingers tapping beneath the barrel now. The rush of fear was ebbing now, leaving John Henry weak. The toothpick was splintering in his mouth.

Junior Cooper, sitting across from John Henry, eased away and tried to speak. "It was really a dude in Cincinnati, Mr. Powers. Not John Henry, sir . . ." He looked into the man's eyes and stopped.

"Don't, Lou . . ." The woman's voice was pleading. Another man, an uncle of Bobbie's whom John Henry recognized, walked slowly up to his brother.

"Don't go to jail behind this no-good boy, Lou." He stood next to Lou Powers, then reached slowly for the gun. John Henry knew that if he were to die today it would have to come in that instant as the man's hand came closer and closer to the barrel. The hand of Bobbie's uncle gripped the barrel and firmly pulled it from Powers. Then he threw an arm around his brother's shoulder and pulled him away.

The man turned to John Henry. "You lucky to be sittin there. You better get the hell away while you can."

The card players had stood up and a few started moving off, not too quickly because now they could afford swagger in the face of the boys with the basketball.

"Damn man's crazy," John Henry said, lighting a cigarette. "Always was crazy as long as I known him." He wanted to pee, his bladder was still strained. He wanted to go someplace and think. If he had died that afternoon, they'd forget him in less than a year and only remember that before he went off to war he was something of a clown and not even a good one. And someone new and slicker would come along to claim the Horse. They'd forget.

A week later as summer chilled toward another fall, John Henry packed two bags. He lied to his mother, telling her he was on his way to a Detroit assembly line. He knew she had heard about Bobbie. He timed his visit to miss his father who was at work and who had cursed him the last time they talked. John Henry had only tried to make a little money to catch up with his tired friends, most of whom were working two jobs. The Horse would have come to his hometown anyway. Someone would have brought it, yes. He turned on the radio as he picked up the expressway outside of town. A bigger town with better contacts might do wonders for his luck.

Ward #3

by Ira Sadoff

I suppose you would have to call our apartment cozy. Two and a half rooms in a basement on Fourth Street, where the coats and the roaches mingle freely in the bathtub, the sink works often as not and the people wash their feet in the toilet. Cozy but not sanitary. Our few friends affectionately call the place Ward #3, but it is officially known as apartment 3. For the moment I am considered the responsible person in the apartment because I am the only one with a job. The fact that this job is night managing the Red Barn, supervising the greaseburgers and the soybean milkshakes, does not seem to disturb anyone here, although my constant inability to hold a job for more than a month is a little more of an apartment concern.

That the four of us ever got together is a mystery to me, that we are still living in the same apartment is more of a miracle or a catastrophe, depending on the day of the week. There is Andy Meltzer, formerly one of the youngest violinists in the New York Philharmonic, later a violinist in a Hollywood movie orchestra, and currently one of the foremost fiddlers in the New York subway system; Josh Wyman, a tall, bleached-blond gigolo, who spends his working hours in the lobbies of Atlantic City hotels; and Janice Kasoff, whose only claim to fame is that since she has been living with three males she has become a very straight-forward lesbian.

I first met Janice when she was serving drinks at the Limelight Cafe, and one night we got to talking after I had lost my job at the Eighth Street Bookstore and she offered to let me stay with

IRA SADOFF (b. 1945) is the author of a book of poetry, *Settling Down* (1975), and has had fiction published in the *Paris Review* and *Transatlantic Review*.

her for a while. She was very sympathetic, almost motherly, and somehow we got involved with each other. Sleeping on the same bed had something to do with it. I moved in permanently, and then, when I was no longer interesting to her (for reasons I am still not certain), instead of asking me to move out, she asked others to move in, to help her pay the rent. She could have made more responsible choices, but not, apparently given the company she keeps. So here we all are, sleeping on one king-size mattress, very little going on between us, doing occasional battle with insomnia and cold feet. Every once in a while we hear one big sigh, almost coming out of the mattress, a sigh of relief that we've made it through another day.

What distinguished the day I stopped sleeping with Janice from other days is hard to say. I remember getting home from work (this time as a runner in the Forty-second Street library) and finding Andy (although I didn't find out his name was Andy until later) in bed with Janice, not doing anything but talking. Although the bed is the apartment's only real piece of furniture, this did not stop me from being a little taken back, even shocked. I fought every bourgeois impulse in my body to keep myself from saying, "What the hell is going on here?" and instead just sat on the mattress and joined in the conversation, finding Andy pleasant enough if not overwhelmingly interesting. Janice and I had never discussed the assumptions of our relationship because there simply weren't any, but when I saw Andy on the bed I began to feel we needed some. I asked her to come out into the hall for a moment, and then asked her what was going on. "Is he an old friend of yours or something?"

"No, I just met him today. On the IRT. He was playing a lovely Bach *partita*."

"Is he going to stay for dinner?"

"No, he's going to live with us."

Somehow I had expected it all along. "Is there something I've done?" I'm ready to let myself in for anything. "Was I becoming too possessive?"

"No, you were becoming too boring."

"I see. You want me to go?"

"Not as long as you're willing to split the rent. What attracted me to Andy, aside from his beautiful playing, was the seventeen dollars plus I saw lying in his violin case. I got fired from my modeling job today. The instructor said they were going to do still-lifes for the rest of the term."

I could think of nothing else to say. I remember being scared to death that first night the three of us slept in bed, with plenty of room but not able to dare touch Janice, and the second night wanting to try anyway but discovering Andy fondling Janice's breasts while she stared at the ceiling, and the third night when nothing happened I began to forget about our intimacy, as though I were sleeping in some kind of decompression chamber. And while I feared I could not sleep in the same bed with them while they were making love, it turned out, when it did happen once, I could, and I was fascinated and horrified at the same time, like a man allowed to witness his own funeral. And I found out that everybody does it primarily the same way, that neither Andy nor I had anything special to offer in the way of lovemaking. It never happened again, so I assume it must not have been all that terrific.

Of course it occurred to me that I should get out, that our living conditions were far from ideal, that I had never been able to take all that stress, but what did not occur to me was where I could get out *to;* my occupational status was even more precarious than Janice's, and in reality there wasn't a person in New York I knew well enough to move in with, even for a short time. So instead I called a meeting of the three of us one night when we all managed to be around at dinner time, and I suggested that there was a way we could eliminate some of the chaos around the apartment. It would not be a bad idea, I said, since we were all living together, if we started sharing some responsibilities.

"What responsibilities?" Janice sneered.

"I can see you're basically an anarchist," I said. "We could plan meals, divide expenses more efficiently, clean the place up, arrange to be away if someone wanted to bring someone over, and so on."

"I can see you're basically an idiot," she said. "There's nothing wrong with the way we do things around here, at least as far as I'm concerned."

"I don't give a shit," Andy said.

"We don't have enough money to pay last month's rent, for

one thing," I said. "If we could get some of our priorities straight, I don't see why we couldn't manage."

Janice became furious and turned to Andy. "How much have you been pocketing out of your take? Honestly, you make me so mad, Andy, I take you off the streets and you cheat me out of the goddamn rent money."

"Janice, what are you so angry about?" I said. "Sometimes I can't believe how rotten you can be to people."

"I guess that's just because I'm a castrating bitch," she said and walked out, slamming the door melodramatically behind her.

"Well, there goes your communal living," Andy said. "Why don't you leave her alone? We'll manage somehow."

"How much did you spend on that Zuckerman concert last week, Andy?"

"Forget it, Mister Military. You're not making enough money to balance my books."

For a couple of days none of us spoke to one another. Janice slept on the floor, restless and without a blanket, and I tried to think of something we could do to pay the rent. But then Janice arrived with Josh, who had tried to hustle her in front of the Saint Marks Cinema. "I usually get twenty-five for the act itself," he said as he walked in the door, "and forty for the entire night. But I can see you're pressed, so I'd take twenty and run." And then, after looking at us, he added, "Unless there are going to be spectators. Then the price goes up accordingly."

"Take it easy, pretty boy, I'd never sleep with a guy who bleaches his hair. But I have a proposition to make. How would you like a permanent base of operations? Where were you planning to sleep tonight?"

"I was planning to make a hit for the night. In fact I'm still planning to."

"Wouldn't it make sense for you to have a real place to stay? Twenty-five dollars a month for everything? You could make that with one half-hour grunt."

"You've really hit bottom, Janice," Andy said, shaking his head.

"No thanks," Josh said. "You just made me lose a good hour of street time."

But three days later Josh came back with a handful of books

and a large collection of cosmetics. "Sometimes the city is real slow," he said. "And I need a place to relax. I work too hard." For two weeks Andy refused to speak to him.

If I had counted on history I would have realized way in advance that I was not destined to be a junior executive at Red Barn. What I did not think about when I took the job was the basic impossibility of motivating a bunch of pimply teen-agers to work when their parents had forced them to get a job and they hated every moment of cooking, cleaning and serving in their waking life. One night an assistant Mr. Red Barn himself came in to inspect the premises while I was providing the employees with my usual deluge of obscenities; what I did not know was that hamburger kings have principles, that I couldn't expect to serve sterile malteds and little fish fries and have a filthy mind at the same time. And I knew after I'd said, "Get those miceburgers rolling," I had buried myself beyond apology.

What bothers me, I suppose, is given that I can't hold a job like this, what job could I hold? And what would happen to me if I just stopped looking? That explains my willingness to trek to the hinterlands of Queens for the Red Barn; and if I walked through the old sites and abandoned exhibitions of the old World's Fair, it was because I secretly hoped I would get mugged. What I really wanted to see was the desperate face of the junkie opening up my wallet and finding it absolutely empty. It would be more satisfying than looking in the mirror.

When I got home to tell everyone I'd been fired, Janice gave me a look that let me know I was absolutely, hopelessly pathetic, and she turned away from me indignantly. It was a look I had seen on her face only once before, and both times it made me shiver. The other time we had gotten free tickets to, of all things, a hockey game, and surprisingly enough to both of us, we went. And even more surprising, we screamed and yelled for blood like all the rest of the fans, almost in spite of ourselves. I threw Janice's hat into the rink, and Janice pushed some adolescent who was rooting for the visiting Blackhawks. When the Rangers lost, we got depressed beyond reason. We went home and made love mournfully. The next morning, when I came to my senses, I told Janice I never wanted to go to a hockey game again. I didn't like what it did to me. That's when Janice gave me that look. "It did what it did to you; why don't you let yourself enjoy it?"

"Because it's horrible, that's why. It brought out the worst in both of us."

"You're a sad case," she said. "You wouldn't know the worst in both of us if it stared you in the face. I'd never let myself get involved with someone like you. I mean that." And the next week Janice went to a hockey game by herself.

When Janice threatens to throw me out unless I come up with my share of last month's rent, Josh generously offers to take me with him to Atlantic City, and I, for some reason, accept his offer. So we take an afternoon bus down and sit in the lobby of the Richmond Hotel, which reminds me of 1940: the faint odor of mildew, the overstuffed chairs, the faded oriental rugs. It is the kind of place where you'd expect to see only geriatrics and degenerates, but it turns out that the majority of the guests are semi-wealthy Jewish widows and divorcées who take their vacations in Atlantic City either because their parents used to take them there or because they have nowhere else to go. Josh is sitting back in his chair smoking a cigarette and I am nervously watching him. Finally a woman comes over to him and asks, "How have you been, Josh? Are you ready for an evening on the town?"

"I'm always ready, Ellie, but I brought a friend along tonight." Ellie looks in my direction as if noticing me for the first time. "Do you think we could find a lovely for him? From what I hear he's very good."

"Don't look at me," she says. "I don't want to break in a new one."

"Well, champ," Josh says, getting up from his chair. "I'll be back in a couple of hours. If someone comes up to you be very nonchalant about it. If not, start hustling the cocktail lounge. By nine, if they haven't found what they want, they're either ready to get drunk out of their minds or try anything."

After Josh leaves me I of course feel foolish, and of course no one comes up to me. In spite of the ridiculous situation, I feel somehow rejected. I must look inexperienced. But I know I can't back out, not unless I want to be thrown out of the apartment. And besides, I have a round-trip busfare invested in the project, so I know I'd better come up with something.

When Josh hasn't returned by ten-thirty, I do go into the bar and nurse a beer with my remaining change. My inability to be aggressive is very disturbing and it must show. Finally sometime after eleven a woman around forty-ish comes up to me and says. "Why the moping? Performance bad or business slow?"

"Oh," I say, trying to keep my voice at an even pitch, "I'm just sitting here."

"Oh," she nods, "I'm just sitting here too. Would you like to sit up in my room? I just love to sit with strange-looking men."

"Thanks," I say.

"Thanks yes, or thanks no?"

"Thanks yes."

She turns to the bartender. "A pint of Gordon's and a six-pack of tonic, Jim." Then she looks at me. "Is that OK?"

"It beats Schlitz."

"Damn right," she smiles. "Don't be so nervous. I have no diseases and I come from a long line of good families."

Somehow she manages to make me feel comfortable. When we get into her room I am surprised to find it's not a flea trap, but that the furniture is antiseptically modern, almost like a dormitory. There is a painting of the Steel Pier over the bed and the usual tourist information under the glass-top desk. The room is painted and not wallpapered as I had expected.

"My name is Marion. How can I put you at ease? Should we talk? Do you have time?"

"I have all night."

"Good. What do you do during the week?"

"Right now, nothing. I used to hold a very responsible position at the Red Barn before I was heard swearing in front of the customers."

"You're kidding."

"No, the Red Barn is no joke."

"I'll say. But I had you pegged as a college-type. Dropout, maybe, but definitely the type."

"You were right."

"But now you're living the underground life, right? It's more romantic."

"It's more nothing. I don't know what I'm doing any more than you do, although it's probably pretty simple. Like it's impossible for me to hold a job."

"Oh you're so dark. If I were the night manager of the Red Barn I probably wouldn't be able to hold a job either."

"Thanks."

"That wasn't a compliment. You're way too grim. Let's talk about me. What do you suppose I'm like?"

"Well, let's see. You must be lonely, unsatisfied, frustrated and generally miserable. And you probably don't have all your own teeth."

"True, I don't have all of my own teeth. All the rest is false."

"You're divorced."

"True."

"You like the seashore."

"False. I like to get away from New York and meet new men."

"Aren't there enough men in New York?"

"Only the ones I work for, and they are notable only for their lack of attractiveness. Listen, we should talk more and I haven't even poured you a drink. Could we go to bed first?"

She doesn't even wait for me to answer before she starts taking off her blouse. Her body is still attractive, more so perhaps because of the way she carries herself. Only now she makes me nervous because she is so accomplished, as though she were the prostitute and I were going to have my first sexual experience. The reversal is impossible to deal with. Moreover she is good in bed, there is no reason why she could not be living with a man and making him happy. Any man. Me.

But afterwards she is so tired she falls asleep in my arms. "We got a late start," she says. "Why don't you take fifty dollars out of my purse? Unless you can stay the night."

Her trust is difficult to understand. I want to tell her fifty dollars is too much, I haven't done anything. I should be paying her, I'd like to talk. When I wake up in the morning she is gone. There is fifty dollars on the dresser, and a note. "Thanks," it says. "I hope I'll see you again. You were very nice. Almost innocent. Marion."

When I get into the lobby Josh is sitting down reading a newspaper; he breaks out into a smile when he sees me coming out of the elevator. "So that's where you've been," he says. "I was beginning to think you'd taken the midnight bus home." When I say nothing he asks, "Was it a beast?"

"No, actually she was pretty terrific. I think I love her." We both laugh for an unreasonable amount of time, drawing attention to ourselves. In the morning the lobby is full of a different kind of clientele, the older people you would expect. They sit here reading newspapers, looking out windows, limping about with or without their canes, smelling the way you would expect old people to smell. I feel very uncomfortable and tell Josh I would like to leave.

"Do you think you'll ever come back?" he asks.

"If I don't get a job I probably might."

"I wouldn't get a job," he says. "I just made a hundred bucks last night."

"I know," I say, "but there's no *future* in it."

I finally found a job that lasted more than a month. Six weeks, to be exact, as a psychological testee for the space program. And this time nobody terminated it, the experiment simply ended. The experiment went as follows: first six of us were closed in the same room for a period of a week, then they studied us individually for another week to test how we had responded to the environment and to one another. Then we went back into the same room for another week. We knew each other by letter only (I was Q, and the other letters were A, G, L, R and Y), in order to protect ourselves in case we did anything embarrassing, which, as it turned out, we did. The purpose of the experiment was to see how enclosure affected group dynamics. My guess is that if they followed our experiment closely, they would never leave the earth again.

Of course the sampling was very strange. Only weird or desperate people would volunteer for such an experiment, and all of us looked slightly more deranged than your average space employee. We began by being very cordial to one another, almost flirtatious, but that broke down by the second day. One of the women, G, took off her clothes before she went to sleep. R said this disturbed him to no end, that given the circumstances it was unnatural and made it difficult for him to get to sleep. G said that was his problem, that it was her body and she was free to deal with it in the way she wanted, and that if she had to worry about every neurotic in the world before she did something she'd never do anything. Y took her side immediately and by the fourth night they were making love on G's bed, noisily and arrogantly. Although I sympathized with G's assertion, somehow I identified with the victim, R, and stayed up with him when he couldn't sleep. I told him it was impossible to control other people's behavior, no matter how much we might want to.

"What are you talking about?" he said. "I live here too. If we're going to have to live together we're going to have to be thoughtful of each other."

"What does being thoughtful mean?" another letter asked. "That no one can do what he or she wants?"

"Maybe since we don't know what thoughtful means, it will be easier to slit each other's throats," R said.

"Maybe it will," Y said.

For some reason they gave us all different kinds of food in differing amounts. At first this angered us all and brought us closer together to protest the way we were being manipulated. We knocked on the doors. Y put his fist through one of the walls and we refused to eat. But by the end of the first evening we were too hungry; those of us who didn't like what we had to eat tried to negotiate for something else. Strawberries made R break out in a rash. They had to know that. A, the quietest of all of us, hated liver vehemently. We made some trades, but eventually everybody felt somebody else was trying to take advantage of him or her, and soon people were throwing their food again, knocking on walls, begging to be let out.

I found myself amazingly attracted to A. Perhaps because she was so quiet, almost intimidated by the group, or because she was so hard to get to know. Or perhaps because she didn't seem to notice me very much. Or because I was locked up in a room with five other people and I felt I had to be attracted to one of them. My choices were limited. Whatever the reason, when I did get up the nerve to tell her I was interested in her, she told me she found me totally unattractive, as ugly as the other letters who were trying to stab each other in the back. I said I needed to know what made her feel that way, that it would help me a lot to find out, that maybe I could change. She said there was no way of explaining something like that, that it was foolish and futile for me to try, that I should just try to accept things the way they were.

"You're so negative," I said.

"Only about you," she said.

For the rest of the week I was quiet, counting the days before I could leave the room. The books they left for us to read were boring, and almost everyone settled into watching TV in a trance; it was the most peaceful we had been with each other, at least after we were able to decide on a program to watch. Besides, I didn't want to read a book the thought mechanics from NASA brought in. What if they *wanted* us to read certain books to see what effect they would have on us. Baudelaire, Ross MacDonald, Desmond Morris, there's no telling what they could do to me.

Josh has been going down to Atlantic City more often, not only on weekends but two or three times during the week. I can't tell if it's because he needs the money or he needs to get out of the apartment. We all seem to be at loose ends, seeing each other only in passing, during occasional meals. The dirt is piling up in the corners. Josh has brought in his own mattress and sleeps in the corner by the door. We are now using paper plates and would use paper pots and pans if they made them. Josh also bought a color TV, which he keeps with him by his bed, but strangely none of us in the apartment find it soothing the way we had in the experiment. As soon as Josh turns it on Andy turns red and begins practicing scales on his violin. Janice says she almost vomits every time he turns it on. Not only is it stupid and boring, she says, but she can't stand the way they treat women on commercials and variety shows, like functional morons. Objectively, I have no objection to the television, but every time it goes on I get the chills, as though I were still locked in that room with all those people. I guess that's what the scientists would call a long-term effect.

Politics. Our world is so small sometimes it seems not to exist. And sometimes I think the television brought it all in. The more than usual crimes of violence, often only blocks away. What the news does is make us all afraid; it is the only show we all watch. Every day when I wake up now I am surprised to find myself here, alone, without our own invading army occupying our apartment house, gathering us all in a big stockade. Only there is a small feeling of satisfaction knowing that there is nothing they could make me do. I am totally unfit to do anything useful. On the other hand maybe they would just gas me to death.

But there is another kind of politics, more personal. Janice brought that into the house. She's now meeting with a group called Radical Lesbians. They meet at the apartment once a week and Josh can't stand it. It is a personal affront to him, to everything he stands for. When he walks in the door he makes dyke jokes, he takes a phony pugilistic stance. "You're all a bunch of psychopaths," Josh says. Most of the women ignore him or laugh at him, but one woman, Lucy Warnick, once spat in his face. He'll never forgive Janice for that. He refuses to leave the apartment when they meet. He turns on the television and makes a general pest of himself. Janice would love to tell him to get out, but by now he pays about two-thirds of the rent, and she is almost afraid he'll force her out of the apartment himself. Josh knows the women hate him as a symbol of oppression, which he is, but personally most of the women in the group seem to feel sorry for him.

Last night I came home and found Janice making love to another woman; it was a night I will not soon forget. For some reason when I was in the same room with her and Andy it did not affect me in the same way; there is a special kind of intimacy between two women I have not been able to break through. Janice looked up from the bed in a daze, almost as though I were not there. She turned away from me and said, "Would you please come back later?" and I left without speaking. I did not see the face of the other woman, only the outline of her body, which was as pale as the sheet she was lying on.

When I came back later that night I asked Janice, "Do you want to talk about it?"

"Talk about what?" she snapped. "My life is my life. Is there something you don't approve of?"

"No, I just thought you might want to talk about it."

"No, I guess I don't want to talk about it," she said with a little more tenderness, her voice fading away as though she were falling down a well.

That night I could not sleep. The smell of the two women was still on the sheets, Janice's aroma was separate and disturbing. Her body fluid spilled on the bed. Melodramatically I got sick to my stomach and walked around the Village all night. In the morning I did a laundry. What I would not admit to myself, what I could not admit to myself, was that Janice was moving further and further away from me, and there was nothing I could do about it.

The results of the study came out, a three hundred and fifty page report, which, as part of our payment, NASA gave us to read. Most of it was as boring as could be expected, but the transcript concerning how each of us responded to the other letters was fascinating. For most people I, as a letter, hardly existed, but when I was mentioned a strange pattern seemed to form: I was the letter most reluctant to express what I was feeling, they never knew if I meant what I said. I always went along with what was easiest for the group. I was never the person to turn on the television or begin an argument. Some people thought this meant I was pretty well-adjusted; others thought I just didn't know what I wanted. One person thought I had been planted there by NASA to watch the other letters. The rest of the report said nothing specific about me, but they concluded it was indeed safe for people to live in space for long periods of time.

When Janice did not come home last night I assumed she was sleeping with one of her friends. Still, it made Andy and me very nervous and we hardly slept. There is something very safe about a woman sleeping between two men, something neither of us had realized before. In the morning, though, one of Janice's friends barged into the apartment and said that Janice was in jail, that she had been arrested in a demonstration in front of the Women's House of Detention. A cop had beaten her head in. She needed two hundred and fifty dollars bail, or else she could rot in jail for months. Immediately Andy and I turned to Josh, the only one of us who could conceivably have scraped up that much money. "Don't look at me," he said, "I'm not giving any of my hard-earned money for a bunch of dykes. Let them go mug an old man."

"Josh," I said, "sometimes you're a first-class jerk."

My response surprised him. "You don't like it," he said, "move into the sewer."

Andy ignored our conversation and picked up his violin. "I'm going to the subway. If I go uptown to Lexington Avenue there's a slight chance I could get arrested, but I should be able to pick up at least forty bucks if I play all day."

"Don't be ridiculous, Andy. She needs two hundred and fifty. Pronto."

The woman had no patience with us. "You guys work it out however you can. Just remember she found this place and gave you all somewhere to stay. I've got a lot of other people to get in touch with. There are thirty sisters in jail and the cops are not very fussy about how they handle them."

"Sisters," Josh said. "Psychos is more like it."

With that comment everyone except Josh left the apartment. I went to the experiment center uptown but they said they had no work for me. They said that in a month they'd be performing a long-term weightless experiment and that if I leave my name, and so on. I left my name and left. The only other thing I could think of was Atlantic City. My only other source of income. I had new courage to face that lobby, strange women, a technical erection. I was only surprised at the immediacy I felt for Janice and the melancholy feeling that she would not appreciate it.

Ironically enough, coming down to Atlantic City to sleep with a forty year old Jewish woman is one of the most moral acts of my life. I am absolutely brazen at this point, coming up to women who look lonely, offering my company, getting refused without embarrassment. But it is a weekday night and things are very slow. It seems that the widows and divorcees must come down only for weekends, and I am surprised to find that until around ten o'clock there are a goodly number of octogenarian types hanging around the lobby. In a fleeting moment of fantasy I think of approaching one of them, but I am afraid they would call the cops and no one would bail *me* out of jail. Finally at ten-thirty, while I am sitting around drinking a beer, a reasonably ugly woman (closer to fifty than forty) comes up to me, very drunk. She reminds me of the woman Josh went off with the first night I was here, but she is obviously someone else.

"You're a fine looking boy," she says.

"Why thank you. Why don't you sit down?"

"And polite too? Have you been hanging around the Rich-mond very long?"

"No, not very."

"I didn't think so. I've never had you before."

"No you haven't. I'm sorry to say." The last phrase hurts as it comes out.

"Are you expensive?"

"Sometimes."

"Well, at my age quantity counts as much as quality. I'm a lady, don't get me wrong, but there's only so much I can do before I get tired or run out of money. Have you had dinner yet?" When I shake my head no, she says, "I can go up to fifty if you spend the night, thirty if you don't."

"That's very generous."

"But you pay for the dinner and the drinks. And that's all the business I want to hear about."

"All right," I say, and I take her out on the boardwalk toward the Ritz-Carleton, which is about a six block walk. The board-walk, except for a few drunks and a couple of police cars cruising on the wooden planks, is virtually empty. The woman, whose name is Edie, tells me this is the first time she's walked down the boardwalk in years. "With so many rapes and muggings it's not safe for a woman my age to walk the streets at night."

"Why do you come here, then, if you stay away from the ocean?"

She gives me a look that lets me know I am an absolute child and then changes the subject. Atlantic City. It seems like the perfect city for corruption.

Dinner is boring but tolerable. I nurse my own drink and discourage Edie from having too much to drink. At this point in the evening she wouldn't know the difference, and every two dollars is two dollars more toward Janice's bail.

I wonder what gave Janice the impetus to get herself in the position of being jailed. What is it that's so important to her about being a lesbian? I know I almost envy it, whatever it is. I know that all my old stereotypes about lesbians (bad relationships with their fathers, bad sex, castration complexes) have gone down the drain, and what I realize about Janice is that she doesn't find men tremendously exciting, and when I look around the apartment at Josh, Andy, and me, I am not surprised. We had nothing to offer her, there was nothing exciting about any of us.

I remember one episode shortly after Janice had been fired from her modeling job. She said that getting fired was the best thing that could have happened to her, that instead of displaying her body she would now make use of it, this break in inertia would lead her to something else. I said that breaks in inertia in my life had only led to more inertia. She looked at me angrily, as if to say; "Don't tell me you're always going to be like this," and although I wanted to say "No," very much, I had said "No" to myself so many times that by now I hesitated to say it to anyone else. We did not talk for a long while. She began to pace. When I got up to touch her she moved away. "I'm not going to feel sorry for anyone," she said. "If you don't get better you'll get out." And while she was never quite strong enough to carry out that threat (she knew the right questions, where would I go? What would happen to me?) she began to keep her distance, as though I had the capacity to contaminate her.

The sexual experience itself, of course, was horrible beyond belief. Edie's body had long ago begun to decay in a way I had not seen before. If she had not been so drunk she would have seen the shock in my expression as she took off her clothes. What struck me was the looseness of skin, as though her bones had shrunk, as though her body had become too much for her tiny frame. I did not become impotent as I had feared, but stayed erect for nearly half an hour by an act of pure will. It amazed me to think of the areas in which I was able to maintain my strengths. What was obvious to me was that Edie did not enjoy a minute of it, she faked heavy breathing in a way that made me think she had forgotten how she used to do it. She called me darling like in the movies. She told me I was as big as she'd ever seen. I was quiet and in a few minutes she either fell asleep or passed out. I had nowhere to go so I lay in bed for my fifty dollars until morning. I did my best to keep from thinking, although I thought some about Janice and the experiment I had taken part in; somehow that was becoming the ultimate failure of my life, although I couldn't say exactly why.

I sat in the lobby with fifty crumpled dollars in my pocket and a promise from Edie that the next time she came to town we would go to the Steel Pier. For two hours I hoped someone would/would not come up to me, and luckily, I think, no one did. I read and re-read the newspaper three or four times, passing over the articles about corruption in government, the secret plans for new wars, the cutbacks of the poverty programs again. It all seemed so improbable to me I couldn't take it seriously. Then I left the hotel and hitched back to New York, still not knowing how we would find the money to get Janice out of jail, knowing furthermore that I would not even be able to keep my job as a gigolo, that my promising beginning had been merely a freak accident.

When I got back to the apartment I found Andy sitting on the front steps holding his violin in his lap, oblivious to everything around him. Before I had a chance to ask him what he was doing, he said, "I wouldn't bother trying to get back into the apartment if I were you. Josh has changed the locks and is standing behind the door with a machete knife."

"Are you serious?"

"If I weren't serious do you think I'd be sitting here on the steps? He's got all my music locked up with him and his two gigolo friends are keeping him company."

"Has he been on junk?"

"I don't think so. You see I pawned his color TV for a hundred bucks, and apparently he's ready to kill us for it."

"You what?"

"I hated that TV, and it was the only way, short of robbing a bank, of getting enough money to get Janice out of jail."

"Andy, how could you be so stupid?"

"If Janice were here he'd never have gotten away with this. She would have thrown him right out on his ass. But now he's pulling some masculine something, holding on to his territory because he can't watch The Hollywood Squares. I told Janice never to let him move in."

I gave Andy what was left of the fifty dollars plus whatever little money I had. It turned out that by pooling our resources, including the money from the TV, we had just enough to get her out. In the meantime, while Andy went to the jail, I said I would try to reason with Josh. But when I knocked on the door he looked through the keyhole and wouldn't let me in. "Josh," I said, "Andy made a stupid mistake. He promised me he'd get your tube out of hock. Today. Honest."

"Why don't you two dyke-loving thieves go find yourselves a place to stay. I've got my property to protect."

"Listen, it was all a mistake. Andy needed the money for Janice, it wasn't for himself. He just wasn't thinking straight."

"Well he's got plenty of time to think straight now. I can't believe how you could have done this to me, after how I showed you how you could make all the money you'd ever need. It's not right."

"I didn't steal anything from you."

"And I could never live in the same house with a dyke and a couple of thieves again. No matter what."

"Josh, I've got my goddamned clothes in there."

"I pawned them. I would have expected something like this from a creep like Andy, but you, what did I ever do to you?"

I was getting tired of trying to explain things to Josh, and it was clear that he had no intention of giving up the apartment. If for no other reason, his pride seemed sufficient to keep us thrown out. I tried to be angry at Andy but it was impossible, and there's a good chance I would have pawned Josh's TV if I had thought of it first. I sat on the steps wondering how Janice would feel about losing her apartment. I thought that if anyone could have changed Josh's mind it was her. But when Andy came back alone I knew that something was wrong. He was out of breath.

"She's already out," he said.

"You mean somebody else supplied the bail?"

"Apparently. Some legal defense committee got the bail lowered and they had some slush fund stored away somewhere."

"Then where is she? Why didn't she come back home?"

"She already did, but Josh wouldn't let her in either. Now she's staying at a women's commune on the West Side. She's apparently getting very involved with one of the women there."

"A commune? After everything I tried to set up here? I don't believe it."

"She said she doesn't want to see you. Or me."

"It figures."

"Here's your sixty bucks. I think I know a place where I can stay near Julliard. There's an old fag professor of mine who always thought I had the cutest bowing technique."

"Very funny."

I watched Andy leave and somehow tried to assess my situation honestly. The woman I cared for was a lesbian and everything I said rubbed her the wrong way. I could not get along with large groups of people. My finest hour was sleeping with a fifty-year-old drunk in a totally futile act. I have somehow hurt Josh in a way I would not have thought possible. In fact, I marvel at how easy it is to hurt people, and wonder why hurting people is not the national sport. Or if it is, how I learned to play so well, and why it has never done me any good.

The Critics' Circle

from *Max Jamison*

by Wilfrid Sheed

The critics' circle was in session when he arrived. They met in the Asshole Room of the Hotel Asshole, as far as Max was concerned. His mind tasted quite foul now, and spewed little bits of garbage into his mouth. He had better not talk too much tonight. He had not written his review, and he felt guilty and hungover about that; not as he had hoped, roguish and liberated. They sat at a long baize-covered table with various-colored potions in front of them, looking, to Max's yellow eye, like wizards, alchemists, dwarfs.

They were talking, his fatheaded circle, about the admission of new members. Jack Flashman, wise guy emeritus at the other news magazine, was on the agenda. "Frankly," said Isabel Nutley of *Women's Thoughts,* "I don't think he quite comes up to our standards." "If we had any standards at all, half of you wouldn't be here," growled the tireless Bruffin. "Gentlemen, gentlemen," said the chairman. "I don't know—who writes the stuff on that magazine anyway? How can you tell? Flashman may be dead, for all we know." "He's a gossip writer, for Christsake. What does he know about the theater?" "What do any of you know about the theater?" "Gentlemen, gentlemen." "Frankly, if Flashman gets in, I quit. I can't stand the guy." "That's too damn bad, we'll miss you, honey, but Flashman happens to write for a very important magazine. You can't just ignore it." "What's wrong with gossip writing? Most of you don't even reach *that* level." "Gentlemen."

WILFRID SHEED (b. 1930) is the author of *The Blacking Factory* and *Pennsylvania Gothic* (1968); *Max Jamison* (1971); *People Will Always Be Kind* (1973); and a recent book about Muhammad Ali, the boxer.

As he looked at their small maniac faces round the table, fighting like cannibals over a dead missionary's pants, Max thought, What you need around here is nothing less than a spiritual rebirth. Let me bring it to you! Let me start the ball rolling. But their eyes were crazed, myopic, their voices high and fanatical; they operated out of little glass bowls, and no one could come in.

"What do you say, Max?"

"I say, why not?" Max said with staring eyes. "Why should any man carry through life the stain of being rejected by this damn fool society?"

"Well, that's true," conceded Bruffin.

Let's hear it now for spiritual rebirth. You too, Bruffin! Down on your knees, you dog. Can't you see that we *all* have to change? I'm not the only one. You're all self-important asses. Or threadbare clowns. Or pretentious hacks. No exceptions, right? You all know that about each other, at least. Take a vote. The room was rimy with contempt; he had never seen such mutual loathing in any group.

So let me lead you into the waters of salvation. My tattered little scout troop, my bee-keepers, my bank clerks. Good enough critics, at least, to know each other's worthlessness. Let us begin with that. Lord, they are not much, I know. But take them for what they are. What's that you say, Lord? You'll call us? I see. Yes, I quite understand.

These meetings always gave Max a sovereign headache. All that trade talk. He couldn't connect with it at all tonight. There are too many serious thoughts to be shuffled solemnly around his own showroom. Did these other critics have lives too? He supposed so. Cold sweats. Silent screaming in the night. Isabel Nutley crouched in a corner of her bathtub watching the water rise. Each must come in here sometimes clamoring for rebirth and deploring the triviality of the others; they probably took turns at it. Tonight was old Max's turn. Nothing important.

"I guess I have to vote against Flashman," he said, reversing himself on Bruffin, "if there's any point to having these meetings at all. He's the kind of guy who'll vote for Jayne Mansfield as actress of the year. A cut-up."

"I'm for him," said Bruffin, swirling his 7-Up. "He writes cleaner prose than anyone in this room. He's also a *complete* sell-out, unlike the rest of you, which gives him a certain kind of integrity. And, above all, he is an *artist* in gossip . . ."

Blood swam across Max's eyes. "Harold, let's make it brief. You give me a pain in the ass."

Bruffin waved a hand. "Is that so? You should take something for it."

"Yes, I think I will." Max stood up awkwardly. He hadn't hit anyone in years and was uncertain of the actual motion of the arm. Was it like a swimming stroke or more like casting a fly? He hadn't done much of those either. Movie punches, stage punches —it would come to him.

Bruffin did not rise to meet him, but sat smirking; as if a punch from Max would be a marvelous giveaway. What did I tell you—hysteria, panic. All these sell-outs are alike. Next he'll be setting fire to the curtains. It gave Max a moment's pause. The obvious way out was verbal. "The trouble with people like you, Bruffin, is that they don't fight when someone calls them a pain in the ass." Not bad, but not good enough. The blood circling his scalp would not settle for that. This was the one spiritual solution he hadn't thought of last night and he was not going to talk himself out of it. He picked up Bruffin by the lapel and removed his glasses as delicately as a dentist, hoping now that Bruffin would hold the smirk just a moment longer; and wheeled his arm round somehow until his knuckles rattled against Bruffin's teeth. Surprisingly hard teeth. A squish of blood traced over his fingers. My God, that felt good. Isabel Nutley screamed pleasantly and rushed for him. Several writhing critics pinned him: it must be a pleasure for them to move their bodies for a change, to be firm with someone. He let them. He had no intention of socking Bruffin again.

The latter had put his hand to his mouth and down again, and it seemed now to contain a tooth. How about that? I knocked a tooth out. Bruffin suddenly darted forward, whimpering like a small animal, and hit Max a soft blow on the eye like a girl. Great! No more talk about hysteria now. Hitting a man when his arms are pinned, indeed. Bruffin was led away still whimpering and staring at his tooth.

Max scooped up his coat and left without speaking to any-body. That seemed best. There was a sense of shock among the critics, which would give way to downright joy as the physical threat receded and they resumed their lives as voyeurs. Critics should do this to each other more often. Magnificent if they fell to clubbing each other right now.

He felt elated all the way home, until with his head down over his shoes, he thought, My God, what was that all about? His new spiritual solution: the gods had made him mad. O.K., O.K., don't take it too hard. Just blowing off steam; lots of good, sane people do that. Bankers and such. And God, did Bruffin ever lose face, crying like a baby over his tooth. But a racking remorse kept Max's neck bent until he could barely raise it. Loss of control was not what he had expected when he started his spiritual odyssey last night.

Max's immediate boss at *Now,* Harvey Salter, tsar of the back of the book, was part of the new wave of *Now* people. If you said to him, as Max had at their first interview, that you thought the magazine was vulgar and superficial, he would scratch his stubby nose and say, "Yes. We're trying to correct that." If you singled out some particular item you especially disliked, Salter would remember it gloomily and say that he hadn't much cared for it either. Given enough time and pressure, he would give up on the whole magazine for you.

Salter was the man who had started hiring people like Max in the first place, and he watched over his eggheads carefully. He lunched with them from time to time, in the bleak executive dining room, and there was talk over the Bloody Marys about the crumby state of the theater. And sometimes at the theater itself, Max would feel Salter breathing gently on his neck from the row in back. Salter never commented on Max's work, but he kept him on edge with this damn intelligent interest of his.

In fact, he spooked Max quite a piece. Harvey had gone to *Now* as a junior seminarian and had been there ever since, no matter how distastefully he appeared to view it; he had survived purges large and small and had moved up steadily under a variety of regimes, getting glummer and more sneaky-diffident as he went. Until now he sat above the world in immaculate white shirt sleeves, and looking like a man who lived on indigestion pills, although no one had ever seen him take one.

Max knew in his bones that if one went to see Salter and told

him that one was suffering a crisis of the spirit, he would understand perfectly ("Oh God, yes—I have those myself"), and
charter a plane to Tibet for you. Now, Inc., was a formidably
kindly organization and they were always sending employees off
on six months' leaves. So what if the employees usually came
back three months early in a muck sweat? It wasn't the magazine's fault that no one could trust such kindness.

Max made an appointment to see Salter on Monday, and then
cancelled it. He imagined the scene afterwards in the power suite.
"Jamison's beginning to crack. Good. Send him away for a while.
They're always weaker and softer when they get back. They're
ours then." A synchronized shifting of cigars. "They can't work
anywhere else after a company vacation. You can do what you
like with them. Put 'em in Religion, put 'em in Finance. They'll
go without a sound." A mighty rustle of trouser legs. "They've
admitted weakness, you see. And that's the name of the game,
isn't it?" A great growl of assent.

Jamison didn't trust any of them a damn inch. He didn't
understand people like that. He had never worked for the power
crowd before; and all he had to go on was fantasy. Salter was the
company spy, the understanding chap in the bar who talked you
into blurting things. He really loved *Now,* old Salter, would lie
and cheat and steal for it. But when he fell, in the inevitable
men's-room fight, his skull would split open and reveal a small
radio.

Max typed a quick, bad review in his old style and, loathing
himself more than ever, handed it in sourly. He went to lunch
with his hands shaking, the way old *Now* hands did. It suddenly
seemed tremendously important not to show his weakness; and as
he looked along the bar, he saw that that was the motive of all of
them.

Jack Flashman cruised up. What was he doing over here? This
wasn't his bar. He must have sniffed carrion. Flashman had
certainly never had a spiritual crisis himself, but he probably
enjoyed them in others. Must not show weakness in front of
Flashman. "Hi Max, how goes?" Notice the probing question, the
sly, gross man behind it. Ah crap, Flashman meant no harm.

"I hear you threw a punch at Bruffin last night."

So that's what he was doing here. Checking out a rumor. "Who
told you that?"

"I have those meetings bugged, didn't you know? I know whose standards I come up to and whose I don't."

"You do, huh? You wouldn't care to name your leak, would you? Our humble meetings are supposed to be confidential."

"Isabel Nutley talks in her sleep. So what did you slug Bruffin for? In your very own words?"

"Don't you know? Or are you trying to spring a second leak?"

"Just double-checking. What I heard was that Bruffin wanted me in the group, and you called him an obscenity and hit him. Is that right?"

It was hard to tell under the stiff clown's face and the shrill bantering voice; but it appeared that Flashman was genuinely angry. Oh great, that's just what I need this morning. A new enemy.

"Your informant is a troublemaker, Jack. Probably Bruffin himself, trying to suck up to you. Did he say I pulled a knife on him?"

Flashman shook his head. "It wasn't Bruffin."

"Well, whoever it was, let me send this message back. Anyone who violates confidence like that is inherently untrustworthy. You buy that?"

Flashman was definitely trying to glower. A grand enemy to find in your In-tray on a Monday morning, a dealer in theatrical gossip who could spread the tale from coast to coast in a matter of hours; or, if his own magazine didn't go for it, could trade it to some dirtier journal and get Max that way.

Max had never imagined worrying about a thing like this. He was not a public figure; his backbiting covered a small area—parts of Manhattan, some houses in Connecticut. He had never realized the jolt to the nerves that went with big-time gossip.

He suddenly found himself almost pleading with Flashman. "For Godsake, Jack—that's the most distorted account I've ever heard of anything. O.K. I voted you down, that's true. But only because I don't think you belong in that particular group. And believe me, that's no insult."

"Nice going, Max babes. Very nice footwork. You voted me down to spare me the pain of not 'belonging.' Of being the only black kid on the block. I appreciate that."

"Listen, it's just a pretentious little group of would-be highbrows, half of whom are certifiably insane . . ."

"In other words, serious critics. Unlike me. Don't go on, Max. I'm very quick. Just tell me about the fight."

"I don't know. It just happened. Harold was being snotty. He called you a never mind." Max hadn't meant to curry favor with Flashman by tattling. This was awful. "I just blew up and hit him. One punch. You're not going to print that, are you?"

Flashman blinked in back of his bifocals. "Print it? Where? Who wants to read about a nothing fight between two unknown critics? Who ever heard of Bruffin outside of Manhattan? Who ever heard of you outside your office?"

Oh God. To beg for mercy and be told that you didn't need it. The ruthless power of the press would spare him after all.

"You eating, or just drinking?" said Flashman.

"Just drinking, it begins to look like."

Flashman's face suddenly slumped, in a surprising gesture. "You know, Max, this is ridiculous, but I'd like to get into that damn society of yours. It would help me at my shop. They have very twisted ideas over there. Also, it would help my confidence, which is not too hot right now."

"*Your* confidence? You're kidding."

"Right. I've been striking out with too many broads lately. Those scores tell you how you're doing. Naming my magazine gets me halfway to bed, at least with the kind of chicks I want to get to bed with. But then I get stuck. They must sense something—job insecurity, identity crisis."

"How's the wife and kids, Jack?"

"They're O.K. So listen, will you put in a word for me at your next outing? I'd appreciate it."

Oh, sure. Why not? "You can have my place if you like, Jack. I only go twice a year, to pick up my gossip." The triviality as suddenly suffocating. What Flashman obviously needed was rebirth, nothing less would do. Maybe we could found a monastery or something together.

"You can afford to be arrogant, Max. I can't." Flashman the Flip having his noonday drinky-poos. Which was better—a vicelike grope, or a voice-like gripe?

"I'm glad you think so. I'd been thinking of giving it up. But you encourage me to persevere."

Max decided to go straight home after lunch. He couldn't face the visual assault of a screening, or the strain of trying to disentangle the sounds. Perhaps he should lie down and recite "God is love" until he fell into a deep, untroubled sleep. Or ring a small bell to summon the monks to prayer.

You know the trouble, Max? No, tell me what the trouble is. All right, I will. You're like the old alcoholic who's too intelligent for AA. You go to the meetings with the best intentions, and you listen to those windbags baring their souls and unwinding their bandages and finding new strength; and you just can't do it. The wise man, the holy man, says, Look, suppose the only road to health lies that way, through stupidity and bad taste? Can't you take a few steps? And your palms sweat, you're scared out of your mind, but no, you can't do it. You leave the meeting and walk back into hell.

As Max wandered home, he imagined a red-light district lined with Christian Science reading rooms, Zen institutes, Scientology labs, faith healers, a gaudy, sleazy gin lane that the Pilgrim must fight his way through. But when he got home, there were no trumpets sounding for him, only a buzzing refrigerator. He pulled the blind and lay down. Go on now, say it. "Love, love, love." "Hara Krishna." Anything. His mouth twisted like a persimmon. I can't do that crap.

The phone rang. This is it! The game is up. He reached out a manicured hand. Why would a man like me care about his nails? Why the twelve suits? Please, some other time perhaps. No more questions today. This here on the phone was Miss Weaver, Mr. Salter's secretary. Having now obtained Mr. Jamison, she must proceed to obtain Mr. Salter. This was a lengthy business, it involved dredging men's rooms and other possible hiding places, and finally a thrilling chase across roofs. That was how long it took for Harvey Salter to answer his own calls.

Max, woozy from Bloody Marys, went through the normal death spasms while waiting. Salter had obviously read Max's latest copy, had seen at once that Max was having a spiritual crisis, and had already made the arrangements to have him spirited out of the country. Two weeks with the Dalai Lama and we'll have you back on your feet. "Max, is that you, Max?"

"Yes, hello there, Harvey."

"Well, Max, how about lunch tomorrow? I'd like to talk to you."

Tomorrow? I'll be dead tomorrow. "Is it something about the

column I handed in? I can do it over this afternoon if you like."

"Column? No, I haven't seen that yet. I'm sure it's fine. All your work is fine."

Oh. Not the column. What a joke on me. Worrying about the column and all that. Max had always despised anxiety cases. But now, as he struggled for rebirth and transcendence, he found the smalls of life getting to him worse than ever. What did he care about his column? Being fired from *Now* would cover him with glory in his old set; his marshal's baton would be restored to him and his old place at the mess. Capital to have you back, Jamison. Yet here he was, writhing along the floor, offering to rewrite when no rewrite was called for. The way of the Pilgrim had strange beginnings.

☆ ☆ The Death of Me
by Bernard Malamud

Marcus was a tailor, long ago before the war, a buoyant man with a bushy head of graying hair, fine fragile brows and benevolent hands, who comparatively late in life had become a clothier. Because he had prospered, so to say, into ill health, he had to employ an assistant tailor in the rear room, who made alterations on garments but could not, when the work piled high, handle the pressing, so that it became necessary to put on a presser; therefore though the store did well, it did not do too well.

It might have done better but the presser, Josip Bruzak, a heavy, beery, perspiring Pole, who worked in undershirt and felt slippers, his pants loose on his beefy hips, the legs crumpling around his ankles, conceived a violent dislike for Emilio Vizo, the tailor—or it worked the other way, Marcus wasn't sure—a thin, dry, pigeon-chested Sicilian, who bore, or returned the Pole a steely malice. Because of their quarrels the business suffered.

Why they should fight as they did, fluttering and snarling like angry cocks, and using, in the bargain, terrible language, loud coarse words that affronted the customers and sometimes made the embarrassed Marcus feel dizzy to the point of fainting, mystified the clothier, who knew their troubles and felt they were as people, much alike. Bruzak, who lived in a half-ruined rooming house near the East River, constantly guzzled beer at work and kept a dozen bottles in a rusty pan packed full of ice. When Marcus, in the beginning, objected, Josip, always respectful to the clothier, locked away the pan and disappeared through the

BERNARD MALAMUD (b. 1914) is the author of *The Natural* (1952); *A New Life* (1961); *Idiots First* (1961); *The Tenants* (1971); *Rembrandt's Ha* (197˙); and other books.

back door into the tavern down the block where he had his glass, in the process wasting so much precious time it paid Marcus to advise him to go back to the pan. Everyday at lunch Josip pulled out of the drawer a small sharp knife and cut chunks of the hard garlic salami he ate with puffy lumps of white bread, washing it down with beer and then black coffee brewed on the one-burner gas stove for the tailor's iron. Sometimes he cooked up a soupy mess of cabbage which stank up the store, but on the whole neither the salami nor the cabbage interested him, and for days he seemed weary and uneasy until the mailman brought him, about every third week, a letter from the other side. When the letters came, he more than once tore them in half with his bumbling fingers; he forgot his work, and sitting on a backless chair, fished out of the same drawer where he kept his salami, a pair of cracked eyeglasses which he attached to his ears by means of looped cords he had tied on in place of the broken side-pieces. Then he read the tissue sheets he held in his fist, a crabbed Polish writing in faded brown ink whose every word he uttered aloud so that Marcus, who understood the language but preferred not to hear, heard. Before the presser had dipped two sentences into the letter, his face dissolved and he cried, oily tears smearing his cheeks and chin so that it looked as though he had been sprayed with something to kill flies. At the end he fell into a roar of sobbing, a terrible thing to behold, which incapacitated him for hours and wasted the morning.

Marcus had often thought of telling him to read his letters at home but the news in them wrung his heart and he could not bring himself to scold Josip, who was, by the way, a master presser. Once he began on a pile of suits, the steaming machine hissed without let-up, and every garment came out neat, without puff or excessive crease, and the arms, legs, and pleats were as sharp as knives. As for the news in the letters it was always the same, concerning the sad experiences of his tubercular wife and unfortunate fourteen-year-old son, whom Josip, except in pictures, had never seen, a boy who lived, literally in the mud with the pigs, and was also sick, so that even if his father saved up money for his passage to America, and the boy could obtain a visa, he would never get past the immigration doctors. Marcus more than once gave the presser a suit of clothes to send to his son, and occasionally some cash, but he wondered if these things ever got to him. He had the uncomfortable thought that Josip, in the last fourteen years, might have brought the boy over had he wanted, his wife too, before she had contracted tuberculosis, but for some reason he preferred to weep over them where they were.

Emilio, the tailor, was another lone wolf. Every day he had a forty-cent lunch in the diner about three blocks away but was always back early to read his *Corriere*. His strangeness was that he was always whispering to himself. No one could understand what he said, but it was sibilant and insistent, and wherever he was, one could hear his hissing voice urging something, or moaning softly though he never wept. He whispered when he sewed a button on, or shortened a sleeve, or when he used the iron. Whispering when he hung up his coat in the morning, he was still whispering when he put on his black hat, wriggled his sparse shoulders into his coat and left, in loneliness, the store at night. Only once did he hint what the whispering was about; when the clothier, noticing his pallor one morning, brought him a cup of coffee, in gratitude the tailor confided that his wife, who had returned last week, had left him again this, and he held up the outstretched fingers of one bony hand to show she had five times run out on him. Marcus offered the man his sympathy, and thereafter when he heard the tailor whispering in the rear of the store, could always picture the wife coming back to him from wherever she had been, saying she was this time—she swore—going to stay for good, but at night when they were in bed and he was whispering about her in the dark, she would think to herself she could never stand this thing and in the morning, was gone. And so the man's ceaseless whisper irritated Marcus; he had to leave the store to hear silence, yet he kept Emilio on because he was a fine tailor, a demon with a needle, who could sew up a perfect cuff in less time than it takes an ordinary workman to make measurements, the kind of tailor who, when you were looking for one, was very rare.

For more than a year, despite the fact that they both made strange noises in the rear room, neither the presser nor the tailor seemed to notice one another; then one day, as though an invisible wall between them had fallen, they were at each other's throats. Marcus, it appeared, walked in at the very birth of their venom, when, leaving a customer in the store one afternoon, he went back to get a piece of marking chalk and came on a sight that froze him. There they were in the afternoon sunlight that flooded the rear of the shop, momentarily blinding the clothier so that he had time to think he couldn't possibly be seeing what he saw—the two at opposite corners staring stilly at one another—a live, almost hairy staring of intense hatred. The sneering Pole in one trembling hand squeezed a heavy wooden pressing block, while the livid tailor, his back like a cat's against the wall, held aloft in his rigid fingers a pair of cutter's shears.

"What is it?" Marcus shouted when he had recovered his voice, but neither of them would break the stone silence and remained as when he had discovered them, glaring across the shop at the other, the tailor's lips moving noiselessly, and the presser breathing like a dog in heat, an eeriness about them that Marcus had never suspected.

"My God," he cried, his body drenched in cold creeping wetness, "tell me what happened here." But neither uttered a sound so he shrieked through the constriction in his throat, which made the words grate awfully, "Go back to work—" hardly believing they would obey; and when they did, Bruzak turned like a lump back to the machine, and the tailor stiffly to his hot iron, Marcus was softened by their compliance and speaking as if to children, said with tears in his eyes, "Boys, remember, don't fight."

Afterwards the clothier stood alone in the shade of the store, staring through the glass of the front door at nothing at all; lost, in thinking of them at his very back, in a horrid world of gray grass and green sunlight, of moaning and blood-smell. They had made him dizzy. He lowered himself into the leather chair, praying no customer would enter until he had sufficiently recovered from his nausea. So sighing, he shut his eyes and felt his skull liven with new terror to spy them both engaged in round pursuit in his mind. One ran hot after the other, lumbering but in flight, who had stolen his box of broken buttons. Skirting the lit and smoking sands, they scrambled high up a craggy cliff, locked in many-handed struggle, teetering on the ledge, till one slipped in slime and pulled the other with him. Reaching forth four hands, they clutched nothing in stiffened fingers, as Marcus, the watcher, shrieked without sound at their evanescence.

He sat dizzily until these thoughts had left him.

When he was again himself, remembrance made it a kind of

dream. He denied any untoward incident had happened; yet knowing it had, called it a triviality—hadn't he, in the factory he had worked in on coming to America, often seen such fights among the men?—trivial things they all forgot, no matter how momentarily fierce.

However, on the very next day and thereafter daily without skipping a day, the two in the back broke out of their silent hatred into thunderous quarreling that did damage to the business; in ugly voices they called each other dirty names, embarrassing the clothier so that he threw the measuring tape he wore like a garment on his shoulders, once around the neck. Customer and clothier glanced nervously at each other, and Marcus quickly ran through the measurements; the customer, who as a rule liked to linger in talk of his new clothes, left hurriedly after paying cash, to escape the drone of disgusting names hurled about in the back yet clearly heard in front so that no one had privacy.

Not only would they curse and heap destruction on each other but they muttered in their respective tongues other dreadful things. The clothier understood Josip shouting he would tear off someone's genitals and rub the bloody mess in salt; so he guessed Emilio was shrieking the same things, and was saddened and maddened at once.

He went many times to the rear, pleading with them, and they listened to his every word with interest and tolerance, because the clothier, besides being a kind man—this showed in his eyes—was also eloquent, which they both enjoyed. Yet, whatever his words, they did no good, for the minute he had finished and turned his back on them they began again. Embittered, Marcus withdrew into the store and sat nursing his misery under the yellow-faced clock clicking away yellow minutes, till it was time to stop—it was amazing they got anything done and their work was prodigious—and go home.

His urge was to bounce them out on their behinds but he couldn't conceive where to find two others who were such skilled and, in essence, proficient workers, without having to pay a fortune in gold. Therefore, with reform uppermost in his mind, he caught Emilio one noon as he was leaving for lunch, whispered him into a corner and said, "Listen, Emilio, you're the smart one, tell me why do you fight? Why do you hate him and why does he hate you and why do you use such bad words?"

Though he enjoyed the whispering and was soft in the clothier's palms, the tailor, who liked these little attentions, lowered his eyes and blushed darkly but either would not or could not reply.

So Marcus sat under the clock all afternoon with his fingers in his ears. And he caught the presser on his way out that evening and said to him, "Please, Josip, tell me what he did to you? Josip, why do you fight, you have a sick wife and boy?" But Josip, who also felt an affection for the clothier—he was, despite Polish, no anti-Semite—merely caught him in his hammy arms, and though he had to clutch at his trousers which were falling and impeding his movements, hugged Marcus into a ponderous polka, then with a cackle, pushed him aside, and in his beer jag, danced away.

When they began the same dirty hullabaloo the next morning and drove a customer out at once, the clothier stormed into the rear and they turned from their cursing—both fatigued and green-gray to the gills—and listened to Marcus begging, shaming, weeping, but especially paid heed when he, who found screeching unsuited to him, dropped it and gave advice and little preachments in a low becoming tone. He was a tall man, and because of his illness, quite thin. What flesh remained had wasted further in these troublesome months, and his hair was white now so that, as he stood before them, expostulating, exhorting, he was in appearance like an old hermit, if not a saint, and the workers showed respect and keen interest as he spoke.

It was a homily about his long-dead dear father, when they were all children living in a rutted village of small huts, a gaunt family of ten—nine boys and an undersized girl. Oh, they were marvelously poor: on occasion he had chewed bark and even grass, bloating his belly, and often the boys bit one another, including the sister, upon the arms and neck in rage at their hunger.

"So my poor father, who had a long beard down to here"—he stooped, reaching his hand to his knee and at once tears sprang up in Josip's eyes—"my father said, 'Children, we are poor people and strangers wherever we go, let us at least live in peace, or if not—' "

But the clothier was not able to finish because the presser, plumped on the backless chair, where he read his letters, swaying a little, had begun to whimper and then bawl, and the tailor, who was making odd clicking noises in his throat, had to turn away.

"Promise," Marcus begged, "that you won't fight any more."

Josip wept his promise, and Emilio, with wet eyes, gravely nodded.

This, the clothier exulted, was fellowship, and with a blessing on both their heads, departed, but even before he was altogether gone, the air behind him was greased with their fury.

Twenty-four hours later he fenced them in. A carpenter came and built a thick partition, halving the presser's and tailor's work space, and for once there was astonished quiet between them. They were, in fact, absolutely silent for a full week. Marcus, had he had the energy, would have jumped in joy and kicked his heels together. He noticed, of course, that the presser occasionally stopped pressing and came befuddled to the new door to see if the tailor was still there, and though the tailor did the same, it went no further than that. Thereafter Emilio Vizo no longer whispered to himself and Josip Bruzak touched no beer; and when the emaciated letters arrived from the other side, he took them home to read by the dirty window of his dark room; when night came, though there was electricity, he preferred to read by candlelight.

One Monday morning he opened his table drawer to get at his garlic salami and found it had been roughly broken in two. With his pointed knife raised, he rushed at the tailor, who, at that very moment, because someone had battered his black hat, was coming at him with his burning iron. He caught the presser along the calf of the arm and opened a smelly purple wound, just as Josip stuck him in the groin, and the knife hung there for a minute.

Roaring, wailing, the clothier ran in, and, despite their wounds, sent them packing. When he had left, they locked themselves together and choked necks.

Marcus rushed in again, shouting, "No, no, please, *please*," flailing his withered arms, nauseated, enervated (all he could hear in the uproar was the thundering clock), and his heart, like a fragile pitcher, toppled from the shelf and bump bumped down the stairs, cracking at the bottom, the shards flying everywhere.

Although the old Jew's eyes were glazed as he crumpled, the assassins could plainly read in them, What did I tell you? *You see?*

✩✩✩ Mailman! Mailman!

from *Post Office*

by Charles Bukowski

1

It began as a mistake.

It was Christmas season and I learned from the drunk up the hill who did the trick every Christmas that they would hire damned near anybody, and so I went and the next thing I knew I had this leather sack on my back and was hiking around at my leisure. What a job, I thought. Soft! They only gave you a block or 2 and if you managed to finish, the regular carrier would give you another block to carry, or maybe you'd go back in and the soup would give you another, but you just took your time and shoved those Xmas cards in the slots.

I think it was my second day as a Christmas temp that this big woman came out and walked around with me as I delivered letters. What I mean by big was that her ass was big and her tits were big and that she was big in all the right places. She seemed a bit crazy but I kept looking at her body and I didn't care.

She talked and talked and talked. Then it came out. Her husband was an officer on an island far away and she got lonely, you know, and lived in this little house in back all by herself.

"What little house?" I asked.

She wrote the address on a piece of paper.

"I'm lonely too," I said, "I'll come by and we'll talk tonight."

I was shacked but the shackjob was gone half the time, off somewhere, and I was lonely all right. I was lonely for that big ass standing beside me.

"All right," she said, "see you tonight."

CHARLES BUKOWSKI (b. 1920) is the author of *Notes of a Dirty Old Man* (1969); *Poems Written Before Jumping Out of an 8 Story Window* (1968); *Post Office* (1971); and at least twenty other works.

She was a good one all right, she was a good lay but like all lays after the 3rd or 4th night I began to lose interest and didn't go back.

But I couldn't help thinking, god, all these mailmen do is drop in their letters and get laid. This is the job for me, oh yes yes yes.

2

So I took the exam, passed it, took the physical, passed it, and there I was—a substitute mail carrier. It began easy. I was sent to West Avon Station and it was just like Christmas except I didn't get laid. Every day I expected to get laid but I didn't. But the soup was easy and I strolled around doing a block here and there. I didn't even have a uniform, just a cap. I wore my regular clothes. The way my shackjob Betty and I drank there was hardly money for clothes.

Then I was transferred to Oakford Station.

The soup was a bullneck named Jonstone. Help was needed there and I understood why. Jonstone liked to wear dark-red shirts—that meant danger and blood. There were 7 subs—Tom Moto, Nick Pelligrini, Herman Stratford, Rosey Anderson, Bobby Hansen, Harold Wiley and me, Henry Chinaski. Reporting time was 5 A.M. and I was the only drunk there. I always drank until past midnight, and there we'd sit, at 5 A.M. in the morning, waiting to get on the clock, waiting for some regular to call in sick. The regulars usually called in sick when it rained or during a heatwave or the day after a holiday when the mail load was doubled.

There were 40 or 50 different routes, maybe more, each case was different, you were never able to learn any of them, you had to get your mail up and ready before 8 A.M. for the truck dispatches, and Jonstone would take no excuses. The subs routed their magazines on corners, went without lunch, and died in the streets. Jonstone would have us start casing the routes 30 minutes late—spinning in his chair in his red shirt—"Chinaski take route 539!" We'd start a halfhour short but were still expected to get the mail up and out and be back on time. And once or twice a week, already beaten, fagged and fucked we had to make the night pickups, and the schedule on the board was impossible—

the truck wouldn't go that fast. You had to skip four or five boxes on the first run and the next time around they were stacked with mail and you stank, you ran with sweat jamming it into the sacks. I got laid all right. Jonstone saw to that.

3

The subs themselves made Jonstone possible by obeying his impossible orders. I couldn't see how a man of such obvious cruelty could be allowed to have his position. The regulars didn't care, the union man was worthless, so I filled out a thirty page report on one of my days off, mailed one copy to Jonstone and took the other down to the Federal Building. The clerk told me to wait. I waited and waited and waited. I waited an hour and thirty minutes, then was taken in to see a little grey-haired man with eyes like cigarette ash. He didn't even ask me to sit down. He began screaming at me as I entered the door.

"You're a wise son of a bitch, aren't you?"

"I'd rather you didn't curse me, sir!"

"Wise son of a bitch, you're one of those sons of bitches with a vocabulary and you like to lay it around!"

He waved my papers at me. And screamed: "MR. JONSTONE IS A FINE MAN!"

"Don't be silly. He's an obvious sadist," I said.

"How long have you been in the Post Office?"

"3 weeks."

"MR. JONSTONE HAS BEEN WITH THE POST OFFICE FOR 30 YEARS!"

"What does *that* have to do with it?"

"I said, MR. JONSTONE IS A FINE MAN!"

I believe the poor fellow actually wanted to kill me. He and Jonstone must have slept together.

"All right," I said, "Jonstone is a fine man. Forget the whole fucking thing." Then I walked out and took the next day off. Without pay, of course.

4

When Jonstone saw me the next 5 A.M. he spun in his swivel and his face and his shirt were the same color. But he said nothing. I didn't care. I had been up to 2 A.M. drinking and screwing with Betty. I leaned back and closed my eyes.

At 7 A.M. Jonstone swiveled again. All the other subs had been assigned jobs or been sent to other stations that needed help.

"That's all, Chinaski. Nothing for you today."

He watched my face. Hell, I didn't care. All I wanted to do was go to bed and get some sleep.

"O.K., Stone," I said. Among the carriers he was known as "The Stone," but I was the only one who addressed him that way.

I walked out, the old car started and soon I was back in bed with Betty.

"Oh, Hank! How nice!"

"Damn right, baby!" I pushed up against her warm tail and was asleep in 45 seconds.

5

But the next morning it was the same thing:

"That's all Chinaski. Nothing for you today."

It went on for a week. I sat there each morning from 5 A.M. to 7 A.M. and didn't get paid. My name was even taken off the night collection run.

Then Bobby Hansen, one of the older subs—in length of service—told me, "He did that to me once. He tried to starve me."

"I don't care. I'm not kissing his ass. I'll quit or starve, anything."

"You don't have to. Report to Prell Station each night. Tell the soup you aren't getting any work and you can sit in as a special delivery sub."

"I can do that? No rules against it?"

"I got a paycheck every two weeks."

"Thanks, Bobby."

6

I forget the beginning time. 6 or 7 P.M. Something like that.

All you did was sit with a handful of letters, take a streetmap and figure your run. It was easy. All the drivers took much more time than was needed to figure their runs and I played right along with them. I left when everybody left and came back when everybody came back.

Then you made another run. There was time to sit around in coffeeshops, read newspapers, feel decent. You even had time for lunch. Whenever I wanted a day off, I took one. On one of the routes there was this big young gal who got a special every night. She was a manufacturer of sexy dresses and nightgowns and *wore* them. You'd run up her steep stairway about 11 P.M., ring the bell and give her the special. She'd let out a bit of a gasp, like, "OOOOOOOOOOhhhhhhhhhHHHH!", and she'd stand close, very, and she wouldn't let you leave while she read it, and then she'd say, "OOOOOoooooh, goodnight, thank YOU!"

"Yes, mam," you'd say, trotting off with a dick like a bull's.

But it was not to last. It came in the mail after about a week and a half of freedom.

> "Dear Mr. Chinaski:
> You are to report to Oakford Station immediately. Refusal to do so will result in possible disciplinary action or dismissal.
> A. E. Jonstone, Supt., Oakford Station."

I was back on the cross again.

7

"Chinaski! Take route 539!"

The toughest in the station. Apartment houses with boxes that had scrubbed-out names or no names at all, under tiny lightbulbs in dark halls. Old ladies standing in halls, up and down the streets, asking the same question as if they were one person with one voice:

"Mailman, you got any mail for me?"

And you felt like screaming, "Lady, how the *hell* do I know who *you* are or I am or anybody is?"

The sweat dripping, the hangover, the impossibility of the schedule, and Jonstone back there in his red shirt, knowing it, enjoying it, pretending he was doing it to keep costs down. But everybody knew why he was doing it. Oh, what a fine man he was!

The people. The people. And the dogs.

Let me tell you about the dogs. It was one of those 100 degree days and I was running along, sweating, sick, delirious, hungover. I stopped at a small apartment house with the box downstairs along the front pavement, I popped it open with my key. There wasn't a sound. Then I felt something jamming its way into my crotch. It moved way up there. I looked around and there was a German Shepherd, full-grown, with his nose halfway up my ass. With one snap of his jaws he could rip off my balls. I decided that those people were not going to get their mail that day, and maybe never get any mail again. Man, I mean he worked that nose in there. SNUFF! SNUFF! SNUFF!

I put the mail back into the leather pouch, and then very slowly, very, I took a half step forward. The nose followed. I took another half step with the other foot. The nose followed. Then I took a slow, very slow full step. Then another. Then stood still. The nose was out. And he just stood there looking at me. Maybe he'd never smelled anything like it and didn't quite know what to do.

I walked quietly away.

8

There was another German Shepherd. It was hot summer and he came BOUNDING out of a back yard and then LEAPED through the air. His teeth snapped, just missing my jugular vein.

"OH JESUS!" I hollered, "OH JESUS CHRIST! MURDER! MURDER! HELP! MURDER!"

The beast turned and leaped again. I socked his head good in mid-air with the mail sack, letters and magazines flying out. He was ready to leap again when two guys, the owners, came out and grabbed him. Then, as he watched and growled, I reached down and picked up the letters and magazines that I would have to re-route on the front porch of the next house.

"You sons of bitches are crazy," I told the two guys, "that dog's a killer. Get rid of him or keep him off the street!"

I would have fought them both but there was that dog growling and lunging between them. I went over to the next porch and re-routed my mail on hands and knees.

As usual, I didn't have time for lunch, but I was still forty minutes late getting in.

The Stone looked at his watch. "You're 40 minutes late."

"You never arrived," I told him.

"That's a write-up."

"Sure it is, Stone."

He already had the proper form in the typer and was at it. As I sat casing up the mail and doing the go-backs he walked up and threw the form in front of me. I was tired of reading his write-ups and knew from my trip downtown that any protest was useless. Without looking I threw it into the wastebasket.

9

Every route had its traps and only the regular carriers knew of them. Each day it was another god damned thing, and you were always ready for a rape, murder, dogs, or insanity of some sort. The regulars wouldn't tell you their little secrets. That was the only advantage they had—except knowing their case by heart. It was gung ho for a new man, especially one who drank all night, went to bed at 2 A.M., rose at 4:30 A.M. after screwing and singing all night long, and, almost, getting away with it.

One day I was out on the street and the route was going well, though it was a new one, and I thought, Jesus Christ, maybe for the first time in two years I'll be able to eat lunch.

I had a terrible hangover, but still all went well until I came to this handful of mail addressed to a church. The address had no street number, just the name of the church, and the boulevard it faced. I walked, hungover, up the steps. I couldn't find a mailbox in there and no people in there. Some candles burning. Little bowls to dip your fingers in. And the empty pulpit looking at me, and all the statues, pale red and blue and yellow, the transoms shut, a stinking hot morning.

Oh Jesus Christ, I thought.

And walked out.

I went around to the side of the church and found a stairway going down. I went in through an open door. Do you know what I saw? A row of toilets. And showers. But it was dark. All the lights were out. How in hell can they expect a man to find a mailbox in the dark? Then I saw the light switch. I threw the thing and the lights in the church went on, inside and out. I walked into the next room and there were priests' robes spread out on a table. There was a bottle of wine.

For Christ's sake, I thought, who in hell but me would ever get caught in a scene like this?

I picked up the bottle of wine, had a good drag, left the letters on the robes, and walked back to the showers and toilets. I turned off the lights and took a shit in the dark and smoked a cigarette. I thought about taking a shower but I could see the headlines: MAILMAN CAUGHT DRINKING THE BLOOD OF GOD AND TAKING A SHOWER, NAKED, IN ROMAN CATHOLIC CHURCH.

So, finally, I didn't have time for lunch and when I got in Jonstone wrote me up for being twenty-three minutes off schedule.

I found out later that mail for the church was delivered to the parish house around the corner. But now, of course, I'll know where to shit and shower when I'm down and out.

10

The rainy season began. Most of the money went for drink so my shoes had holes in the soles and my raincoat was torn and old. In any steady downpour I got quite wet, and I mean wet—down to soaked and soggy shorts and stockings. The regular carriers called in sick, they called in sick from stations all over the city, so there was work everyday at Oakford Station, at all the stations. Even the subs were calling in sick. I didn't call in sick because I was too tired to think properly. This particular morning I was sent to Wently Station. It was one of those 5 day storms where the rain comes down in one continuous wall of water and the whole city gives up, everything gives up, the sewers can't swallow the water fast enough, the water comes up over the curbings, and in some sections, up on the lawn and into the houses.

I was sent off to Wently Station.

"They said they need a good man," the Stone called after me as I stepped out into a sheet of water.

The door closed. If the old car started, and it did, I was off to Wently. But it didn't matter—if the car didn't run, they threw you on a bus. My feet were already wet.

The Wently soup stood me in front of this case. It was already stuffed and I began stuffing more mail in with the help of another sub. I'd never seen such a case! It was a rotten joke of some sort. I counted 12 tie-outs on the case. That case must have covered half the city. I had yet to learn that the route was all steep hills. Whoever had conceived it was a madman.

We got it up and out and just as I was about to leave the soup walked over and said, "I can't give you any help on this."

"That's all right," I said.

All right, hell. It wasn't until later that I found out he was Jonstone's best buddy.

The route started at the station. The first of twelve swings. I stepped into a sheet of water and worked my way downhill. It was the poor part of town—small houses and courts with mailboxes full of spiders, mailboxes hanging by one nail, old women inside rolling cigarettes and chewing tobacco and humming to their canaries and watching you, an idiot lost in the rain.

When your shorts get wet they slip down, down down they slip, down around the cheeks of your ass, a wet rim of a thing held up by the crotch of your pants. The rain ran the ink on some of the letters; a cigarette wouldn't stay lit. You had to keep reaching into the pouch for magazines. It was the first swing and I was already tired. My shoes were caked with mud and felt like boots. Every now and then I'd hit a slippery spot and almost go down.

A door opened and an old woman asked the question heard a hundred times a day:

"Where's the *regular* man, today?"

"Lady, PLEASE, how would *I* know? How in the hell would I know? I'm here and he's someplace else!"

"Oh, you *are a gooney* fellow!"

"A gooney fellow?"

"Yes."

I laughed and put a fat water-soaked letter in her hand, then went on to the next. Maybe uphill will be better, I thought.

Another Old Nelly, meaning to be nice, asked me, "Wouldn't you like to come in and have a cup of tea and dry off?"

"Lady, don't you realize we don't even have time to pull up our shorts?"

"Pull up your shorts?"

"YES, PULL UP OUR SHORTS!" I screamed at her and walked off into the wall of water.

I finished the first swing. It took about an hour. Eleven more swings, that's eleven more hours. Impossible, I thought. They must have hung the roughest one on me first.

Uphill was worse because you had to pull your own weight.

Noon came and went. Without lunch. I was on the 4th or 5th swing. Even on a dry day the route would have been impossible. This way it was so impossible you couldn't even think about it.

Finally I was so wet I thought I was drowning. I found a front porch that only leaked a little and stood there and managed to light a cigarette. I had about 3 quiet puffs when I heard a little old lady's voice behind me:

"Mailman! Mailman!"

"Yes, mam?" I asked.

"YOUR MAIL IS GETTING WET!"

I looked down at my pouch and sure enough, I had left the leather flap open. A drop or two had fallen in from a hole in the porch roof.

I walked off. That does it, I thought, only an idiot would go through what I am going through. I am going to find a telephone and tell them to come get their mail and jam their job. Jonstone wins.

The moment I decided to quit, I felt much better. Through the rain I saw a building at the bottom of the hill that looked like it might have a telephone in it. I was halfway up the hill. When I got down I saw it was a small cafe. There was a heater going. Well, shit, I thought, I might as well get dry. I took off my raincoat and my cap, threw the mailpouch on the floor and ordered a cup of coffee.

It was very black coffee. Remade from old coffeegrounds. The worst coffee I had ever tasted, but it was hot. I drank 3 cups and sat there an hour, until I was completely dry. Then I looked out: it had stopped raining! I went out and walked up the hill and began delivering mail again. I took my time and finished the route. On the 12th swing I was walking in twilight. By the time I returned to the station it was night.

The carrier's entrance was locked.

I beat on the tin door.

A little warm clerk appeared and opened the door.

"What the hell took you so long?" he screamed at me.

I walked over to the case and threw down the wet pouch full of go-backs, miscased mail and pickup mail. Then I took off my key and flipped it against the case. You were supposed to sign in and out for your key. I didn't bother. He was standing there.

I looked at him.

"Kid, if you say one more word to me, if you so much as sneeze, so help me God, I am going to kill you!"

The kid didn't say anything. I punched out.

The next morning I kept waiting for Jonstone to turn and say something. He acted as if nothing had happened. The rain stopped and all the regulars were no longer sick. The Stone sent 3 subs home without pay, one of them me. I almost loved him then.

I went on in and got up against Betty's warm ass.

11

But then it began raining again. The Stone had me out on a thing called Sunday Collection, and if you're thinking of church, forget it. You picked up a truck at West Garage and a clipboard. The clipboard told you what streets, what time you were to be there, and how to get to the next pickup box. Like 2:32 P.M., Beecher and Avalon, L3 R2 (which meant left three blocks, right two) 2:35 P.M., and you wondered how you could pick up one box, then drive 5 blocks in 3 minutes and be finished cleaning out another box. Sometimes it took you over 3 minutes to clean out a Sunday box. And the boards weren't accurate. Sometimes they counted an alley as a street and sometimes they counted a street as an alley. You never knew where you were.

It was one of those continuous rains, not hard, but it *never* stopped. The territory I was driving was new to me but at least it was light enough to read the clipboard. But as it got darker it was harder to read (by the dashboard light) or locate the pickup boxes. Also the water was rising in the streets, and several times I had stepped into water up to my ankles.

Then the dashboard light went out. I couldn't read the clipboard. I had no idea where I was. Without the clipboard I was like a man lost in the desert. But the luck wasn't all bad—yet. I had two boxes of matches and before I made for each new pickup box, I would light a match, memorize the directions and drive on. For once, I had outwitted Adversity, that Jonstone up there in the sky, looking down, watching me.

Then I took a corner, leaped out to unload the box and when I got back the clipboard was GONE!

Jonstone in the Sky, have Mercy! I was lost in the dark and the rain. *Was* I some kind of idiot, actually? Did I make things happen to myself? It was possible. It was possible that I was subnormal, that I was lucky just to be alive.

The clipboard had been wired to the dashboard. I figured it must have flown out of the truck on the last sharp turn. I got out of the truck with my pants rolled up around my knees and started wading through a foot of water. It was dark. I'd never find the god damned thing! I walked along, lighting matches—but nothing, nothing. It had floated away. As I reached the corner I had sense enough to notice which way the current was moving and follow it. I saw an object floating along, lit a match, and there it WAS! The clipboard. *Impossible!* I could have kissed the thing. I waded back to the truck, got in, rolled my pantlegs down and really *wired* that board to the dash. Of course, I was way behind schedule by then but at least I'd found their dirty clipboard. I wasn't lost in the backstreets of Nowhere. I wouldn't have to ring a doorbell and ask somebody the way back to the post office garage.

I could hear some fucker snarling from his warm frontroom:

"Well, well. You're a post office employee, *aren't* you? Don't you know the way back to your own garage?"

So I drove along, lighting matches, leaping into whirlpools of water and emptying collection boxes. I was tired and wet and hungover, but I was usually that way and I waded through the weariness like I did the water. I kept thinking of a hot bath, Betty's fine legs, and—something to keep me going—a picture of myself in an easychair, drink in hand, the dog walking up, me patting his head.

But that was a long way off. The stops on the clipboard seemed endless and when I reached the bottom it said "Over" and I flipped the board and sure enough, there on the backside was *another* list of stops.

With the last match I made the last stop, deposited my mail at the station indicated, and it was a *load,* and then drove back toward the West Garage. It was in the west end of town and in the west the land was very flat, the drainage system couldn't handle the water and anytime it rained any length of time at all, they had what was called a "flood." The description was accurate.

Driving on in, the water rose higher and higher. I noticed stalled and abandoned cars all around. Too bad. All I wanted was to get in that chair with that glass of scotch in my hand and watch Betty's ass wobble around the room. Then at a signal I met Tom Moto, one of the other Jonstone subs.

"Which way you going in?" Moto asked.

"The shortest distance between 2 points, I was taught, is a straight line," I answered him.

"You better not," he told me. "I know that area. It's an ocean through there."

"Bullshit," I said, "all it takes is a little guts. Got a match?"

I lit up and left him at the signal.

Betty, baby, I'm coming!

Yeah.

The water got higher and higher but mail trucks are built high off the ground. I took the shortcut through the residential neighborhood, full speed, and water flew up all around me. It continued to rain, hard. There weren't any cars around. I was the only moving object.

Betty baby. Yeah.

Some guy standing on his front porch laughed at me and yelled, "THE MAIL MUST GO THROUGH!"

I cursed him and gave him the finger.

I noticed that the water was rising above the floorboards, whirling around my shoes, but I kept driving. Only 3 blocks to go!

Then the truck stopped.

Oh. Oh. Shit.

I sat there and tried to kick it over. It started once, then stalled. Then it wouldn't respond. I sat there looking at the water. It must have been 2 feet deep. What was I supposed to do? Sit there until they sent a rescue squad?

What did the Postal Manual say? Where *was* it? I had never known anybody who had seen one.

Balls.

I locked the truck, put the ignition keys in my pocket and stepped into the water—nearly up to the waist—and began wading toward West Garage. It was still raining. Suddenly the water rose another 3 or 4 inches. I had been walking across a lawn and had stepped off the curbing. The truck was parked on somebody's front lawn.

For a moment I thought that swimming might be faster, then I thought, no, that would look ridiculous. I made it to the garage and walked up to the dispatcher. There I was, wet as wet could get and he looked at me.

I threw him the truck keys and the ignition keys.

Then I wrote on a piece of paper: 3435 Mountview Place.

"Your truck's at this address. Go get it."

"You mean you left it out there?"

"I mean I left it out there."

I walked over, punched out, then stripped to my shorts and stood in front of a heater. I hung my clothes over the heater. Then I looked across the room and there by another heater stood Tom Moto in *his* shorts.

We both laughed.

"It's hell, isn't it?" he asked.

"Unbelievable."

"Do you think The Stone planned it?"

"Hell yes! He even made it rain!"

"Did you get stalled out there?"

"Sure," I said.

"I did too."

"Listen, baby," I said, "my car is 12 years old. You've got a new one. I'm sure I'm stalled out there. How about a push to get me started?"

"O.K."

We got dressed and went out. Moto had bought a new model

car about 3 weeks before. I waited for his engine to start. Not a sound. Oh Christ, I thought.

The rain was up to the floorboards.

Moto got out.

"No good. It's dead."

I tried mine without any hope. There was some action from the battery, some spark, though feeble. I pumped the gas, hit it again. It started up. I really let it roar. VICTORY! I warmed it good. Then I backed up and began to push Moto's new car. I pushed him for a mile. The thing wouldn't even fart. I pushed him into a garage, left him there, and picking the highland and the drier streets, made it back to Betty's ass.

12

The Stone's favorite carrier was Matthew Battles. Battles never came in with a wrinkled shirt on. In fact, everything he wore was new, looked new. The shoes, the shirts, the pants, the cap. His shoes really shined and none of his clothing appeared to have ever been laundered even once. Once a shirt or a pair of pants became the least bit soiled he threw them away.

The Stone often said to us as Matthew walked by:

"Now, *there* goes a carrier!"

And The Stone meant it. His eyes damn near shimmered with love.

And Matthew would stand at his case, erect and clean, scrubbed and well-slept, shoes gleaming victoriously, and he would fan those letters into the case with joy.

"You're a real carrier, Matthew!"

"Thank you, Mr. Jonstone!"

One 5 A.M. I walked in and sat down to wait behind The Stone. He looked a bit slumped under that red shirt.

Moto was next to me. He told me: "They picked up Matthew yesterday."

"Picked him up?"

"Yeah, for stealing from the mails. He'd been opening letters for the Nekalayla Temple and taking money out. After 15 years on the job."

"How'd they get him, how'd they find out?"

"The old ladies. The old ladies had been sending in letters to Nekalayla filled with money and they weren't getting any thank-you notes or response. Nekalayla told the P.O. and the P.O. put the Eye on Matthew. They found him opening letters down at the soak-box, taking money out."

"No shit?"

"No shit. They caught him in cold daylight."

I leaned back.

Nekalayla had built this large temple and painted it a sickening green, I guess it reminded him of money, and he had an office staff of 30 or 40 people who did nothing but open envelopes, take out checks and money, record the amount, the sender, date received and so on. Others were busy mailing out books and pamphlets written by Nekalayla, and his photo was on the wall, a large one of N. in priestly robes and beard, and a painting of N., very large too, looked over the office, watching.

Nekalayla claimed he had once been walking through the desert when he met Jesus Christ and Jesus Christ told him everything. They sat on a rock together and J.C. laid it on him. Now he was passing the secrets on to those who could afford it. He also held a service every Sunday. His help, who were also his followers, rang in and out on timeclocks.

Imagine Matthew Battles trying to outwit Nekalayla who had met Christ in the desert!

"Has anybody said anything to The Stone?" I asked.

"Are you *kidding?*"

We sat an hour or so. A sub was assigned to Matthew's case. The other subs were given other jobs. I sat alone behind The Stone. Then I got up and walked to his desk.

"Mr. Jonstone?"

"Yes, Chinaski?"

"Where's Matthew today? Sick?"

The Stone's head dropped. He looked at the paper in his hand and pretended to continue reading it. I walked back and sat down.

At 7 A.M. The Stone turned:

"There's nothing for you today, Chinaski."

I stood up and walked to the doorway. I stood in the doorway. "Good morning, Mr. Jonstone. Have a good day."

He didn't answer. I walked down to the liquor store and bought a half pint of Grandad for my breakfast.

13

The voices of the people were the same, no matter where you carried the mail you heard the same things over and over again.

"You're late, aren't you?"

"Where's the regular carrier?"

"Hello, Uncle Sam!"

"Mailman! Mailman! This doesn't go here!"

The streets were full of insane and dull people. Most of them lived in nice houses and didn't seem to work, and you wondered how they did it. There was one guy who wouldn't let you put the mail in his box. He'd stand in the driveway and watch you coming for 2 or 3 blocks and he'd stand there and hold his hand out.

I asked some of the others who had carried the route:

"What's wrong with that guy who stands there and holds his hand out?"

"What guy who stands there and holds his hand out?" they asked.

They all had the same voice too.

One day when I had the route, the man-who-holds-his-hand-out was a half a block up the street. He was talking to a neighbor, looked back at me more than a block away and knew he had time to walk back and meet me. When he turned his back to me, I began running. I don't believe I ever delivered mail that fast, all stride and motion, never stopping or pausing, I was going to kill him. I had the letter half in the slot of his box when he turned and saw me.

"OH NO NO NO!" he screamed. "DON'T PUT IT IN THE BOX!"

He ran down the street toward me. All I saw was the blur of his feet. He must have run a hundred yards in 9.2.

I put the letter in his hand. I watched him open it, walk across the porch, open the door and go into his house. What it meant somebody else will have to tell me.

14

Again I was on a new route. The Stone always put me on hard routes, but now and then, due to the circumstances of things, he was forced to place me on one less murderous. Route 511 was peeling off quite nicely, and there I was thinking about *lunch* again, the lunch that never came.

It was an average residential neighborhood. No apartment houses. Just house after house with well-kept lawns. But it was a *new* route and I walked along wondering where the trap was. Even the weather was nice.

By god, I thought, I'm going to make it! Lunch, and back in on schedule! Life, at last, was bearable.

These people didn't even own dogs. Nobody stood outside waiting for their mail. I hadn't heard a human voice in hours. Perhaps I had reached my postal maturity, whatever that was. I strolled along, efficient, almost dedicated.

I remembered one of the older carriers pointing to his heart and telling me, "Chinaski, someday it will get you, it will get you right *here!*"

"Heart attack?"

"Dedication to service. You'll see. You'll be proud of it."

"Balls!"

But the man had been sincere.

I thought about him as I walked along.

Then I had a registered letter with return attached.

I walked up and rang the doorbell. A little window opened in the door. I couldn't see the face.

"Registered letter!"

"Stand back!" said a woman's voice. "Stand back so I can see your face!"

Well, there it was, I thought, another nut.

"Look lady, you don't *have* to see my face. I'll just leave this slip in the mailbox and you can pick your letter up at the station. Bring proper identification."

I put the slip in the mailbox and began to walk off the porch.

The door opened and she ran out. She had on one of those see-through negligees and no brassiere. Just dark blue panties. Her hair was uncombed and stuck out as if it were trying to run away from her. There seemed to be some type of cream on her face, most of it under the eyes. The skin on her body was white as if it never saw sunlight and her face had an unhealthy look. Her mouth hung open. She had on a touch of lipstick, and she was *built* all the way . . .

I caught all this as she rushed at me. I was sliding the registered letter back into the pouch.

She screamed, "Give me my letter!"

I said, "Lady, you'll have to . . ."

She grabbed the letter and ran to the door, opened it and ran in.

God damn! You couldn't come back without either the registered letter or a signature! You even had to sign in and out with the things.

"HEY!"

I went after her and jammed my foot into the door just in time.

"HEY. GOD DAMN YOU!"

"Go away! Go away! You are an evil man!"

"Look, lady! Try to understand! You've got to sign for that letter! I can't let you have it that way! You are robbing the United States mails!"

"Go away, evil man!"

I put all my weight against the door and pushed into the room. It was dark in there. All the shades were down. All the shades in the house were down.

"YOU HAVE NO RIGHT IN MY HOUSE! GET OUT!"

"And you have no right to rob the mails! Either give me the letter back or sign for it. Then I'll leave."

"All right! All right! I'll sign."

I showed her where to sign and gave her a pen. I looked at her breasts and the rest of her and I thought, what a shame she's crazy, what a shame, what a shame.

She handed back the pen and her signature—it was just scrawled. She opened the letter, began to read it as I turned to leave.

Then she was in front of the door, arms spread across. The letter was on the floor.

"Evil evil evil man! You came here to rape me!"

"Look lady, let me by."

"THERE IS EVIL WRITTEN ALL OVER YOUR FACE!"

"Don't you think I know that? Now let me out of here!"

With one hand I tried to push her aside. She clawed one side of my face, good. I dropped my bag, my cap fell off, and as I held a handkerchief to the blood she came up and raked the other side.

"YOU CUNT! WHAT THE HELL'S WRONG WITH YOU!"

"See there? See there? You're evil!"

She was right up against me. I grabbed her by the ass and got my mouth on hers. Those breasts were against me, she was all up against me. She pulled her head back, away from me—

"Rapist! Rapist! Evil rapist!"

I reached down with my mouth, got one of her tits, then switched to the other.

"Rape! Rape! I'm being raped!"

She was right. I got her pants down, unzipped my fly, got it in, then walked her backwards to the couch. We fell down on top of it.

She lifted her legs high.

"RAPE!" she screamed.

I finished her off, zipped my fly, picked up my mail pouch and walked out leaving her staring quietly at the ceiling . . .

I missed lunch but still couldn't make the schedule.

"You're 15 minutes late," said The Stone.

I didn't say anything.

The Stone looked at me. "God o mighty, what happened to your face?" he asked.

"What happened to yours?" I asked him.

"Whadda you mean?"

"Forget it."

15

I was hungover again, another heat spell was on—a week of 100 degree days. The drinking went on each night, and in the early mornings and days there was The Stone and the impossibility of everything.

Some of the boys wore African sun helmets and shades, but me, I was about the same, rain or shine—ragged clothing, and the shoes so old that the nails were always driving into my feet. I put pieces of cardboard in the shoes. But it only helped temporarily—soon the nails would be eating into my heels again.

The whiskey and beer ran out of me, fountained from the armpits, and I drove along with this load on my back like a cross, pulling out magazines, delivering thousands of letters, staggering, welded to the side of the sun.

Some woman screamed at me:

"MAILMAN! MAILMAN! THIS DOESN'T GO HERE!"

I looked. She was a block back down the hill and I was already behind schedule.

"Look, lady, put the letter outside your mailbox! We'll pick it up tomorrow!"

"NO! NO! I WANT YOU TO TAKE IT NOW!"

She waved the thing around in the sky.

"Lady!"

"COME GET IT! IT DOESN'T BELONG HERE!"

Oh my god.

I dropped the sack. Then I took my cap and threw it on the grass. It rolled out into the street. I left it and walked down toward the woman. One half block.

I walked down and snatched the thing from her hand, turned, walked back.

It was an advertisement! 4th class mail. Something about a 1/2 off clothing sale.

I picked my cap up out of the street, put it on my head. Put the sack back onto the left side of my spine, started out again. 100 degrees.

I walked past one house and a woman ran out after me.

"Mailman! Mailman! Don't you have a letter for me?"

"Lady, if I didn't put one in your box, that means you don't have any mail."

"But I know you have a letter for me!"

"What makes you say that?"

"Because my sister phoned and said she was going to write me."

"Lady, I don't have a letter for you."

"I know you have! I know you have! I know it's there!"

She started to reach for a handful of letters.

"DON'T TOUCH THE UNITED STATES MAILS, LADY! THERE'S NOTHING FOR YOU TODAY!"

I turned and walked off.

"I KNOW YOU HAVE MY LETTER!"

Another woman stood on her porch.

"You're late today."

"Yes, mam."

"Where's the regular man today?"

"He's dying of cancer."

"Dying of cancer? Harold is dying of cancer?"

"That's right," I said.

I handed her mail to her.

"BILLS! BILLS! BILLS!" she screamed. "IS THAT ALL YOU CAN BRING ME? THESE BILLS?"

"Yes, mam, that's all I can bring you."

I turned and walked on.

It wasn't my fault that they used telephones and gas and light and bought all their things on credit. Yet when I brought them their bills they screamed at me—as if *I* had asked them to have a phone installed, or a $350 t.v. set sent over with no money down.

The next stop was a small two storey dwelling, fairly new, with ten or twelve units. The lock box was in the front, under a porch roof. At last, a bit of shade. I put the key in the box and opened it.

"HELLO UNCLE SAM! HOW ARE YOU TODAY?"

He was loud. I hadn't expected that man's voice behind me. He had *screamed* at me, and being hungover I was nervous. I jumped in shock. It was too much. I took the key out of the box and turned. All I could see was a screen door. Somebody was back in there. Air-conditioned and invisible.

"God damn you!" I said, "don't call me Uncle Sam! I'm *not* Uncle Sam!"

"Oh you're one of those *wise* guys, eh? For 2 cents I'd come out and whip your ass!"

I took my pouch and slammed it to the ground. Magazines and letters flew everywhere. I would have to reroute the whole swing. I took off my cap, and smashed it to the cement.

"COME OUT OF THERE, YOU SON OF A BITCH! OH,

GOD O MIGHTY, I BEG YOU! COME OUT OF THERE!
COME OUT, COME OUT OF THERE!"

I was ready to murder him.

Nobody came out. There wasn't a sound. I looked at the
screen door. Nothing. It was as if the apartment were empty. For
a moment I thought of going on in. Then I turned, got down on
my knees and began rerouting the letters and magazines. It's a
job without a case. Twenty minutes later I had the mail up. I
stuck some letters in the lock box, dropped the magazines on the
porch, locked the box, turned, looked at the screen door again.
Still not a sound.

I finished the route, walking along, thinking, well, he'll phone
and tell Jonstone that I threatened him. When I get in I better
be ready for the worst.

I swung the door open and there was The Stone at his desk,
reading something.

I stood there, looking down at him, waiting.

The Stone glanced up at me, then down at what he was
reading.

I kept standing there, waiting.

The Stone kept reading.

"Well," I finally said, "what about it?"

"What about what?" The Stone looked up.

"ABOUT THE PHONE CALL! TELL ME ALL ABOUT
THE PHONE CALL! DON'T JUST SIT THERE!"

"What phone call?"

"You didn't get a phone call about me?"

"A phone call? What happened? What have you been doing
out there? What did you do?"

"Nothing."

I walked over and checked my stuff in.

The guy hadn't phoned in. No grace on his part. He probably
thought I would come back if he phoned in.

I walked past The Stone on my way back to the case.

"What did you *do* out there, Chinaski?"

"Nothing."

My act so confused The Stone that he forgot to tell me I was
30 minutes late or write me up for it.

16

I was casing next to G.G. early one morning. That's what they called him: G.G. His actual name was George Greene. But for years he was simply called G.G. and after a while he looked like G.G. He had been a carrier since his early twenties and now he was in his late sixties. His voice was gone. He didn't speak. He croaked. And when he croaked, he didn't say much. He was neither liked nor disliked. He was just there. His face had wrinkled into strange runs and mounds of unattractive flesh. No light shone from his face. He was just a hard old crony who had done his job: G.G. The eyes looked like dull bits of clay dropped into the eye sockets. It was best if you didn't think about him or look at him.

But G.G., having all that seniority had one of the easiest routes, right out on the fringe of the rich district. In fact, you might call it the rich district. Although the houses were old, they were large, most of them two stories high. Wide lawns mowed and kept green by Japanese gardeners. Some movie stars lived there. A famous cartoonist. A best-selling writer. Two former governors. Nobody ever spoke to you in that area. You never saw anybody. The only time you saw anybody was at the beginning of the route where there were less expensive homes, and here the children bothered you. I mean, G.G. was a bachelor. And he had this whistle. At the beginning of his route, he'd stand tall and straight, take out the whistle, a large one, and blow it, spit flying out in all directions. That was to let the children know he was there. He had candy for the children. And they'd come running out and he'd give them candy as he went down the street. Good old G.G.

I'd found out about the candy the first time I got the route. The Stone didn't like to give me a route that easy but sometimes he couldn't help it. So I walked along and this young boy came out and asked me.

"Hey, where's my candy?"

And I said, "What candy, kid?"

And the kid said, *"My* candy! I want *my* candy!"

"Look, kid," I said, "you must be crazy. Does your mother just let you run around loose?"

The kid looked at me strangely.

* * *

But one day G.G. got into trouble. Good old G.G. He met this new little girl in the neighborhood. And gave her some candy. And said, "My, you're a *pretty* little girl! I'd like to have you for my own little girl!"

The mother had been listening at the window and she ran out screaming, accusing G.G. of child molestation. She hadn't known about G.G., so when she saw him give the girl candy and make that statement, it was too much for her.

Good old G.G. Accused of child molestation.

I came in and heard The Stone on the phone, trying to explain to the mother that G.G. was an honorable man. G.G. just sat in front of his case, transfixed.

When The Stone was finished and had hung up, I told him:

"You shouldn't suck up to that woman. She's got a dirty mind. Half the mothers in America, with their precious big pussies and their precious little daughters, half the mothers in America have dirty minds. Tell her to shove it. G.G. can't get his pecker hard, you know that."

The Stone shook his head. "No, the public's dynamite! They're dynamite!"

That's all he could say. I had seen The Stone before—posturing and begging and explaining to every nut who phoned in about anything . . .

I was casing next to G.G. on route 501, which was not too bad. I had to fight to get the mail up but it was *possible,* and that gave one hope.

Although G.G. knew his case upsidedown, his hands were slowing. He had simply stuck too many letters in his life—even his sense-deadened body was finally revolting. Several times during the morning I saw him falter. He'd stop and sway, go into a trance, then snap out of it and stick some more letters. I wasn't particularly fond of the man. His life hadn't been a brave one, and he had turned out to be a hunk of shit more or less. But each time he faltered, something tugged at me. It was like a faithful horse who just couldn't go anymore. Or an old car, just giving it up one morning.

The mail was heavy and as I watched G.G. I got death-chills. For the first time in over 40 years he might miss the morning dispatch! For a man as proud of his job and his work as G.G., that could be a tragedy. I had missed plenty of morning dispatches, and had to take the sacks out to the boxes in my car, but my attitude was a bit different.

He faltered again.

God o mighty, I thought, doesn't anybody notice but me?

I looked around, nobody was concerned. They all professed, at one time or another, to be fond of him—"G.G.'s a good guy." But the "good old guy" was sinking and nobody cared. Finally I had less mail in front of me than G.G.

Maybe I can help him get his magazines up, I thought. But a clerk came along and dropped more mail in front of me and I was almost back with G.G. It was going to be close for both of us. I faltered for a moment, then clenched my teeth together, spread my legs, dug in like a guy who had just taken a hard punch, and winged the mass of letters in.

Two minutes before pull-down time, both G.G. and I had gotten our mail up, our mags routed and sacked, our airmail in. We were both going to make it. I had worried for nothing. Then The Stone came up. He carried two bundles of circulars. He gave one bundle to G.G. and the other to me.

"These must be worked in," he said, then walked off.

The Stone knew that we couldn't work those circs in and pull-down in time to meet the dispatch. I wearily cut the strings around the circs and started to case them in. G.G. just sat there and stared at his bundle of circs.

Then he put his head down, put his head down in his arms and began to cry softly.

I couldn't believe it.

I looked around.

The other carriers weren't looking at G.G. They were pulling down their letters, strapping them out, talking and laughing with each other.

"Hey," I said a couple of times, "hey!"

But they wouldn't look at G.G.

I walked over to G.G. Touched him on the arm: "G.G.," I said, "what can I do for you?"

He jumped up from his case, ran up the stairway to the men's locker room. I watched him go. Nobody seemed to notice. I stuck a few more letters, then ran up the stairs myself.

There he was, head down in his arms on one of the tables. Only he wasn't quietly crying now. He was sobbing and wailing. His whole body shook in spasms. He wouldn't stop.

I ran down the steps, past all the carriers, and up to The Stone's desk.

"Hey, hey, Stone! Jesus Christ, Stone!"

"What is it?" he asked.

"G.G. has flipped out! Nobody cares! He's upstairs crying! He needs help!"

"Who's manning his route?"

"Who gives a damn? I tell you, he's *sick!* He needs help!"

"I gotta get somebody to man his route!"

The Stone got up from his desk, circled around looking at his carriers as if there might be an extra one somewhere. Then he hustled back to his desk.

"Look, Stone, somebody's got to take that man home. Tell me where he lives and I'll drive him home myself—off the clock. Then I'll carry your damned route."

The Stone looked up:

"Who's manning your case?"

"Oh, God damn the case!"

"GO MAN YOUR CASE!"

Then he was talking to another supervisor on the phone: "Hello, Eddie? Listen, I need a man out here . . ."

There'd be no candy for the kids that day. I walked back. All the other carriers were gone. I began sticking in the circulars. Over on G.G.'s case was his tie-up of unstuck circs. I was behind schedule again. Without a dispatch. When I came in late that afternoon, The Stone wrote me up.

I never saw G.G. again. Nobody knew what happened to him. Nor did anybody ever mention him again. The "good guy." The dedicated man. Knifed across the throat over a handful of circs from a local market—with its special: a free box of a brand name laundry soap, with the coupon, and any purchase over $3.

17

After 3 years I made "regular." That meant holiday pay (subs didn't get paid for holidays) and a 40 hour week with 2 days off. The Stone was also forced to assign me as relief man to

5 different routes. That's all I had to carry—5 different routes. In time, I would learn the cases well plus the shortcuts and traps on each route. Each day would be easier. I could begin to cultivate that comfortable look.

Somehow, I was not too happy. I was not a man to deliberately seek pain, the job was still difficult enough, but somehow it lacked the old glamour of my sub days—the not-knowing-what-the-hell was going to happen next.

A few of the regulars came around and shook my hand.

"Congratulations," they said.

"Yeh," I said.

Congratulations for what? I hadn't done anything. Now I was a member of the club. I was one of the boys. I could be there for years, eventually bid for my own route. Get Xmas presents from my people. And when I phoned in sick, they would say to some poor bastard sub, "Where's the *regular* man today? You're late. The regular man is never late."

So there I was. Then a bulletin came out that no caps or equipment were to be placed on top of the carrier's case. Most of the boys put their caps up there. It didn't hurt anything and saved a trip to the locker room. Now after 3 years of putting my cap up there I was ordered not to do so.

Well, I was still coming in hungover and I didn't have things like caps on my mind. So my cap was up there, the day after the order came out.

The Stone came running with his write-up. It said that it was against rules and regulations to have any equipment on top of the case. I put the write-up in my pocket and went on sticking letters. The Stone sat swiveled in his chair, watching me. All the other carriers had put their caps in their lockers. Except me and one other—one Marty. And The Stone had gone up to Marty and said, "Now, Marty, you read the order. Your cap isn't supposed to be on top of the case."

"Oh, I'm sorry, sir. Habit, you know. Sorry." Marty took his cap off the case and ran upstairs to his locker with it.

The next morning I forgot again. The Stone came with his write-up.

It said that it was against rules and regulations to have any equipment on top of the case.

I put the write-up in my pocket and went on sticking letters.

* * *

The next morning, as I walked in, I could see The Stone watching me. He was very deliberate about watching me. He was waiting to see what I would do with the cap. I let him wait awhile. Then I took the cap off my head and placed it on top of the case.

The Stone ran up with his write-up.

I didn't read it. I threw it in the wastebasket, left my cap up there and went on sticking mail.

I could hear The Stone at his typewriter. There was anger in the sound of the keys.

I wondered how he managed to learn how to type? I thought.

He came again. Handed me a 2nd write-up.

I looked at him.

"I don't have to read it. I know what it says. It says that I didn't read the first write-up."

I threw the 2nd write-up in the wastebasket.

The Stone ran back to his typewriter.

He handed me a 3rd write-up.

"Look," I said, "I know what all these things say. The first write-up was for having my cap on top of the case. The 2nd was for not reading the first. This 3rd one is for not reading the first or 2nd write-ups."

I looked at him, and then dropped the write-up into the wastebasket without reading it.

"Now I can throw these away as fast as you can type them. It can go on for hours, and soon one of us is going to begin looking ridiculous. It's up to you."

The Stone went back to his chair and sat down. He didn't type anymore. He just sat looking at me.

I didn't go in the next day. I slept until noon. I didn't phone. Then I went down to the Federal Building. I told them my mission. They put me in front of the desk of a thin old woman. Her hair was grey and she had a very thin neck that suddenly bent in the middle. It pushed her head forward and she looked up over the top of her glasses at me.

"Yes?"

"I want to resign."

"To *resign?*"

"Yes, resign."

"And you're a regular carrier?"

"Yes," I said.

"Tsk, tsk, tsk, tsk, tsk, tsk, tsk," she went, making this sound with her dry lips.

She gave me the proper papers and I sat there filling them out.

"How long have you been with the post office?"

"Three and one half years."

"Tsk, tsk, tsk, tsk, tsk, tsk, tsk, tsk," she went, "tsk, tsk, tsk, tsk."

And so there it was. I drove home to Betty and we uncapped the bottle.

Little did I know that in a couple of years I would be back as a clerk and that I would clerk, all hunched-up on a stool, for nearly 12 years.

✲✲ Working the Woods
✲✲

from *Sometimes a Great Notion*

by Ken Kesey

We're running a little late, what with waiting breakfast on the kid. The sun's already coming through the trees. We head out up Blueclay Road toward the North Spur of Breakneck, where the show is, and after about a half-hour bouncing and bumping and nobody saying word one to nobody else we get up to the site. The slashing piles are still smoking from yesterday's burning, and the sun's rose out of the branches and is promising to make a long hot sticky sonofabitch of a day of it. I slide out from behind the wheel and go around and open the door and stand there stretching and scratching my belly while the truck empties, kind of not looking at him. "What do you think?" I ask Joe Ben. "Did we or did we not come up with a fine day to welcome old Leland Stanford home to the woods?" Joe, he tips an eye up for a check with his Big Time Weatherman just to be sure and says, "Oh *yeah!* Maybe get a little on the toasty side before the sun sets, but the way I looked at it all the signs point to a day with a heart of gold. Ain't that the way you read it, Leland?"

The boy is shaking like a dog shitting peach pits, still cold from the river ride. He frowns over at Joe like he isn't sure whether he's being spoofed or not, then he grins and says, "I'm afraid I failed to take any courses on astrological signs, Joe; I'll have to trust to your interpretation." This tickles Joe to pieces. Joe digs big words, especially when they're aimed at him. He giggles and spits and goes to hauling out all the paraphernalia for the day—maps and hard hats and "Boy, be sure an' take these gloves!" and candy bars and snuff cans and pocket knives, and,

KEN KESEY (b. 1935) is the author of *One Flew Over the Cuckoo's Nest* (1962); *Sometimes a Great Notion* (1964); and *Garage Sale* (1973).

naturally, the little transistor radio he keeps near him all day—passing them around like a munitions officer issuing arms before a big battle. He hands Lee his hard hat and goes prancing around, tilting his head this way and that to get a good look at the way it sits, saying "Um . . . oh yeah . . . say there . . . wait . . . here we go," and fooling with it till he gets it settled the way he wants it. Then he starts giving Lee a rundown on what to expect and what's happening and what to look out for working the woods.

"The main thing," Joe says, "oh yeah, the *mainest* thing . . . is, when you fall, fall in the *direction* of your work. Con*serve* yourself." He demonstrates how to conserve yourself by doing a couple of nose dives as we amble along. "The whole notion of loggin' is *very* simple if you get onto it. It comes to this: the idea is to make a tree into a log and a log into a plank. Now, when it's standin' up vertical it's a *tree,* and when it's laid down it's a *felled tree.* And when we buck it into lengths of thirty-two feet an' them lengths are *logs.* Then we drag them logs acrost to where the truck is and lift 'em up onto the truck an' then the truck drives 'em down to the bridge at Swedesgap where the government scalers cheat us an' then we take 'em on down to our mill an' dump 'em into the water. When we get enough of 'em in the water we drag 'em up into the mill and we cut 'em up an' we got planks, *lumber.*" He stops to twiddle with the dial of his transistor, trying to pick up one of the Eugene stations. "Or, sometimes, instead of cuttin', we just sell the logs outright." I look over at him to see how he means that, but he's holding the radio to his ear. "Ah. Now it's comin' through. Oh man, Lee, you ever see the beat of one of these little outfits? Listen to that tone." He shakes his head at his little radio and twists the dial loud as it'll go. The tinny screech of some awful Western is squeezed out into the forest. "Makes the day a joy," he says, grinning till you'd think he'd pop; a little thing like that radio could give Joe Ben a thousand dollars' worth of kicks, just about any little thing could.

> *You broke my heart an' tol' me lies,*
> *Left me cold without good-bys;*
> *Oh, your frosty eyes . . .*

We stop walking right near where Andy's starting his chain saw. The saw chokes and barks and dies and barks again with a rising snarl. Andy grins over at us and hollers, "Commencin'!" cocks an eye up above for widow-makers, then touches the saw's blurred teeth against the flank of a big fir. A fountain of white fir sparks spew against the sun. We stand and watch him make his undercut and sight the tree. He's made it a little too much sloped, so he cuts him a dutchman and slides it in to account for the extra inch or so, and goes around to the other side and goes at it with the saw again. When the tree creaks and tips and goes whooshing down I glance over to check the boy and see he's impressed by it. That makes me feel better. I'd begun to wonder if it's possible at all to talk with him; I'd begun to wonder if maybe what a man learns over twelve years in a world so different is like a foreign language that uses some of the words from our world but not enough to be familiar to us, not enough so we can talk. But when I see him watch that tree come down I think, There's that; just like any man I ever knew, he likes to see a tree felled. There is that, by Christ.

"Well," I say, "we ain't makin' anything but shadows. Let's get hold of it." And we start walking again.

Joby leaves to fire up the donkey. Lee follows me across a clearing toward the edge of the woods. At the edge of a pile of slashing and dozed berry vine the clearing quits and the trees plunge into the sky. It's the part of the show I like best, this edge, where the cutting stops and the forest starts. I'm always reminded of the edge of a grain field where the reaper has stopped.

Behind us the donkey engine begins wheezing and gagging. I see Joe sitting like a twisted bird high up in his spiny nest of levers and cables and wires, grabbing at the throttle. The radio sits in front of him, sometimes carrying across to us, sometimes swallowed up by the noise. A ball of blue smoke explodes from the exhaust and I think the whole machine is going to shake itself to death. "That goddamned outfit should of been retired with the old man," I say. The boy doesn't say anything. We start walking again. Somewhere I hear the knock of an ax where John is chopping off branches. Like a wooden bell ringing. And that squeal of Joe's radio coming and going on little breezes. All these things, the way a day gets going, the sound and all, and seeing Lee dig that tree falling, make me feel a whole lot better. I decide maybe it's not going to be such a bear as I thought.

Overhead the highlines that swoop to the spar tree are commencing to bob and jiggle and strum the air. I point up at them. "That's your row to hoe, bub, that line, I aim to see if you can stand up under the strain of setting choker, by god, so just resign your ass to your fate." I'm meaning to rib him a little. "Course, I don't expect you to last out the morning but we got a stretcher handy." I grin over at him. "That boy of Orland's is handlin' the other line . . . he can take over when you fall behind." He looks like he's being ordered up to the front lines, standing all at attention and his jaw set. I'm intending to kind of kid him but, try as I may, I can hear myself sounding just exactly like old Henry doing some first-rate ass-chewing, and I know I couldn't pick a worse way to talk to Lee. But I'm damned if I can stop it.

"You ain't gonna like it at first. As a matter of fact you're gonna think I'm givin' you the dirtiest end of the dirtiest stick on the whole operation." (And he wouldn't of been far from the truth.) "But it can't be helped. The easier jobs, the machinery jobs, it'd take too long to teach you and they're risky even when a guy knows what he's about. Besides, we're hurting for time. . . ."

(And maybe that right there is why I couldn't help sounding angry, because of knowing just how tough setting choker was going to be on a tenderfoot. Maybe I really was trying to be extra tough and was hacked at myself for loading him with it. I do that sometimes . . .)

"But one thing: it'll make a man of you."

(I just don't know. All I know is I thought I was relaxing a little around him, then tied up, the same as I tied up trying to talk with Viv the night before, explaining our deal with Wakonda Pacific. Same as I tie up with anybody except Joe Ben; and me and him didn't really *have* to talk a whole lot . . .)

"If you can make it through the first few days you'll have it whipped; if you can't, well, you just can't is all. There's lots of other niggers can't cut it neither and they ain't all in Dixie."

(I've always had a tough time trying to talk to others without barking. With, say, Viv, I'd start out trying to sound like Charles Boyer or somebody and come off, every time, sounding like the old man telling Sheriff Layton how to deal with the boogin' Reds in this country, how to take care of them Commy bastards *right!* And believe me, sounding like that is sounding pretty damn hard. When old Henry got going on the Reds he could really come on fierce . . .)

"But all I ask is you give it a fair go for a while."

(Because Henry always claimed he was convinced that the only thing worse than Reds was Jews, and the only thing worse than Jews was high-and-mighty niggers, and the only thing worse than the whole lot of them was them goddamned hardheaded Southern bigots he was always reading about. "Oughta poison everybody south of the Mason-Dixon line . . . 'stead sending Northern tax money down to feed 'em . . .")

"So if you're ready, grab hold of that piece of cable and drag it here. I'll show you how to look for a choker hole. C'mon, snap out of it. Bend down here an' watch . . ."

(I wouldn't argue much with the old man myself, mainly because I didn't *know* Reds here in America, and didn't feel much one way or the other about uppity jigs, and was just a little vague about what a bigot was . . . but I tell you, for a while him and *Viv* used to really lock horns about just that very subject, that race business. Really get into it. I remember . . . well, let me recall the thing that *stopped* the whole business. Let's see . . .)

"Okay, now, you watch this."

Lee stands with his hands in his pocket while Hank explains the job with the slow patience of a man who is explaining something once and it had better be picked up because it isn't about to be repeated. He shows Lee how to loop the length of cable over a fallen and bucked log and how to hook the cable to the big line that runs in a circle from the pulley at the anchor stump to the rigging at the top of the spar. ". . . and when you get it hooked you'll have to be your own whistle-punk till things level out. We're too shorthanded for such luxuries. You savvy?" I nodded and Hank went on outlining my duties for the day. "Okay, listen." *Hank gives the cable a kick to make sure it is secure, then leads Lee up the slope to a high stump where a small wire runs in a gleaming arch to the donkey puffing and clanging seventy-five yards away.* "One jerk means take 'er away." *He pulls the wire. A shrill peep from a compressed-air whistle on the donkey sets the tiny figure of Joe Ben into action. The cable tightens with a deep twanging. The donkey engine strains; an outraged roar; the log lurches out of its groove and goes bumping up the hill toward the yarder. When the log reaches the spar they watch Joe Ben leap from the donkey cab and scuttle over the pile*

*of logs to unhook the choker. Then one of Orland's boys creaks
the neck of the yarder forward, like the skeleton of some prehis-
toric reptile painted yellow and brought flashless to life; Joe Ben
gouges the tongs into each side of the log and jumps clear as he
waves to the boy in the yarder cab. Again the gigantic piece of
wood lurches and is jerked into the air as Joe Ben hustles back to
the donkey controls.* "Joe's bein' his own chaser. It's tough on
him, but like I said, it can't be helped." *By the time the yarder
has pivoted and swung the log onto the bed of the truck and
nudged it into place, Joe Ben is back in the donkey and the cable
is reeling back out again. It comes snaking through the brush and
torn earth toward the place where Lee and Hank stand waiting.*
I listened, hoping Hank would explain more about the task,
cursing him for presuming he needed to explain as much as he
had. We were standing alongside each other at the "show," going
through last minute instructions before my big First Day . . .

(Viv, see, spends a lot of her time reading and is up on a lot of
things—that's trouble right there, because there's nothing in the
whole world makes old Henry madder than somebody, especially
some woman, having the common gall to be up on a lot of things
he's already got opinions on . . . so, anyhow, this once, they
got into it about what the *Bible* of all things says about this race
business . . .)

They watch the cable draw nearer. "Then, you see, when the
choker gets close to where you want it, give her *two* jerks." *The
whistle peeps twice. The highline stops. The choker cable hangs
shuddering in its own dust.* "Okay, watch now; I'll set it one
more time for you."

(The old man, see, was claiming the Bible said the spooks
were born to be bondservants because their blood was black like
the blood of Satan. Viv disagreed a while, then got up, walked to
the gun case where we keep the big family Bible with the birth-
days in it, and went to flipping through with Henry just aglower-
ing . . .)

When Hank has repeated the procedure he turns to Lee . . .
"You got it now?" I nodded, determined and dubious, Brother
Hank then took a wristwatch from his pocket and looked at it,
wound it, and returned to the same pocket. "I'll check with you
when I can," he told me. "I got to see about rigging a spar on
that peak yonder this morning because we'll have to move the

yarding and loading later this afternoon or tomorrow. You sure you got it now?"

Lee nods again, his mouth tight. Hank says, "Okeedoke, then," and goes crashing off through the vine and brush toward the crummy truck. "Hey." A few yards away he stops and turns . . . "I bet you didn't think to bring those gloves, did you? No, I mighta known. Here. Use mine." Lee catches the wadded gloves and mutters, "Thanks, thanks ever so much." Hank resumes his crashing through the brush . . .

(When Viv found what she's after in that big Bible she read, "The blood of all men is as one," and shut the Bible. And I tell you: that pissed the old man *so* . . . that I don't know if he would of *ever* spoke to her again, not another word ever, if it hadn't been for the *lunches* she started packing for us to take to work. . . .)

Lee holds the gloves one in each hand, burning with frustrated and confused anger as his brother walks away: You prick, he calls wordlessly after Hank, you pompous prick! Use mine, huh, as though he was giving me his right arm. Why I'll wager every nickel I can lay my hands on that he has at the very least a dozen such pairs in that truck!

Hank finished his instructions and walked away, leaving me to have at it. I looked after him stomping off through brush and brambles, then looked at the cable he had left with me, then at the nearest log, and, fired by that long-shot challenger's elation that I had experienced earlier, pulled on my gloves and had at it . . .

As soon as Hank is gone Lee curses again and jerks on the first of the gloves in a stylized parody of drawing-room fury, but the elegance of his style is marred when he is forced to inspect the second glove, and the fury turns abruptly back on itself when he withdraws from the last two fingers the dirty, sweat-packed cotton padding Hank uses to protect the ends of his tender stumps . . .

The job was actually simple enough—on the surface—simple, backbreaking labor. But if there is one thing you learn in college it is that the first snowstorm is the most important—score high in your first test and you can coast out the rest of the term. So I had at it that first day with a will, dreaming that I might snow Brother

Hank fast and measure up early and be finished with the whole
ridiculous business before it broke my back . . .

*The first log he chooses lies at the top of a small knoll, in a
patch of firecracker weed. He heads toward it; the little red
flowers with sulphur-yellow tips seem to part to make way for
him and the cable. He throws the bell around the end of the log
that is lifted free of the earth where the knoll drops sharply
toward the canyon, then secures it in its hook. He steps back to
examine the job, a little puzzled: "There doesn't seem anything so
difficult about this. . . ." and walks back to the jerk-wire. The
whistle on the donkey peeps. The log tips and heads for the spar
tree. "Nothing so very difficult . . ." He turns to see if Hank has
been watching and sees his brother just disappearing over another
ridge where a second line leads from the spar tree. "Where is he
going?" He glances around, deciding quickly on the next log he
will hook. "Is he going to that other cable over there?"* (Yeah, it
was the lunches that Viv packed . . .) *Hank passes the boy at
the other anchor stump, telling him he'd better get it in gear,
"Lee's already tooted one in" and continues on into the woods
. . .* (Lunches, see, are about twice as big a deal in the woods
as at home, because you get terrible hungry by noon; and the way
the old man appreciates eating anyhow, they are like a Major
League event. So when Viv took over the lunchbag packing from
Jan—on account of Jan being pregnant, was Viv's story, but I've
always suspected it was more to get back in the old man's good
graces—well, Henry just somehow forgot all about Bibles and
black blood. Not that Jan's lunches weren't all right, because they
were; but that's all they were. Viv's lunches were always all right
and then a good deal more than all right to boot. They were a
goddamned feast sometimes. But more than there just being
plenty, there was generally something *special* about them . . .)

*The second log goes as easy as the first. And as it is being
unhooked he looks back toward the other anchor stump some
hundred yards away on that other ridge. There still has been no
whistle signal. As he watches he see a figure struggling through a
thicket of red alder, the cable still over his shoulder. Though the
figure is not even wearing the same color sweat shirt, Lee is
suddenly certain that it is Hank "Taking over the other choker
job!" The line above his head strums and with rising excitement*

he looks and sees his second log is unhooked and his cable is scrambling back to him. He takes it up before it has completely stopped and jogs, dragging the heavy cable as fast as he can, toward the next log, not even taking time to glance at the progress of the figure he supposes to be his brother . . . (Something special and *different* in her lunches—something other than sandwiches, cookies, and an apple; something you could strut and brag about when you were sitting with a bunch of jacks eating out of their ordinary old nosebags—but, mostly, it was that Viv's lunches gave you a little piece of the day to look forward to in the morning and think back on in the afternoon. . . .) *The cable snags briefly, but he wrenches it loose. A berry vine trips him and he falls to his knees, grinning as he recalls Joe Ben's advice, but he is still able to secure the log and jerk the take-it-away signal just seconds before the second signal comes from the other ridge. In the distance Joe Ben's head swings back in surprise; he has been sitting, his hands already on the levers controlling the cables running to that southern ridge, not expecting a call so soon from Lee. "That boy is really humping it." Joe changes levers. Lee holds his panting, then sees the highline above him tauten and his log jump out of the vines: he is a log ahead, two if you count that first one! How about that, Hank?* (Her lunches sure changed the old man's point of view . . .) *Two logs ahead!*

The next log has fallen on a clear, almost perfectly level piece of ground. Unhampered by vines or brush, Lee reaches the log easily, noticing with elation that he is gaining on the other figure, who is fighting through the red alder again. But the very flatness of the ground beneath Lee's log presents a problem; how do you get the cable under it? Lee hurries along the length of the big stick of wood all the way to its stump, then crosses and hurries puffing back, bent at the waist as he tries to peer through the tangle of limbs lining its length where Andy's saw has stripped them from the trunk . . . *but there is no hole to be found: the tree has fallen evenly, sinking a few inches into the stony earth from its butt to its peak. Lee chooses a likely place and falls to his knees and begins pawing at the ground beneath the bark, like a dog after a gopher. Behind him he hears the peep of the other ridge's signal and his digging becomes almost frenzied.* The trouble was, with my plan to put in a good first day even if it broke my back: I almost broke my back that first day. . . . *He finishes the hole and gets the cable through and hooked and jerks his whistle wire* . . . But *only* during the first half of that first day. *Then, panting rapidly, hurries to inspect the next log; "He should have told me about the holes, the prick. . . ."* (And see, the funny thing is it was also Viv's lunches that finally broke the ice and gave me the chance I was waiting for to talk with the boy . . .) The second half of the day went easier—because by then I had learned that I was breaking my back for naught . . . *The line strums overhead. The cable comes back. The moss begins to stream softly on the old stumps* . . . and that I was *never* going to measure up to Brother Hank, simply because he had rigged the scale, making it impossible. *As the sun gets higher and higher.*

☆☆☆ A Lesson in Pawnbroking

from *The Pawnbroker*

by Edward Lewis Wallant

Maybe I have a tumor, Sol thought with bitter amusement. He tried to visualize that peculiar knot of pressure, tried even to localize it. It would seem to be here, just below the breastbone and then . . . up here near his neck . . . no, more toward his back and down. For a moment he thought of death, that old companion of his youth. Ortiz feather-dusted quietly, and he watched him. That sourly anticlimactic joke; it only made him feel cold, not fearful at all.

"Mail this on the corner," he said.

Ortiz took the envelope and studied the address.

Sol sighed mildly. "Just mail it, will you," he said. "Don't waste time. Maybe when you get back I'll tell you a few things, give you a *lesson* in pawnbroking. You are always after me to."

Ortiz smiled and walked swiftly out on his errand. Sol studied his debts while he was waiting. He made a dozen small calculations which proved he didn't make enough money to pay all his bills. Then he just let the pencil meander over the paper in small, amoebic doodles until his assistant returned.

"All right. That thing you just mailed was the list of yesterday's hocks, the things I loaned money on."

The eager acolyte leaned on the counter, his eyes on the Pawnbroker's mouth, all of him narrowed to that mundane information. It occurred to him that great secrets could come from tiny perforations, inadvertently. He must be patient and receptive.

EDWARD LEWIS WALLANT (1926–1962) wrote *The Human Season* (1960); *The Pawnbroker* (1961); *The Tenants of Moonbloom* (1963); and *The Children at the Gates* (1964); the last two were published after his death.

"All the information about an item of jewelry, for example, must be on that list; the amount loaned on it, the complete description. In describing a watch, you must have the case and movement numbers, the size, any unusual markings, any engraved inscriptions. In jewelry, you use the loupe to . . ."

The store creaked under the grotesque weight of its merchandise, and the air was respectful of the teacher's voice. No customers came in; the street in front of their doorway seemed deserted and even the traffic sounded distant. It seemed to Jesus that all the city found the time suddenly hallowed, and he offered himself to the Pawnbroker's dark, indrawn voice with an unconscious sensation of privilege.

"To find the purity of gold in something, up to fourteen karat, you scratch a tiny mark. I say *tiny* in the ethical sense. Actually, this is an area for dishonest profit, too; the filings from a year's gouging can add up to a pretty penny. Anyhow, you drop nitric acid on the scratch. If there is brass, you will get a bright green, silver will show up a dirty gray, and iron will give you a blackish-brown color. Now if the gold is about fourteen karat, you must use these special gold-tipped needles and a touchstone. The acid we use for this is secret to the trade. . . ."

"*Secret,* huh," Jesus echoed in a languid voice as the Pawnbroker gave him the barest outlines of the mysteries.

And it seemed to him that many things of great significance just lay in the quality of the big Jew's voice, that he might, at any moment, surprise the great complexity of his employer just in the ponderous breath that carried the droning words. Horror and exaltation seemed to reside in the Pawnbroker's mysterious history, oddly eased and enriched in the imminence of revelation, oddly eased and enriched in the things beyond what he could form in thought, beyond what the older man said.

". . . so you must watch out for the professional confidence men, the gyp-artists. They are shrewd and practiced and they have a huge bag of tricks. In jewelry, for instance. Take a good-quality pearl which has been accidentally ruined by acid or sweat. The con man will peel the vital top layer to expose the second layer. This layer *will* have a similar appearance to the unspoiled pearl. For a few months! But then you will realize that you are stuck with a dull, worthless nothing. It is important to examine the apparently beautiful pearl, for only the original top layer is really smooth; the other layers are coarse by close comparison."

Sol's voice rolled on in the stillness, disdainful of this latter-day craft of his, echoing his vast bitterness for the things he had once considered important and which he now hated because in his loss of them he had been left deprived and ugly.

Yet, not knowing this (nor would he have cared if he had), the smooth-skinned youth with the sly, delicate face basked in his exposure to ancient, terrible wonders, things only faintly shaped by his scattered knowledge of the Pawnbroker's peculiar heritage, his strange survival of fantastic horrors. So he looked at the blue numbers on his employer's arm and tried to work back from that cryptic sum to the figures that had made it; and, more and more, he was involved in an odd current of emotions, softened and blinded and bound.

Until, finally, the Pawnbroker pushed at him almost gently and said, "Enough with the lessons. Get to work now, Ortiz."

And then, to make the severance complete, Mrs. Harmon came in with three suits; Jesus took them upstairs to the loft and went reluctantly back to his cross-indexing, which now must include Willy Harmon's two Sunday suits and the invalid younger Harmon's rare festive change. And Jesus Ortiz muttered about nothing, really cursing the elusiveness of the Nazerman spirit.

"Fee time at my Edith's secretary school," Mrs. Harmon said in her chuckling voice. Then she laughed out loud and shook her head in wonder at the precariousness of her life. "Man d'lifeboats again, another bill. Honest and true, it like bailin' out a leaky ol' boat fill with holes. Pawn somethin' to buy somethin' else, then pawn that. Each time it seem like the boat gettin' lower in d'water. Ain't it a *wonder* a body stay afloat long as it do?" She sighed at her ridiculous resignation. "But you do, somehow you do, one way or another. I declare, sometimes I don't know if the good Lord plan it all this way to test or if he jus' so busy he get to you again and again jus' in time to keep you from goin' under for the third time." And then her rich, imperishable laughter struck on all the objects in the place, stealing all their value by implying that nothing had value without human hands to coax life into it.

"Five dollars for the three suits," Sol said, feeling the buried pressure again. It sent a streak of apprehension through him; he recalled the power of a few blades of grass to grow through and split solid stone.

"I jus' ain't up to horse-tradin' today, Mistuh Nazerman. No use threatenin' to take my suits someplace else. Too tired to bother." She held out her hand for the money. As she buried the bills deep in the shabby purse, she muttered, "Jus' keep them ol' pawn tickets, these and the ones from the candlesticks, too. You an' me both know that what you bury might jus' as well stay dead." For a moment she looked at the gray, untouchable face of the Pawnbroker. "Ain't that right, Mistuh Nazerman?"

"I suppose it is," he answered, his face sightless and only coincidentally directed toward her.

Two women came in with wedding rings to pawn, apparently arrived at similar desperations at the same time. An old Orthodox Jew, wearing a long gabardine coat despite the heat, offered a tiny diamond stickpin; he argued feebly in Yiddish for a few minutes and then took the small loan with a little clucking noise. A Puerto Rican youth brought in a Spanish guitar and took the first price offered without a word; only he plucked a two-note farewell to the instrument on its own strings before abandoning it. A jet-black girl with the face of a fourteen-year-old and a pregnant body gave him her engagement "diamond," which was glass. The Pawnbroker sent her out with it in her hand, stunned and lost.

At noon a man with nut-colored skin and white hair came into the store. He walked over to the counter with an amiability that indicated he had nothing he wished to get a loan on.

"I'm Savarese," he said. He had black eyes and puffy, fighter's features. "I'm agonna giva you d'estimate."

"I expected you yesterday," Sol said.

"I wasa busy." He ran his eyes in mock appraisal over the store and grinned. "Well, after carefula study, I'ma estimate the complete redecoratin' gonna costa you five G's."

"Who do I make the check out to?"

"Acame Contractin' Corporation," Savarese said, picking at his teeth with a toothpick.

"How do you spell it?"

"It'sa A C M E, *Acame!*"

As Sol began to write, Savarese looked furtively around for a moment, then silently took a thick envelope from his breast pocket and dropped it in front of the Pawnbroker. Sol pocketed it without looking up as he continued writing.

Savarese took the check from him with a parting chuckle.

"Give you a gooda job, Mr. Pawnabroker, paint the whole goddama place pink anda yellow."

Sol waved him away with the offhand gesture he would have used to brush a bug off the counter.

He opened the envelope, and the inside was greasy-green with money. Fifty hundred-dollar bills bulged out. As he stared dully at it, the steps behind him creaked. He turned quickly to see his assistant gazing innocently at the money.

"I guess Thursdays are paydays," Jesus said flatly.

"Mind your own business," Sol said. He took the money back to the huge safe and, hiding the combination with his body, locked it in. Later, as was his custom, he would take it to the night depository of the bank down the street.

A well-dressed woman, white with mortification, brought in a diamond watch. He loaned her ninety dollars on it, and she took the money with a little wince before hurrying out with the pawn ticket clutched in her hand.

"Now she not a virgin any more," Jesus said. "She been in to a pawnshop, sell her soul to the devil."

"I can do without your jokes," Sol said, involved with that peculiar kernel inside him. What was the matter with him, worrying invisible aches like his fearful brother-in-law, Selig? "You have time to be funny? Go instead to the cafeteria and get me some coffee."

Jesus raised his eyes in mocking surprise at his employer's unusual self-indulgence. "Next thing you be takin' afternoons off to go to the track."

"You must be patient with me," Sol answered sourly. "I am getting on in years." He flipped a coin to Jesus.

The youth snapped it out of the air with a dart of his hand and then winked at Sol for his own prowess. "Black, no sugar?"

Sol nodded impatiently.

While Jesus was gone, Mabel Wheatly came in.

"This here a expensive locket," she said challengingly. "No sense foolin' around, I *know* it's gold."

It *was* gold, heavy and pure. Obligatorily, he scratched and tested, but he knew all the time by the very feel of it.

"Fifty dollars," he said.

"Gimme the locket."

"Seventy-five," he revised, offering the figure she would get from anyone else.

"That worth a hundred easy," she said, taking up her property with an assaying glance at his face, emboldened by his one retreat.

"Not to me," he said, looking into her face as though it were a hollow well.

She saw finality in his expression. For a moment she rubbed the gold with her thumb, massaging prodigious value into it. Then she nodded and dropped it on the counter before him.

As he wrote up the article and made out the pawn ticket, she talked her relief like a man who, after a hard day's work, takes satisfaction in his pay, in the money he thinks will advance him along the road to a particular aspiration.

"Ah, you know all about *me*, Pawnbroker," she said in an easy, confiding voice. "You know what I'm in. I don't have to tell you how hard *I* work for my money."

"It is peculiar work," he agreed without judgment.

"Oh brother, peculiar is right." She lit a cigarette and looked back with comfortable melancholy at those hardships already behind her. "Like a woman could go right out of her mind if she thinks on it too much."

"Then I suppose you should not think about it," he said with a little serrated edge to his voice.

"I suppose," she said. She watched her exhaled smoke as it was caught suddenly by the fan and torn to pieces. "Got me a hard boss there, too."

"The woman in charge?" he inquired politely as he finished the little bit of paper work.

"Oh no, she all right. No, I mean the big boss, the owner. He one hard man. Not that he do anything I know of. Only the way he look at us girls, talk in a quiet weird voice. Like you just *know* what he threatenin', if you mess around. Big man, too, got lots of irons in the fire, you know."

Sol looked up for a few seconds to stare at the slow-moving cigarette smoke between them. He was teased with an almost imperceptible sense of recognition, of connection. But the smoke caught in the fan's arc and was wafted away, so he found himself looking at the girl's ordinary brown features, and whatever it was ducked down in his consciousness.

That night, before he left, Jesus asked Sol if he wanted him to accompany him to the bank. "I take one of them duelin' pistols and guard you, huh?"

"If you would only do those things I ask you to, I would be satisfied. Never mind volunteering; I do not appreciate it. Just go on home, I will ask you for what I want."

"You gonna smother my initiative," Jesus said with his wild smile.

"Good night already," Sol said, raising his hand and turning his head away in exasperation. And when he looked back, Ortiz was gone.

He went to the safe and took the money out. For the first time he found himself apprehensive over that half-block walk. Formerly, he had always had the policeman on the beat escort him the short way. But in recent weeks, since Leventhal had become so annoying, he had gone alone.

Anyhow, it was still quite light on the street. There were many people around and police were never more than a block or so away. He locked up the store and started down the street.

When he was almost to the bank, he noticed the three men on the far corner, recognized the ash-gray suit, Tangee, the great bulk of Buck White. He hurried the last few dozen feet, and his hands shook as he slipped the envelope into the brass, revolving chamber. But when he looked back at the men after the money was safely deposited, they appeared quite innocent, like any three men commenting idly on the passing scene. And he felt a growing rage at himself, as though his greatest enemy had invaded his body to leave him shaken and unknown to himself.

☆☆
☆

Dark Came Early in That Country

by Nelson Algren

"We'll fight you on condition you don't knock Reno out in the first two rounds," DeLillo's manager told me, "after two it's every man for hisself."

"Honor Word?" I asked him.

"A hundred dollars and you pay your own expenses to Chicago, Honor Word," he told me.

"Do we take it?" I asked Beth.

"We take it," she told me.

"I don't have the expenses," I told her.

Beth gave me the expenses.

We were the semi-windup. A place called Marigold.

During instructions I asked DeLillo where was he from. He didn't answer. I didn't expect him to. I just wanted him to think about where he was from while I was working the lace of my left glove loose.

I caught him light with the lace across the eye early in the round. He stepped back and complained to the ref. The ref tightened the lace and waggled his finger at me: naughty Roger. By the middle of the round DeLillo's eyelid had begun to swell. By the end of the round he couldn't see on that side. I could have reached over and belted him out but I didn't. I'd give my Honor Word.

In the second I got on his blindy side and clipped him under the ear. He sagged. I could have finished him off but I didn't. I

NELSON ALGREN (b. 1909) published his first novel in 1935 (*Somebody in Boots*); others have appeared since, including *The Man with the Golden Arm* (1949); *A Walk on the Wild Side* (1956); his most recent collection is *The Last Carousel* (1973).

danced him up and down till his ear stopped ringing. You see I'd give my Honor Word.

When we came out for the third I extended my gloves to him.

"It ain't the last round," DeLillo told me.

"It is for you," I told him, and reached over and knocked him cold. I always did have color.

I sent the hundred to Beth by money order. It got back to Shawneetown before I did. When I got there I still had some expenses.

"It shows I can fight a *little,* don't it?" I asked Beth.

"A little; but not much," Beth told me.

"Well, I know the *moves,* anyhow."

"You know the moves alright," Beth told me, "but you can't fight much."

Friday, that week, we caught the Fight of the Week. The room would have been warm enough without a fire, but Beth has to keep one going all year round because of my Pa. The old man was sitting in his overcoat, like he does all year round, helping us watch Pete Mathias, the middleweight titleholder. Being a fighter is a step up from the mines, to Pa.

Mathias was having trouble against an opponent no smarter than Reno DeLillo.

"He wouldn't be taking chances like that against *you,* Roger," Pa told me, "he wouldn't let hisself open against *you.*"

We let the old man say what he wants so long as he don't complain. Pa don't have the right to complain anymore.

Around the eighth round I got the feeling I *could* whip Mathias. I got the feeling so strong I switched the fight off. Beth smiled just as if she understood.

Beth always smiles like she understands everything about everything. Maybe she does. The idea of my quitting the ring and opening a diner was hers. She found one for sale, too. Two thousand dollars. In Carriers Mills. But we were no nearer buying it than we were four years ago when we first got engaged. Maybe she don't really understand anything.

My hundred-dollar kayo at the Marigold wasn't featured by *Ring Magazine* and I greatly doubt it will be listed in *Boxing Year Book* under *Great Battles of All Time.* When I got into San

Antonio I had forty dollars left and I had to fight some fellow Sweetmouth Jenkins at the Army Post there. He got a white manager.

A couple hours before fight time there was a polite rap at my hotel door. The door wasn't locked. I didn't bother getting off the bed.

"I'm Jenkins' manager," a little man in white seersucker, holding his hat in his hand, told me. I still didn't get off the bed. I'd never seen a fight manager holding his hat before. It was my first time.

"My boy is a nice boy with a wife and family," this Polite Manager let me know. "Ah hope you don't bust him up *unnecessarily,* Roger. I'm not asking you not to beat him. Just don't bust him up. His wife is hardly more than a girl, Roger."

"Am I fighting Jenkins or his family?" I asked this Polite Manager.

"His wife will be down front, Roger. She's expecting."

I got off the bed.

"My name isn't 'Roger,' " I told the man, "it's 'Holly.' Now what *is* this anyhow? Would your boy take it easy on *me* if I had a wife expecting?"

"Ah purely regret having brought the matter up, Mr. Holly," he told me; and left just as if I were letting him down. " 'Holly' is my *last* name!" I hollered after him.

But he kept on walking like he didn't hear.

Mr. Sweetmouth Jenkins, sitting across the ring from me, had a mouth like a tribal drum. And here he comes at me with his piano-key teeth sticking out too far. I can feint him with my shoulders. I can feint him with my feet. I can feint him with my eyes or hands. But Mr. Sweetmouth is so busy doing everything wrong he don't even know I'm feinting him. How can I take a man out I can't set up? He got away from me six times in the first two rounds and in the third he begun looking good. I could almost hear Mrs. Jenkins saying, "Daddy, you looked *wonderful* the first three rounds." Daddy wouldn't be able to answer because his jaw would be wired. I *decided* that. I went out for the fourth to nail that tribal drum.

I couldn't nail it. He was too strong. He kept grabbing my arms in the clinches and squeezing the muscle. He made me ache all over with his chopping and butting and scratching my face and chest with his head full of wire bristles. Nigger fighters know how to use that patch against you. I made up my mind: "I got to start outthinking this cat."

I outthought him from the sixth round straight through to the final bell. And all the while I was outthinking him he was chopping me from one side of the ring to the other till my arms were paralyzed and I was swallowing blood.

"By unanimous decision, Sweetmouth Jenkins!" the announcer made it, "over Roger Holly!"

I got a scattering of applause for having two front names.

But Sweetmouth Jenkins hadn't beat me. His manager had. It's what you get for not making yourself hostile right from the go. I can still beat Mr. Sweetmouth Jenkins.

But when you're thirty-two and have been at this trade thirteen years you've pretty well used up your hostility. I caught a midnight bus to Galveston. I had to fight somebody there I didn't even know his name.

After the bus lights dimmed and the other riders were sleeping, I tried to get to sleep by remembering the names of men I'd fought. I couldn't remember more than two or three. I remember the fights. It was just the names I couldn't remember.

So I remembered the names of the places I'd fought in. I did better on those. I remembered the Camden Convention Hall in South Jersey and the Grotto Auditorium in San Antonio and the Moose Temple in Detroit and the Marigold in Chicago and the New Broadway in Philly and the Norristown Auditorium and the Arcadia Ballroom in Providence.

And that week at Presque Isle near the St. John River, with potato pickers being trucked in from all over the country, and Evergreen Shows put up a canvas with a sixteen foot ring, on a platform two feet high in the center, and billed me as The Penobscot Strongboy—"Don't be afraid, folks, he is only a little man and his hands are gloved."

They were gloved alright. Right after supper the merry-go-round electrician bandaged my hands and I soaked them in a bucket of salt brine to toughen the bandages till they were like rocks. I had to keep my hands in my pockets when I strolled the midway with the early evening crowd.

Dark came early in that country. We used old carbon lights to light up the banner, strung between two poles in front of the tent, showing two boxers squaring off. It would already be dark, and the carbon lights flaring, when the electrician would bang on an iron ring, the barker would get up on the bally with a big horn and holler "Ladies and gentlemen! We are bringing you here tonight and every night this week, meeting all comers, the Penobscot Strongboy, undefeated in the State of Maine! This show will pay twenty silver dollars to any man who will last three rounds with him! Mind you, gentlemen—*you don't have to win! Just stay three rounds!* He is only a little man and his hands are gloved."

That was when I'd step up on the bally wearing a bathrobe over my fighting trunks. I was eighteen then and weighed 142 pounds.

"Ladies and gentlemen, the best carnival fighter ever seen in this part of the country. The Penobscot Strongboy!"

He'd keep talking until he'd get some smalltown fighter, only half-willing yet ashamed to back down in front of friends, to step up. Even if he *could* fight a little, I could do a little more. But he'd always tell the fellow, in front of the crowd, that he couldn't hold the show liable if he got hurt in the ring.

On the third night we ran out of heel-walkers. I had to slip the electrician ten dollars to fake three rounds with me just to get a crowd watching. It worked. For the second show gave a big hand to a rough-looking redhead around 175 pounds. The crowd knew him and liked him. I began smelling money. The show manager came in and told me, "Roger, we got a full house out there and four nights to go. You know what to do."

I knew what to do alright. If you have a full house, and a man wasn't dangerous, you let him stay and win twenty silver dollars. Because the crowd would file out and pay again for the next show. So I whipped a light right high to Red's head to get up his guard, then shot a jab low on his belt—*very* light—just low enough to get the crowd to hating me. Then he hit me a solid punch and began carrying the fight to me. Red wasn't simply trying to stay—and he *had* a good right. But his left was just good enough to fill his coat sleeve.

Toward the end of the third round I began throwing wild rights, like I was desperate to knock him out so as to save twenty dollars. I made sure I missed every one. To make it look even better I went down on one knee as if he'd hit me really solid. Even Red thought he'd hurt me.

When the bell rang ending the third round the crowd was screaming, "Kill him, Red! Kill him! He's no good!"

"Ladies and gentlemen!"—The manager came out—"The Penobscot Strongboy admits your man is a very good man, and that he would *rather* fight somebody else. But *our* man is a sport, he is going to give *your* man another chance. We will now pay *your* man twenty silver dollars—But"—pause—"if *he* is as good a sport as *our* man, he will let the twenty ride and this show will now pay him *fifty* silver dollars if he stays the second three rounds! If he fails to stay the show owes him nothing."

The crowd, of course, was all for it. So was Red. Those two hundred and fifty fools rushed out and bought tickets and were back in the tent in no time at all. The ticket agent had to stop selling because we couldn't get any more into the tent.

I felt sorry for Red but it couldn't be helped. When he rushed out at the bell I slid along the ropes, threw a terrific right to his gut that doubled him over, shifted for leverage and threw a left hook that had everything I owned behind it. Red rolled under the bottom rope onto the edge of the ring. He was out almost two minutes.

I still remember that manager ballying the crowd as they filed out, one by one and not one saying a word—"Don't be afraid, folks, he's only a little man and his hands are gloved!"

And the Rainbow Garden in Little Rock and the Garden Palace in Passaic and the Armory A.C. in Wilkes-Barre and the Fenwick Club in Cincinnati and Antler's Auditorium in Lorain, Ohio. I went back to Detroit and remembered the Grand River Gym and the old Tuxedo A.C. on Monroe Avenue.

Just before I fell asleep I knew those were the names of the places where I'd used up my hostility.

It was getting light across that Gulf Road land between the Gulf Road towns when I woke up. I'd made this scene before. The land looked to me the way beds do in cheap hotels where you don't get clean sheets unless you pay a week in advance.

Bed after bed.

I got a room like that in Galveston. Then I went to look for a corner man. I had to fight somebody calls hisself Indian Mickey Walker.

It isn't always easy to find somebody to work your corner in these east Texas towns. Sometimes you can find an out-of-work fruit-picker to carry your bucket. If you're lucky you'll find an old-timey fighter, fight-manager, or fight-follower to handle you. Them kind are the ones who don't take money off you. Yes, I've carried my own bucket. Into rings where the ropes were unpadded.

At the Ocean Athletic Club I found a skinny little hustler from New Jersey, calls hisself Dominoes because he's been hustling domino parlors in the Rio Grande Valley. He'd kept one hand in his pocket so long one shoulder was higher than the other. I bought him a meal. Then I took him back to my room and emptied my little green-and-white Ozark Air bag on the bed: cotton swabs, surgical scissors, carpenter's wax, liquid adrenalin, smelling salts, Spirits of Ammonia, iodine, Monsel's Solution, Vaseline, adrenalin chloride, and half a pint of brandy. I showed him what everything was for except the brandy. Dominoes already knew what brandy was for.

I asked him did he know anything about some clown calls hisself Indian Mickey Walker.

"Strictly an opponent," Dominoes told me, "I seen him fight a prelim at the Garden when he come up from the bushes; but he come up too fast. Went down even faster."

"All the same he done better than I done," I had to admit. "Closest I've got to the Garden was McArthur Stadium in Brooklyn."

"Never been there."

"McArthur Stadium or Brooklyn?"

"Neither," he told me, "but I'll tell you what I think. I think you need a manager."

"What for?" I asked the man, "I never needed somebody to tell me the best hand to hit an opponent with is the one closest to his jaw. I never needed somebody to teach me that when you clobber someone it's a shrewd idea to duck. What can a manager do for me beside robbing me blind?"

"He might get you in at the Garden," Dominoes decided—"or wouldn't you like that?"

"There's people in hell would like ice water," I told him, "but that don't mean anyone's bringing the pitcher."

Indian Walker was a shoeshine fighter. Stands in the middle of the ring with his head down and flails both arms like he's shining shoes. Built like a weight lifter. More hair on his chest than I got on my head. Some Indian.

The ref was one of them Elks Club athletes who'd refereed so many fights he'd gotten punchy. He likes to show who's the boss by sticking his head between us and hollering "Break!" so you could hear him in the back of the hall.

He stuck his head in there once too often. The stupid Indian nails him and down goes the ref onto one knee. The whole house began counting him out. He made it up at eight. After that he stayed out from between us. But every time we clinched somebody would holler "Break!"

Indian Walker won seven of the eight rounds. One was about even. The ref give me the fight on points. I got the winner's end, a hundred dollars, for not knocking the referee down.

I hung around home a week or so. Then I got a call from Minneapolis.

Some businessmen up there had "discovered" a six-foot-five schoolboy and had bought him half a dozen fast knockouts. They offered me five hundred and expenses to fight him. The reason they wanted me, I guessed, was because nobody has ever had me off my feet in a ring. It would be a boost for the Schoolboy Giant if he should be the first. I told the men to send me a hundred for expenses in front, that I'd want the other five before I got in any ring with a Real Live Giant. Then I phoned Dominoes to meet me in St. Paul.

"It ought to be worth fifteen hundred," I told Dominoes. He understood what I meant. So did Beth. They *had* to want a tank job. Beth didn't say anything. She wanted that diner in Carriers Mills.

I took a look at the Schoolboy Giant working out. Some giant. It didn't seem possible that they were going to let me go after him. He was *all* schoolboy.

Yet nobody rapped my hotel door. Nobody stopped me on the street. Nobody phoned me for a meet. "Something funny is going on," I told Dominoes. "Something funny *isn't* going on," Dominoes corrected me.

The weighing-in was in a downtown newspaper office. The room was full of bush sportswriters. The Giant was undressing in a corner. I began undressing too. I let him walk toward the scales first. He was about to step on the scale but I hollered right in his ear "Get off that scale!" and shoved him so hard he almost toppled. I pointed my finger right up at his nose—"Don't *ever* let me catch you trying to get on a scale in front of *me!* Do you *hear?*"

After I'd weighed in I stepped down.

"You can weigh yourself now," I told him.

He weighed 232. I weighed 172. They billed me at 180.

It wasn't till after the instructions, waiting in my corner for the bell, that Dominoes whispered, "They're dropping him."

The Giant's people were betting against him.

Well, all right. So was I.

He came out into the middle of the ring, put his left foot into one bucket and his right foot into another, extended his left hand and poised his right exactly as he had been told to do. I walked right up on his big flat feet, worked the ball of my wrist into his right eye; then held. I stepped back at the break, missed deliberately with my right in order to catch his other eye with my elbow; then held.

He put both gloves across his eyes; so I walked up on his feet again and butted him in the mouth. He half-turned toward the referee and said, "He's walking on my feet," and I reached over and knocked him into a spin. He caught himself going down by his forearms.

I didn't go in on him. I waited till the ref got out from between us. The Giant put both arms around me and held me till the bell. I went back to my corner wobbling from his hug.

Sometimes you can feint a man into position for an uppercut. You can feint him with your hands, your head, your shoulders, your eyes or your feet. I was always best at feinting with my feet. I let the Giant work me into my own corner and feinted him into the ropes. Then I let him work me into his corner and feinted him the same way—this time he went sprawling.

I was just trying him out. Feinting isn't enough. The idea of feinting isn't to send a man sprawling. The idea of it is to get him just enough off balance so that when you hit him a shot at the same second you feint him, he goes down. If he feints you right back you go down. In the middle of the second round he spread those big flat feet again.

I walked right up on them and butted him in the mouth. He turned his head to the ref to complain and I hit him on the jaw again. This time he went to both knees. He got up on one with one eye shut, the other cut and his mouth bleeding. Yet he got up at nine and still seemed to be in his right mind. So I followed him and he smashed my nose in with a big right hand.

I grabbed his middle and held; just held. I'd never been hit that hard before in my life. And all the while he was weaving from side to side it was me weaving from side to side trying to keep the ref from getting me off him. I didn't let go until I was sure I wouldn't hit the floor.

Then I came up fast and skulled him in his bloody mouth and he skulled me back so hard I had to hold again. The Schoolboy Giant was catching on.

I felt Dominoes pressing my skull with his fingers as hard as he could. Then he used the liquid adrenalin. "It's a *bad* cut," I heard him tell me, "*real* bad."

A right uppercut is a sucker punch. If you don't time it exactly you leave yourself open to your opponent's cross or jab. You have to think ahead to land it, anticipate your man's moves. It's a good punch to throw at an opponent who fights a little lower than you. But if you're fighting one a full head higher, you have to bring him down to you. I went for the Schoolboy Giant's body. A right to the heart, a left to the solar plexus. He lowered his head, his arms crossed level with his heart; with my right glove almost touching the floor I pivoted on the ball of my left foot. And brought it up. He pitched face forward as if he'd been mugged with a crowbar.

I watched his legs while the ref counted him out. The doctor was working on him a full half-minute before his calves twitched. The last I saw of the Schoolboy Giant two handlers were dragging him to his corner with his toes scraping the canvas.

Dominoes gave me interference to the locker room. Some kid threw a handful of popcorn in my face on the way.

"Lock the door," I told Dominoes as soon as we got inside. I didn't get up on the rubbing table. I didn't take off my robe. I just looked at Dominoes a long time.

"Mister," I finally told him, *"never* tell me I got a bad cut. *Never* tell *anybody* he got a bad cut. Tell him it's nothing. Only a scratch." Then I began throwing up.

A postcard from Shawneetown was waiting for me at Boise. All it said was *Everyone Here Fine Don't Get Hurt.*

I read it sitting on a locker-room bench. After I'd read it I put it with Beth's other cards telling me Don't Get Hurt. Then I put on my trunks and went upstairs to the gym.

There was a poster next to the door. It said Cowboy Goldie Williams *vs.* Roger Holly. I began throwing my left into the heavy bag.

A good many people don't even remember I began fighting as a left-hander. A good many people don't even remember I began fighting.

A lanky young fellow in blue jeans and Spanish boots stopped to watch me. I paid him no heed.

"You left-handed?" he finally asked me.

"No," I told him, "right-handed."

"Then *hit* it right-handed," he told me.

"I'm developing my left," I explained.

"Developing?" He looked like he couldn't believe his ears—"at your age you're *developing* something? Hell, you're old enough to be Cowboy's old man."

"Reckon I could be his old man," I admitted, "if I'd married when I was fourteen."

"Nobody gets married that young," he decided.

"But it don't make no difference," he filled *me* in—"Cowboy Williams is going to beat you silly. He's going to gouge you 'n' bust your eardrums, too. He's going to pound your kidneys. He's going to crack your ribs. He's going to bust your jaw. He'll give you con-*cussions!"*

"What do we do following *that?"* I asked him, "Play unnatural games?" and went back to the bag. I wondered who had sent him.

When I climbed into the ring that night I found out who'd sent him. The fellow who came down the aisle in a white satin robe was the same fellow. Cowboy Williams had sent hisself.

A fighter so keyed up as to play trick-or-treat before a fight is likely to start fast, I guessed.

I guessed just right. He came tearing across the ring and I caught him coming.

All I had to do was to step aside to let him fall.

I kept an eye out for kids holding popcorn bags on the way to the locker.

While I was dressing the promoter came in and sat down on the bench.

"I can get you on at the Tulane Club," he told me, "five hundred and expenses."

"I'll take it," I told the man, "who do I have to kill?"

"Your worry will be how to keep from getting killed. You're fighting The Pride of New Orleans."

"Who's New Orleans proud of now?"

"Jesus St. James. *Stay in shape.*"

"I don't have to stay in shape to beat somebody named St. James," I told the man.

I stay in shape all the time. I don't drink or cat after women. If you stay out late on Monday you still feel it Friday in this trade.

I didn't find out till we got to New Orleans that Mr. James was unbeaten. Twenty-two professional fights, fourteen wins by kayo, six by decision, one no-decision and one draw. Mr. James could hit, it looked by the record.

He didn't look like he could hit in his corner. A college boy, no more than twenty, six foot high and not a mark on him. Carrying his left like he was just walking down the street. I'd have to watch that hand for certain. He also looked like he could move around. I didn't need anymore to tell me I wouldn't last ten rounds against this athlete. I went out and bought a pair of Sammy Frager five-ounce gloves, of which three ounces is in the wrists. I thought that just *maybe* I might get away with them. At the weigh-in I gave them to the referee. He looked like a doctor.

"Do me a small favor," I asked him, "let me use these tonight."

We were standing right next to a scale but he didn't put them on it.

"Beautiful gloves," he told me. "How much do we owe you?"

"Not a dime," I told him, "they're on the house."

He came into the dressing room that night and handed me the gloves and then left me and Dominoes *alone*. No deputy. Nobody. I'd never had anything like it happen to me before.

Dominoes pulled on white tape tight as I could stand it without stopping the circulation. Then he put black tape over the white. Then he put white tape over the black. I was loaded.

We'd hardly finished taping when someone knocked. Dominoes stepped out to see who. He stepped back in and shut the door behind him.

"There's a fellow out here wants to know if you'll take five hundred to let St. James go the distance," Dominoes told me.

"We take it," I told Dominoes. So out he steps again and steps back in and shuts the door and hands me five c-notes.

"I don't have pockets in my trunks," I told him, "you hold it."

All I did the first two minutes of the first round was to test myself to see how I felt. I felt kind of limber. So I go in and hit Mr. James with a left hook and he starts to go down. I grab him and we're still falling. We're both falling all around the ring, me trying to make it look like it's *me* that's out on his feet. I leaned him against the ropes with my weight against him so he wouldn't slide onto the floor. And all the while the crowd hollering for *him* to finish *me!* I leaned on him till the referee pried me off. By that time the athlete had come around.

All I did the next two rounds was miss punches by the yard, dance Mr. James up and down, duck, bob, weave, clinch, and complain to the ref to keep this stinker going. The crowd didn't care for it.

"If you don't start fighting you're not getting paid," the ref told me at the end of the fourth.

"I got to get rid of this kid," I told Dominoes in the corner, "he's going to faint on me."

"Better not," Dominoes reminded me, touching the five bills in his shirt pocket.

The crowd had its blood up. They'd paid to see a fight. I hit the Pride of New Orleans with another left hook and he went out cold. Flat on his back and arms stiff at his sides.

Dominoes picked up the stool with its legs sticking out and ran interference again back to the dressing room. As soon as he'd locked the door someone began pounding on it.

"Coming under the door," I hollered; and slipped the five bills underneath it.

I'd beaten three unbeatables in a row all by kayo. So a magazine did a story on bush league fighters without managers and said I was the best of a bad lot.

"You're not in the bushes no more," Dominoes decided, "you got a manager now."

"Who?" I asked him.

"Me," he told me.

I didn't say anything. I just let him go ahead.

Oh, that Dominoes. He signed me up for three ten rounders in a single week: Monday night, Wednesday night and Saturday night.

"What are we doing Thursday?" I asked him.

Beth took it well. "I always knew you were a bad lot," she told me when she read that magazine piece, "but I never dreamed you were the *very best* of it. At least you fight a lot. And you do have color."

The poster said Sol Schatzer Proudly Presents—I couldn't read the rest because Dominoes was sitting with his head against it, pretending to be on the nod.

I read the contract in front of me through twice. Both times I stopped where it said *In event challenger establishes legitimate claim to title, he herewith agrees to purchase managerial services of co-signer.*

"I can beat Pete Mathias without a manager," I told Schatzer.

"It's the customary contract," he told me, "I don't have all day. So sign."

I pushed it back to Schatzer.

"You know what you are, Roger?" Schatzer told me, "you're an Agony Fighter, *that's* what you are. You know what else you are, Roger? You're an Agony *Man, that's* what you *also* are. You can't fight and you won't let an opponent fight. You can't make money for yourself, and you won't let somebody who can make it for you. You don't *want* a manager? Has somebody been around here lately asking? Somebody phoning to ask could he manage Roger Holly? *Who* been asking? *Who* been phoning? I'll tell you who: *nobody. That's* who been phoning to manage Roger Holly."

"I just *got* me a manager," I told Schatzer and nodded toward Dominoes; on the nod under the poster of Peter Mathias.

"That's a manager?"

Schatzer jumped up, raced around his desk with the contract in his hand, and shook Dominoes like a half-empty sack. Dominoes opened one eye. Schatzer pushed the contract into his hand.

"Manager! Read a contract your fighter won't sign! *Read,* Manager!"

Dominoes tore the contract in two and let the halves fall to the floor.

"I don't know what you're getting so excited about, Roger," Schatzer told me when he'd caught his breath, "all I'm doing is protecting myself. If you should get lucky against Mathias, *I* lose *my* title. All the contract means is I manage you. Don't I have a right to protect my own interest?"

"How much does the co-signer take?" I asked Schatzer.

"Twenty-five percent, clown," Dominoes said like talking in his sleep.

"All right, Roger, I'll level with you," Schatzer began leveling. "Just for the sake of the argument, let's pretend you *do* have a chance against Mathias."

"I didn't say I had a *chance,* Mr. Schatzer," I told him in a respectful tone. "I said I *would,* I *can.* I *know* I'll beat Mathias."

"OK. So you *can* beat Mathias. So can Al Ostak. So can Vince Guerra. So can Lee Homan. So can Indian Walker—and every one of them can whip you and hold the title longer and draw better, too. Am I right or am I wrong?"

"I have a decision over Walker," was all I could think to say.

"I know about that decision," Schatzer found me out. "Indian Walker is a washed-up Has-Had-It-Has-Been. But he can still beat *you.*"

"Then why not offer *him* the fight? Why offer it to *me?*" I really wanted to know.

"Because then he'll get thirty percent of each man in a re-match," Dominoes cut in again, "and three guys he can get thirty-five percent out of."

"You stay out of this," Schatzer told Dominoes.

"I can whip Indian Walker," I told Schatzer.

"You can't even whip Sweetmouth Jenkins," Schatzer told me.

"I couldn't untrack myself that night."

"All right," Schatzer said, glancing at his watch, "go ahead and whip him. Whip anybody you want. Whip Mathias if you want to. How you're going to get into a ring with him without me is where *you* got a problem."

It was true that any one of those fighters could whip Mathias as easy as I could. It was true that there were just as many fighters who could take *me*. It was true that, if I got the title, I wouldn't be able to hold it long. It was true I never drew big.

And what was truest of all was that if I didn't get this chance, I'd never get another.

"Give me the damned paper," I told Schatzer, and signed it.

"I'm sorry I had to speak to you like I did, Roger," Schatzer told me. "I did so for your own good. Actually I have nothing but admiration for you."

Three days before the fight Schatzer sent for me. He came right to the point.

"I'm seeing you get five thousand dollars before the fight, Roger," he told me.

"I don't get it," I told him.

"In small bills. The day before the fight."

"I still don't get it."

"For not straining yourself to win, clown."

"Let me maul it over in my mind a couple days," I told Schatzer.

I didn't tell him I wasn't going to take the five thousand.

If I let him know I wasn't going to take it, he might have Mathias fake a training injury. If the fight were postponed, I'd never get another chance. Nobody would be demanding to know when these two tigers were going to do battle. It would just mean somebody else taking the title off Mathias, that was all.

I put Dominoes in the gym to watch Mathias.

"He don't have to fake no injury," Dominoes reported back; "when he cuts out of the gym, he puts on a pair of foggy-type magnifying glasses so he can tell a taxi from a police car. But he's going to go through with it all the same. Schatzer must have a fix with the Commission medics."

"He must need the money pretty bad," I told Dominoes, "he must need the money *real* bad."

It's never bothered me to climb into a ring first and wait in my corner until an opponent comes down the aisle and climbs through the ropes to the house's applause.

When Mathias came up the aisle everyone applauded; and half the house stood up to get a better look.

I could see him coming better than most, being higher up. He was in a flashy green silk robe. But the way he was coming, between two handlers, both of them half a head higher than he was, I saw what Dominoes meant. They kept him between their shoulders as they came to keep him walking straight. When they reached the ring they waited till he got a hand on the top rope. Then one kind of half-boosted him into the ring. Mathias raised his gloves over his head and held them there until one of the handlers shouldered him toward the corner. Then he just stood there until the other handler put a stool up.

"He don't see me," I whispered to Dominoes.

"Hell, he can't even see the stool," Dominoes whispered back.

What went through my mind was: This is going to be awful.

I didn't know how awful it was going to be.

Mathias kept his eyes on the floor during instructions. All I could see of his head was where he'd combed back a few strings of red hair to cover a bald spot; and a little pink horseshoe at the tip of his nose where the bone had been taken out. It must be filled with wax, I thought. When I tap him in the forehead the horseshoe will get red. When I hit him squash on it, it's going to *pour* blood. But something about the way he was standing made me think he wasn't listening to the referee. Then the crowd whooped and he didn't hear the whoop. Something more than his eyes was wrong with Pete Mathias. His handlers steered him back to his corner.

He came out of his corner and hit me in the mouth with his head. He slipped my lead and threw a right hand that near tore my head off at the neck. I moved back, mulling him to give my head a chance to clear. He caught the nape of my neck in his glove, jammed his iron jaw into my shoulder, and *whack-whack-whack-right-left-right,* I got hit by three house bricks from his deaf-blind tiger. *What has he got in his gloves* went through my mind, holding on hard. I stepped back to ask the ref to examine his gloves. What he hit me with I never felt. I came to in my corner feeling Dominoes' fingers pressing the skin above my right eye. "Did I go down?" I asked him. "No, you got back here by yourself," he told me. By the way he kept pressing I knew it was a deep cut.

"Is it bad?" I asked him. "Only a scratch," he told me. Mathias was standing in his corner waiting for the bell to spring upon me. I only hoped he'd wait until it rang.

"He's blind as a bat," Dominoes said.

"Then how does he know where I'm at?"

"He's *listening.*"

"He can't hear neither."

"Stop scraping your shoes on the canvas. He's catching vibrations. Get up on your toes—*if he can't hear you he can't find you.*"

And the bell.

I came out tippy-toe, stuck a glove in Mathias' face, and tippy-toed quietly away. Mathias wheeled and went for the opposite corner.

"Other corner!" every fink in that house stood up hollering.

Talk about your informers! If there'd been a Stool Pigeon's Convention in town, every single delegate had come to help Pete Mathias find me.

Between rounds he didn't sit down. Just stood there boggling his head about trying to find out where I'd gone. Just before the bell his handler would whisper to him where I was hiding and push him. He'd come right over there. All I could hope was he wouldn't put his glasses on.

The way I lasted through that fight was by grabbing his left glove in both of my own and holding on to it for dear life for as long as the referee would let me. Once I stuck my head under his armpit to keep him from digging that iron chin into my shoulder and striking me. From this purely defensive position Mathias was so hampered he couldn't do anything but smash the wind out of my lungs, bang my ears till they rang, pound my kidneys to shreds, and rabbit-punch me at will—"you got him, Roger," someone hollered in the dark behind the press row, "you're gettin' your blood all over him!" I don't know whether Mathias heard this—but something suddenly got him *mad* at me. He got my lower lip in his glove in a clinch and gave it a twist that almost tore it off. I grabbed his Adam's apple and sunk my teeth into the lobe of his left ear—the ref got my teeth out by pulling my head back by the hair— but I was still choking him to death. Then he split my right cheek wide open with the point of his elbow.

"I didn't *mean* to hurt him," I told the referee.

"If that's how you men want to fight it's alright with me," the referee gave us the go-ahead.

Mathias wasn't cute-dirty. He wasn't even scientific-dirty. He was temper-dirty. All I could do those last two rounds was grab his elbow, spin him, give him a choke job, chop him in the groin and try a butt on that tender nose now and then. Just to let him know I was in the fight, too.

And then on an old scarred bench was a swab stick, the cardboard core of a roll of gauze, the top of a Vaseline jar and half a bottle of liquid adrenalin.

That was what I had to show for getting my face punched in for fourteen years.

On the evening of the first day that we opened the diner at Carriers Mills, Beth switched on the Fight of the Week for our two customers.

It was Sweetmouth Jenkins, challenger, against Pete Mathias, title-holder. Jenkins kayoed old Pete in two minutes and eleven seconds of the first round. I switched the set off and went back to waiting on the two customers.

People around here say I never could fight much, I just knew the moves. Beth says I had color.

The Marigold in Chicago and the Armory A.C. in Wilkes-Barre and the Valley Arena at Holyoke and Joe Chap's Gym in Brooklyn and The Grotto in Jersey City and The Casino at Fall River and Provenzano A.C. in Rochester and the St. Cloud Music Hall and Antlers Auditorium in Lorain and Billow Abraham's Gym in Wilkes-Barre and Conforto's Gym on Canal Street and Sportsman's Bar in Covington and the Council Bluffs Ballpark and the Hesterly Arena in Tampa and the Tacoma Ice Palace and the Great Lakes Club in Buffalo and the Century

A.C. in Baltimore and the Paterson Square Garden and the Coliseum Bowl in Frisco.

If just people didn't keep running so fast these days, backwards sometimes.

You never can be sure what they might do to you by mistake.

☆☆☆ My Death

by Lynda Schor

It was cool in the hallway as I locked the stroller to the filthy balustrade. I considered for a moment whether it would be easier to make two trips upstairs with the contents of the stroller, and decided to try for one. I didn't like trying to make the decision of whether I preferred my bundles ripped off or the baby kidnapped, so I decided to unload everything. With the baby in my arms, I bent down, took out his blanket, bottle, and his toys, put them alongside him in one arm; then with the other hand I lifted the huge bag of groceries out by the top of the bag—balancing it gently so the whole top didn't tear off—and settled it in my other arm. The cool, musty air felt good as it dried my perspiration. One more flight, I thought. Then, at the bottom of the second flight of stairs, something happened. I broke out into a cold sweat as I felt the blood leave my head and all my extremities. My heart began beating wildly, in an incredible arrhythmia. Then I felt an explosion so large that it was audible too, a sort of light surrounded by blackness which fell down over my eyes, leaving a residue of tiny sparks sparkling at the edges, then an incomparable nausea of the whole body, a deep nausea which included even my extremities.

This is it, I thought. What I was always afraid of. Death. I'd always thought it would be a stroke—cerebral accident, as it was called. Maybe this was a heart attack, or diabetic shock, but most likely it was a large blood vessel bursting in the brain in a sort of explosion, the blood, out of its boundaries in a rush, flooding all

LYNDA SCHOR (b. 1938) has published stories in *Ms.*, *Fiction*, and *Redbook* and has a collection entitled *Appetites* (1975).

over, rushing down over my eyes. That's what my grandmother had died of, and I always knew it would feel like that. It actually felt familiar.

When I didn't feel my heart anymore I knew I was dead, but I didn't want to drop the baby so I thought I'd just try to get upstairs, and, too, the thought of all the groceries splattered all along the hall, the ketchup spilled, broken glass, oranges falling down the stairs all the way to the front door—and what the tenant's committee would think—filled me with dismay. I made a supreme effort, and continued carrying it all upstairs. I rested the groceries against my raised knees as I unlocked the door, fully intending to lay the baby down, and then lie down myself, being dead. But as I put the baby down and saw him kicking there on the couch, I felt sudden remorse. I knew I couldn't leave him there because as soon as I actually gave up the ghost he'd probably roll off the couch and cry piteously for hours, with no one to hear him. Just as I was trying to figure out what to do with the little guy he began to cry, and I realized that it was time for him to nurse, and it would be better if I left him fed and comfortable; so I left the food in the bag and lifted my shirt, cradling the baby, who felt hot next to my cooling flesh, which must by now be way below body temperature, and wondering whether there was still milk in a dead woman's breast. The baby sucked greedily, unaware of my condition. Certain body processes must continue from inertia for a while. I burped him conscientiously, and then he shit on me, right out the edges of his Pampers. I decided not to leave him in that condition, and also I myself didn't want anyone to find me dead with shit on my lap, which brought me to the whole thing of what I should wear. I looked in the mirror and I didn't look good, but I looked as I imagined I'd look after I saw my grandfather dead, though when I saw him he had more makeup than I. My face was whiter, his was the bluish-black of a heart attack. Probably one of the arterioles in my brain had burst. And I had thought that those small lapses into senility I had experienced lately were the result of too much housework. I looked white and solid, as if I were made of marble, an article rather than a person. In a lifeless state, my face was really ugly; since I wasn't really pretty, the only thing I'd had in my favor was a sort of life, some sex appeal emanating from a type of expressiveness, which, when gone, left my face frightening in its blank, sheer ugliness of form.

Just as I'm about to lie down—with great misgivings, as I watch the baby paddle about on the rug, arms and legs moving frantically, but luckily unable to move an inch in any direction except round in a circle—I realize that it's time to pick up the other two kids from school. A person can't even die here, I think as tears (where can they be welling from?) actually fill my eyes. Maybe I can get someone to pick them up for me. I've already considered calling Dave, but would he leave the store early just because his wife has died? What about when I had the baby and he made me come home two days early from the hospital because he couldn't watch the other two and didn't want to close the store, even for a day? And the time I nearly bled to death from a hemorrhaging extracted wisdom tooth and the dentist wouldn't answer his answering service, and I asked Dave to come home and watch the three kids so I could find an emergency clinic that dispensed dental treatment, and he said he couldn't leave yet because a customer was there. So do you think he'd leave in the middle of the day for a mere death? I decided to call Ruth Roth. Maybe she'd take them to her house; then I wouldn't have to worry about them and Dave could pick them up when he closed his shop.

"Hello, Ruth?"

"Hi."

"Listen, Ruth, I'm dead. Could you pick up the kids for me and keep them a while till Dave picks them up?"

"I'm dead too. I was going to call you and ask you whether you could pick up Rosalee."

"I would, but I'm really dead, I mean *dead*."

"I'm worse than dead—I have this virus. Just pick up Rosalee today, I'll do yours tomorrow."

I decided not to hassle. I got ready to pick up my two kids, plus Rosalee.

The outside of the school is sickening even when one's feeling well. I suppose it could be uglier aesthetically, but it becomes ugly when one has to go there every day for so many years, stand in the same place, and at a certain moment see mobs of kids begin pouring out, an effusive discharge, a percolating, inundating deluge, almost as if the building itself is writhing in the throes of an enormous peristalsis.

Timothy and Rosalee, in the same class, are out, running wildly around the stroller, the baby's head swiveling around in complete circles, watching them. The two kids, increasingly wild, disturb me. There's no part of me that's sympathetic with the speed of them. I become dizzy and lean on a parked car for support.

"Stop being so wild," I say, thinking to myself that it's all because Rosalee's here, which is mostly a lie.

"You're going to hurt yourselves," I warn, like an oracle. Their movements accelerate as they interweave with other children, moving in and out, spreading along the whole street—books, noise, and food flying, like a dance choreographed by my worst enemy—and sure enough, Timothy is on the pavement, on his chin. As he cries, blood drips in drops to the spot on the concrete where his chin hit, leaving a mark. Everyone crowds around, sympathetic, telling me about all the cases they knew of where a fall on the chin bone required stitches, as I stare at the split flesh hanging at the bottom of my little boy's chin. In a semistupor, I raise my ass off the royal-blue Volkswagen, whose fender fits so neatly to my body, and rummage around in my purse for something to stanch the blood. I find a diaper without too much spit-up on it. As soon as the wound is covered with the diaper, some of the people who had become vampires pull in their teeth and begin moving away again. Timothy is at last quiet and we wait for Alex. Rosalee is also subdued. It would be very pleasant except for the fact that when Alex comes out we'll have to run over to the emergency room at St. Vincent's, which, fortunately, is right across the street from the school. Who knows how much foresight went into that seeming coincidence? I see Alex, minus her usual smile.

"What's wrong?" I ask, barely having time to be interested.

No answer. This is very common. I consider taking advantage of the situation in order not to have to hear what's the matter.

"What's the matter?"

"Ggaaaoo ooooieu mmnn . . . ooiiiiffo." She's said that

whole sentence without once opening her mouth, which is excellent except for the fact that I didn't understand a word.

"Timothy fell from being wild with Rosalee," I tell her, "and we have to take him to the clinic. I think he needs stitches."

"Ggooor gigo," she says with her mouth still closed.

What I'd like to do is leave the kids at David's store before I take Timo to the hospital. It's only about a block and a half out of the way. I peer under the diaper and see that the bleeding seems to have stopped, but I know he'll need stitches by the way the wound hangs open.

"Let's go," I say. We all start moving, Timo and Alex each holding one side of the stroller handle; then I notice that Rosalee's not with us. She's standing there, fifteen feet behind us.

"Come on!" I say. My teeth are clenched. Anger or rigor mortis?

"I can't. My mommy didn't tell me to go with you."

"Well, she called me up, but by then it was too late to tell you."

"She said never to go with anybody."

"I'm Timo's mother."

"Well, I'm not going."

"Then you'll be here forever, because I'm supposed to take you."

"I don't care. I'll wait here forever for my mommy, and when she sees I'm not with you she'll come and get me."

"Your ass," I say, and I pull her as hard as I can and place her hand around the stroller handle with as much pressure as I can, as if I am gluing it there and don't want it to come off.

When we get to David's store he comes out to meet us, probably in the hope that if he gets to us first, he can deflect us from coming into the store and distract us into going home. He's wearing his sneakers and a work shirt open to the waist. His brown, slender chest, tanned and hairless, is charming, as are his gently hairy ankles, emerging from the bottoms of his shrunken slacks and flowing, unbroken by the presence of socks, into his sneakers. He glares.

"I have to leave the kids here to take Timo to the hospital. He fell in front of the school."

"Why can't you take them? You know they'll be wild here. They might break something."

"Because I think Timo needs stitches, and the other kids will be disturbing and running around and there's no place to put the stroller and the baby will breathe infected air. Aside from that, I died this afternoon. I shouldn't even be doing anything. I could lie down right now and no one would be able to call me down for it."

"You always complain," he says.

I then rip the diaper from where Timo is holding it to his chin, taking advantage of the fact that David can't bear to see any injury, no matter how slight, in order to impress upon him that it's not just for nothing I'm asking him to do this favor. He looks, turns white, puts his arm across his eyes, and runs for the store. I park the stroller, stuff the pacifier in the baby's mouth, and take off in the opposite direction with Timothy. It takes a few minutes for me to get used to walking without a stroller in front of me without falling over, but when I do, it feels so good that I don't even mind going for stitches. Timo isn't crying. He wants to know whether he can have some candy.

I know where the emergency room is; I've been there before. We wait in a long line to register. Timothy is holding the diaper to his chin and eating Good & Plenty. It's our turn.

"Name," says the secretary.

"Timothy Schor."

"Timothy? That's a strange name for a woman."

"It's not for me—it's my son."

"I thought it was you, you look so terrible," she says.

"Dead people usually look bad," I say.

She looks around in a moment of panic, as if she's trying to spot a psychiatrist on duty. She decides to terminate any communication with me other than the application for treatment. I show her his chin.

"Oh, it's bad. Looks like another mouth," she says coolly.

"Fuck you," I whispered with my death breath.

"Go to the third room on your left after the large room where that sign is, and wait," she says.

We wait. My fear is that after we wait for four hours or so, we'll find out that they lost the pink paper that the secretary filled out. A nurse comes in.

"Timothy Schor?"

"Yes?"

She slips a thermometer under his tongue, and times his pulse as Good & Plenty juice streams out along the sides of the thermometer and dribbles onto the diaper. We wait more. Timothy is sitting on a tiny crib, one side of which is down, and I'm holding his hand because the crib frightens him. A woman comes in with a baby. She undresses the baby in another crib. Even though it's summer, the baby has on a sweater-and-legging ski set and a light woolen bonnet, which have to be removed; then, underneath, little shoes, tights, a dress, a tiny slip, a minuscule undershirt. She undresses the baby leisurely, carefully, right down to its medals and one Pampers, weeping gently onto its belly. She folds all the clothes neatly in a pile, takes out a soft baby's hairbrush from her large pink carrying case, and begins to gently brush its almost nonexistent hair. This must be the grooming instinct, I think. As I look at Timo, I wonder why I lack it. His hair is long; it hasn't been combed for a year and a half. He has various food stains on his face which extend down over his shirt in matching and contrasting colors. His face is long, his chin sharp. I'm considering taking him home and taping his chin together myself. Waiting so long makes me angry. I'm thinking of lying down right here and now so they can say, "She died waiting for service in the emergency clinic," but I'm afraid to leave Timo at their mercy.

A doctor comes in. He says *"¿Que Pasa?"*

"He fell," I say.

"Let's have a look. Ugh. What happened?" he asks Timo.

"He fell on the concrete in front of the school."

"What happened, sonny?" he asks Timo.

"I fell on the concrete in front of the school."

"Are you trying to accuse me of child beating?" I ask.

"Cool it, lady. This must have upset you—you don't look well. Have a seat."

"I'm already sitting."

"Well, relax. I'll tell the nurse to bring you some smelling salts. I'm going to have to take a couple of stitches. You wait here."

"I want to come with him."

"I'd rather you didn't. You look so bad, you might faint."

"If I look bad, it's because I'm dead. Smelling salts and waiting here aren't going to help. You think I'm just a hysterical woman," I screamed, "but I'm not—I'm simply dead. A person could die waiting here!" I shrieked, filling the halls with my mausoleum, Creature-Feature scream. The doctor ran from the room. A minute later a nurse came back and took Timo out. The coward is probably waiting, trembling in the sewing room. Where did the doctor learn to sew? In Home Economics? Will they bring back my child? Maybe they'll take me upstairs to the loony section. There's no need to fear that—loony space is at a premium these days. If you really go insane bad, you have to check in at Bellevue and wait for an opening here. It's the Concord of mental hospitals. And on the wall, to minimize my sufferings is a crucifix, a painted metal Christ on a wooden cross: passive, limp, blood painted with a metallic glow streaming from every nail wound. Actually he's beyond suffering. As depicted here, he must already be dead. They bring in Timo, with shiny dried tear rivulets and a stretched mouth.

At the cashier's I say, "How much is it?"

"Sixteen dollars for a visit to the emergency room plus four stitches at ten dollars a stitch—that's forty plus sixteen—plus the X-rays that they took to see whether the bone was chipped and the entire-body X-rays they took to see whether he showed signs of previous child battering."

"You expect me to pay for the unauthorized X-rays that you took for your own use, having nothing to do with my child's injury? You get a special grant for that! I should sue you for exposing him to unnecessary X-rays!

"Lady, I didn't take the X-rays, so don't say 'you.' I'm only the cashier."

"Just send me a bill, I don't carry that much money—even Rockefeller doesn't. He has credit cards. Do you accept credit? How about BankAmericard?" She hid under the desk.

As we walk away, I get a glimpse of red carpet and scarlet armchairs, matching the red costume in the portrait of the Cardinal that's hanging above the chairs. Incredible interior, I think, planning to return someday and shoot it with color film. I feel genuine regret when I realize that I'll never be back to shoot anything. I'll be lucky if I can lie down before I decompose. But who shall I leave my Minolta Autocord to? Let David keep it all, even though he prefers 35 mm.

"Where were you for so long?" asks Dave when we return to the store. Does he think we lied to him in order to go see a movie or something? "How much did it cost?" he asks.

"I'm not sure—they want to charge for X-rays I didn't tell them to do."

"Well, you'll have to pay out of the household money, since it was all due to your neglect."

I held Timothy to me and wept into his bandage.

"Don't get it wet," Timo says.

On the way home the baby begins to cry. I buy some milk, not knowing when a dead woman's milk gives out. I recall photos I've seen in *Life* and *Look* of dead Indian women, starved to death, with emaciated babies at the breast, but I never could tell whether they were still sucking. Or if they were, were they getting anything? At home, baby at my breast, I see I was wise to buy the milk. After a few sucks, he cries, tries again, screams. I make a bottle. The best way to wean someone from you is to die. Alex still looks unhappy. I asked her what's the matter; she gives me a pathetic look and bares her teeth. There's nothing there. She has no front teeth anymore. And they can't have just fallen out—on the contrary, new, permanent ones have just grown in, just achieved their full growth within the past week or two. And since they were enormous, it isn't hard to miss them now.

"What happened," I say. I don't yell.

Her face turns into a prune and tears run like streams in and out of creases and into her mouth.

"Why are you crying?"

"Because I thought you were going to yell."

Well, to tell you the truth, I feel like yelling, I feel like screaming, but it's really stupid to yell at a kid because her teeth are knocked out. And they aren't completely knocked out, just chipped off almost to the top. A good dentist could cap them.

Actually, I had thought that when David finally came home he'd take over, so that I could just die normally. It isn't so much that I wanted to die, but being already dead, I had no choice—

There was something compelling about lying down. I did have dinner ready for him so that things wouldn't be too much of a strain. I also prepared food for the next four days, cold things, and wrapped them and labeled them with instructions for warming or serving or eating.

When he came in he looked at me for a minute and said, "You don't look well."

I said, "Well, it's because I'm dead, and usually dead people aren't well."

"Don't be so sarcastic," he said. "You always complain. Think of something more positive. For instance, at least you can't get cancer now. Why don't you make some coffee to take your mind off it?"

"Look," I said, "I'm dead and I'm going to lie down. Make yourself some instant coffee."

"I don't like instant coffee."

"Then make yourself some regular."

"But I don't know how much coffee to put in."

I made the coffee, trying to figure out where to lie down when I finally could. The whole thing seemed so unnatural at this point. It's best to just lie down the moment you die, no matter where it is? Did that mean I should descend the hall stairs and collapse at the point where I originally died? The kids were watching *Gilligan's Island* and the baby was sleeping. I lay down on the bed and was pervaded by a gentle peace, which was shattered by David calling, "Hey, where's my dinner?" He called again. I wondered whether I was capable of ever getting up. I ignored him. Eventually he'd see that something was wrong and that I'd never be able to make his dinner again, or he'd get his own fucking dinner. He continued calling an endless number of times. Finally he came in and throttled me.

"What's wrong?" he said.

"I told you. I'm dead."

"You're just a hypochondriac. Move over." He lay down beside me—squeezed in because I didn't move over. Then he moved over on top of me.

"How can you do this to a dead person?" I was really indignant over the indignity.

"Well, I'll try. It's sort of exciting." He disembarked for one mad moment while he ripped off his clothes. Then he proceeded to rip off mine, which was more difficult, since I didn't even raise my hips so he could pull down my underpants. He sublimated himself onto my body again, kissing my limp lips and pumping into my unresponsive limbs. Obviously he wasn't enjoying it, he was spending all the time trying to arouse me.

"Why can't you move just a little?" he said. "I feel like a necrophiliac."

"If you were a necrophiliac you'd dig making it with me like this," I said. He tried some more.

"Oh, fuck it," he said, dismounting. "Why can't you excite me?"

"Why does your excitement depend on mine? You're insecure. You take it too personally. It's a known fact that dead people don't respond even if Paul Newman were wiggling his cock into their pubic hair."

He went to put water into the tub for his bath, which is too bad because it occurred to me to take a bath too, and I was in a hurry. I put the kids to bed. I looked in the mirror. My face was already thinner; my eyes looked like melted fish eyes. My skin was like cheese cake with birthday-candle blue lips. I heard Dave shouting from the bathroom over the sloshings of water, "Too bad I never took out insurance for you. I never dreamed you'd die so young. I'd never have to work again." I felt like weeping but not a tear came to my concave fish eye.

I rested on the toilet while I let my bath water in, nice and hot. I left my hand under the faucet, where it flipped to and fro like a seal's flippers. When the tub was full I ingressed into the water gently, insinuating my body in a bit at a time, enjoying the sensual pleasure of the extreme heat on the lower part of my body and the goose flesh on the upper, unimmersed portions. When the sensation mitigated, I rested my back against the curved back of the tub and slowly slid downward. I continued sliding down until I felt the water crawling up over my lips, feeling the water in my nose, over my eyes, and tickling my scalp as it flooded fluidly through my hair. I never bothered to come up. I noticed that the oblivion I was experiencing was not that much different from the usual.

☆ Undercover Work

from *On Ice*

by Jack Gelber

6:55 A.M. Fred and Al are hereby notified that the alarm clock is of a criminal nature. It caused the suspect (me, no one else here to . . .) pain in the calf, coccyx, the nape of the neck, and the chest. Washed, the skin feeling as if it were blown up to my size and supported by heavier-than-air gas.

7:07 A.M. Manhattan gasoline pumped into the nose, filtered through the brain covering by capillary action, and caused slight nausea. Although not unpleasant, suggest you take isle of Manhattan to Albany for incarceration.

7:27 A.M. Three out of four motorists were speeding. Fifteen dollars or fifteen days. Ah, to be up in the early aggressive morn, braving horn blowers and other phallic worshipers.

7:47 A.M. Approaches to the shopping center left unguarded. If they are not careful, New York construction workers will move entire center to another site. No guards in the parking lot. Tut. Fat, near-sighted guard watching people punch clock. Easily diverted. Asked him for camera department, and he forgot to check badge. Could have been K. and he would not have known.

7:55 A.M. You will be happy to hear, boss (collective expression), that the camera department was still intact. Assistant Mgr. blew nose. (Germ warfare.) Counted out money. The fool turned his back to me. Didn't he know that I could sprint out with it? Fellow with pimples (5′ 10″, 155 lbs., brown hair, brown eyes)

JACK GELBER (b. 1932) is the author of *On Ice* (1964) and a number of plays, including *The Connection* (1960); *The Cuban Thing* (1968); and *Sleep* (1972).

introduced himself as Shel-don Ashkenasie (will check spelling later) and immediately started a harangue about the New York Yankees. At that hour of the morning there was nothing more repulsive than a pimply-faced schmuck Yankee fan who never had been in a ball park yet was very authoritarian. For out-of-season palaver: suggested sentence of 5 yrs. sol. confinement.

8:00 A.M. Work officially began. Where's the coffee machine? Ber-nard ordered all to clean the area. He singled me out as the newest clerk and told me to learn the merch-n-dise. Ber-nard has the disconcerting habit of patting one on the ass as a sign of friendliness. Ber-nard retreated to his office.

8:02 A.M. Everyone smoked, hiding their butts in glass display cases.

8:05 A.M. The only female in the camera department arrived. All cleaning stopped; now smoking in an open manner. She gave all a smile, the space between her front two teeth adding an idiot sexuality to her other attractions. (5′ 4″, 110 lbs., dark blond hair, brown eyes, and if this investigator had been properly trained by MARCO he could tell her cup size.) Shel-don won in edging over to her area. Anger changed to amusement as he rubbed a large pimple on his cheek.

8:11 A.M. Looked over fellow employees. Can't work too fast, boss. After all, boss, you don't want me to look suspicious. It looks like a long job, boss. I'm going to dig here and wouldn't be a bit surprised if it took the best part of a year to figure out this caper. Keep up the insurance premiums on Oldsmobile. Ber-nard stuck his head out of his office and yelled, "Stop smoking and clean up."

8:13 A.M. Went to storeroom and discovered a method of sneaking a smoke. Loss of five minutes work. If every worker did this once a day, it would mean, boss, a loss of 60 work hours a day, 300 a week, or about 15,000 work hours per year. Suggest company hire a detective to frisk employees for cigarettes and thereby improve their efficiency. Anyway, cigarettes are poison.

8:20 A.M. Trouble with hiring a detective (just wanted to get more work for MARCO) would be in driving slothfulness underground. A tour of the basement (in quest of coffee) revealed a dozen or so hung-over, snoring employees, not so hidden away behind enormous crates. By the way, will MARCO please supply a wristwatch as it is getting increasingly difficult to guess the time of each one of my amazing discoveries?

8:35 A.M. Ber-nard showed me how to work cash register. Didn't look easy to beat, but a confederate could scoop up a wad and run. Not a customer in sight. Other departments had the *Daily News* spread out on counters, with languorous smoking employees reading. Country ladies must shop in the afternoon.

8:36 A.M. Found out store didn't open until 9:00.

8:50 A.M. Joe Bigelow (5' 11", 175 lbs., crew-cut blond, blue eyes) complained about the pay (which is low) and threatened to quit as he has two children. Sympathized with the notion (I have an imaginary child which I will explain), but can't say that I liked him: something about a service button in the lapel that annoyed me. However, he informed me that the girl's name was Dorothy Hoak.

9:02 A.M. Watched assistant manager (Raffles, 6' 2", 195 lbs., black hair, Mexican eyes) demonstrate a slide projector. Habitually used the pronoun "your" preceding all nouns. He blew nose often, and once the snot dribbled onto his tie. No sale.

10:45 A.M. No customers. Doldrums. Asked Ber-nard if I could look over the store to get an idea of Company Spirit, etc. He said that it was a wonder that those pricks upstairs hadn't sent someone down to do just that, but they always came for new workers during a rush period for that purpose.

11:00 A.M. Ducked into candy room. Yes, boss, they have a special room devoted to satisfying sugar lust. Contained within four walls were eleven nickel and dime candy machines, and it was here that this undercover agent incurred his first expense. Item 1—four bars of chocolate.

11:10 A.M. The old trick of walking into a department (dressed properly) ostensibly to move merchandise and then walking out of the store with it will work. Don't consider it wise to gamble my cover by testing it.

11:50 A.M. Met another new man. Marcus Headfort (5′ 5″, 105 lbs., brown eyes, brown hair) seemed too happy to get such a lousy job. Gave the impression that he had fulfilled his lifelong ambition by being a camera clerk.

11:59 A.M. Ate a cheese sandwich because the old bankroll is dipping faster than a Dow-Jones average during a steel strike. (MARCO, baby, shell out an advance.) Obvious that all the young ones in lunchroom were at the same high school and/or live in the same neighborhood. That seemed to leave the girls out of this spy's hands.

12:35 P.M. Impossible to eat lunch in half hour.

1:00 P.M. Finally waited on a customer. Felt everyone watching. Firmly believe no one, including customer, noticed the mistake in change.

5:00 P.M. Time to go home. And sleep. Honest, chief, there was so much to do that no note was taken of the entire afternoon's misdealings, if any. Joe Bigelow confided that some Jewish person owned this chain of stores. Indeed, Ber-nard confirmed this and added that many of the managers had been in the service with Al-bert Weinstock. That was one source of inefficiency that could never be wiped out! Never hire your army buddies. Right, chief? Raffles advised me to keep my nose clean. Shel-don claimed Mantle would hit 60 next season. Dorothy H. said she didn't like fast workers.

✩✩ Widow Water
✩✩
by Frederick Busch

I spent the afternoon driving to New Hartford to the ice cream plant for twenty-five pounds of sliced dry ice. I had them cut the ice into ten-inch long slivers about three-quarters of an inch in width, wrapped the ice in heavy brown paper and drove it back to Brookfield and the widow's jammed drill-point. It's all hard-water country here, and the crimped-pipe points they drive down for wells get sealed with calcium scales if you wait enough years, and the pressure falls, the people call, they worry about having to drill new wells and how much it will cost and when they can flush the toilets again, how long they'll have to wait.

I went in the cellar door without telling her I was there, disconnected the elbow joint, went back out for the ice and, when I had carried the second bundle in, she was standing by her silent well in the damp of her basement, surrounded by furniture draped in plastic sheets, firewood stacked, cardboard boxes of web-crusted Mason jars, the growing heaps of whatever in her life she couldn't use.

She was small and white and dressed in sweaters and a thin green housecoat. She said "Whatever do you mean to do?" Her hands were folded across her little chest, and she rubbed her gnarled throat. "Is my well dead?"

"No ma'am. I'd like you to go upstairs while I do my small miracle here. Because I'd like you not to worry. Won't you go upstairs?"

She said "I live alone—"

I said "You don't have to worry."

FREDERICK BUSCH (b. 1941) is the author of *I Wanted a Year Without Fall* (1971); *Breathing Trouble* (1973); *Hawkes: A Guide to His Fictions* (1973); and *Manual Labor* (1974).

"I don't know what to do about—this kind of thing. It gets more and more of a problem—this—all this." She waved her hand at what she lived in and then hung her hands at their sides.

I said "You go on up and watch the television. I'm going to fix it up. I'll do a little fixing here and come back tonight and hook her up again and you be ready to make me my after-dinner coffee when I come back. You'll have water enough to do it with."

"Just go back upstairs" she said.

"You go on up while I make it good. And I don't want you worrying."

"Alright, then," she said, "I'll go back up. I get awfully upset now. When these—things. These—I don't know what to do anymore." She looked at me like some thing that was new. Then she said "I knew your father, I think. Was he big like you?"

"You know it" I said. "Bigger. Didn't he court you one time?"

"I think everybody then must have courted me one time."

"You were frisky" I said.

"Not like now" she said. Her lips were white on her white face, the flesh looked like flower petals: pinch them and they crumble, wet dust.

"Don't you feel so good now?"

"I mean kids now."

"Oh?"

"They have a different notion of frisky now."

"Yes they do" I said. "I guess they do."

"But I don't feel so good" she said. "This. Things like this. I wish they wouldn't happen. Now. I'm very old."

I said "It keeps on coming, doesn't it?"

"I can hear it come. When the well stopped, I thought it was a sign. When you get like me, you can hear it come."

I said "Now listen: you go up. You wrap a blanket around you and talk on the telephone or watch the teevee. Because I guarantee. You knew my father. You knew my father's word. Take mine. I guarantee."

I said "That's my girl." She was past politeness so she didn't smile or come back out of herself to say goodbye. She walked to the stairs and when she started to shuffle and haul the long way up, I turned away to the well pipe, calling "You make sure and have my coffee ready tonight. You wait and make my after-

dinner coffee, hear? There'll be water for it." I waited until she
went up, and it was something of a wait. She was too tired for
stairs. I thought to tell Bella that it looked like the widow hadn't
long.

But when she was gone I worked. I put my ear to the pipe and
heard the sounds of hollowness, the emptiness under the earth
that's not quite silence—like the whisper you hear in the long-
distance wires of the telephone before the relays connect. Then I
opened the brown paper packages and started forcing the lengths
of dry ice down into the pipe. I carried and shoved, drove the ice
first with my fingers and then with a piece of copper tube, and I
filled the well pipe until nothing more would go. My fingers were
red, and the smoke from dry ice misted up until I stood in an
underground fog. When nothing more would fit, I capped the
pipe, kicked the rest of the ice down into the sump—it steamed
as if she lived above a fire, as if always her house was smolder-
ing—and I went out, drove home. I went by the hill roads, and
near Excell's farm I turned the motor off, drifted down the dirt
road in neutral, watching. The deer had come down from the
high hills and they were moving delicately through the fields of
last year's cornstumps, grazing like cattle at dusk, too many to
count. When the truck stopped I heard the rustle as they pulled
the tough silk. Then I started the motor—they jumped, stiffened,
watched me for a while, went back to eating: a man could come
and kill them, they had so little fear—and I drove home to Bella
and a tight house, long dinner, silence for most of the meal, then
talk about the children while I washed the dishes and she put
them away.

And then I drove back to the house that was dark except for
one lighted window. The light was yellow and not strong. I
turned the engine off and coasted in. I went downstairs on the
tips of my toes because, I told myself, there was a sense of silence
there, and I hoped she was having some rest. I uncapped the
well pipe and gases blew back, a stink of the deepest cold, and
then there was a sound of climbing, filling up, and water banged
to her house again. I put the funnel and hose on the mouth of the
pipe and filled my jeep can, then capped the check valve, closed
the pipe that delivered the water upstairs, poured water from the
jeep can through the funnel in to prime the pump, switched it on,
watched the pressure needle climb to thirty-eight pounds, opened

the faucet to the upstairs pipes and heard it gush. I hurried to get the jeep can and hose and funnel and tools to the truck, and I had closed the cellar door and driven off before she made the porch to call me. I wanted to get back to Bella and tell her what a man she was married to—who could know so well the truths of ice that he could calculate its gases would build up pressure enough to force the scales from a sealed-in pipe and make a dead well live.

I-80 Nebraska M.490-M.205

by John Sayles

This is that Alabama Rebel, this is that Alabama Rebel, do I have a copy?"

"Ahh, 10-4 on that, Alabama Rebel."

"This is that Alabama Rebel westbound on 80, ah, what's your handle, buddy, and where you comin from?"

"This is that, ah, Toby Trucker, eastbound for that big O town, round about the 445 marker."

"I copy you clear, Toby Trucker. How's about that Smokey Bear situation up by that Lincoln town?"

"Ah, you'll have to hold her back a little through there. Alabama Rebel, ah, place is crawling with Smokies like usual. Saw three of em's lights up on the overpass just after the airport here."

"And how bout that Lincoln weigh station, they got those scales open?"

"Ah, negative on that. Alabama Rebel, I went by the lights was off, probably still in business back to that North Platte town."

"They don't get you coming they get you going. How bout that you-know-who, any sign of him tonight? That Ryder P. Moses?"

"Negative on that, thank God. Guy gives me the creeps."

"Did you, ah, ever actually hear him, Toby Trucker?"

"A definite 10-4 on that one, Alabama Rebel, and I'll never forget it. Coming down from that Scottsbluff town three nights ago I copied him. First he says he's northbound, then he says he's southbound, then he's right on my tail singing 'The Wabash

JOHN SAYLES (b. 1950) is the author of *Pride of the Bimbos* (1975).

Cannonball.' Man blew by me outside of that Oshkosh town on 26, must of been going a hundred plus. Little two-lane blacktop and he thinks he's Parnelli Jones at the Firecracker 500."

"You see him? You see what kind of rig he had?"

"A definite shit-no negative on that, I was fighting to keep the road. The man aint human."

"Ah, maybe not. Toby Trucker, maybe not. Never copied him myself, but I talked with a dozen guys who have in the last couple weeks."

"Ahh, maybe you'll catch him tonight."

"Long as he don't catch me."

"Got a point there, Alabama Rebel. Ahhhh, I seem to be losing you here—"

"10-4. Coming up to that Lincoln town, buddy, I thank you kindly for the information and ah, I hope you stay out of trouble in that big O town and maybe we'll modulate again some night. This is that Alabama Rebel, over and out."

"This is Toby Trucker, eastbound, night now."

Westbound on 80 is a light-stream, ruby-strung big rigs rolling straight into the heart of Nebraska. Up close they are a river in breakaway flood, bouncing and pitching and yawing, while a mile distant they are slow-oozing lava. To their left is the eastbound stream, up ahead the static glare of Lincoln. Light. The world in black and white and red, broken only by an occasional blue flasher strobing the ranger hat of a state policeman. Smokey, the Bear's campfire. Westbound 80 is an insomniac world of lights passing lights to the music of the Civilian Band.

"This that Arkansas Traveler, this that Arkansas Traveler, do you copy?"

"How bout that Scorpio Ascending, how bout that Scorpio Ascending, you out there, buddy?"

"This is Chromedome at that 425 marker, who's that circus wagon up ahead? Who's that old boy in the Mrs. Smith's pie-pusher?"

They own the highway at night, the big rigs, slip-streaming in caravans, hopscotching to take turns making the draft, strutting the thousands of dollars they've paid in road taxes on their back ends. The men feel at home out here, they leave their cross-eyed headlights eating whiteline, forget their oily-aired, kidney-jamming cabs to talk out in the black air, to live on the Band.

"This is Roadrunner, westbound at 420, any you eastbound people fill me in on the Smokies up ahead?"

"Ahh, copy you, Roadrunner, she's been clean all the way from that Grand Island town, so motormotor."

(A moving van accelerates.)

"How bout that Roadrunner, this is Overload up to 424, that you behind me?"

(The van's headlights blink up and down.)

"Well come on up, buddy, let's put the hammer down on this thing."

The voices are nasal and tinny, broken by squawks, something human squeezed through wire. A decade of televised astronauts gives them their style and self-importance.

"Ahh, breaker, Overload, we got us a code blue here. There's a four-wheeler coming up fast behind me, might be a Bear wants to give us some green stamps."

"Breaker break, Roadrunner. Good to have you at the back door. We'll hold her back a while, let you check out that four-wheeler."

(The big rigs slow and the passenger car pulls alongside of them.)

"Ahh, negative on that Bear, Overload, it's just a civilian. Fella hasn't heard bout that five-five limit."

"10-4 and motormotor."

(Up front now, the car is nearly whooshed off the road when the big rigs blow past. It wavers a moment, then accelerates to try and take them, but can only make it alongside before they speed up. The car falls back, then tries again.)

"Ah, look like we got us a problem, Roadrunner. This uh, Vega—whatever it is, some piece of Detroit shit, wants to play games."

"Looks like it, Overload."

"Don't know what a four-wheeler is doing on the Innerstate this time of night anyhow. Shunt be allowed out with us working people. You want to give me a hand on this, Roadrunner?"

"10-4, I'll be the trapper, you be the sweeper. What we got ahead?"

"There's an exit up to the 402 marker. This fucker gets off the ride at Beaver Crossing."

(The trucks slow and the car passes them, honking, cutting

sharp to the inside lane. They let it cruise for a moment, then the lead rig pulls alongside of it and the second closes up behind, inches from the car's rear fender. The car tries to run but they stay with it, boxing it, then pushing it faster and faster till the sign appears ahead on the right and the lead truck bulls to the inside, forcing the car to squeal off onto the exit ramp.)

"Mission accomplished there, Roadrunner."

"Roger."

They have their own rules, the big rigs, their own road and radio etiquette that is tougher in its way than the Smokies' law. You join the club, you learn the rules, and woe to the man who breaks them.

"All you westbound! All you westbound! Keep your ears peeled up ahead for that you-know-who! He's on the loose again tonight! Ryder P. Moses!"

There is a crowding of channels, a buzzing on the airwaves. Ryder P. Moses!

"Who?"

"Ryder P. Moses! Where you been, trucker?"

"Who is he?"

"Ryder—!"

"—crazy—"

"—weird—"

"—P.—!"

"—dangerous—"

"—probly a cop—"

"—Moses!"

"He's out there tonight!"

"I copied him going eastbound."

"I copied him westbound."

"I copied him standing still on an overpass."

Ryder P. Moses!

On 80 tonight. Out there somewhere. Which set of lights, which channel, is he listening? Does he know we know?

What do we know?

Only that he's been copied on and around 80 every night for a couple weeks now and that he's a terminal case of the heebie-jeebs, he's an overdose of strange. He's been getting worse and worse, wilder and wilder, breaking every trucker commandment and getting away with it. Ryder P. Moses, he says, no handle, no Gutslinger or Green Monster or Oklahoma Crude, just Ryder P. Moses. No games with the Smokies, no hide-and-seek, just an open challenge. This is Ryder P. Moses eastbound at 260, going ninety per, he says. Catch me if you can. But the Smokies can't, and it bugs the piss out of them, so they're thick as flies along Nebraska 80, hunting for the crazy son, nailing poor innocent everyday truckers poking at seventy-five, Ryder P. Moses. Memorizes your license, your make, and your handle, then describes you from miles away, when you can't see another light on the entire plain, and tells you he's right behind you, watch out, here he comes right up your ass, watch out watch out! Modulating from what must be an illegal amount of wattage, coming on sometimes with "Ici Radio Canada" and gibbering phony frog over the CB, warning of ten-truck pileups and collapsed overpasses that never appear, leading truckers to put the hammer down right into a Smokey with a picture machine till nobody knows who to believe over the Band anymore. Till conversations start with "I am not now nor have I ever been Ryder P. Moses." A truck driver's gremlin that everyone has either heard or heard about, but no one has ever seen.

"Who is this Ryder P. Moses? Int that name familiar?"

"Wunt he that crazy independent got hisself shot up during the Troubles?"

"Wunt he a leg-breaker for the Teamsters?"

"Dint he use to be with P.I.E.?"

"—Allied?"

"—Continental Freightways?"

"—drive a 2500-gallon oil tanker?"

"—run liquor during Prohibition?"

"—run nylons during the War?"

"—run turkeys during Christmas?"

"Int that the guy? Sure it is."

"Short fella."

"Tall guy."

"Scar on his forehead, walks with a limp, left hand index finger is missing."

"Sure, right, wears a leather jacket."

"—and a down vest."

"—and a lumber jacket and a Hawaiian shirt and a crucifix round his neck."

"Sure, that's the fella, medium height, always dressed in black. Ryder P. Moses."

"Dint he die a couple years back?"

"Sheeit, they aint no such person an never was."

"Ryder P. who?"

"Moses. This is Ryder P. Moses."

"What? Who said that?!"

"I did. Good evening, gentlemen."

Fingers fumble for volume knobs and squelch controls, conversations are dropped and attention turned. The voice is deep and emphatic.

"I'm Ryder P. Moses and I can outhaul, outhonk, outclutch any leadfoot this side of truckers' heaven. I'm half Mack, half Peterbilt, and half Sherman don't-tread-on-me tank. I drink fifty gallons of propane for breakfast and fart pure poison, I got steel mesh teeth, a chrome-plated nose, and three feet of stick on the floor. I'm the Paul mother-lovin Bunyan of the Interstate system and I don't care who knows it. I'm Ryder P. Moses and all you people are driving on *my* goddamn road. Don't you spit, don't you litter, don't you pee on the pavement. Just mind your p's and q's and we won't have any trouble."

Trucks pull alongside each other, the drivers peering across suspiciously, then both wave hands over head to deny guilt. They change channels and check each other out—handle, company, destination. They gang up on other loners and demand identification, challenge each other with trivia as if the intruder were a Martian or a Nazi spy. What's the capital of Tennessee. Tennessee Stomper? How far from Laramie to Cheyenne town. Casper Kid? Who won the '38 World Series, Truckin Poppa?

Small convoys form, grow larger, posses ranging eastbound and westbound on I-80. Only the CB can prove that the enemy is not among them, not the neighboring pair of taillights, the row of red up top like Orion's belt. He scares them for a moment, this Ryder P. Moses, scares them out of the air and back into their jarring hotboxes, back to work. But he thrills them a little, too.

"You still there fellas? Good. It's question and answer period.

Answer me this: do you know where your wife or loved one is right now? I mean *really know* for sure? You been gone a long time fellas, and you know how they are. Weak before Temptation. That's why we love em, that's how we get next to em in the first place, int it, fellas? There's just no telling *what* they're up to, is there? How bout that Alabama Rebel, you know where that little girls of yours is right now? What she's gettin herself into? This minute? And you there, Overload, how come the old lady's always so tired when you pull in late at night? What's she done to be so fagged out? She aint been haulin freight all day like you have. Or has she? I tell you fellas, take a tip from old Ryder P., you can't ever be certain of a *thing* in this world. You out here ridin the Interstate, somebody's likely back home ridin that little girl. I mean just *think* about it, think about the way she looks, the faces she makes, the way she starts to smell, the things she says. The *noises* she makes. Now picture them shoes under that bed, ain't they a little too big? Since when did you wear size twelves? Buddy, I hate to break it to you but maybe she's right now giving it, giving it all to some other guy.

"Some size twelve.

"You know how they are, those women, you see them in the truck stops pouring coffee. All those Billie Raes and Bobbi Sues, those Debbies and Annettes, those ass-twitching little things you marry and try to keep in a house. You know how they are. They're not built for one man, fellas, it's a fact of nature. I just want you to think about that for a while, chew on it, remember the last time you saw your woman and figure how long it'll be before you see her again. Think on it, fellas."

And, over the cursing and threats of truckers flooding his channel, he begins to sing.

> *In the phone booth—at the truckstop*
> *All alone.*
> *I listen to the constant ringing—of your phone.*
> *I'd try the bars and hangouts where*
> *You might be found.*
> *But I don't dare.*
> *You might be there.*
> *You're slippin round.*

They curse and threaten but none of them turn him off. And some do think on it. Think as they have so many times before, distrusting with or without evidence, hundred-mile stretches of loneliness and paranoia. How can they know for sure their woman is any different from what they believe all women they meet to be—willing, hot, eager for action? Game in season. What *does* she do, all that riding time?

> *I imagine—as I'm hauling*
> *Back this load.*
> *You waiting for me—at the finish*
> *Of the road.*
> *But as I wait for your hello*
> *There's not a sound.*
> *I start to weep,*
> *You're not asleep,*
> *You're slippin round.*

The truckers overcrowd the channel in their rush to copy him, producing only a squarking complaint, something like a chorus of "Old MacDonald" sung from fifty fathoms deep. Finally the voice of Sweetpea comes through the jam and the others defer to her, as they always do. They have almost all seen her at one time or another, at some table in the Truckers Only section of this or that pit stop, and know she is a regular old gal, handsome looking in a country sort of way and able to field a joke and toss it back. Not so brassy as Colorado Hooker, not so butch as Flatbed Mama, you'd let that Sweetpea carry your load any old day.

"How bout that Ryder P. Moses, how bout that Ryder P. Moses, you out there, sugar? You like to modulate with me a little bit?"

The truckers listen, envying the crazy son for this bit of female attention.

"Ryder P.? This is that Sweetpea moving along bout that 390 mark, do you copy me?"

"Ah yes, the Grande Dame of the Open Road! How's everything with Your Highness tonight?"

"Oh, passable, Mr. Moses, passable. But you don't sound none too good yourself, if you don't mind my saying. I mean we're just worried *sick* about you. You sound a little—over*strained?*"

"*Au contraire,* Madam, *au contraire.*"

She's got him, she has. You catch more flies with honey than with vinegar.

"Now tell me honey, when's the last time you had yourself any sleep?"

"Sleep? *Sleep* she says! Who sleeps?"

"Why just *ev*rybody, Mr. Moses. It's a natural fact."

"That, Madam, is where you are mistaken. Sleep is obsolete, a thing of the bygone ages. It's been synthesized, chemically duplicated and sold at your corner apothecary. You can load up on it before a long trip—"

"Now I just don't know *what* you're talkin bout."

"Insensibility Madam, stupor. The gift of Morpheus."

"Fun is fun, Ryder P. Moses, but you just not making sense. We are *not* amused. And we all getting a little bit *tired* of all your prankin around. And we—"

"Tired, did you say? Depressed? Overweight? Got that run-down feeling? Miles to go before you sleep? Friends and neighbors I got just the thing for you, a miracle of modern pharmacology! Vim and vigor, zip and zest, bright eyes and bushy tails—all these can be *yours,* neighbor, relief is just a swallow away! A couple of Co-Pilots in the morning orange juice. Purple Hearts for lunch, a mouthful of Coast-to-Coast for the wee hours of the night, and you'll droop no more. Ladies and gents, the best cure for time and distance is Speed. And we're all familiar with that, aren't we folks? We've all popped a little pep in our day, haven't we? Puts you on top of the world and clears your sinuses to boot. Wire yourself home with a little methamphetamine sulfate, melts in your mind, not in your mouth. No chocolate mess. Step right up and get on the ride, pay no heed to that man with the eight-ball eyes! Start with a little propadrine maybe, from the little woman's medicine cabinet? Clear up that stuffy nose? Then work your way up to the full-tilt boogie, twelve-plus grams of Crystal a day! It kind of grows on you, doesn't it, neighbor? Start eating that Sleep and you won't want to eat anything else. You know all about it, don't you, brothers and sisters of the Civilian Band, you've all been on that roller coaster. The only way to fly."

"Now Ryder, you just calm—"

> *"Benzedrine, Dexedrine,*
> *We got the stash!"*

he chants like a high-school cheerleader.

> *"Another thousand miles*
> *Before the crash."*

"Mr. Moses, you can't—"

> *"Coffee and aspirin,*
> *No-Doz, Meth.*
> *Spasms, hypertension,*
> *Narcolepsy, death.*
>
> *"Alpha, methyl,*
> *Phenyl too,*
> *Ethyl-amine's good for you!*
>
> *"Cause when you're up you're up,*
> *An when you're down you're down,*
> *But when you're up behind Crystal*
> *You're upside down!"*

The airwaves crackle with annoyance. Singing on the CB! Sassing their woman, their Sweetpea, with drug talk and four-syllable words!

"—man's crazy—"
"—s'got to go—"
"—FCC ever hears—"
"—fix his wagon—"
"—like to catch—"
"—hophead—"
"—pill-poppin—"
"—weird talkin—"
"—turn him *off!*"

"Now boys," modulates Sweetpea, cooing soft and smooth, "I'm sure we can talk this whole thing out. Ryder P., honey, whoever you are, you must be runnin out of *fuel*. I mean you been going at it for *days* now, flittin round this Innerstate never coming to light. Must be just all *out* by now, aren't you?"

"I'm going strong, little lady, I got a bottle full of energy left and a thermos of Maxwell House to wash them down with."

"I don't mean *that,* Mr. Moses, I mean fuel *awl.* Int your tanks a little low? Must be runnin pert near empty, aren't you?"

"Madam, you have a point."

"Well if you don't fuel up pretty soon, you just gon be out of *luck,* Mister, they isn't but one more place westbound between here and that Grand Island town. Now Imo pull in that Bosselman's up ahead, fill this old hog of mine up. Wynch you just join me, I'll buy you a cup of coffee and we'll have us a little chitchat? That truck you got, whatever it is, can't run on no *pills.*"

"Madam, it's a date. I got five or six miles to do and then it's Bosselman's for me and Old Paint here. Yes indeedy."

The other channels come alive. Bosselman's, on the westbound, he's coming down! That Sweetpea could talk tears from a statue, an oyster from its shell. Ryder P. Moses in person, hotdamn!

They barrel onto the off-ramp, eastbound and westbound, full tanks and empty, a steady caravan of light bleeding off the main artery, leaving only scattered four-wheelers to carry on. They line up behind the diner in rows, twin stacks belching, all ears.

"This is that Ryder P. Moses, this is that Ryder P. Moses, in the parking lot at Bosselman's. Meet you in the coffee shop, Sweetpea."

Cab doors swing open and they vault down onto the gravel, some kind of reverse Grand Prix start, with men trotting away from their machines to the diner. They stampede at the door and mill suspiciously. Is that him, is that him? Faces begin to connect with handles, remembered from some previous nighttime break. Hey, there's old Roadrunner, Roadrunner, this is Arkansas Traveler, I known him from before, he aint it, who's that over there? Overload, you say? You was up on I-29 the other night, north of Council Bluffs, wunt you? What you mean no, I had you on for pert near a half hour! You were where? Who says? Roadrunner, how could you talk to him on Nebraska 83 when I'm talking to him on I-29? Overload, somebody been takin your name in vain. What's that? You modulated with me yesterday from Rawlins? Buddy, I'm out of that Davenport town last evening. I'm *west* bound. Clutch Cargo, the one and only, always was and always will be. You're kidding! The name-droppin snake! Fellas we got to get to the bottom of this, but quick.

It begins to be clear, as they form into groups of three or four who can vouch for each other, that this Ryder P. Moses works in mysterious ways. That his voice, strained through capacitors and diodes, can pass for any of theirs, that he knows them, handle and style. It's outrageous, it is, it's like stealing mail or wiretapping, like forgery. How long has he gotten away with it, what has he said using their identities, what secrets spilled or discovered? If Ryder P. Moses has been each of them from time to time, what is to stop him from being one of them now? Which old boy among them is running a double life, which has got a glazed look around the eyes, a guilty twitch at the mouth? They file in to find Sweetpea sitting at a booth, alone.

"Boys," she says, "I believe I just been stood up."

They grumble back to their rigs, leaving waitresses with order pads gaping. The civilians in the diner buzz and puzzle—some mass, vigilante threat? Teamster extortion? Paramilitary maneuvers? They didn't like the menu? The trucks roar from the Bosselman's abruptly as they came.

On the Interstate again, they hear the story from Axle Sally. Sally broadcasts from the Husky three miles up on the eastbound side. Seems a cattle truck is pulled up by the pumps there, left idling. The boy doesn't see the driver, all he knows is it's pretty ripe, even for a stock-hauler. Something more than the usual cowshit oozing out from the air spaces. He tries to get a look inside but it's hard to get that close with the smell and all, so he grabs his flashlight and plays it around in back. And what do you think he sees? Dead. Dead for some time from the look of them, ribs showing, legs splayed, a heap of bad meat. Between the time it takes the boy to run in to tell Sally till they get back out to the pumps, whoever it was driving the thing has pumped himself twenty gallons and taken a powder. Then comes the call to Sally's radio, put it on my tab, he says, Ryder P. Moses, westbound.

They can smell it in their minds, the men who have run cattle or have had a stock wagon park beside them in the sleeping lot of some truck stop, the thought of it makes them near sick. Crazy. Stone wild crazy.

"Hello there again, friends and neighbors, this is Ryder P. Moses, the Demon of the Dotted Line, the Houdini of the Highways. Hell on eighteen wheels. Sorry if I inconvenienced anybody with the little change of plans there, but fuel oil was going for two cents a gallon cheaper at the Husky, and I never could pass up a bargain. Funny I didn't see any of you folks there, y'ought to be a little sharper with your consumer affairs. These are hard times, people, don't see how you can afford to let that kind of savings go by. I mean us truckers of all people should see the writing on the wall, the bad news in the dollars and cents department. Do we 'Keep America Moving' or don't we? And you know as well as me, there ain't shit moving these days. Poor honest independent don't have a Chinaman's chance, and even Union people are being unsaddled left and right. Hard times, children. Just enough stuff has to get from here to there to keep us in business. Hell, the only way to make it is to carry miscellaneous freight. Get that per-item charge on a full load and you're golden. Miscellaneous—"

(The blue flashers are coming now, zipping by the westbound truckers, sirenless in twos and threes, breaking onto the channel to say don't panic, boys, all we want is the cattle truck. All the trophy we need for tonight is Moses, you just lay back and relax. Oh those Smokies, when they set their minds to a thing they don't hold back, they hump after it full choke and don't spare the horse. Ryder P. Moses, your ass is *grass*. Smokey the Bear on your case and he will douse your fire. Oh yes.)

"—freight. Miscellaneous freight. Think about it, friends and neighbors, brothers and sisters, think about what exactly it is we haul all over God's creation here, about the goods and what they mean. About what they actually mean to you and me and everyone else in this great and good corporate land of ours. Think of what you're hauling right now. Ambergris for Amarillo? Gaskets for Gary? Oil for Ogalalla, submarines for Schenectady? Veal for Vermillion?"

(The Smokies moving up at nearly a hundred per, a shooting stream in the outside lane, for once allied to the truckers.)

"Tomato for Mankato, manna for Tarzana, stew for Kalamazoo, jerky for Albuquerque. Fruit for Butte."

(Outdistancing all the legitimate truckers, the Smokies are a blue pulsing in the sky ahead, the whole night on the blink.)

"Boise potatoes for Pittsburgh pots. Scottsbluff sugar for Tampa tea. Forage and fertilizer. Guns and caskets. Bull semen and hamburger. Sweet-corn, soy, stethoscopes and slide rules.

Androids and zinnias. But folks, somehow we always come back empty. Come back less than we went. Diminished. It's a law of nature, it is, a law—"

They come upon it at the 375 marker, a convention of Bears flashing around a cattle truck on the shoulder of the road. What looks to be a boy or a very young man spread-eagled against the side of the cab, a half-dozen official hands probing his hidden regions. The trucks slow, one by one, but there is no room to stop. They roll down their co-pilot windows, but the only smell is the thick electric-blue of too many cops in one place.

"You see im? You see im? Just a kid!"

"—prolly stole it in the first place—"

"—gone crazy on drugs—"

"—fuckin hippie or somethin—"

"—got his ass but good—"

"—know who he is?"

"—know his handle?"

"—seem im before?"

"—the end of him, anyhow."

All order and etiquette gone with the excitement, they chew it over among themselves, who he might be, why he went wrong, what they'll do with him. Curiosity, and already a kind of disappointment. That soon it will be all over, all explained, held under the dull light of police classification, made into just some crackpot kid who took a few too many diet pills to help him through the night. It is hard to believe that the pale, skinny boy frisked in their headlights was who kept them turned around for weeks, who pried his way into their nightmares, who haunted the CB and outran the Smokies. That he could be the one who made the hours between Lincoln and Cheyenne melt into suspense and tension, that he could be—

"Ryder P. Moses, westbound on 80. Where *are* all you people?"

"Who?"

"What?"

"Where?"

"Ryder P. Moses, who else? Out here under that big black sky, all by his lonesome. I sure would preciate some company. Seems like you all dropped out of the running a ways back. Thought I seen some Bear tracks in my rear view, maybe that's it. Now it's just me an a couple tons of beef. Can't say these steers is much for conversation, though. Nosir, you just can't beat a little palaver with your truckin' brothers and sisters on the old CB to pass the time. Do I have a copy out there? Anybody?"

They switch to the channel they agreed on at the Bosselman's, and the word goes on down the line. He's still loose! He's still out there! The strategy is agreed on quickly—silent running. Let him sweat it out alone, talk to himself for a while and haul ass to catch him. It will be a race.

(Coyote, in an empty flatbed, takes the lead.)

"You're probably all wondering why I called you together tonight. Education. I mean to tell you some things you ought to know. Things about life, death, eternity. You know, tricks of the trade. The popular mechanics of the soul. A little exchange of ideas, communication, I-talk-you-listen, right?"

(Up ahead, far ahead, Coyote sees taillights. Taillights moving at least as fast as he, almost eighty-five in a strong crosswind. He muscles the clutch and puts the hammer down.)

"Friends, it's all a matter of wheels. Cycles. Clock hand always ends up where it started out, sun always dips back under the cornfield, people always plowed back into the ground. Take this beef chain I'm in on. We haul the semen to stud, the calves to rangeland, the one-year-olds to the feedlot, then to the slaughterhouse the packer the supermarket the corner butcher the table of J.Q. Public. J.Q. scarfs it down, puts a little body in his jizz, pumps a baby a year into the wife till his heart fattens and flops, and next thing you know he's pushing up grass on the lone pray-ree. You always end up less than what you were. The universe itself is shrinking. In cycles."

(Coyote closes to within a hundred yards. It is a cattle truck. He can smell it through his vent. When he tries to come closer it accelerates over a hundred, back end careening over two lanes. Coyote feels himself losing control, eases up. The cattle truck eases too, keeping a steady hundred yards between them. They settle back to eighty per.)

"Engines. You can grease them, oil them, clean their filters and replace their plugs, recharge them, antifreeze and STP them, treat them like a member of the family, but poppa, the miles take their toll, Time and Distance bring us all to rust. We haul engines from Plant A to Plant B to be seeded in bodies, we haul them to the dealers, buy them and waltz around a couple numbers, then drag them to the scrapyard. Junk City, U.S.A., where they break down into the iron ore of a million years from now. Some cycles take longer than others. Everything in this world is a long fall, a coming to rest, and an engine only affects where the landing will be.

The cure for Time and Distance is Speed. Did you know that if you could travel at the speed of light you'd never age? That if you went any faster than it, you would get younger? Think about that one, friends and neighbors, a cycle reversed. What happens when you reach year zero, egg and tadpole time, and keep speeding along? Do you turn into your parents? Put that in your carburetor and slosh it around."

And on he goes, into Relativity, the relationship of matter and energy, into the theory of the universe as a great Mobius strip, a snake swallowing its own tail. Leaving Coyote far behind, though the hundred yards between stays constant. On he goes, into the life of a cell, gerontology, cryogenics, hibernation theory. Through the seven stages of man and beyond, through the history of aging, the literature of immortality.

(Through Grand Island and Kearney, through Lexington and Cozad and Gothenburg, with Coyote at his heels, through a hundred high-speed miles of physics and biology and lunatic-fringe theology.)

"You can beat them, though, all these cycles. Oh yes, I've found the way. Never stop. If you never stop you can outrun them. It's when you lose your momentum that they get you.

"Take Sleep, the old whore. The seducer of the vital spark. Ever look at yourself in the mirror after Sleep has had hold of you, ever check your face out? Eyes pouched, neck lined, mouth puckered, it's all been worked on, cycled. Aged. Wrinkle City. The cycle catches you napping and carries you off a little closer to the ground. Sleep, ladies, when it has you under, those crows come tiptoeing on your face, sinking their tracks into you. Sleep, gents, you wake from her half stiff with urine, stumble out to do an old man's aimless, too-yellow pee. It bloats your prostate, pulls your paunch, plugs your ears, and gauzes your eyes. It sucks you, Sleep, sucks you dry and empty, strains the dream from your mind and the life from your body.

(Reflector posts ripping by, engine complaining, the two of them barreling into Nebraska on the far edge of control.)

"And you people let it have you, you surrender with open arms. Not me. Not Ryder P. Moses. I swallow my sleep in capsules and keep one step ahead. Rest not, rust not. Once you break from the cycle, escape that dull gravity, then, people, you travel in a straight line and there is nothing so pure in this world. The Interstate goes on forever and you never have to get off.

"And it's beautiful. Beautiful. The things a sleeper never sees open up to you. The most beautiful dream is the waking one, the one that never ends. From a straight line you see all the cycles going on without you, night fading in and out, the sun's arch, stars forming and shifting in their signs. The night especially, the blacker the better, your headlights making a ghost of color on the road side, focusing to climb the white line. You feel like you can ride deeper and deeper into it, that night is a state you never cross, but only get closer and closer to its center. And in the daytime there's the static of cornfields, cornfields, cornfields, flat monotony like a hum in your eye, like you're going so fast it seems you're standing still, that the country is a still life on your windshield."

(It begins to weave gently in front of Coyote now, easing to the far right, nicking the shoulder gravel, straightening for a few miles, then drifting left. Nodding. Coyote hangs back a little further, held at bay by a whiff of danger.)

"Do you know what metaphor is, truckin mamas and poppas? Have you ever met with it in your waking hours? Benzedrine, there's a metaphor for you, and a good one. For sleep. It serves the same purpose but makes you understand better, makes everything clearer, opens the way to more metaphor. Friends and neighbors, have you ever seen dinosaurs lumbering past you, the road sizzle like a fuse, night drip down like old blood? I have, people. I've seen things only gods and the grandfather stars have seen, I've seen dead men sit in my cab beside me and living ones melt like wax. When you break through the cycle you're beyond the laws of man, beyond CB manners or Smokies' sirens or statutes of limitations. You're beyond the laws of nature, time, gravity, friction, forget them. The only way to win is never to stop. Never to stop. Never to stop."

The sentences are strung out now, a full minute or two between them.

"The only escape from friction is a vacuum."

(Miles flying under North Platte glowing vaguely ahead on the horizon, Coyote, dogged, hangs on.)

There is an inexplicable crackling on the wire, as if he were growing distant. There is nothing for miles to interfere between them. "The shortest distance—between two points—ahh—a straight line."

(Two alone on the plain, tunneling Nebraska darkness.)

"Even the earth—is falling. Even—the sun—is burning out."

(The side-to-side drifting more pronounced now, returns to the middle more brief. Coyote strains to pick the voice from electric jam, North Platte's display brightens. Miles pass.)

"Straight—"

There is a very loud crackling now, his speaker open but his words hung, a crackling past the Brady exit, past Maxwell. (Coyote creeping up a bit, then lagging as the stock-hauler picks up speed and begins to slalom for real, Coyote tailing it like a hunter after a gut-ripped animal spilling its last, and louder crackling as it lurches, fishtails, and lurches ahead wheels screaming smoke spewing saved only by the straightness of the road and crackling back when Coyote breaks into the Band yelling Wake up! Wake up! Wake up! pulling horn and flicking lights till the truck ahead steadies, straddling half on half off the right shoulder in direct line with the upspeeding concrete support of an overpass and he speaks. Calm and clear and direct.)

"This is Ryder P. Moses," he says. "Going west. Good night and happy motoring."

(Coyote swerves through the flameout, fights for the road as the sky begins a rain of beef.)

✰✰✰ The Floating Truth

by Grace Paley

The day I knocked, all the slats were flat. "Where are you, Lionel?" I shouted. "In the do-funny?"

"For goodness' sake, be quiet," he said, unlatching the back door. "I'm the other side of the coin."

I nicked him with my forefinger. "You don't ring right, Charley. You're counterfeit."

"Come on in and settle," he said. "Keep your hat on. The coat rack's out of order."

I had visited before. The seats were washable plaid plastic— easy to care for—and underfoot was the usual door-to-door fuzz. In graceful disarray philodendrons rose and fell from the back window ledge.

"How in the world can you see to drive, Marlon?"

"Well, baby, I don't drive it much," he said. "It isn't safe."

He offered me an apple from the glove compartment.

"Nature's toothbrush," I said dreamily. "How've you been, Eddie?"

He sighed. "Things never looked better."

He hopped out the front door and crawled in the rear. He was not a seat climber. "Truthfully, I would have phoned you no later than tonight," he said. He snapped the blinds horizontal, and from the east the morning glared at our pale faces. He took a paper and pencil out of a small mahogany file cabinet built along the rear of the front seat. "Let's get down to brass tacks," he said. "What do you want to do?"

"What does anyone want to do?"

GRACE PALEY (b. 1922) is the author of *The Little Disturbances of Man* (1959) and *Enormous Changes at the Last Minute* (1974).

"Let me ask the questions," he said. "What do *you* want to do?"

"Oh . . . something worth-while," I said. "Well, make a contribution . . . you know what I mean . . . help out somehow . . . do good."

"Please!" he said bitterly. "Don't waste my time. Every sonofabitch wants to do good."

"Why, that's nice," I said. "What a wonderful social trend. In these terrible times it's marvelous news."

"It's marvelous news . . ." he squeaked in a high girl-voice. "Don't be an idiot. All of time is terrible. You should have lived in a little farming village during the Hundred Years' War. Anyway, do you realize you're paying me by the hour? Let's get started. What can you *do?*"

I was surprised to hear that I was paying him by the hour. Still, for all I know, despite their appearance, these times may not be terrible at all.

"I can type. I went to business school for three months and I can type."

"Don't worry," he said. "I've gotten jobs for virgins. I could place a pediatrician in the Geriatric Clinic."

"If you're so great, Bubbles, how come you don't even have a home?"

"I've only just found myself," he said, turning inward. On the outside he was a mirror image of a face with a dead center. His eyes were blue. The pupils were dark and immovable. He never saw anything out of the corner of his eye but swiveled his whole head to stare at it. His hair was blond, darkening in a terrible rush before the gray could become general. All his sex characteristics were secondary, which did not prevent him from asking me after our first day's work, "Give me a bunny hug, baby?" I didn't mind at all and did, goosing him gently. It seemed to me he'd like that a lot. I am not considered wild, but I am kind.

I scraped a ham sandwich out of my dungarees and offered him half. "*Gasoline* is what I need," he said peevishly. "I was going to call for a man who invited me to La Vie for a business deal."

Just then the phone rang. He lunged over the front seat for it. "What good luck, Edsel," he chortled. "You got me just as I was pulling up to a meter. Hold it a moment while I disengage." He made grunting noises as though great effort were involved because of tonnage, then resumed his conversation. "Yes? About tonight? I'm not sure I can make it . . . I've got to be out all day . . ."

I waved a one-dollar bill across the windshield mirror. "Ah . . . make it quarter to ten, so I have time to eat. . . . No, that's not necessary . . . No . . . Well, if you insist, at least allow me to call for you. I'll stop by at eight-thirty. . . . Great . . . It'll be marvelous to talk with you again. *A riverderci.*"

"Here," I said, "is a dollar. Petrol."

"I appreciate it," he said.

The Edsel he met at eight-thirty, honking his horn before a canopied doorman, was Jonathan Stubblefield, but don't try to reach him because he's unlisted. His eyes were pale as the moon. They drove here and yon, hip-flasked, unwatered and unsodaed, uniced and defrosted, looped in one another's consonants. Lack of communication made them appear to be lovers.

"Do you have a friend?" asked Jonathan Stubblefield. "Yes, a girl," said my pal, his nose always to the grindstone. Jonathan Stubblefield misunderstood. "Hotcha!" he replied. "I have a friend myself, but the goddamn family—— What do you think of the family?" he asked, trying to make sense of his entire life.

"The Family of Man? Oh, I believe in it. But look here, Edsel . . . this girl I'm talking about is not a sexual partner. She's a business associate. Lively, alert, young, charming, clever, enthusiastic. How can you use her?"

"Oh boy," said Jonathan Stubblefield, stupefied. "Upside down, cross-country, her choice. Any way she says."

"You still misunderstand me. It's her business affairs I'm in charge of."

"Oh," said Jonathan Stubblefield. "Oh," he said, "in that case send me a résumé," and passed out.

"But you didn't tell him anything about me," I complained the following afternoon.

"Why should I? He didn't tell me anything about himself. Do you think his real name is Stubblefield? What's the matter with you? Don't put yourself on a platter. What are you—a roast duck, everything removable with a lousy piece of flatware? Be secret. Turn over on your side. Let them guess if you're stuffed. That's how I got where I am."

The organization of his ideas was all wrong; I was drawn to the memory of myself—a mere stripling of a girl—the day I learned that the shortest distance between two points is a great circle.

"Anyway, you ought to think in shorter sentences," he suggested, although I hadn't said a word. Old Richard-the-Liver-Headed, he saw right through to the heart of the matter, my syntax.

"Well, now, just go somewhere for a couple of days. Home, maybe. How about home? Go to the movies. I don't give a damn where you go. I'll have the résumé ready. I've pinpointed Edsel. He's avid to have an employee."

"I'll do what you say." I had to get started somehow. I had been out of school six weeks and was beginning to feel nearly unemployable.

I ducked out of the car. A cop came to the door and squinted authoritatively. "Listen, Squatface, I told you Tuesday, get this hearse to a mummery." He was one of those college cops, in it for the pension. Security is an essential. How else face the future?

"Ran out of gas," my chum whispered as soft as soup.

"Here's a dollar," I replied. "More petrol."

It rained for three days. On the fourth morning, I received a telegram. PHONE OUT OF ORDER. MEET ME USUAL PLACE. SEE EDSEL. LIKE FLYNN, YOU'RE IN.

At noon I found them admiring new white tires. (These are the good times.) I was all dressed up and they were all dressed up. Jonathan Stubblefield, observed me. His eyes *were* pale as the moon. He winked and a tear rolled down his smooth cheek. "I have an occluded lachrymal duct," he explained.

"Let's go to the Vilamar Cafeteria where we can talk." He added with pride, "It's on me."

We proceeded at once, single file, Stubblefield leading. In the cafeteria we seated ourselves deferentially around a rotating altar of condiments and began in communal reverence.

"You seem so young," said Jonathan Stubblefield. "I can't really believe that time has passed. Take a good look at me. A

man of thirty-one. Inside my head, a photostatic account of Pearl
Harbor. I can still see it so clear . . . the snow just stippling the
rocks——"

"Snow?"

"Snow. The absolute quiet and then that wild hum and then
the noise. And then the whole world plunged into disaster."

"Oh my!"

"You were too young. But I remember—Geneva, Yalta, the
San Francisco conference, much-scoffed-at Acheson; those days
were the hope of the world. I remember it like yesterday."

"You do?"

"What sort of memories can you young people of today have?
You have a reputation for clothes and dope. You have no sense
of history; you have no tragic sense. What is Alsace-Lorraine?
Can you tell me, my dear? What problem does it face, even
today? You don't know. Not innocent, but ignorant."

"You're right," I said.

"Of course," he said. "You can't deny it. The truth finds its
own level and floats."

"Coffee?" asked Roderick the middleman.

"Not me," said Edsel. "Baked apple for me. And salmon
salad. Jello maybe. I'm on a diet." He patted his tummy. "Now
tell me about yourself. I want to know you better."

I tossed my pony tail, agleam with natural oils, and said:
"What can I say?"

"You can tell me about yourself. Who you are, where you
come from, what your interests are, your hobbies. Who's your
favorite boy friend, for instance?"

I told him who I was, where I came from, what my interests
and my hobbies were. "But I'm still waiting for Mr. Right to
come out of the West."

"You and I have a lot in common," he said sadly. "I'm still
waiting for Mr. Right too. I'm paraphrasing, of course. I mean
Miss Right.

"You know, you dress beautifully. You look like a rose. Yes, a
rose is what is indicated." He touched gently that part of the
décolletage furthest from my chin.

He looked at his watch, which had a barometer tucked in
somewhere along its circumference. "Pressure rising; I've got to
run. Tell our friend 'excuse me' for me. Tell him you're hired,

pending résumé. I've got to have that résumé. I don't do business without documentation."

He stood up and transported his gaze slowly from the lady's rest room to the steam counter, the short order table, the grand coffee urns, and finally to the great doors which rested where their rubber stoppers had established them.

"I am lord of all I survey," he murmured. He smiled benefi- cently on my shining face, then turned on his heels, like the sound of the old order changing, and disappeared into the Götter- dämmerung of the revolving doors.

"Oh, Everett, what an interesting man!" I said. We split the salmon salad, but jello reminds me of junket.

"Well, what do you think of him? Not bad. He's the wave of the future. A man who can use leisure. Here's the résumé." He was very businesslike and continued, as he buttered a hard seeded roll, to give me orders for my own good. "Type it. Do a nice job . . . only it has to look home-typed; the only one of its kind. Maybe you ought to make a mistake. If he thinks you've plastered the city with them, you're finished . . . Look it over. It's a day's work, and I'm kind of proud of it."

I riffled and read. "Say, it's three pages, legal size. Do you know it's three pages?"

"Aha!" he said in pride.

"Oh, please, it's ridiculous. What'll I do if he calls any of these people?"

"No, no, no. He *wants* to hire you. He's crazy about you; he wants to be your friend. When he sees all these words, he'll be happy and feel free. He may not even read them."

I looked it over again. These are only a few of the jobs with which he had papered my past. The first, in advertising:

THE GREEN HOUSE: In eight exciting months I brought THE GREEN HOUSE'S name before the public in seven ways —all inexpensive: Two-color posters were distributed. No copy used. A green house on an eggshell-white background. Two-color matchbooks—no copy. Two-color personal cards for all person- nel. THE GREEN HOUSE itself was finally painted green. Here and there throughout the city where people least expected it (park benches, lamp posts, etc.), the question asked in green paint: What Is Green? In infinitesimal green print below and to the right the reply: THE GREEN HOUSE is green.

"What in hell is THE GREEN HOUSE?"

"I don't know," he giggled.

Here's another; this, under the heading of Public Relations:

The Philadelphia: An association of professionals working in the Law and allied fields hired me to bring Law and its possibilities to women everywhere. I traveled throughout the country for five months by bus, station wagon, train, and also by air under the name of Gladys Hand. Within nine months there were 11 per cent more users of legal services. The average fee had jumped $7.20 over the previous year. Crowded court calendars required statute revisions in seven states. *The Philadelphia* ascribed these improvements to my work in their behalf.

And more:

THE KITCHEN INSTITUTE: Through the medium of The Kitchen Institute Press's "The Kettle Calls," we inaugurated a high-pressure plan to return women to the kitchen. "The kitchen you are leaving may be your home," was one of many slogans used. By radio and television, as well as by ads taken in Men's publications and on Men's pages in newspapers (sports, finance, etc.), Men were told to ask their wives as they came in the door each night: "What's cooking?" In this way the prestige of women in kitchens everywhere was enhanced and the need and desire for kitchens accelerated.

At the very end, as though it were of no importance whatsoever, he had typed "More Facts" and then listed: Single, twenty-three, Grad. Green Valley College for Women. Additional Courses, Sorbonne, in Short Story Writing and Public Speaking. Social Chairman of G O in High School.

"Oh, for God's sake," I said. "That last is pretty silly."

"It may be silly to you, but if he reads it at all he'll certainly read the last line and he'll like that. 'A girl who was lightheaded enough to be social chairman in high school may still be spinning,' is the way I see it."

"But listen," I told him two days later. "I'm not twenty-three."

"You will be, you will be," he assured me.

That afternoon I was helping him water the philodendrons. I was a little excited about being on the threshold of my future, and some water dripped down the back seat and filled the crevices of the upholstery.

"My God, you infuriate me sometimes," he said, tearing the

watering can from my hand. "Can't you watch what you're doing?" Poor Dick, he was a covey of twittering angers. "You're so damn stupid!" he screamed. He poured the dregs into an open ash tray and sprinkled the windows. "Get something, get something," he cried. I ran down to the store and bought an old Sunday *Times* to help clean up the mess. I realized that, against great odds, he was only trying to make a home. When I returned he was on the phone: "Can't have you down here. Place is incredible! Let me pick you up. I want to close the deal. It's been pending too long . . . I said 10 per cent . . . 10 per cent is what I want. That's not excessive."

"What deal?" I asked.

"Big deal," he replied sotto voce. "O.K."

The phone rang again. "Edsel!" he beamed. "Long time no see. Long time no hear also . . . Of course," he said. "Ha-ha. 'Can she do shorthand?' Baby, he wants to know if you can do shorthand! Ha-ha, Edsel, she's a speed demon!"

"I can't," I whispered.

He twisted his trunk to reach me and then kicked me on the shin.

He hung up. "O.K.," he said. "Go on over. He's all yours. Good luck. You'll get my bill in the morning mail."

Well, that is how I got my first job. I entered the business world, my senses alert. I quietly watched and voraciously listened. Every 9 A.M. in the five-day week I opened the heavy oak door on which a sign in Old Regal said STUBBLEFIELD. I kept my pencils sharpened. I read the morning papers in the morning and the evening papers in the afternoon, in case some question about current events should arise.

It was true, he had been avid to have an employee and seemed happy. Often his mother called to ask him to please come to lunch or cocktails. Occasionally his father called but left no name. At decent intervals I was instructed to say he was out of town on business. He entrusted me with the key, and when he was away for two or three days, I was in full charge.

I had planned to remain with the job for at least a year, to learn office procedure and persistence.

But one Monday at about 10 A.M. the door opened and a camel-hair blonde, all textured in cashmere, appeared. "I've just been hired by Mr. Stubblefield," she said, "via Western Union."

She flapped a manila half sheet under my nose. "I met him in Bronxville last graduation day." She looked around. There were mauve walls and army colored file cabinets. "I just love a two-girl office," she said, expecting to be my friend. "What's he like? Does he give severance pay?"

She was followed by a desk and a Long Island boy from the Bell Telephone Company. I didn't say anything to anyone but filed my *Time* and unfolded my New York *Herald Tribune*. I resharpened my pencil and proceeded to underline whatever required underlining.

"A lot of paper work?" asked Serena, a cool revision of my former self. I had nothing to say.

Jonathan Stubblefield poked his snout out of the inner office. "Get to know each other, girls. You're exactly the same age."

That information unsettled me.

"You don't know how old I am," I said. "Anyway, what do you need her for? I'm doing a job. I'm doing as good a job as you require. This is a deliberate slap in my face. It is."

"We're in the middle of an expanding economy, for goodness' sake!" said Jonathan Stubblefield. "Don't be sentimental. Besides, I thought we could do with some college people."

"But there isn't enough work to go around," I said bravely. "There's nothing to do."

"It's my company, isn't it?" he said belligerently. "If I want to, I can hire forty people to do nothing. NOTHING."

I looked at Jonathan Stubblefield, a man in tears—but only because of his lachrymal ducts—a man nevertheless with truth on his side.

"There's room for everybody," he said. But he would not reconsider. He probably never really liked me in the first place.

As I had never used the phone for private conversations, I had to wait until five to call my vocational counselor from a phone booth.

"Come on down, baby," he said, giving me his latitude and longitude. "I don't know what you want to talk about. You owe me fifteen dollars already."

Because of cross-town traffic, it was nearly dark by the time I reached him. I had purchased a rare roast beef sandwich with coleslaw and gift-wrapped it with two green rubber bands. But he laughed in my face. "I only eat out these days; I hate puttering around with drinks and dishes." We gave the sandwich to a passing child who immediately ripped off the aluminum foil and dumped the food into the gutter. She folded the foil neatly and slipped it into her pocket.

Surly Sam turned on the car heater and dimmed the lights. "Oh my," I said, "it's lovely here now. What are those—crocuses?"

"Yes," he said, "crocuses. I take some pride in raising them in the fall."

"Lovely!" I repeated.

"Well," he said, "what's on your mind? How's the job?"

"What job? You call that a job?"

"You're a character!" he said, laying it all at my door. "What'd you expect to do—give polio shots?"

"What's so wrong with that? That's not the most terrible thing in the world."

He entangled all my hopes in one popeyed look. "And where would you go from there? Let me tell you something. I sent you to Edsel . . . I worked three days on the résumé for him, because I believe that Edsel is going places and anyone on board will be going with him. Believe me, what you're now doing constitutes some of the finest experience available to a young person who wants to set sail for tomorrow.

"Ah yes," he continued philosophically, swiveling slightly to see how absorbent I looked, "ah yes—you could do more. Now if you were really sincere, you could take your shoes off and stand on a street corner with a sign saying: 'He died for me.'" He paused. I didn't comment, because I was waiting for that particular hint that would tell me where I was going, in case it was there. "Or else," he suggested, brightening, "leave the habitations of men—like me."

My heart sank in terror.

He felt he had gone far enough, and we leaned back in the rosy décor, smoking across one artless silence after another. Finally he grimaced out of his usual face, raised an eyebrow, and swiveled. "Ah, what's the use, baby?"

"How true," I said. I owed him something, and in due time I paid him something. Beyond that it was the Sabbath. "It's morning, Morton," I said. "Good night!"

He walked me to the rump of the car.

"I'm not mad," I said. We shook hands and I went my way.

I was directed to the future, but it is hard for me to part with experience. Before I reached the subway entrance, I turned for a last look. He stood in front of the car, glancing up and down the street. There wasn't a soul in his sight. Not even me.

Then he peed. He did not pee like a boy who expects to span a continent, but like a man—in a puddle.

"Good night!" I called, hoping to startle him. He never heard me but stared at the dusty trash he had driven out of the gutters through oblique tunnels that led to the sea. He tightened his belt and hunched his shoulders against the weather. Having left the habitations of men, you can understand he had a special problem. When he was conveniently located he stopped in the city park. At other times he had to use dark one-way streets to help maintain the water levels of this airsick earth.

I gathered fifteen cents from several pockets and started down the subway steps when I heard him shout. In all modesty, I think he was calling me. . . . "Hey, beautiful!" he asseverated. "You're pretty damn diurnal yourself."

✩✩✩ The Maggot Principle
by William O'Rourke

I do two things each day that I hate to do. I go to sleep and I wake up. Knowing this, it is not as easy to rail against that which I do that I have no wish to do. We are all extorted by chance, though the guise makes a difference, and it is not unusual to come to a place and find yourself engaged in an enterprise opposite your original intentions.

A small town is different from a large city that any grotesques you see, you are likely to see again, as in a recurrent bad dream. And this is not even a small town, but a summer resort, the bait on the tip of this hook of New England. When winter comes, those who remain are the stragglers any traveling thing leaves behind. You may think of touring circuses, fairs, religious zealots with tent compounds, or a retreating army, and that is close to the situation. There is a meanness in the shut-up buildings: plywood over the windows as if the glass has grown cataracts. What makes people stay is the same inclination that brings them to the lip of an extinct volcano or a notable man's grave.

Through the winter there is only one institution that functions; it is the Fish Factory. It appears another ruin, cited for extinction. Listing walls nonwithstanding, it still prospers within. The building is kept together by what it is: three floors of cold storage is its center and the ice gives solid structure. If the freezers were shut off, it is said by those who have worked there longest, the building would collapse. The ice is like anger, which steadies men.

WILLIAM O'ROURKE (b. 1945) is the author of *The Harrisburg 7 and the New Catholic Left* (1972) and *The Meekness of Isaac* (1974).

* * *

The employees of the Fish Factory have a grim cheerfulness that comes to people who are glad to have a job, any job. The manager who hired me, seeing drawn across my face a map of Midwestern industry, advised me to take other employment, if I could find it, though his expression was that of the only grocer in town who tells you to buy your produce elsewhere if you don't like the price.

The stench, the unskinned odor, though never gotten used to, becomes familiar and then unrecognised. My training began in the packing room, where lobster tails are weighed and sorted and put in packages ready for stores. One thousand frozen lobster tails smell like caged white mice. Stainless steel tables, a cement floor, Toledo scales, gray plastic pans, and cartons of frozen lobster tails from South Africa. Who packed these across the Atlantic? I wonder as I crack a block of frozen lobster tails across the edge of the table. It shatters, an ancient clay pot filled with coins, into fifty little tails.

Could any machine equal the chaotic precision of four people sorting lobster tails? Flinging them, after checking their weight, into eight stainless steel pans, separated in two by wooden dividers. The air is as full of flying lobster tails as the sky above Kennedy Airport is with planes.

Casey, an aging lesbian, who does the final weighing, has masculinized every woman in the room by circumcising their names. Alice is Al, Lucy is Lu, Frieda is Fred. Casey is boss of the radio, a tiny plastic thing that sits on a crate. Its cord snakes up the wall to a high socket as if the music coming from it held it erect like a summoned cobra.

Frozen lobster tails hit pans sounding like cutlery dropped in a sink. The windows are covered with polyethylene; a few late summer flies cling to it. Furry, they evolved short cilia against the cold; and it is cold in the large room. A heater suspended from the ceiling comes on at intervals suddenly, like a man bolting up from troubled sleep.

There are the stuffers, usually four, lobster tails piled in front of them. The tails come wrapped in cellophane, and the stuffers put them into boxes and then onto a conveyor belt that brings them to two elderly women who select an additional lobster tail from one of the pans I and another have been filling, which will bring the weight up to what is marked on the box. From there to Casey and then through a machine that seals the ends of the cardboard boxes. The air is filled with the smell of melting wax. An old man, Sammy, takes them into the freezer, where they wait to be shipped out. On the wall is taped the record amount of lobster tails ever to be packed in a day.

Four of us, poker-faced, stand around a table, dealing lobster tails into pans. Each tail is given an inspection, a multiplicity of single observations of identical articles. Having seen each for a second, you have seen one for eight hours. The dark brown carapace which is spotted with reds and greens is no longer a crustacean's but an insect's. The white meat of the lobster is the starch inside a withered twig. The little fins folded over in death across its belly are the hands of children in their abbreviated coffins.

At the end of the day, when the room is filled with fluorescent light, a giddiness sets in, a hilarity takes over. After a spurt of feverish activity, crackling laughter. I have seen it happen elsewhere, this spasm of silent activity ended by laughter. The infirm have it, the insane and the employed.

"Oh, look at this, Casey," a small Portuguese woman says upon finding a lobster tail brown with eggs. The women gather around her as around a newborn. "They should have thrown her back in, the damn fisherman," Casey says, "I've seen them sit on the dock during summer and scrub off the eggs so they could sell them. They'll kill them all off." The women continue to coo over the lobster, halved as ever the babe would have been if Solomon had carried out his intentions.

I keep forgetting these are corpses. Dismembered ones at that, since they're frozen, hard little shards of ice. Sometimes, through excessive handling and being in a lot that is unpacked but not repacked, and then returned to the freezer to come out again and not find its way into a finished package, they get to be a little limp. But these are supposed to be terminally discarded.

There is a break at ten after beginning at eight in the morning. The men go for coffee, the women into a room that has benches. The packing room empties and takes on a coldness that is present whenever humans depart, like a fire gone completely out.

* * *

There is an hour for lunch. Atop a nearby firehouse a siren screams out noon. A generator that is hooked up to nothing, and its wail is mechanized frustration. It gives a split-second warning of its coming, a mere electrical click, and as I walk away from the factory to a luncheonette I put my gloved hands up to my ears. It takes fifteen steps for it to end. Every day at noon; a reminder, a flag at half-mast; whatever machines are buried in me mourn with it.

I worry for the first week that my work in the Fish Factory will brand me. That the stink will be too odious to those not directly involved with the work. That my uniform of boots and sweaters and coarse coat with a cap pulled over my hair will ostracize me, make me stand out, put the town off-limits. But the populace surprises me and takes no notice. Even when I get to the luncheonette, the stools next to me are not vacated, even though I smell of death and flounder. Soon I have no sense of shame.

Walking the one main street of town, I see the daily grotesques. The man with his hair shaved away from two sullen lumps that show the remains of their stitches like the teeth marks a child leaves playfully on your arm. Some hack's proud work, though I cannot know what ill caused the surgery, though the man has an addled smile. The main street of town is the common recreation area for a number of lost homes. There is the man with the nervous disorder who has to generate more stationary thrust than a Saturn rocket before he can propel himself ten feet. Then he rests against the fender of a car. He once asked me a question and spoke so fast that I had to learn to listen to him. By slowing down his speech, a seventy-eight record to thirty-three-and-a-third, I could understand him. But then the only answer his question required was "No." By the time I reach the luncheonette the parade is half over, though usually at the counter there is a gentle spastic who is having a cup of coffee, continually stirring his sugar, sounding all the while through my desiccated meal like he is calling a meeting to order.

The Fish Factory system can assimilate anyone immediately. Without notice, one afternoon the packing room emptied out and we filed through the door, up narrow steps attached to the outside of the building. High tide is in, right up to the pilings which begin where the building stops. There is a long wharf extending into the bay. Next to the Fish Factory is a boat-restoring yard, and a large fishing boat lies beached on its side, a peeling underbelly exposed like an obese patient waiting for an injection. The steps we climb continue over the roof and up to a high third floor to which I have never come. From here everything is motionless, stilled by distance, and silent except for the squalls of the gulls who perch around and along a track that descends to the wharf. There is a large cage that is run on cable, ascending now, loaded with fresh fish. The trap slams against a metal tank and then the load of fish drops. Hollow sounds, distant, far-off explosions. The cage descends again as we enter the room, leaving the gulls to rip the fish that make a path of carcasses underneath the cage's track.

Machinery, water on the floor, mounds of ice go undiminished in the cold. Cartons thrown down a hole in the ceiling; Dominic, the foreman, herds his gang together, the old women beside the conveyor, herring comes over the elevated ridge on one belt like an unexpected assault and flops into cartons that are to hold fifty pounds each. They are sent down over rollers to be weighed and then transferred to carts, and when fifteen are stacked they are hauled to the freezer. I lift them from the weighing table to the carts. Round silver scales stick to my black gloves. Soon they are covered by this soft mail. The boxes of herring get backed up. "Stop the belt!" Dominic yells. Herring spills over the filled boxes onto the floor, sounding like strokes of a tired whipping. They are scooped up later with a shovel. It is hard work and doesn't slow down unless the belts stop. During the pause my wrists ache, the delayed burning that cold produces when you just start to get warm. The body gets used to it, new rhythms are learned. I keep forgetting the fish are dead, I pay such little attention to them, lost to the rapid motions that are required to keep up. They do not have whites to their eyes, but are clear. All their small mouth are open. Thousands and thousands of herring. My feet slip on the ones fallen around me. The iron wheels of the cart flatten them. My heels gash open orange bellies. I get used to the queasy footing.

Three young men are clustered around the end of the initial conveyor belt. They wear thick aprons and gloves, shoving boxes just filled down the line. At times they find an odd fish among the school of herring and they are discarded into one large box. The monster box. They look like excited physicians throwing spare organs back over their shoulders.

Sarge trips the cage, releasing fish into the tank. There is a fury behind the work that is always present during a siege. The long whine of the steel cable, the crash of the cage against metal, the thud of two hundred pounds of herring. They drop onto the fish below, which are continually slithering out a small opening onto the conveyor belt. In their convex and concave mesh they resemble the race of the sperm for the egg, down the narrow channel, each forcing the other with helpless collaborators' weight. Cattle do the same thing in their stalls that lead to slaughterhouses. A Judas goat is not necessary in every case. Confined numbers can cause deadly momentum.

We get caught up. Over two hundred barrels of herring packed. Dominic, now bored with driving the crew, descends to the floor beneath and I wander over to see the beginnings of the process of which I am the end. I pass the monster box like a cemetery a young boy encounters unavoidably at night on his way home. A spiny fish that still breathes like a tattered bellows. A starfish adhering to a pink stingray like a sea spider. A squid twisted around a scupp. Kelp forms a reticule around the ooze. The monster box: a synposis of a nightmare.

There is a tank into which large cod have been thrown that were caught with the herring. One cod has already been gutted. Its emptied carcass, whch is now nothing but a wide flat head and a long handle of backbone, stretches out on the cement like a lost shovel you find rotting in the ground after a winter's snow has gone and uncovered it. The two filleted sections rest atop a crate. They are washed off and very white.

In the tank are the sleek cod, so huge they seem after the herring which never got beyond eight inches. Big-mouthed, an olive-drab color without any of the iridescence of the herring. Some of the cod have, stuck halfway out of their mouths, three or four half-swallowed herring. Death has prevented the cod from consuming them. A macabre *in flagrante delicto*. Stories to inspire chastity in my high-school youth leap to mind like spawning salmon. During a Retreat, a gray priest telling of two "fornicating youths in the back seat of a car, crushed by a brakeless truck, found by their parents and the authorities still locked in their carnal embrace, their sin embossed in death, their guilt preserved as surely as by the lava of Vesuvius . . ."

I pick up one of the cod from whose mouth four half-swallowed herring protrude, and in death his startled eyes give back some excuse of innocence, like all the heads at that boys' school seemed to want to extend by the amused and shocked shaking of their heads. *Somebody stuffed them in my mouth. I can't even breathe . . .*

I try to pull one herring out by its tail, till its reluctance overwhelms me, so tenacious is their graved epoxy, and I drop the cod back in the tank. I had begun to get an erection.

It is seven-fifty in the morning and I am the first to leave tracks in the snow. As I come around the corner of the pump house a man leans out the window and pours a coffee can full of steaming water over a pipe's frozen valve.

May, an old woman who is very short and whenever she looks at you to speak she turns her head, so it appears she's looking at you from around some nonexistent corner, says to me as I weigh lobster, "Maybe they'll give us medals depending on how many lobsters we get done."

How could people have worked eighteen hours a day? The same incomprehension as a soldier has viewing the armor of a knight. Finally five o'clock comes; it is terrible; the death wish of killing time. We file from the room each day like surgeons who keep losing their patients under the knife.

The men who assemble near a truck in the early morning, cold vapors seeping from their mouths, the departing cast of their slumbering hopes, come rubbing their hands, standing near the empty trailer like seconds who arrive early for a duel in order to survey the clearing.

The resignation of men before they take to their jobs. It is the same, regardless of the task, as long as it is one they have resigned themselves to. Shrugged shoulders, jokes made, sour as coffee grinds that collapse garbage bags. They shame reluctance by action. We are used to the earth's passings, its relays, its handings-over.

So we load the truck. The freezer door swings open onto the loading dock. Aluminum tracks are set up down the middle of the empty trailer, the truck driver and myself at the far end. An air-conditioning unit sticks out, for this truck carries perishables, the cold air channeled down the length of the trailer by a canvas tube that hangs close to the ceiling. It is primitive but works, something Archimedes would have figured out. The truckdriver and I do not introduce ourselves, but the speed with which we handle the cartons describes us to one another, the archaic dance of manual labor. Midway, he tells me his name and asks for mine, and because I am ten years younger than he and youth will be forgiven most anything, he overlooks the length of my hair, and because I will take eight cartons to his seven (a subtle dowry I have to pay because it is *his* truck). The others he has met before and for the sake of good comradeship they recall him, or if not exactly him, a truckdriver they did remember, as if it is good enough to say kind things about a member of the species if not the exact individual.

The truck fills up completely, a queen bee brimming with eggs, and for a while we are somber with the idea of procreation, stacking the cartons, but it wanes.

"Boy, whoever it is that runs that coffee place, is that a man or a woman?" the truckdriver asks.

I reply it is indeed a woman but in a voice full of regret at her mannishness, the same tone a hunter uses when he speaks of a favorite coon dog that has lost the ability to follow the scent. With this cleared up, other testings go on, exchanged assurances in the muted air of the trailer as we pile up frozen whiting.

"You don't exactly clean up around here," Sammy had said. Clean up. Hygiene. Money douche. Five-dollar ablutions.

Sarge talks like a motor that will never quite turn over. Short, breathy sentences that end completely before they are finished, then start up again, only to end. He tells about an old man who would pay money for your socks, the mangier the better, which he would stuff into his mouth. Sarge makes movements with his hand like he's tossing peanuts in between his teeth. The truck-driver tells about a friend of his who would walk twenty miles through a blizzard if he knew there was a sure piece of ass waiting for him. Sarge, because of his excited speech, seems to bubble, telling about a retarded girl who has to be taken out of school because she would remove her clothes in class.

"Slap. Her titties." Sarge using his hands like there's fluttering wash hanging below his chest. "Hump. Around in. The aisles." Sarge juggling his three hundred pounds around the loading dock as if he were offering his thrusting middle to a fire hydrant. Common men load trucks and we are common men.

Who saw the first one? Behind me, at the table of stuffers, someone says quietly, "Is that a maggot?" Lippy, who sounds like Radio Free Europe jammed by the Russians, replies, "Naaaahissparrtaadulobstir," and brushes aside whatever it is.

It was a bad day for lobster packing; the law of averages had given us the wrong sizes, too many big ones, too many small ones, not enough medium-sized and the correct weight was hard to come by. A computer could figure the variations possible to get four separate lobster tails to weigh out to 6.8 ounces and it is easy if you have all different sizes; but a preponderance of one will impede the natural selection, and boxes are rejected, and the race of 6.8-ounce boxes of Cap'n Ahab's South African Lobster Tails will die out, disappear from the face of the earth, if the balance in sizes is not restored. Boxes would come back and be emptied out, repacked and sent back again—not many, but just enough to make it a bad day, like yesterday, when the same thing happened. There was a box of lobster tails that had been put back in the freezer the day before that had begun to thaw out and so there would be today.

"Look," Casey let out with an unaccustomed girlish screech, "there *are* maggots!" She held up a blue box on which could be seen a small silhouette climbing along one wall, like a mountain climber descending a sheer cliff.

The stuffers pushed aside the pile of lobster tails, and there on the top of that stainless-steel table are about a dozen maggots. Maggots! Though on top of the bright silver table they look like shoots of wild rice. Their backs hump like babies flexing little fists.

"It's these loose ones," Casey yells, holding up an almost completely thawed lobster tail that bends over in her hand like a man collapsed across barbed wire.

"I told Dominic they were getting no good, but he wanted to get rid of them," Casey goes on exultantly, glad to have her day's grumblings vindicated. Maggots in the lobster tails! That'll show them!

Maggots. An American housewife, fresh from Food World, comes into her kitchen, puts down her brown sacks, takes off her car coat, sets aside her new checkbook which pictures in color the first A-Bomb explosion on each check, and gets out a box of Cap'n Ahab's Apartheid Lobster Tails, tearing its quick-zip opener to throw out her hors d'oeuvres for tonight's pre-bridge dinner party, and out crawls a maggot. Her throat parches. She steps back, irises widening. She puts out a hand to reach for the absolute axis that Food World spins on, and finds it gone! Stumbling, only to knock over her Osterizer, which trips the switch that sets growling her disposal, and finding nothing to cling to as the terror of that vision becomes entire and lucid, cracking open an evil that falls onto her Teflon mind like a black egg, she grabs her Arctic Chest's door handle, reeling, swings it open and collapses at its feet, slowly being covered with ice cubes from the mini-igloo-icemaker till she revives.

What must she think we are? We who have packed MAGGOTS into her lobster tails. That our factory is a geodesic dome of cobwebs. Our lobsters hauled in fetid garbage cans. She sees not ground zero, but the periphery, the sores, the ooze, the tracks left by the skittering rats which imprint the new cuneiform on the clay tablets of Mesopotamia!

But all the while, it is just our Fish Factory. Quiet as a battlefield when they come to strip the weapons from the dead. Clean, brightly lit, the cement floor washed as spotlessly as front walks by summer gardeners. And on the silver table the dozen grains of wild rice.

Casey is still yelling, vilifying Dominic, as if he is the First Cause, the uncaused cause, the harborer of spontaneous generation.

I hear a faint rambunctious tapping. I look over to the window covered with cloudy plastic, and trapped in there are several hairy flies. One of whose knocking against that plastic sounds as proud as an old man who has been accused of being the impregnator of a young girl thought to be virginal. A Joseph fly.

Dominic comes through the door, his upper and lower jaw

meshing badly, the missing teeth cause his bite to be sinister. He grumbles against the elements, that it is not his fault, that it is the general policy to use lobster tails if they have thawed out a bit, possibly exposed to contamination by our little club of flies. He rips open sealed cartons and discovers no maggots in them, but Casey takes a box and finds a maggot perched on a tail.

Dominic's broken face for a minute resembles Robert Mc-Namara's as he stares at the pile of boxes ready to be taken into the freezer. A whole day's work! His brow knits into an abacus, cost accounting, tabulating, the number of employees, wages, hours worked, cost of recycling, and makes the humane, the only decision: Check all the boxes! Open them up and check them and repack them all. He continues to mutter against the cosmos and quits the room, a king who chooses not to see the execution he has just decreed.

We all set to the sealed boxes. Savagely tearing them open, transfixed smiles as we ravage the work we did, a chance to open what we heretofore had only been able to close. The battered boxes we empty lay at our feet like the fruit that falls too soon from the tree and is trampled by the pickers. Young men grunt as they rip into large cartons which contain the smaller baby-blue boxes. The first minutes of this are elating, then the dark zeal abates and the monotony that is our true condition reclaims us. No other maggots are discovered.

Casey looks at the rising pyramid of repacked cartons with a bitterness that I know can only mean she let one contaminated box through, to lurk on the shelf of Food World, under the frosty breath of their air conditioning which continually bathes the produce with a white eminence like the red glow of a sacristy lamp. The unsuspecting mother will pick it out and take it into her home and finally unwrap for herself a putrescence that even if hell were our three floors of freezers could not be preserved forever from her gaze. We deal in perishables.

The repacking resumes its usual pace. Any lobster tail that is even partially thawed is discarded. The work is done. The day over. Sammy hauls the last load into the freezer.

"Maybe we should tell the Board of Health," May whispers around her invisible corner, but the refrain is not picked up. If someone tells, and they do something about it, if they close this place down, then we won't have jobs, and anyway, nothing really happened. The maggots were here, but they didn't get through; the maggots didn't get into Food World. If they got into Food World and crawled along America's kitchen counter that would be one thing, but they were stopped *here,* where they began. At the Fish Factory.

☆☆☆ A Wrestler with Sharks
by Richard Yates

Nobody had much respect for *The Labor Leader*. Even Finkel and Kramm, its owners, the two sour brothers-in-law who'd dreamed it up in the first place and who somehow managed to make a profit on it year after year—even they could take little pride in the thing. At least, that's what I used to suspect from the way they'd hump grudgingly around the office, shivering the bile-green partitions with their thumps and shouts, grabbing and tearing at galley proofs, breaking pencil points, dropping wet cigar butts on the floor and slamming telephones contemptuously into their cradles. *The Labor Leader* was all either of them would ever have for a life's work, and they seemed to hate it.

You couldn't blame them: the thing was a monster. In format it was a fat biweekly tabloid, badly printed, that spilled easily out of your hands and was very hard to put together again in the right order; in policy it called itself "An Independent Newspaper Pledged to the Spirit of the Trade Union Movement," but its real pitch was to be a kind of trade journal for union officials, who subscribed to it out of union funds and who must surely have been inclined to tolerate, rather than to want or need, whatever thin sustenance it gave to them. The *Leader's* coverage of national events "from the labor angle" was certain to be stale, likely to be muddled, and often opaque with typographical errors; most of its dense columns were filled with flattering reports on the do-

RICHARD YATES (b. 1926) is the author of *Revolutionary Road* (1961); *Eleven Kinds of Loneliness* (1962); *A Special Providence* (1969); *Disturbing the Peace* (1975); and *The Easter Parade* (1976).

ings of the unions whose leaders were on the subscription list, often to the exclusion of much bigger news about those whose leaders weren't. And every issue carried scores of simple-minded ads urging "Harmony" in the names of various small industrial firms that Finkel and Kramm had been able to beg or browbeat into buying space—a compromise that would almost certainly have hobbled a real labor page but that didn't, typically enough, seem to cramp the *Leader's* style at all.

There was a fast turnover on the editorial staff. Whenever somebody quit, the *Leader* would advertise in the help-wanted section of the *Times,* offering a "moderate salary commensurate with experience." This always brought a good crowd to the sidewalk outside the *Leader* office, a gritty storefront on the lower fringe of the garment district, and Kramm, who was the editor (Finkel was the publisher), would keep them all waiting for half an hour before he picked up a sheaf of application forms, shot his cuffs, and gravely opened the door—I think he enjoyed this occasional chance to play the man of affairs.

"All right, take your time," he'd say, as they jostled inside and pressed against the wooden rail that shielded the inner offices. "Take your time, gentlemen." Then he would raise a hand and say, "May I have your attention, please?" And he'd begin to explain the job. Half the applicants would go away when he got to the part about the salary structure, and most of those who remained offered little competition to anyone who was sober, clean and able to construct an English sentence.

That's the way we'd all been hired, the six or eight of us who frowned under the *Leader's* sickly fluorescent lights that winter, and most of us made no secret of our desire for better things. I went to work there a couple of weeks after losing my job on one of the metropolitan dailies, and stayed only until I was rescued the next spring by the big picture magazine that still employs me. The others had other explanations, which, like me, they spent a great deal of time discussing: it was a great place for shrill and redundant hard-luck stories.

But Leon Sobel joined the staff about a month after I did, and from the moment Kramm led him into the editorial room we all knew he was going to be different. He stood among the messy desks with the look of a man surveying new fields to conquer, and when Kramm introduced him around (forgetting half our names) he made a theatrically solemn business out of shaking hands. He was about thirty-five, older than most of us, a very small, tense man with black hair that seemed to explode from his skull and a humorless thin-lipped face that was blotched with the scars of acne. His eyebrows were always in motion when he talked, and his eyes, not so much piercing as anxious to pierce, never left the eyes of his listener.

The first thing I learned about him was that he'd never held an office job before: he had been a sheet-metal worker all his adult life. What's more, he hadn't come to the *Leader* out of need, like the rest of us, but, as he put it, out of principle. To do so, in fact, he had given up a factory job paying nearly twice the money.

"What'sa matter, don'tcha believe me?" he asked, after telling me this.

"Well, it's not that," I said. "It's just that I—"

"Maybe you think I'm crazy," he said, and screwed up his face into a canny smile.

I tried to protest, but he wouldn't have it. "Listen, don't worry, McCabe. I'm called crazy a lotta times already. It don't bother me. My wife says, 'Leon, you gotta expect it.' She says, 'People never understand a man who wants something more outa life than just money.' And she's right! She's right!"

"No," I said. "Wait a second. I—"

"People think you gotta be one of two things: either you're a shark, or you gotta lay back and let the sharks eatcha alive—this is the world. Me, I'm the kinda guy's gotta go out and wrestle with the sharks. Why? I dunno why. This is crazy? Okay."

"Wait a second," I said. And I tried to explain that I had nothing whatever against his striking a blow for social justice, if that was what he had in mind; it was just that I thought *The Labor Leader* was about the least likely place in the world for him to do it.

But his shrug told me I was quibbling. "So?" he said. "It's a paper, isn't it? Well, I'm a writer. And what good's a writer if he don't get printed? Listen." He lifted one haunch and placed it on the edge of my desk—he was too short a man to do this gracefully, but the force of his argument helped him to bring it off. "Listen, McCabe. You're a young kid yet. I wanna tellya something. Know how many books I wrote already?" And now his hands came into play, as they always did sooner or later. Both stubby fists were thrust under my nose and allowed to shake there for a moment before they burst into a thicket of stiff, quivering fingers—only the thumb of one hand remained folded down. "Nine," he said, and the hands fell limp on his thigh, to rest until he needed them again. "Nine. Novels, philosophy, political theory —the entire gamut. And not one of 'em published. Believe me, I been around awhile."

"I believe you," I said.

"So finally I sat down and figured: What's the answer? And I figured this: The trouble with my books is, they tell the truth. And the truth is a funny thing, McCabe. People wanna read it, but they only wanna read it when it comes from somebody they already know their name. Am I right? So all right. I figure, I wanna write these books, first I gotta build up a name for myself. This is worth any sacrifice. This is the only way. You know something, McCabe? The last one I wrote took me two years?" Two fingers sprang up to illustrate the point, and dropped again. "Two years, working four, five hours every night and all day long on the weekends. And then you oughta seen the crap I got from the publishers. Every damn publisher in town. My wife cried. She says, 'But why, Leon? Why?' " Here his lips curled tight against his small, stained teeth, and the fist of one hand smacked the palm of the other on his thigh, but then he relaxed. "I told her, 'Listen, honey. You know why.' " And now he was smiling at me in quiet triumph. "I says, 'This book told the truth. That's why.' " Then he winked, slid off my desk and walked away, erect and jaunty in his soiled sport shirt and his dark serge pants that hung loose and shiny in the seat. That was Sobel.

It took him a little while to loosen up in the job: for the first week or so, when he wasn't talking, he went at everything with a zeal and a fear of failure that disconcerted everyone but Finney, the managing editor. Like the rest of us, Sobel had a list of twelve or fifteen union offices around town, and the main part of his job was to keep in touch with them and write up whatever bits of news they gave out. As a rule there was nothing very exciting to write about: the average story ran two or three paragraphs with a single-column head:

PLUMBERS WIN
3¢ PAY HIKE

or something like that. But Sobel composed them all as carefully as sonnets, and after he'd turned one in he would sit chewing his lips in anxiety until Finney raised a forefinger and said, "C'mere a second, Sobel."

Then he'd go over and stand, nodding apologetically, while Finney pointed out some niggling grammatical flaw. "Never end a sentence with a preposition, Sobel. You don't wanna say, 'gave the plumbers new grounds to bargain on.' You wanna say, 'gave the plumbers new grounds on which to bargain.' "

Finney enjoyed these lectures. The annoying thing, from a spectator's point of view, was that Sobel took so long to learn what everyone else seemed to know instinctively: that Finney was scared of his own shadow and would back down on anything at all if you raised your voice. He was a frail, nervous man who dribbled on his chin when he got excited and raked trembling fingers through his thickly oiled hair, with the result that his fingers spread hair oil, like a spoor of his personality, to everything he touched: his clothes, his pencils, his telephone and his typewriter keys. I guess the main reason he was managing editor was that nobody else would submit to the bullying he took from Kramm: their editorial conferences always began with Kramm shouting "Finney! Finney!" from behind his partition, and Finney jumping like a squirrel to hurry inside. Then you'd hear the relentless drone of Kramm's demands and the quavering sputter of Finney's explanations, and it would end with a thump as Kramm socked his desk. *"No,* Finney. No, no, *no!* What's the matter with you? I gotta draw you a picture? All right, all right, get outa here, I'll do it myself." At first you might wonder why Finney took it—nobody could need a job that badly—but the answer lay in the fact that there were only three by-lined pieces in *The Labor Leader:* A boiler-plated sports feature that we got from a syndicate, a ponderous column called "LABOR TODAY, by Julius Kramm," that ran facing the editorial page, and a double-column box in the back of the paper with the heading:

BROADWAY BEAT
by WES FINNEY

There was even a thumbnail picture of him in the upper left-hand corner, hair slicked down and teeth bared in a confident smile. The text managed to work in a labor angle here and there—a paragraph on Actors' Equity, say, or the stagehands' union—but mostly he played it straight, in the manner of two or three real Broadway-and-night-club columnists. "Heard about the new thrush at the Copa?" he would ask the labor leaders; then he'd give them her name, with a sly note about her bust and hip measurements and a folksy note about the state from which she "hailed," and he'd wind it up like this: "She's got the whole town talking and turning up in droves. Their verdict, in which this department wholly concurs: the lady has class." No reader could have guessed that Wes Finney's shoes needed repair, that he got no complimentary tickets to anything and never went out except to take in a movie or to crouch over a liverwurst sandwich at the Automat. He wrote the column on his own time and got extra money for it—the figure I heard was fifty dollars a month. So it was a mutually satisfactory deal: for that small sum Kramm held his whipping boy in absolute bondage; for that small torture Finney could paste clippings in a scrapbook, with all the contamination of *The Labor Leader* sheared away into the wastebasket of his furnished room, and whisper himself to sleep with dreams of ultimate freedom.

Anyway, this was the man who could make Sobel apologize for the grammar of his news stories, and it was a sad thing to watch. Of course, it couldn't go on forever, and one day it stopped.

Finney had called Sobel over to explain about split infinitives, and Sobel was wrinkling his brow in an effort to understand. Neither of them noticed that Kramm was standing in the doorway of his office a few feet away, listening, and looking at the wet end of his cigar as if it tasted terrible.

"Finney," he said. "You wanna be an English teacher, get a job in the high school."

Startled, Finney stuck a pencil behind his ear without noticing that another pencil was already there, and both pencils clattered to the floor. "Well, I—" he said. "Just thought I'd—"

"Finney, this does not interest me Pick up your pencils and listen to me, please For your information, Mr. Sobel is not supposed to be a literary Englishman He is supposed to be a literate American, and this I believe he is. Do I make myself clear?"

And the look on Sobel's face as he walked back to his own desk was that of a man released from prison.

From that moment on he began to relax; or almost from that moment—what seemed to clinch the transformation was O'Leary's hat.

O'Leary was a recent City College graduate and one of the best men on the staff (he has since done very well; you'll often see his by-line in one of the evening papers), and the hat he wore that winter was of the waterproof cloth kind that is sold in raincoat shops. There was nothing very dashing about it—in fact its floppiness made O'Leary's face look too thin—but Sobel must secretly have admired it as a symbol of journalism, or of nonconformity, for one morning he showed up in an identical one, brand new. It looked even worse on him than on O'Leary, particularly when worn with his lumpy brown overcoat, but he seemed to cherish it. He developed a whole new set of mannerisms to go with the hat: cocking it back with a flip of the index finger as he settled down to make his morning phone calls ("This is Leon Sobel, of *The Labor Leader* . . ."), tugging it smartly forward as he left the office on a reporting assignment, twirling it onto a peg when he came back to write his story. At the end of the day, when he'd dropped the last of his copy into Finney's wire basket, he would shape the hat into a careless slant over one eyebrow, swing the overcoat around his shoulders and stride out with a loose salute of farewell, and I used to picture him studying his reflection in the black subway windows all the way home to the Bronx.

He seemed determined to love his work. He even brought in a snapshot of his family—a tired, abjectly smiling woman and two small sons—and fastened it to his desk top with cellophane tape. Nobody else ever left anything more personal than a book of matches in the office overnight.

One afternoon toward the end of February, Finney summoned me to his oily desk. "McCabe," he said. "Wanna do a column for us?"

"What kind of a column?"

"Labor gossip," he said. "Straight union items with a gossip or a chatter angle—little humor, personalities, stuff like that. Mr. Kramm thinks we need it, and I told him you'd be the best man for the job."

I can't deny that I was flattered (we are all conditioned by our surroundings, after all), but I was also suspicious. "Do I get a by-line?"

He began to blink nervously. "Oh, no, no by-line," he said. "Mr. Kramm wants this to be anonymous. See, the guys'll give you any items they turn up, and you'll just collect 'em and put 'em in shape. It's just something you can do on office time, part of your regular job. See what I mean?"

I saw what he meant. "Part of my regular salary too," I said. "Right?"

"That's right."

"No thanks," I told him, and then, feeling generous, I suggested that he try O'Leary.

"Nah, I already asked him," Finney said. "He don't wanna do it either. Nobody does."

I should have guessed, of course, that he'd been working down the list of everyone in the office. And to judge from the lateness of the day, I must have been close to the tail end.

Sobel fell in step with me as we left the building after work that night. He was wearing his overcoat cloak-style, the sleeves dangling, and holding his cloth hat in place as he hopped nimbly to avoid the furrows of dirty slush on the sidewalk. "Letcha in on a little secret, McCabe," he said. "I'm doin' a column for the paper. It's all arranged."

"Yeah?" I said. "Any money in it?"

"Money?" he winked. "I'll tell y' about that part. Let's get a cuppa coffee." He led me into the tiled and steaming brilliance of the Automat, and when we were settled at a damp corner table he explained everything. "Finney says no money, see? So I said okay. He says no by-line either. I said okay." He winked again. "Playin' it smart."

"How do you mean?"

"How do I mean?" He always repeated your question like that, savoring it, holding his black eyebrows high while he made you wait for the answer. "Listen, I got this Finney figured out. *He* don't decide these things. You think he decides anything around that place? You better wise up, McCabe. Mr. *Kramm* makes the decisions. And Mr. Kramm is an intelligent man, don't kid yourself." Nodding, he raised his coffee cup, but his lips recoiled from the heat of it, puckered, and blew into the steam before they began to sip with gingerly impatience.

"Well," I said, "okay, but I'd check with Kramm before you start counting on anything."

"Check?" He put his cup down with a clatter. "What's to check? Listen, Mr. Kramm wants a column, right? You think he cares if I get a by-line or not? Or the money, either—you think if I write a good column he's gonna quibble over payin' me for it? Ya crazy. *Finney's* the one, don'tcha see? *He* don't wanna gimme a break because he's worried about losing his *own* column. Get it? So all right. I check with nobody until I got that column written." He prodded his chest with a stiff thumb. "On my own time. Then I take it to Mr. Kramm and we talk business. You leave it to me." He settled down comfortably, elbows on the table, both hands cradling the cup just short of drinking position while he blew into the steam.

"Well," I said. "I hope you're right. Be nice if it does work out that way."

"Ah, it may not," he conceded, pulling his mouth into a grimace of speculation and tilting his head to one side. *"You* know. It's a gamble." But he was only saying that out of politeness, to minimize my envy. He could afford to express doubt because he felt none, and I could tell he was already planning the way he'd tell his wife about it.

The next morning Finney came around to each of our desks with instructions that we were to give Sobel any gossip or chatter items we might turn up; the column was scheduled to begin in the next issue. Later I saw him in conference with Sobel, briefing him on how the column was to be written, and I noticed that Finney did all the talking: Sobel just sat there making thin, contemptuous jets of cigarette smoke.

We had just put an issue to press, so the deadline for the column was two weeks away. Not many items turned up at first—it was hard enough getting news out of the unions we covered, let alone "chatter." Whenever someone did hand him a note, Sobel would frown over it, add a scribble of his own and drop it in a desk drawer; once or twice I saw him drop one in the wastebasket. I only remember one of the several pieces I gave him: The business agent of a steamfitters' local I covered had yelled at me through a closed door that he couldn't be bothered that day because his wife had just had twins. But Sobel didn't want it. "So, the guy's got twins," he said. "So what?"

"Suit yourself," I said. "You getting much other stuff?"

He shrugged. "Some. I'm not worried I'll tellya one thing, though—I'm not using a lotta this crap. This chatter. Who the hell's gonna read it? You can't have a whole column fulla crap like that. Gotta be something to hold it together. Am I right?"

Another time (the column was all he talked about now) he chuckled affectionately and said, "My wife says I'm just as bad now as when I was working on my books. Write, write, write. She don't care, though," he added. "She's really getting excited about this thing. She's telling everybody—the neighbors, everybody. Her brother come over Sunday, starts asking me how the job's going—you know, in a wise-guy kinda way? I just kept quiet, but my wife pipes up: 'Leon's doing a column for the paper now'—and she tells him all about it. Boy, you oughta seen his face."

Every morning he brought in the work he had done the night before, a wad of handwritten papers, and used his lunch hour to type it out and revise it while he chewed a sandwich at his desk. And he was the last one to go home every night; we'd leave him there hammering his typewriter in a trance of concentration. Finney kept bothering him—"How you coming on that feature, Sobel?"—but he always parried the question with squinted eyes and a truculent lift of the chin. "Whaddya worried about? You'll get it." And he would wink at me.

On the morning of the deadline he came to work with a little patch of toilet paper on his cheek; he had cut himself shaving in his nervousness, but otherwise he looked as confident as ever. There were no calls to make that morning—on deadline days we all stayed in to work on copy and proofs—so the first thing he did was to spread out the finished manuscript for a final reading. His absorption was so complete that he didn't look up until Finney was standing at his elbow. "You wanna gimme that feature, Sobel?"

Sobel grabbed up the papers and shielded them with an arrogant forearm. He looked steadily at Finney and said, with a firmness that he must have been rehearsing for two weeks: "I'm showing this to Mr. Kramm. Not you."

Finney's whole face began to twitch in a fit of nerves. "Nah, nah, Mr. Kramm don't need to see it," he said. "Anyway, he's not in yet. C'mon, lemme have it."

"You're wasting your time, Finney," Sobel said. "I'm waiting for Mr. Kramm."

Muttering, avoiding Sobel's triumphant eyes, Finney went back to his own desk, where he was reading proof on BROADWAY BEAT.

My own job that morning was at the layout table, pasting up the dummy for the first section. I was standing there, working with the unwieldly page forms and the paste-clogged scissors, when Sobel sidled up behind me, looking anxious. "You wanna read it, McCabe?" he asked. "Before I turn it in?" And he handed me the manuscript.

The first thing that hit me was that he had clipped a photograph to the top of page 1, a small portrait of himself in his cloth hat. The next thing was his title:

SOBEL SPEAKING
by Leon Sobel

I can't remember the exact words of the opening paragraph, but it went something like this:

This is the "debut" of a new department in *The Labor Leader* and, moreover, it is also "something new" for your correspondent, who has never handled a column before. However, he is far from being a novice with the written word, on the contrary he is an "ink-stained veteran" of many battles on the field of ideas, to be exact nine books have emanated from his pen.

Naturally in those tomes his task was somewhat different than that which it will be in this column, and yet he hopes that this column will also strive as they did to penetrate the basic human mystery, in other words, to tell the truth.

When I looked up I saw he had picked open the razor cut on his cheek and it was bleeding freely. "Well," I said, "for one thing, I wouldn't give it to him with your picture that way—I mean, don't you think it might be better to let him read it first, and then—"

"Okay," he said, blotting at his face with a wadded gray handkerchief. "Okay, I'll take the picture off. G'ahead, read the rest."

But there wasn't time to read the rest. Kramm had come in, Finney had spoken to him, and now he was standing in the door of his office, champing crossly on a dead cigar. "You wanted to see me, Sobel?" he called.

"Just a second," Sobel said. He straightened the pages of SOBEL SPEAKING and detached the photograph, which he jammed into his hip pocket as he started for the door. Halfway there he remembered to take off his hat, and threw it unsuccessfully at the hat stand. Then he disappeared behind the partition, and we all settled down to listen.

It wasn't long before Kramm's reaction came through. *"No* Sobel. No, no, *no!* What *is* this? What are you tryna put *over* on me here?"

Outside, Finney winced comically and clapped the side of his head, giggling, and O'Leary had to glare at him until he stopped.

We heard Sobel's voice, a blurred sentence or two of protest, and then Kramm came through again: " 'Basic human mystery'—this is gossip? This is chatter? You can't follow instructions? Wait a minute—Finney! Finney!"

Finney loped to the door, delighted to be of service, and we heard him making clear, righteous replies to Kramm's interrogation: Yes, he had told Sobel what kind of a column was wanted; yes, he had specified that there was to be no by-line; yes, Sobel had been provided with ample gossip material. All we heard from Sobel was something indistinct, said in a very tight, flat voice. Kramm made a guttural reply, and even though we couldn't make out the words we knew it was all over. Then they came out, Finney wearing the foolish smile you sometimes see in the crowds that gape at street accidents, Sobel as expressionless as death.

He picked his hat off the floor and his coat off the stand, put them on, and came over to me. "So long, McCabe," he said. "Take it easy."

Shaking hands with him, I felt my face jump into Finney's idiot smile, and I asked a stupid question. "You leaving?"

He nodded. Then he shook hands with O'Leary—"So long, kid"—and hesitated, uncertain whether to shake hands with the rest of the staff. He settled for a little wave of the forefinger, and walked out to the street.

Finney lost no time in giving us all the inside story in an eager whisper: 'The guy's *crazy!* He says to Kramm, 'You take this column or I quit'—just like that. Kramm just looks at him and says, 'Quit? Get outa here, you're fired.' I mean, what *else* could he say?"

Turning away, I saw that the snapshot of Sobel's wife and sons still lay taped to his desk. I stripped it off and took it out to the sidewalk. "Hey, Sobel!" I yelled. He was a block away, very small, walking toward the subway. I started to run after him, nearly breaking my neck on the frozen slush. "Hey *Sobel!*" But he didn't hear me.

Back at the office I found his address in the Bronx telephone directory, put the picture in an envelope and dropped it in the mail, and I wish that were the end of the story.

But that afternoon I called up the editor of a hardware trade journal I had worked on before the war, who said he had no vacancies on his staff but might soon, and would be willing to interview Sobel if he wanted to drop in. It was a foolish idea: the wages there were even lower than on the *Leader,* and besides, it was a place for very young men whose fathers wanted them to learn the hardware business—Sobel would probably have been ruled out the minute he opened his mouth. But it seemed better than nothing, and as soon as I was out of the office that night I went to a phone booth and looked up Sobel's name again.

A woman's voice answered, but it wasn't the high, faint voice I'd expected. It was low and melodious—that was the first of my several surprises.

"Mrs. Sobel?" I asked, absurdly smiling into the mouthpiece. "Is Leon there?"

She started to say, "Just a minute," but changed it to "Who's calling, please? I'd rather not disturb him right now."

I told her my name and tried to explain about the hardware deal.

"I don't understand," she said. "What kind of a paper is it, exactly?"

"Well, it's a trade journal," I said. "It doesn't amount to much, I guess, but it's—*you* know, a pretty good little thing, of its kind."

"I see," she said. "And you want him to go in and apply for a job? Is that it?"

"Well I mean, if he *wants* to, is all," I said. I was beginning to sweat. It was impossible to reconcile the wan face in Sobel's snapshot with this serene, almost beautiful voice. "I just thought he might like to give it a try, is all."

"Well," she said, "just a minute, I'll ask him." She put down the phone, and I heard them talking in the background. Their words were muffled at first, but then I heard Sobel say, "Ah, I'll talk to him—I'll just say thanks for calling." And I heard her answer, with infinite tenderness. "No, honey, why should you? He doesn't deserve it."

"McCabe's all right," he said.

"No, he's not," she told him, "or he'd have the decency to leave you alone. Let me do it. Please. I'll get rid of him."

When she came back to the phone she said, "No, my husband says he wouldn't be interested in a job of that kind." Then she thanked me politely, said goodbye, and left me to climb guilty and sweating out of the phone booth.

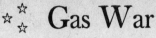

Gas War

from *Turkey Hash*

by Craig Nova

The gas station, a new one, has a large canopy that looks like an airplane wing, six islands, twelve pumps, a sign with bursts of red and blue flak that reads GAS WAR. In front of the garage and office there are cases of soft drinks, neat, bullionlike piles of Tahitian Treat and Canada Dry. And all around the canopy there's a welcome-home banner, GRAND OPENING.

I hear a drilling sound in the back of the station. The office and garage are made of some tinny alloy, and all the walls rumble. I find Cap behind the cases of oil, his head in a cleared shelf, a new drill in his hand. Corkscrew strips of metal spin at the end of the bit. It's Cap's first day on the job.

"It ain't got a peephole," says Cap. "Now what kind of station is that?"

Manager leaves at five. Cap has the place to himself until twelve, when he's supposed to close up.

"Shit," says Cap. "Well, I'm going to make a peephole."

Horse-T sits quietly on the cases of soft drinks.

"He's got to stew for a couple of days," I say, meaning Duckbill.

"Right," says Horse-T. "Fine. Just leave me out of it. Crazy people are more your line, Niles."

Horse-T has a school's-out expression.

I walk around the station, looking at the display models of hydrocarbons, the smooth, professional Tinker Toys. They're everywhere, on top of the pumps, hanging from wires, stacked in the office, sitting on cases of soft drinks.

CRAIG NOVA (b. 1945) is the author of *Turkey Hash* (1972) and *The Geek* (1975).

"Hey," yells Cap over his stage-thunder drilling, "watch the pumps."

An automotive sheriff: Cap points the drill at a car that's just pulled up to one of the islands. It's a yellow Studebaker, a '51, with mud flaps and custom hubcaps. It's a convertible, too. The mud flaps have reflectors and the paint job looks like it was done in someone's front yard. The driver's got a brown three-dollar wig, but you can see gray around the sides of his head, in his natural hair. Powdered face, rouged cheeks, his cruising complexion.

I stand on the island and wring my hands.

"Ethyl," says Three-Dollar Wig.

"I pumped my last drop of ethyl," I say. "There's a gas war! Oh, where am I going to get more gas?"

"What about him?" says Three-Dollar Wig, pointing to Horse-T, who's filling Ford with gas.

"He's getting my last drop of regular!" I say. "You there," I yell at Horse-T, "stop that!"

"Huh?" says Horse-T.

"Oh, no," I say. "What am I going to do?"

"I'll come back tomorrow," says Three-Dollar Wig.

"Oh, would you," I say, "would you?"

"Sure," says Three-Dollar Wig.

"Thanks," I say, "thanks an awful lot."

Three-Dollar Wig bounces over the curb, honks the horn, grinds the gears, and finally pulls into the street.

"This place is right in the creep belt," I say to Cap, "ain't it?"

But he ignores me, intent on his drilling.

"It's got to be right beneath the toilet paper," says Cap, "otherwise they'll see."

The station is filled with new tools, buffed and shiny, as sterile as a surgeon's instruments, and sophisticated equipment, oscilloscopes and jacks run by compressed air. In a metal cabinet I find a uniform that fits. *Jim* is stitched onto the shirt. Talk about starch, I think. The cuffs and collar feel like smooth cardboard. Shiny strip down one leg. Some uniform.

The bit squeals, slips all the way through the wall.

"You got to keep the door locked," says Cap with a sly smile, holding the key to the women's bathroom, "so you can tell when they're in there. They've got to ask for it."

Cap sees me hanging the uniform on a new hook.

"You leaving at twelve?" I say.

He nods.

"But there's a gas war," I say. "The place should be open a little later."

"There ain't any gas war," says Cap. "That's just for suckers."

"Looks like a gas war," I say. "That uniform fits."

Cap smiles and says, "Let me think about it."

Horse-T brings chicken dinners in cardboard boxes. We wash them down with warm Tahitian Treat.

"They take inventory once a week," says Cap, pointing to the racks of tires and batteries. "I got a few days."

Business is slow, but the bathroom's busy. It doesn't matter to Cap: young, old, fat, thin. He leans his head into the shelf, watches, not moving a muscle, holding his breath. He's got an eye like Long John Silver's.

"Whew," says Cap, "I'm going to miss that."

But he brings his car, the Mercury, around, and we load it with batteries, cases of oil, new tires wrapped with golden tape.

"You're in business," he says. "The manager comes at nine."

He takes the oscilloscope, too, puts it in the front seat: Lord's going to be a happy man.

"I got to see Lord," says Cap.

"Sure you do," I say.

Horse-T climbs into the Mercury, too, and says, "Enough. I'm going home."

Grand opening! I think, Come on in! But the station's empty. I watch with shopkeeper's anxiety the passing cars. The drunks roll in at midnight.

"Fill'er up."

I pump gasoline. Hydrocarbons for the kids, coupons for the little woman. Cigarettes at cut-rate prices. Two packages for the woman who comes out of the bar across the street.

"My name's Ethyl," she says, "like the gasoline."

She's depression heavy, potato-fed, has a rotten tooth, greasy hair, one black eye. She has to navigate: walking isn't easy. A stained dress, shoes that almost match.

I offer her more cigarettes, but she refuses.

"I can only carry two," she says.

She looks behind the station, at the open ground there on which there's a few abandoned cars, their hoods open, engines gone, but otherwise in pretty good shape, the large wooden spools left by the power company, oil drums, lawn furniture without webbing, the station's overflowing trash bin. She looks at me, begins to speak, but then turns and walks back to the bar.

I pump gasoline: my pocket fills. A hundred dollars and some change. A drunk runs into the coffee machine, but I reassure him, fill his tank for nothing. I give him the last of the hydrocarbon models. The station has a pleasant odor. Coffee runs in the gutters of the islands.

"Look," says Ethyl, a half hour later, after walking across the street again, "lemme use that lot, huh?"

"Sure," I say.

"My name's Ethyl," she says, "like the . . ." But she stops giggling, squints at me, and says, "Oh."

In two hours she brings three of them from the bar, one shy and embarrassed, wearing glasses with large plastic rims, another with a scowl on his face, as though his dentures hurt. Honey, sweetheart, she says to them as they climb with her into the back seat of a castaway De Soto. The third, a thin and stunted man with quick movements and the drawn face of a baboon, who walks bent at the waist as though he were leaning into wind, spends a moment or two picking up papers in the lot to cover the De Soto's windows.

"You hold the money," she says to me. "I've got no place to put it."

"What's his pleasure?" I say, pointing to the third man, who walks now with a slow and careful gait, as though lingering sensation were a full tub of water.

"For six bucks," she says without smiling, "you can find out."

When the bar closes I have twenty-four dollars for her.

"Twenty-four rubles," she says with farmer's pride, as though she had grown them. She counts the greasy pile twice and is still convinced I cheated her.

"Beats me," she says, "how you did it. New way of folding bills or something."

"I didn't cheat you," I say. But she shakes her head and says, "You'll show me the trick sometime, huh?"

"Sure," I say.

She smiles, walks up the street to buy a chicken dinner and two bottles of wine, one of which she gives to me.

"Brrr-gun-dee," she says. "Straight to the head."

After her dinner I give her a uniform that has *Sam* stitched onto it and lead her to the bathroom, pulling in behind us the semicircular tub used for checking leaks in inner tubes.

"Make yourself at home," she says, taking off her dress and changing the water in the tub. "I ain't modest."

But both of us avoid her body, evidence of heavy years, sagging flesh that looks as though she were slowly melting. I sit on the closed toilet lid, explain about the peephole, tell her that every gas station has one. She asks if she can look sometime.

"I been in Europe," she says, momentarily awkward, smiling at some time-locked incident, some pleasant misunderstanding. She squats over the tub and cleans herself with quick, patted splashes, bidet-style. She washes her dress, too, and hangs it on the aerial of the De Soto to dry.

"You've got to be out of there by nine," I say, pointing to the De Soto when she goes there to sleep. "The manager comes then."

"Fuck him," she says. "I'm sleeping till noon."

I pump gasoline, count my money, decide that a hundred fifty is enough for me: I ain't greedy.

The city wakes by color; dark sky, dark faces, garbage men sitting high up in the cabs of their trucks; yellow sky, yellow faces, Orientals in their pickups, buying gas for the lawn mower; white faces appear at dawn.

"Gas war's starting," I say to a man dressed in white, his face and arms covered with flour. "Price is going down."

"What's it at now?' The asks.

"Half the price on the pump."

"Fill 'er up!"

Ping! Ping! Bells in the pump mark gallons.

"Gas war!" I say, startling a woman in a Plymouth station wagon. "We're going to run the competition clean out of business."

"Is it going down more?" she asks. "Maybe I should come back later."

I'm tired of making change: it slows business down.

"Don't leave!" I say. "I'll find out for you."

I run to the office, make a hurried phone call to the time operator: seven forty-five. Bad news for the competition.

"It's dropped to nothing," I say with wild eyes, my body trembling with disbelief. "Nothing at all."

"Fill 'er up!"

"Gas war!" I scream at a '53 Ford. "We're giving it away!"

"So what," says the driver. "Gimme a buck's worth and shut up."

But the word spreads: people ask to use the telephone, speak into the mouthpiece with tense, conspiratorial expressions. I run from car to car, setting each nozzle on automatic, finally get all of them working. The station fills. Every pump is chiming.

"Fill 'er up!"

Cars come and go quickly, as though from a pit stop. I give away the last of the tires and the batteries. The lines into the station grow: two lanes all the way down the block. There's a minor accident down the street and I see the drivers shouting at one another, pointing to a broken headlight, a creased door.

"How much longer is it going to last?" a driver asks.

"Until the competition folds," I say with a grim face.

But I watch the clock: eight-fifteen.

"Fill 'er up!"

I can't help it: I begin to laugh. Down the street at the Standard station someone climbs a ladder to the sign where prices are advertised. Petroleum! I think. The nation needs petroleum! Oil company executives, sitting in pajamas, wait for conference calls to go through.

Strategy? says one. We'll just run the lying bastards out of business. Agreements be damned. I always knew it would come to this.

I take the nozzle from a Dodge truck with a TV repair shop sign painted on its side, but the driver stops me. He has dyed, thinning hair, a black triangle that's combed straight back from his brow. A face so wrinkled it looks like an accordion. He peers into the opening of the gas tank, sees there's enough for a quart more, and says to me; "When I say fill 'er up, I mean fill 'er up. You son of a bitch."

"Sorry," I say.

On the other side of the station two women begin to fight over a nozzle. A man takes from the trunk of his Chevrolet a case of empty jars and begins to fill them. A child begins to scream. Soon most of the drivers are helping themselves, showing others how to work the pumps. A line forms at the telephone, too.

"Gas war," a man screams into the mouthpiece. "Free cigarettes and oil, too!"

Eight-thirty: I change in the bathroom, park Ford across the street, and go into the bar. In the window there's a sign that reads: 8 A.M. TO 10 A.M. EYE OPENER, WINE, 15 CENTS.

Cap pulls up in front of the bar, sees Ford, and looks inside. He's driving a new Buick.

"I'm going to Phoenix," he says.

Where else? I think.

"You take care now," says Cap. And then he's gone.

The manager skids up in his Rambler, jumps onto the top of a pump, but no one will listen to him. A driver knocks him down. Manager has a smashed, bleeding mouth, a horrified expression: he stands on an island, not knowing what to do, listening to the pumps ring.

I walk across the street and say to him, "Turn off the power."

He's still stunned: large pupils, the color of oil.

"In the office," I say, giving him a gentle push. "The switch."

"Oh," he says.

I swear at Farmer, explain my anger, race Ford all the way to the beach, the shack.

"How's the gas war?" says Horse-T.

"Shh," I say, "quiet."

I hang my uniform on a hook.

"How's the gas war?" says Horse-T, laughing as he sees me count out half of the take.

☆☆ # The Network

from *Americana*

by Don DeLillo

I was an extremely handsome young man. The objectivity which time slowly fashions, and the self-restraint it demolishes, enable me to make this statement without recourse to the usual modest disclaimers which give credit to one's parents or grandparents in the manner of a sires-and-dams book. I suppose it's true enough that I inherited my mother's fine fair skin and my father's athletic physique, but the family album gives no clue to the curiously Grecian perspective of my face. Physical identity meant a great deal to me when I was twenty-eight years old. I had almost the same kind of relationship with my mirror that many of my contemporaries had with their analysts. When I began to wonder who I was, I took the simple step of lathering my face and shaving. It all became so clear, so wonderful. I was blue-eyed David Bell. Obviously my life depended on this fact.

I was exactly six feet two inches tall. My weight varied between 185 and 189. Despite my fair skin I tanned unusually well. My hair was more blond than it is now, thicker and richer; my waistline was thirty-two; my heartbeat was normal. I had a trick knee but my nose had never been broken, my feet were not ugly and I had better than average teeth. My complexion was excellent.

My secretary told me once that she had overheard Strobe Botway, one of my superiors at the network, refer to me as being "conventionally" handsome. We had a good laugh over that. Strobe hated me because I was taller and younger than he was, when smoking, of slowly rotating the cigarette with his thumb,

DON DELILLO (b. 1936) is the author of *Americana* (1971); *End Zone* (1972); *Great Jones Street* (1973); and *Ratner's Star* (1976).

index and middle fingers, as Bogart did in an early film of his. Strobe hated me because I was taller and younger than he was, and somewhat less extraterrestrial. He talked often of the Bogart mystique, using Germanic philosophical terms which nobody understood, and he subverted many parties by quoting long stretches of dialogue from obscure Bogart films. He also had his favorite character actors, men whose names nobody could ever connect with a face, men who played prison wardens for seven consecutive movies, who were always attacking Japanese machine-gun nests with a grenade in each hand, who were drunkards, psychotic killers, crooked lawyers, or test pilots who had lost their nerve. Strobe seemed to admire the physical imperfections of people, their lisps, scar tissue, chipped teeth; in his view these added up to character, to a certain seedy magnetism. His world was not mine. I admired Humphrey Bogart but he made me nervous. His forehead bothered me; it was the forehead of a man who owes money. My own instincts led me to Kirk Douglas and Burt Lancaster. These were the American pyramids and they needed no underground to spread their fame. They were monumental. Their faces slashed across the screen. When they laughed or cried it was without restraint. Their chromium smiles were never ambiguous. And they rarely had time to sit down and trade cynical quips with some classy society dame or dumb flatfoot. They were men of action, running, leaping, loving with abandon. When I was a teenager I saw Burt in *From Here to Eternity*. He stood above Deborah Kerr on that Hawaiian Beach and for the first time in my life I felt the true power of the image. Burt was like a city in which we are all living. He was that big. Within the conflux of shadow and time, there was room for all of us and I knew I must extend myself until the molecules parted and I was spliced into the image. Burt in the moonlight was a crescendo of male perfection but no less human because of it. I deny that he was a mere exhibit, plastic and sexless in some hall of science. I deny that he was pure anatomy, a diagram in a medical primer. Burt lives! I carry that image to his day, and so, I believe, do millions of others, men and women, for their separate reasons. Burt in the moonlight. It was a concept; it was the icon of a new religion. That night, after the movie, driving my father's car along the country roads, I began to wonder how real the landscape truly was, and how much of a dream is a dream.

Strobe died in the middle of a meeting. He had a heart attack at his desk. He is conventionally dead. But he would have been happy to know that his reaction to my physical traits was shared by others at the network. Hidden energies filled the air, small secret currents, as happens in every business which thrives in the heat of the image. There was a cult of the unattractive and the clever. There were points scored for ruthlessness. There were vendettas against the good-looking. One sought to avoid categories and therefore confound the formulators. For to be neither handsome nor unattractive, neither ruthless nor clever, was to be considered a hero by the bland, a nice fellow by the brilliant and the handsome, a nonentity by the clever, a homosexual by the lunatic fringe of the unattractive, a bright young man by the ruthless, a threat by the dangerously neurotic, an intimate and loyal friend by the alienated and the doomed. I did my best to keep low, I moved quietly close to walls and up and down the stairwells. A small incident confirmed the value of these tactics. It happened one day, after lunch, when I found myself crossing Madison Avenue stride for stride with Tom Maples, a young man who had joined the network at roughly the same time I had. We exchanged the usual cautious pleasantries. When we reached the sidewalk, a lovely teen-age girl wearing pink eyelashes asked me for my autograph. "I don't know who you are," she said, "but I'm sure you must be somebody." Her smile was rather winning, and blithely I signed her fold-out map of the subway system, thinking Maples might be amused. He avoided me for the next six months. After that I did my best to be exceedingly humble and withdrawing. I felt it was essential to the well-being of others.

It's time now to run the film again. I mean that quite literally, for I still have in my possession a movie made in those years, and many tapes as well. There isn't much to do on an island this remote and I can kill (or rather redistribute) a fair amount of time by listening to the soundtrack and taking yet another look at some of the footage.

I went down the corridor to my office. My secretary was at her desk eating a jelly donut and writing a letter. Her name was Binky Lister. She was a cheerful girl, a few pounds overweight in a pleasant way. She was having an affair with my immediate superior, Weede Denney, but continued to be a trustworthy secretary, which means she lied on my behalf and defended me on all counts against charges made by the secretaries of men who feared and hated me. She followed me into the office.

"Mr. Denney wants you for a ten o'clock meeting."

"What's it all about?"

"He doesn't tell me everything for chrissake."

"Don't get mad, Binky. It was just an idle question."

Standing there she crossed her ankles awkwardly, a sort of nonfacial pout. I sat behind my enormous desk and at once imagined myself naked. Then I pushed the chair back slightly and began to revolve in a magisterial 180-degree arc, surveying my land. The walls were covered with blow-ups of still photographs from programs I had written and coordinated. My bookcase was full of bound scripts. There were plants in two corners of the room and a dozen media periodicals arranged neatly on the end table. The ashtrays were all from Jensen. I had a black leather sofa and a yellow door. Weede Denney's sofa was bright red and he had a black door.

"What else?" I said.

"A woman called. She didn't leave her name but she said to tell you the frogs' legs weren't as tasty as usual."

"My life," I said, "is a series of telephone messages which nobody understands but me. Every woman I meet thinks she's some kind of Delphic phrasemaker. My phone rings at three in the morning and it's somebody stranded at some airport calling to tell me that the animal crackers have left the zoo. The other day I got a telegram—a schizogram—from a girl on the Coast and all it said was: MY TONSILS WENT TO A FUNERAL. Do you ever send messages like that, Bink? My life is a telex from Interpol."

"If it's all so annoying, why did you smile when I told you about the frogs' legs?"

"It was good news," I said.

I went around to Weede's office. He was sitting in his restyled barber chair. For a desk he used a low round coffee table made of teak. Across the room was his three-screen color TV console. The barber chair, being an eccentricity permitted someone in Weede's position, hadn't bothered me much, but the coffee table was a bit frightening, seeming to imply that my titanic desk was all but superfluous. Weede was a master of the office arts, specializing in the tactic of reaction. Some time after I had joined the network, a subordinate of Weede's named Rob Claven decided to decorate his office with exactly fourteen of his wife's paintings. It was a fairly horrifying sight. Weede didn't say a word. But a week later a few of us, including Rob Claven, went to a meeting in Weede's office. What we saw startled us. All the paintings and old schooner prints had vanished and in their place was hung a single eight-by-twelve-inch reproduction of a detail from the Sistine Chapel. The almost bare walls were Rob Claven's death sentence. The Michelangelo was the dropping of the blade.

Finally Weede nodded me out of the doorway and directed me to the blue chair. He did this with a movement of hand or eye so close to imperceptibility that even as I sat down I could not determine how I knew that I was supposed to sit in the blue chair. Reeves Chubb was already there, smoking one of his mentholated cigars. Weede told us an anecdote that concerned golf and adultery. Within a few minutes five more people entered, one a woman, Isabel Mayer, and the meeting began.

I looked out the window. Men in yellow helmets were working on a building that was going up across the street. They weaved in and out of its hollow bones, shooting acetylene, and catwalked over shaky planks. Strangely they did not seem to move with any special caution. Perhaps they had come to terms with the fear of falling. They had probably seen others fall and despised those deaths for the relief that followed the shock, a relief that must have risen with the wind, floor to floor, up the raw spindling shanks of the building. What could you do but go quickly to a dark bar and drink three burning whiskies? At one level two men squatted, riveting, and another, a level above, jumped from plank to plank, his arms held out slightly, hands at hip length. In mid-jump, at a certain angle against the open side of the building, he had the sky behind him, a rich and early blue, and they were framed in girders, man and sky, for what seemed an impossible second. I could see the riveters and the man jumping but they could not see each other. I watched for a long time, simultaneously trying to map the office voices and make them mean something. Then another man appeared from behind a girder, a tall man whose pants did not quite reach the top of his workboots. He stood motionless for a moment, hand canted against the rim of his helmet, shielding his eyes from the sun. He seemed to be looking at us. Then he lifted his hand above his head and began to wave. He was looking right at me, waving. I didn't know what to do. The cool voices clicked, measuring, compromising, destroying, pressuring. I felt he had to be acknowledged. I didn't know why but I felt it had to be done. It was absolutely imperative; a sign had to be given.

"Look," I said. "Look at that man over there. He's waving at us."

"Look," Isabel said. "He's waving. That construction worker. Do you see him, Weede?"

Then we were all on our feet, all eight of us, crowding before the window, waving back at him. It was exhilarating. We were all weaving and laughing. Weede began to shout: "We see you! We see you!" We shoved each other to get more room. Isabel was trying to climb onto the wide radiator shelf that edged out from the bottom of the window. I helped her up and she knelt there, waving with both hands now. The sky was cloudless. We were laughing uncontrollably.

We finished the meeting in high spirits. Weede suggested we all go to lunch together. Reeves Chubb begged off, saying he had a lot of work to get done, and I knew that sooner or later Weede would make him suffer for that little bit of whitewash. We went to the Gut Bucket, a nouveau speakeasy with spittoons and sawdust where you paid $4.50 for a hamburger. It was full of network people, actors and models. There were hundreds of photographs of George Raft on the wall. We sat at a circular oak table. Nobody said anything for fully three minutes. Then the waiter came and took our orders.

Across the room a very attractive couple sat drinking. Their legs touched beneath the table. I stared at the girl, trying to catch her eye. All I wanted was a brief smile, nothing more. It would have pleased me a great deal. There was an energy in me which demanded release in these small ways. To thieve one smile from that man's afternoon. I hoarded such ego-moments, remembering every one. The nod. The pretty smile. The deep glance over the tip of the cigarette. Anything more would have been too much. I didn't want to cause any pain.

"Good meeting," Weede said. "Are we agreed on that?"

The waiter brought the food before we were finished with our second drinks. The place was filled with fantastic women. Weede told us about his camera safari in Kenya. He and his wife Kitty had spent a month there in the autumn. He said that we all had to come up to his apartment and look at the slides some time. At the network, people were always making vague invitations. Someone you hadn't seen in months would materialize in your doorway, a seraphic image above your morning coffee. "Let's have lunch some day," he'd say, and that would be the end of him. Or one of your superiors, lifting his soapy head from a washroom basin, would squint in your direction and mumble: "When are you going to come over and have dinner with Ginny (Billie, Ellie, Sandy) and me?" Genuine invitations were usually delivered in secrecy, either in confidential memos or behind closed doors.

Weede excused himself before dessert arrived and he left in an atmosphere of unbending silence. We all knew where he was going—to the Penn-Mar Hotel on Ninth Avenue where Binky would be waiting for him. They met every Thursday for an hour or so. After he'd gone Isabel decided to order a brandy and we joined her. She was a short mashed woman of forty-five or so. Four months earlier, at a party aboard a tugboat repeatedly circling the Statue of Liberty, she had gone around telling everyone that she had dropped one of her pubic hairs into Mastoff Panofsky's scotch and soda. Everybody was afraid of her. There was no logical reason for this; her job, in some obscurely defined way, dealt with fashion coordination, and she was not competitive with anyone in the entire network. Yet we all went to shameful extremes to prove our friendship and loyalty. It may have been that we sensed a dangerous feline perversity. Competitive or not, she seemed to be a woman who might attack at any moment, making no concessions at all to the etiquette of office combat. Now she began to tell us about the graffiti in the ladies' rooms of various restaurants around town. She hit the table after each recitation. The brandies came and we talked about the winter schedule, agreeing it was first-rate. A very tall girl wearing candy-cane trousers walked across the room; her legs seemed joined directly to her shoulders. Then Reeves Chubb came in. He saw us and waved. He dropped into the vacated chair with a burst of relief that seemed worthy of some historic moment, as if he had been gouging through a rain forest for months before finding us, the lost battalion.

"Did I miss Weede?" he said. "Guess I missed him, damn it. Thought I'd come down for a quickie before tackling that China thing. What's everybody drinking? I just heard Phelps got the ax. He doesn't know about it yet so don't say anything. They'll probably wait until after the first of the year. Paul Joyner thinks he's next. His door has been closed all morning. Hallie said he's been calling everybody he's ever known since high school. But he's been saying he's next for the last eight years. I guess he figures if he says it, it won't happen. Reverse jinx. The last few weeks have been hell on wheels. I've been in the office every weekend this month. If there's no letup soon, my child bride says she's going home to mother. Did you read where MBO is using recons for the depth skeds? I ran into Jones Perkins on my way down. He said Warburton's got some kind of rare fatal blood thing. I'd love to go out to Aspen for the holidays but I don't see how I can swing it. My secretary's going though. I don't know how they do it. Hallie's going to Europe again in the spring. Have you heard what Merrill did, that perfect ass? Which reminds me. Blaisdell told me he saw Chandler Bates' wife in San Juan last weekend. Hanging around El Convento with some tacky scuba type. Isabel, those are the most stunning gloves. If I don't take a vacation soon, you're going to walk into my office and see nothing there but a heap of ashes. What's everybody drinking?"

We went back to the office. In the early afternoon it was always quiet, the whole place tossing slowly in tropical repose, as if the building itself swung on a miraculous hammock, and then the dimming effects of food and drink would begin to wear off and we would remember why we were there, to buzz and chime, and all would bend to their respective machines. But there was something wonderful about that time, the hour or so before we remembered. It was the time to sit on your sofa instead of behind the desk, and to call your secretary into the office and talk in soft voices about nothing in particular—films, books, water sports, travel, nothing at all. There was a certain kind of love between you then, like the love in a family which has shared so many familiar moments that not to love would be inhuman. And the office itself seemed a special place, even in its pale yellow desperate light, so much the color of old newspapers; there was the belief that you were secure here, in some emotional way, that you moved in known terrain. If you had a soul, and it had the need to be rubbed by roots and seasons, to be comforted by familiar things, then you could not walk among those desks for two thousand mornings, nor hear those volleying typewriters, without coming to believe that this was where you were safe. You knew where the legal department was, and how to get a package through the mailroom without delay, and whom to see about tax deductions, and what to do when your water carafe sprang a leak. You knew all the things you wouldn't have known if you had suddenly been placed in any other office in any other building anywhere in the world; and compared to this, how much did you know, and how safe did you feel, about, for instance, your wife? And it was at that time, before we remembered why we were there, that the office surrendered a sense of belonging, and we sat in the early afternoon, pitching gently, knowing we had just returned to the mother ship.

There was a phone ringing in the corridor. Nobody bothered to pick it up. Then another one began ringing. I walked slowly around my office, stretching as I went. I tried to remember whether Burt or Kirk had ever acted in an office film, one of those dull morality tales about power plays and timid adulteries. I noticed a memo on my desk. I knew immediately, from the brevity of the message, that it was another of the strange memos that had been appearing at irregular intervals for over a year. I picked it up and read it.

To Tech Unit B
From: St. Augustine
   And never can a man be more disastrously in death than
   when death itself shall be deathless.

Nobody knew who sent these memos. Investigations had been made, people questioned, but nothing came of it. Whoever sent them had to overcome two difficulties. He had to get into the multilith room and run off enough copies for our entire sub-section without being discovered. And he had to distribute the memos, one by one, to every desk and office in the area. The multilith operators had been cleared of any suspicion and so had all the mailboys. No one had ever seen these particular memos delivered; they simply appeared, either in the morning or early afternoon. This was the first of the St. Augustines. Previous memos had borne messages from Zwingli, Lévi-Strauss, Rilke, Chekhov, Tillich, William Blake, Charles Olson and a Kiowa chief named Satanta. Naturally the person responsible for these messages became known throughout the company as the Mad Memo-Writer. I never referred to him that way because it was much too obvious a name. I called him Trotsky. There was no special reason for choosing Trotsky; it just seemed to fit. I wondered if he was someone I knew. Everybody seemed to think he was probably a small grotesque man who had suffered many disappointments in life, who despised the vast impersonal structure of the network and who was employed in our forwarding department, the traditional repository for all sex offenders, mutants and vegetarians. They said he was most likely a foreigner who lived in a rooming house in Red Hook; he spent his nights reading an eight-volume treatise on abnormal psychology, in small type, and he told his grocer he had been a Talmudic scholar in the old country. This was the consensus and maybe it had a certain logic. But I found more satisfaction in believing that Trotsky was one of our top executives. He made eighty thousand dollars a year and stole paper clips from the office.

I sat at my desk and with a ballpoint pen traced the outline of my left hand on a blank piece of note paper. Then I called Sullivan but she didn't answer the phone. I walked around the office some more and looked out into the corridor. Many of the girls were back at work, unhooding their typewriters and storing squalid Kleenex in the bottom drawers of their desks where it would rest with old love letters, rag dolls, and pornographic books their bosses had given them in the spirit of the new liberalism, and also to see if anything would happen. I closed the door. Then I unzipped my pants and took out my cock. I walked around the office like that for a while. It felt good. I put it back and then filed Trotsky's memo in the folder that held all of his other work as well as some poems I had written in the office from time to time and some schizograms from girls I knew. (HELLO FROM THE SCENIC COAST OF NEBRASKA.) I opened the door. Binky was at her desk. She took a sandwich and a paper container out of a white bag. The sandwich, when she unwrapped it, looked wet and gummy. There was something very touching about that moment.

"Welcome back to the big rock candy mountain."

"Hi," she said. "I spent two solid hours at goddamn Saks without buying a thing. And now I'm about to eat a Coca-Cola sandwich. Merry Christmas."

"Trotsky struck again."

"I saw it," she said. "I still think it's you."

She knew that would flatter me. Often she said things that seemed intended to do me some good. I never knew why. In many ways Binky was a good friend to me and I used to wonder what would happen if I tried, in the jargon of the day, to complicate our relationship. Once, working late in the office, she removed her shoes while taking dictation. The sight of a woman taking off her shoes has always stirred me, and I kissed her. That was all, a kiss between paragraphs, but maybe it wasn't mere tenderness which made me do it, nor a desire to challenge the blandness of our attachment. Maybe it was just another of my ego-moments. It was only several days before that I had learned about Binky and Weede.

"Come on in," I said.

She brought her lunch with her and we sat on the sofa.

"Phelps Lawrence just got bounced," she said.

"I heard."

"There's a rumor that Joyner's next."

"Joyner started it," I said. 'It's part of his survival kit. If he's not careful it's going to blow up in his face one of these days."

"Jody thinks it's the beginning of a purge. There's been a rash of confidential memos. She thinks Stennis might be forced to resign. But keep it quiet. She made me promise not to breathe a word."

"I've noticed all the closed doors. Sometimes I think they close their doors just to frighten us. Everybody knows closed doors mean secret discussions and secret discussions mean trouble. But maybe they're in there watching guitar lessons on Channel 31."

"Grove Palmer is getting a divorce," Binky said.

Suddenly I realized that I hadn't brushed my teeth after lunch. I kept some toothpaste and a toothbrush in my office and always brushed my teeth after a lunch that included a few drinks. The washroom after lunch was always full of men brushing their teeth and gargling with mouthwash. There were times when I thought all of us at the network existed only on videotape. Our words and actions seemed to have a disturbingly elapsed quality. We had said and done all these things before and they had been frozen for a time, rolled up in little laboratory trays to await broadcast and rebroadcast when the proper time-slots became available. And there was the feeling that somebody's deadly pinky might nudge a button and we would all be erased forever. Those moments in the washroom, with a dozen men sawing away at their teeth, were perhaps the worst times of all. We seemed to be no more than electronic signals and we moved through time and space with the stutter and shadowed insanity of a TV commercial.

"What's happening with your Navaho project?" Binky said.

"Quincy keeps jamming up the works. I'm going to talk to Weede and see if I can get to work on it alone. But don't mention it to anybody."

"David," she said.

"What?"

"They may drop 'Soliloquy.' "

"Are you sure?"

"The person who told me said the crappy sponsor wasn't interested in renewing."

"Why not?"

"The person didn't say."

"There's always the Navahos," I said.

"David, I think it's the third or fourth best show on TV."

"Soliloquy" was a series I had worked out on my own. It was the first major thing I had done since joining Weede's group—a small, elite and experimental unit put together for the purpose of developing new concepts and techniques. The rest of the network despised us because of our relative freedom and because of the industry prizes we had won for our warcasts, which were done independently of the news division. "Soliloquy" had won nothing. Each show consisted, very simply, of an individual appearing before the camera for an hour and telling his life story. I wanted to ask her what else Weede had said about the series. But that wouldn't have been fair. She had already taken a chance in telling me as much as she had. Just then Weede went by my office, moving swiftly, head down, body tilted forward as if on skis. He always came back to the office at least half an hour after Binky on Thursday afternoons; this maneuver, obviously, was an attempt to avoid suspicion. I liked to think that he walked around the block five times during that half hour, or stood in a phone booth in the lobby and pretended he was talking to someone, moving his lips over the mouthpiece, perhaps actually speaking, carrying on a normal businesslike conversation with the dial tone. And he always walked by my office very quickly, then tried to avoid me for the rest of the day. He must have possessed an extraordinarily complex sense of guilt. I think he was afraid of me on those Thursdays. But on Friday morning he would come looking for me, breathing smoke and vengeance, as if I were the engineer of his guilt.

Binky went back to her desk. I loosened my tie and rolled up my sleeves. I had managed to deceive myself into believing that people would be deceived into believing that a man so untidy (in an atmosphere so methodically spruce) must be driving himself mercilessly. The phone rang. It was Wendy Judd, a girl I had dated in college. She was living in New York now, having traveled for a year right after she divorced her husband, one of the top production people at either Paramount or Metro.

"I'm dying, David."

"Don't generalize, Wendy."

"New York is vicious. Listen, before I forget, can you come to a dinner party tomorrow night? Come alone. You're the only one who can save me."

"You know I go bowling with the fellas on Friday night, Wendy."

"David, please. This is no time for jokes."

"Our team is called the Steamrollers. We play the Silver Jets for the all-league title tomorrow. Winner gets a cup with a naked Greek bowling ace embossed on the side."

"Come early," she said. "You can help me toss the salad. We'll talk over old times.'

"There are no old times, Wendy. The tapes have been accidentally destroyed."

"Eightish," she said, and hung up.

Outside the girls were hammering at their little oval keys. I went for a walk. Everybody was busy. All the phones seemed to be ringing. Some of the girls talked to themselves while typing, muttering *shit* whenever they made a mistake. I went around to the supply area. The cabinets were the same color as troops in the field. Hallie Lewin was in there, leaning over a bottom drawer. There is no place in the world more sexually exciting than a large office. It is like a fantasy of some elaborate woman-maze; wherever you go, around corners, into cubicles, up or down the stairwells, you are greeted by an almost lewd tableau. There are women standing, sitting, kneeling, crouching, all in attitudes that seem designed to stun you. It is like a dream of jubilant gardens in which every tree contains a milky nymph. Hallie saw me and smiled.

"I hear Reeves Chubb got canned," I said.

"Really? I had no idea he was in trouble."

"Don't breath a word."

"Of course not."

"Hallie, you've got the sweetest little ass I've ever seen."

"Why thank you."

"Not a word about Reeves now."

"I promise," she said.

I went around toward Weede Denney's office. On the way I saw Dickie Slater, the sixty-five-year-old mailboy, standing behind Jody Moore's desk rubbing his groin. When he saw me he grinned, man to man, and kept rubbing. Jody was on the phone, speaking Portuguese for some reason. I turned a corner and saw James T. Rice running down a hallway at top speed. I had no idea what I wanted to say to Weede. I was upset about the series being dropped and I felt venomous. In similar situations I usually reacted as a child might react after he has been disappointed or rebuked, with a child's petty genius for reprisal. I told bizarre and pointless lies. I broke my typewriter. I stole things from the office. I wrote snake-hissing memos to my subordinates. Once, after an idea of mine had been criticized by a senior vice-president named Livingston, I went back to my office, blew my nose several times, and that night sneaked up to Livingston's office and put the soiled handkerchief in the top drawer of his desk.

Weede was standing in the middle of his office, deep in thought, one hand absently grooming his bald head. He looked at me carefully.

"Can't talk to you now, Dave; wires are burning up; see you first thing in the morning."

On the way back to my office I stopped at Binky's desk to talk some more but she looked busy. I went inside and dialed Sullivan's number again. She was there. .

"Utah," I said.

"Hello, David."

"Montana, Wyoming, Nevada, Arizona."

"I didn't see you leave last night. You abandoned me to all those keening necrophiles."

"Steamboat Springs, the Sawtooth Mountains, Big Timber, Aztec, Durango, Spanish Fork, Monument Valley."

"I hear America singing," she said, but not as if she meant it.

"I know a guy with a camp trailer. He's living in Maine somewhere. We can pick him up and then all head west in the camper."

"All I need is an hour's notice."

"Blasting through New Mexico in the velvet dawn."

"I'm late for an appointment," Sullivan said.

I tried to get some work done. It was dark now and I went to the window. Looking south, from as high as we were, I could see the stacked lights extending almost the entire length of Manhattan, and that delicate gridiron tracery in the streets. I opened the window slightly. The whole city was roaring. In winter, when the darkness always comes before you expect it and all those lights begin to pinch through the stale mist, New York becomes a gigantic wedding cake. You board the singing elevator and drop an eighth of a mile in ten seconds flat. Your ears hum as you are decompressed. It is an almost frighteningly impersonal process and yet something of this kind seems necessary to translate you from the image to what is actually impaled on that dainty fork.

I strolled around to Carter Hemmings' office. He was at his desk, smelling the nicotine on his fingers. When he saw me he tried to neutralize the flow of panic by standing up, absurdly, and spreading his arms wide, an Argentinian beef baron welcoming a generalissimo to his villa.

"Hey Dave," he said. "What's happening, buddy?"

"I understand Mars Tyler got the sack," I said.

"No kidding. No kidding. Jesus."

"There's a big purge on. The tumbrels are clattering through the streets."

"Sit down," he said. "I'll get Penny to order some coffee."

"Can't spare the time, Carter. All the circuits are overloaded. How's that laser beam project shaping up? They're starting to put pressure."

"I'm trying to hammer it into workable form, Dave."

"Have a good time with B.G. last night?"

"I didn't know you knew her, Dave."

"Slightly," I said.

"Beautiful girl. But we didn't really hit it off. Dinner. Then I took her home."

"Weede was talking about you during lunch today. He's a curious man, Weede. Sometimes given to rash judgments. Better get cracking on that laser beam thing. I'll be in early tomorrow to take a look at it. Weede'll be in early tomorrow too. We're all coming in very early tomorrow. Have a nice evening, Carter. Say hello to your wife for me."

"Dave, I'm not married."

I went back to my office. Binky was in there trying to straighten out my files. It was almost time to leave. I fixed my tie and buttoned my shirtcuffs. In the corridor all the phones were ringing. I wondered who Trotsky was.

✩✩✩ The Sons of Abolition

by R. D. Skillings

The barracks was warm with afternoon sun. Gloomy Gerald Macey stared at the chessboard. "Please, move," he said.

"I can't concentrate," said Ben Flack, who only played to please Gerald. "Let's go in town and lush."

"Move," said Gerald. "It's mate in three."

"Your great-grandfather's dusty balls!" cried Ed Peacock, kibitzing from the bunk above. Graduate of an Ohio law school, with a wife at home, his language had lately acquired the exuberance of a binge. He did not mind the military. He had never been so free before; he might never be so free again. Ben Flack had been in the demolition business. Gerald Macey, because he liked to read, wanted to be a writer.

All were draft dodgers, doing six months in the Air Force National Guard to avoid the Army. Civilian life awaited them, and nothing they did in McGee, Mississippi in April of 1960 seemed to matter; nothing that happened had consequences.

"Speaking of balls," said Ben Flack, "I think I'll get laid tonight."

"That was what you thought last night, too," Gerald recalled with discomfort.

"Black bitch!" said Flack, turning red.

"Let go my arm, jus' let go my arm." Ed Peacock's mimicry of the girl's voice did not conceal derision.

Gerald had stepped aside, disassociating himself from his friends, while Flack tried to persuade the black waitress at the soda fountain to come with him to a dance at the Service Club.

R. D. SKILLINGS (b. 1937) is the author of *Alternative Lives* (1974), a collection of stories.

She dutifully smiled as at some inane remark well-meant, and continued sponging the counter. Flack asked if she had a husband, what time did she get off? Sure of the world, he slouched on his elbow as if he were at a bar and she were there to be picked up.

The druggist, who looked like William Faulkner, watched from the cash register, and Ed Peacock in levity asked Gerald, who did not answer, when was the last lynching in town.

"Baby, there's no segregation on Base," Flack said, in earnest now.

The girl started to move away, but he leaned across and caught her arm. "Baby, you got nothing to be afraid of," he said, "you can go anywhere you want with me."

"Let go my arm," the girl said, "jus' let go my arm."

Then the druggist squeezed around the cash register, crossed almost quickly the aisle of floor. "That's all right, Julie," he murmured, "I'll finish up here. You can start the floor, if you like."

Without looking at anyone the girl went to a closet, got a broom and began sweeping behind the racks of medicines.

"Almost nine o'clock," the druggist said to Flack. "We always close a little early on Fridays, you know." He glanced out the window at the grey starless twilight, touched his mustache. "I sure do hope it don't rain. I went out this morning without my raincoat and my wife said. . . ."

"Mister," said Flack, "I hope it rains shit."

"But she does not *want* to go anywhere with you," the druggist cried quietly.

"Everyone in Mississippi is either a nigger or deserves to be," said Flack, glowering at the chessboard.

"Move!" Gerald cried. "Move! Move! Move!"

Flack sprang up with inspiration. "I resign," he declared.

Robbed of victory, Gerald removed his glasses and peered out the window. There was nothing to see but another barracks. Time began to gape again. "Your position was completely untenable," he insisted.

Ed Peacock smiled down on him. "At the rate you're going you'll get an ulcer. What d'you want an ulcer for at your young age?"

Gerald lay down opposite Freddy Pommer who was asleep

with his eyes open and tried to remember why he was here. He had quit college to seek life, but found himself still a student, this time in a school for administrative technicians, whose classroom was a barracks, whose faculty had fought in Korea, and whose curriculum consisted of the regulations, manuals and paperwork by which the daily business of the Air Force is conducted. He felt like a misprint on a table of statistics, would have been a pacifist but for Hitler, worried about war, and got into angry arguments. "Ulcers," Ed Peacock mocked, and Gerald half agreed. On the firing line, shooting at human-shaped targets, it calmed him to think the meaning of consent lay deeper than the surface obedience he shared with the others, who did not doubt all America's enemies were evil.

Toward evening they drove into town to drink. The road went through a hollow where a stream trickles between grassless banks. Under ancient trees crouched a community of shanties. The earth around was packed flat by feet. Vapor rose from chimneys. Dogs yawned in the yards and naked black children sat on the sagging porches. Ed Peacock slowed the car to miss a hen.

"Makes you proud to be white, doesn't it?" Gerald said, embittered by this daily ordeal.

No one answered.

"America the beautiful," Gerald said, furious at their ease.

"Animals!" Freddy Pommer growled. "They ain't no better than apes!"

"Down here they aren't," said Flack, who was from Boston.

"They don't know anything else," Ed Peacock said philosophically. "I know it'll sound illiberal, but ignorance really is bliss."

Behind them the shanties vanished round a bend in the road like a vision of original sin.

"Some day America will be destroyed," Gerald promised in a voice that shook.

Ed Peacock began to hum to himself. The others wore expressions of patience, tolerant of his tumult.

On the outskirts of McGee, in the traffic, they came on garages with tier on tier of windshields priced in red paint $345, $420, $600, Dairyqueens, billboards, bars— it was like the road through all the hopeful little towns across America, it was like home. A car of kids roared by and Gerald in rage stared after it. Let none be spared, he thought, let me not be spared.

At the next corner he got out to catch the McGee bus. The others were going across the river into Arkansas to look for girls. Gerald was going off to get drunk by himself, plot an apocalypse, and meet them later at the Crystal Ball.

When the bus came it was full. He moved down the aisle and stood, holding a strap. Without turning he could feel the jury of blacks in the back of the bus. It troubled him for the first time to see Negroes in numbers. Ben Flack, who said they were better in bed, called them spades and claimed acquaintance with their culture, but to Gerald they seemed fearful, a conquered people, and he did not wish to be mistaken for one of the masters. He wanted to wear a badge saying, I'm from New England where the greens honor our grandfathers who died for your liberty.

The bus stopped in the middle of a block. The pleasant driver came down the aisle to Gerald, then smiled, almost bowing, and spoke softly to the Negro sitting in the split-seat by the door:

"Would j'all please be kind enough to let the gentleman sit down?"

The Negro, a man seventy, in a black suit, also smiled, and in a voice equally fond, even grateful, said, "Certainly, certainly," then rose with easy alacrity, smiling from Gerald the gentleman to the driver and back again.

"Thank you," murmured the driver and the three stood for a moment, smiling and murmuring, before Gerald, his heart stopped with astonishment, slipped safely into the seat.

He stumbled off at the next stop. The Crystal Ball was a mile away and he walked toward it in a horror from which he tried to escape into fantasies of making atonement to the man whose seat he had stolen by marrying his beautiful daughter, of executing the driver before the assembled peoples of the world, of leading a black rebellion in which white blood filled the gutters.

"Shine, Mister?" said a black boy on the corner.

Gerald drew breath, nodded, and bravely put one foot up on the boy's box, accepting in penance the terrible tableau. He stared down in shame, watching the fast fingers work.

"Are y'all in the Air Force?"

Gerald confessed it.

"I can tell by your shoes," the boy said happily. "They're Air Force shoes. Are y'all a General?"

"I wish I were," Gerald said. "I'd make some changes."

"Uh-huh," said the boy. His fingers slipped, smearing polish on the cuff. He gazed up aghast. "Aw," he whined, "aw, General, I'm sorry."

"That's all right," said Gerald, "don't worry about it."

"Wait, I'll get it out, it ain't much, I'll get it right out, yes sir." The boy darted a brown hand into his box, brought forth a rag and began scrubbing the cuff, spreading the stain. "See, it don't hardly show," he sang triumphantly, "it don't hardly show at all, no sir."

"What's the damage?" said Gerald feebly.

"Jus' a dime," the boy said with energy, putting his equipment back in the box, "jus' a dime for the best shine in town."

Gerald had no coins but a half-dollar which he handed over, saying, "Keep the change, and thank you very much."

"Thank *you*, General," the boy said, and gave him a grin that hit like a fist.

Gerald turned away, hoping to summon the dignity of sorrow, but knew he was in flight, pursued by the boy's contempt.

The Crystal Ball was a crowded sanctuary. In the depths of the place, at one of the tables, a dispute was in progress; voices, blurred by passion and dogma, were raised above the jukebox. He did not look to see who it was: there were fights every night. He did not look for his friends. He drank alone at the bar like a hermit among the locals, staring into the mirror, but could not quench the burning in his stomach.

"You out at the Base?" at last inevitably said the drunk beside him. "I useta be in the Air Force myself. Had some times, had some real times, had the best times of my life in the Air Force, you know that? You jus' a young fella. How old d'you think I am? I'm old enough to be your father. I'm gon buy you a beer. I like you, you know why? You know why I like you? Because you're such a damn good kid."

An Act of Prostitution

by James Alan McPherson

When he saw the woman the lawyer put down his pencil and legal pad and took out his pipe.

"Well," he said. "How do you want to play it?"

"I wanna get outta here," the whore said. "Just get me outta here."

"Now get some sense," said the lawyer, puffing on the pipe to draw in the flame from the long wooden match he had taken from his vest pocket. "You ain't got a snowball's chance in hell."

"I just want out," she said.

"You'll catch hell in there," he said, pointing with the stem of his pipe to the door which separated them from the main courtroom. "Why don't you just get some sense and take a few days on the city."

"I can't go up there again," she said. "Those dike matrons in Parkville hate my guts because I'm wise to them. They told me last time they'd really give it to me if I came back. I can't do no time up there again."

"Listen," said the lawyer, pointing the stem of his pipe at her this time, "you ain't got a choice. Either you cop a plea or I don't take the case."

"*You* listen, you two-bit Jew shyster." The whore raised her voice, pointing her very chubby finger at the lawyer. "*You* ain't got no choice. The judge told you to be my lawyer and you got to do it. I ain't no dummy, you know that?"

"Yeah," said the lawyer. "You're a real smarty. That's why

JAMES ALAN McPHERSON (b. 1943) is the author of *Hue and Cry* (1969), a collection of short stories.

you're out on the streets in all that snow and ice. You're a real smarty all right."

"You chickenshit," she said. "I don't want you on my case anyway, but I ain't got no choice. If you was any good, you wouldn't be working the sweatboxes in this court. I ain't no dummy."

"You're a real smarty," said the lawyer. He looked her up and down: a huge woman, pathetically blonde, big-boned and absurd in a skirt sloppily crafted to be mini. Her knees were ruddy and the flesh below them was thick and white and flabby. There was no indication of age about her. Like most whores, she looked at the same time young but then old, possibly as old as her profession. Sometimes they were very old but seemed to have stopped aging at a certain point so that ranking them chronologically, as the lawyer was trying to do, came hard. He put his pipe on the table, on top of the police affidavit, and stared at her. She sat across the room, near the door in a straight chair, her flesh oozing over its sides. He watched her pull her miniskirt down over the upper part of her thigh, modestly, but with the same hard, cold look she had when she came in the room. "You're a real smarty," he commented, drawing on his pipe and exhaling the smoke into the room.

The fat woman in her miniskirt still glared at him. "Screw you, Yid!" she said through her teeth. "Screw your fat mama and your chubby sister with hair under her arms. Screw your brother and your father and I hope they should go crazy playing with themselves in pay toilets."

The lawyer was about to reply when the door to the consultation room opened and another man came into the small place. "Hell, Jimmy," he said to the lawyer, pretending to ignore the woman, "I got a problem here."

"Yeah?" said Jimmy.

The other man walked over to the brown desk, leaned closer to Jimmy so that the woman could not hear and lowered his voice. "I got this kid," he said. "A nice I-talian boy that grabbed this Cadillac outta a parking lot. Now he only done it twice before and I think the Judge might go easy if he got in a good mood before the kid goes on, this being Monday morning and all."

"So?" said Jimmy.

"So I was thinking," the other lawyer said, again lowering his voice and leaning much closer and making a sly motion with his head to indicate the whore on the chair across the room. "So I was thinking. The Judge knows Philomena over there. She's here almost every month and she's always good for a laugh. So I was thinking, this being Monday morning and all and with a cage-load of nigger drunks out there, why not put her on first, give the old man a good laugh and then put my I-talian boy on. I know he'd get a better deal that way."

"What's in it for me?" said Jimmy, rapping the ashes from his pipe into an ashtray.

"Look, I done *you* favors before. Remember that Chinaman? Remember the tip I gave you?"

Jimmy considered while he stuffed tobacco from a can into his pipe. He lit the pipe with several matches from his vest pocket and considered some more. "I don't mind, Ralph," he said. "But if she goes first the Judge'll get a good laugh and then he'll throw the book at her."

"What the hell, Jimmy?" said Ralph. He glanced over at the whore who was eying them hatefully. "Look, buddy," he want on, "you know who that is? Fatso Philomena Brown. She's up here almost every month. Old Bloom knows her. I tell you, she's good for a laugh. That's all. Besides, she's married to a nigger anyway."

"Well," said Jimmy. "So far she ain't done herself much good with me. She's a real smarty. She thinks I'm a Jew."

"There you go," said Ralph. "Come on, Jimmy. I ain't got much time before the Clerk calls my kid up. What you say?"

Jimmy looked over at his client, the many pounds of her rolled in great logs of meat under her knees and around her belly. She was still sneering. "O.K." He turned his head back to Ralph. "O.K., I'll do it."

"Now look," said Ralph, "this is how we'll do. When they call me up I'll tell the Clerk I need more time with my kid for consultation. And since you follow me on the docket you'll get on pretty soon, at least before I will. Then after everybody's had a good laugh, I'll bring my I-talian on."

"Isn't *she* Italian?" asked Jimmy, indicating the whore with a slight movement of his pipe.

"Yeah. But she's married to a nigger."

"O.K.," said Jimmy, "we'll do it."

"What's that?" said the whore, who had been trying to listen all this time. "What are you two kikes whispering about anyway? What the hell's going on?"

"Shut up," said Jimmy, the stem of his pipe clamped far back in his mouth so that he could not say it as loud as he wanted. Ralph winked at him and left the room. "Now listen," he said to Philomena Brown, getting up from his desk and walking over to where she still sat against the wall. "If you got a story, you better tell me quick because we're going out there soon and I want you to know I ain't telling no lies for you."

"I don't want you on my case anyway, kike," said Philomena Brown.

"It ain't what *you* want. It's what the old man out there says you gotta do. Now if you got a story let's have it *now*."

"I'm a file clerk. I was just looking for work."

"Like *hell!* Don't give *me* that shit. When was the last time you had your shots?"

"I ain't never had none," said Mrs. Brown.

Now they could hear the Clerk, beyond the door, calling the Italian boy into court. They would have to go out in a few minutes. "Forget the story," he told her. "Just pull your dress down some and wipe some of that shit off your eyes. You look like hell."

"I don't want you on the case, Moses," said Mrs. Brown.

"Well you got me," said Jimmy. "You got me whether you want me or not." Jimmy paused, put his pipe in his coat pocket, and then said: "And my name is *Mr. Mulligan!*"

The woman did not say anything more. She settled her weight in the chair and made it creak.

"Now let's get in there," said Jimmy.

II

The Judge was in his Monday morning mood. He was very ready to be angry at almost anyone. He glared at the Court Clerk as the bald, seemingly consumptive man called out the names of six defendants who had defaulted. He glared at the group of drunks and addicts who huddled against the steel net of the prisoners' cage, gazing toward the open courtroom as if expecting mercy from the rows of concerned parties and spectators who sat in the hot place. Judge Bloom looked as though he wanted very badly to spit. There would be no mercy this Monday morning and the prisoners all knew it.

"Willie Smith! Willie Smith! Come into Court!" the Clerk barked.

Willie Smith slowly shuffled out of the prisoners' cage and up to the dirty stone wall, which kept all but his head and neck and shoulders concealed from the people in the musty courtroom.

From the bench the Judge looked down at the hungover Smith.

"You know, I ain't never seen him sitting down in that chair," Jimmy said to one of the old men who came to court to see the daily procession, filling up the second row of benches, directly behind those reserved for court-appointed lawyers. There were at least twelve of these old men, looking almost semi-professional in faded gray or blue or black suits with shiny knees and elbows. They liked to come and watch the fun. "Watch old Bloom give it to this nigger," the same old man leaned over and said into Jimmy Mulligan's ear. Jimmy nodded without looking back at him. And after a few seconds he wiped his ear with his hand, also without looking back.

The Clerk read the charges: Drunkenness, Loitering, Disorderly Conduct.

"You want a lawyer, Willie?" the Judge asked him. Judge Bloom was now walking back and forth behind his bench, his arms gravely folded behind his back, his belly very close to pregnancy beneath his black robe. "The Supreme Court says I have to give you a lawyer. You want one?"

"No sir," the hung-over Smith said, very obsequiously.

"Well, what's your trouble?"

"Nothing."

"You haven't missed a Monday here in months."

"Yes sir."

"All that money you spend on booze, how do you take care of your family?"

Smith moved his head and shoulders behind the wall in a gesture that might have been a shuffle.

"When was the last time you gave something to your wife?"

"Last Friday."

"You're a liar. Your wife's been on the City for years."

"I help," said Smith, quickly.

"You help, all right. You help all right. You help her raise her belly and her income every year."

The old men in the second row snickered and the Judge eyed them in a threatening way. They began to stifle their chuckles. Willie Smith smiled.

"If she has one more kid she'll be making more than me," the Judge observed. But he was not saying it to Smith. He was looking at the old men.

Then he looked down at the now bashful, smiling Willie Smith. "You want some time to sleep it off or you want to pay?"

"I'll take the time."

"How much you want, Willie?"

"I don't care."

"You want to be out for the weekend, I guess."

Smith smiled again.

"Give him five days," the Judge said to the Clerk. The Clerk wrote in his papers and then said in a hurried voice: "Defendant Willie Smith, you have been found guilty by this court of being drunk in a public place, of loitering while in this condition, and of disorderly conduct. This court sentences you to five days in the House of Correction at Bridgeview and one month's suspended sentence. You have, however, the right to appeal in which case the suspended sentence will not be allowed and the sentence will then be thirty-five days in the House of Correction."

"You want to appeal, Willie?"

"Naw sir."

"See you next week," said the Judge.

"Thank you," said Willie Smith.

A black fellow in a very neatly pressed Army uniform came on next. He stood immaculate and proud and clean-shaven with his cap tucked under his left arm while the charges were read. The prosecutor was a hard-faced black police detective, tieless, very long-haired in a short-sleeved white shirt with wet armpits. The detective was tough but very nervous. He looked at his notes while the Clerk read the charges. The Judge, bald and wrinkled and drooping in the face, still paced behind his bench, his nose twitching from time to time, his arms locked behind the back. The soldier was charged with assault and battery with a dangerous weapon on a police officer; he remained standing erect and silent, looking off into the space behind the Judge until his lawyer, a plump, greasy black man in his late fifties, had heard the charge and motioned for him to sit. Then he placed himself beside his lawyer and put his cap squarely in front of him on the table.

The big-bellied black detective managed to get the police officer's name, rank and duties from him, occasionally glancing over at the table where the defendant and his lawyer sat, both hard-faced and cold. He shuffled through his notes, paused, looked up at the Judge, and then said to the white officer: "Now, Officer Bergin, would you tell the Court in your own words what happened?"

The white policeman put his hands together in a prayer-like gesture on the stand. He looked at the defendant whose face was set and whose eyes were fixed on the officer's hands. "We was on duty on the night of July twenty-seventh driving around the Lafayette Street area when we got a call to proceed to the Lafayette Street subway station because there was a crowd gathering there and they thought it might be a riot. We proceeded there, Officer Bigelow and me, and when we got there sure enough there was a crowd of colored people running up and down the street and making noise and carrying on. We didn't pull our guns because they have been telling us all summer not to do that. We got out of the car and proceeded to join the other officers there in forming a line so's to disperse the crowd. Then we spotted that fellow in the crowd."

"Who do you mean?"

"That fellow over there." Officer Bergin pointed to the defendant at the table. "That soldier, Irving Williams."

"Go on," said the black detective, not turning to look at the defendant.

"Well, he had on this red costume and a cape, and he was wearing this big red turban. He was also carrying a big black shield right outta Tarzan and he had that big long cane waving it around in the air."

"Where is that cane now?"

"We took it off him later. That's it over there."

The black detective moved over to his own table and picked up a long brown leather cane. He pressed a small button beneath its handle and then drew out from the interior of the cane a thin, silver-white rapier, three feet long.

"Is this the same cane?"

"Yes sir," the white officer said.

"Go on, Officer."

"Well, he was waving it around in the air and he had a whole lot of these colored people behind him and it looked to me that he was gonna charge the police line. So me and Tommy left the line and went in to grab him before he could start something big. That crowd was getting mean. The looked like they was gonna try something big pretty soon."

"Never mind," said the Judge. He had stopped walking now and stood at the edge of his elevated platform, just over the shoulder of the officer in the witness box. "Never mind what you thought, just get on with it."

"Yes sir." The officer pressed his hands together much tighter. "Well, Tommy and me, we tried to grab him and he swung the cane at me. Caught me right in the face here." He pointed his finger to a large red and black mark under his left eye. "So then we hadda use force to subdue him."

"What did you do, Officer?" the black detective asked.

"We hadda use the sticks. I hit him over the head once or twice, but not hard. I don't remember. Then Tommy grabbed his arms and we hustled him over to the car before these other colored people with him tried to grab us."

"Did he resist arrest?"

"Yeah. He kicked and fought us and called us lewd and lascivious names. We hadda handcuff him in the car. Then we took him down to the station and booked him for assault and battery.

"Your witness," said the black detective without turning around to face the other lawyer. He sat down at his own table and wiped his forehead and hands with a crumpled white handkerchief. He still looked very nervous but not as tough.

"May it please the Court," the defendant's black lawyer said slowly, standing and facing the pacing Judge. "I move . . ." And then he stopped because he saw that the Judge's small eyes were looking over his head, toward the back of the courtroom. The lawyer turned around and looked, and saw that everyone else in the room had also turned their heads to the back of the room. Standing against the back walls and along the left side of the room were twenty-five or so stern-faced, cold-eyed black men, all in African dashikies, all wearing brightly colored hats, and all staring at the Judge and the black detective. Philomena Brown and Jimmy Mulligan, sitting on the first bench, turned to look too, and the whore smiled but the lawyer said, "Oh hell," aloud. The men, all big, all bearded and tight-lipped, now locked hands and formed a solid wall of flesh around almost three-quarters of the courtroom. The Judge looked at the defendant and saw that he was smiling. Then he looked at the defendant's lawyer, who still stood before the Judge's bench, his head down, his shoulders pulled up towards his head. The Judge began to pace again. The courtroom was very quiet. The old men filling the second rows on both sides of the room leaned forward and exchanged glances with each other up and down the row. "Oh hell," Jimmy Mulligan said again.

Then the Judge stopped walking. "Get on with it," he told the defendant's lawyer. "There's justice to be done here."

The lawyer, whose face was now very greasy and wet, looked up at the officer, still standing in the witness box, but with one hand now at his right side, next to his gun.

"Officer Bergin," said the black lawyer. "I'm not clear about something. Did the defendant strike you *before* you asked him for the cane or *after* you attempted to take it from him?"

"Before. It was before. Yes sir."

"You *did* ask him for the cane, then?"

"Yes sir. I asked him to turn it over."

"And what did he do?"

"He hit me."

"But if he hit you before you asked for the cane, then it must be true that you asked him for the cane *after* he had hit you. Is that right?"

"Yes sir."

"In other words, after he had struck you in the face you were still polite enough to keep your hands off him and ask for the weapon."

"Yes sir. That's what I did."

"In other words, he hit you twice. Once, *before* you requested the cane and once *after* you requested it."

The officer paused. "No sir," he said quickly. "He only hit me once."

"And when was that again?"

"I thought it was before I asked for the cane but I don't know now."

"But you did ask for the cane before he hit you?"

"Yeah." The officer's hands were in prayer again.

"Now, Officer Bergin, did he hit you *because* you asked for the cane or did he hit you in the process of giving it to you?"

"He just hauled off and hit me with it."

"He made no effort to hand it over?"

"No, no sir. He hit me."

"In other words, he struck you the moment you got close enough for him to swing. He did not hit you as you were taking the cane from him?"

The officer paused again. Then he said: "No sir," He touched his face again, then put his right hand down to the area near his gun again. "I asked him for the cane and he hauled off and hit me in the face."

"Officer, are you telling this court that you did not get hit until you tried to take the cane away from this soldier, this Vietnam veteran, or that he saw you coming and immediately began to swing the cane?"

"He swung on me."

"Officer Bergin, did he swing on you, or did the cane accidentally hit you while you were trying to take it from him?"

"All I know is that he *hit me.*" The officer was sweating now.

"Then you don't know just when he hit you, before or after you tried to take the cane from him, do you?"

The black detective got up and said in a very soft voice: "I object."

The black lawyer for the defendant looked over at him contemptuously. The black detective dropped his eyes and tightened his belt, and sat down again.

"That's all right," the oily lawyer said. Then he looked at the officer again. "One other thing," he said. "Was the knife still inside the cane or drawn when he hit you?"

"We didn't know about the knife till later at the station."

"Do you think that a blow from the cane by itself could kill you?"

"Object!" said the detective. But again his voice was low.

"Jivetime Uncle Tom motherfucker!" someone said from the back of the room. "Shave that Afro off your head!"

The Judge's eyes moved quickly over the men in the rear, surveying their faces and catching what was in all their eyes. But he did not say anything.

"The prosecution rests," the black detective said. He sounded very tired.

"The defense calls the defendant, Irving Williams," said the black lawyer.

Williams took the stand and waited, head high, eyes cool, mouth tight, militarily, for the Clerk to swear him in. He looked always toward the back of the room.

"Now Mr. Williams," his lawyer began, "tell this court in your own words the events of the night of July twenty-seventh of this year."

"I had been to a costume party." William's voice was slow and deliberate and resonant. The entire courtroom was tense and quiet. The old men stared, stiff and erect, at Irving Williams from their second-row benches. Philomena Brown settled her flesh down next to her lawyer, who tried to edge away from touching her fat arm with his own. The tight-lipped Judge Bloom had reassumed the pacing behind his bench.

"I was on leave from the base," Williams went on, "and I was coming from the party when I saw this group of kids throwing rocks. Being in the military and being just out of Vietnam, I tried to stop them. One of the kids had that cane and I took it from him. The shield belongs to me. I got it in Taiwan last year on R and R. I was trying to break up the crowd with my shield when this honkie cop begins to beat me over the head with his club. Police brutality. I tried to tell . . ."

"That's enough," the Judge said. "That's all I want to hear." He eyed the black men in the back of the room. "This case isn't for my court. Take it upstairs."

"If Your Honor pleases," the black lawyer began.

"I don't," said the Judge. "I've heard enough. Mr. Clerk, make out the papers. Send it upstairs to Cabot."

"This court has jurisdiction to hear this case," the lawyer said. He was very close to being angry. "This man is in the service. He has to ship out in a few weeks. We want a hearing today."

"Not in my court you don't get it. Upstairs, and that's *it!*"

Now the blacks in the back of the room began to berate the detective. "Jivetime cat! Handkerchief-head flunky! Uncle Tom motherfucker!" they called. "We'll get *you,* baby!"

"Get them out of here," the Judge told the policeman named Bergin. "Get them the hell out!" Bergin did not move. "Get them the hell out!"

At that moment Irving Williams, with his lawyer behind him, walked out of the courtroom. And the twenty-five bearded black men followed them. The black detective remained sitting at the counsel table until the Clerk asked him to make way for counsel on the next case. The detective got up slowly, gathered his few papers, tightened his belt again and moved over, his head held down, to a seat on the right side of the courtroom.

"Philomena Brown!" the Clerk called. "Philomena Brown! Come into Court!"

The fat whore got up from beside Jimmy Mulligan and walked heavily over to the counsel table and lowered herself into one of the chairs. Her lawyer was talking to Ralph, the Italian boy's counsel.

"Do a good job, Jimmy, please," Ralph said. "Old Bloom is gonna be awful mean now."

"Yeah," said Jimmy. "I got to really work on him."

One of the old men on the second row leaned over the back of the bench and said to Jimmy: "Ain't that the one that's married to a nigger?"

"That's her," said Jimmy.

"She's gonna catch hell. Make sure they give her hell."

"Yeah," said Jimmy. "I don't see how I'm gonna be able to try this with a straight face."

"Do a good job for me, please, Jimmy," said Ralph. "The kid's name is Angelico. Ain't that a beautiful name? He ain't a bad kid."

"Don't you worry, I'll do it." Then Jimmy moved over to the table next to his client.

The defendant and the arresting officer were sworn in. The arresting officer acted for the state as prosecutor and its only witness. He had to refer to his notes from time to time while the Judge paced behind his bench, his head down, ponderous and impatient. Then Philomena Brown got in the witness box and rested her great weight against its sides. She glared at the Judge, at the Clerk, at the officer in the box on the other side, at Jimmy Mulligan, at the old men smiling up and down the second row, and at everyone in the courtroom. Then she rested her eyes on the officer.

"Well," the officer read from his notes. "It was around one-thirty A.M. on the night of July twenty-eighth. I was working the night duty around the combat zone. I come across the defendant there soliciting cars. I had seen the defendant there soliciting cars on previous occasions in the same vicinity. I had then on previous occasions warned the defendant there about such activities. But she kept on doing it. On that night I come across the defendant soliciting a car full of colored gentlemen. She was standing on the curb with her arm leaning up against the door of the car and talking with these two colored gentlemen. As I came up they drove off. I then arrested her, after informing her of her rights, for being a common streetwalker and a public nuisance. And that's all I got to say."

Counsel for the whore waived cross-examination of the officer and proceeded to examine her.

"What's your name?"

"Mrs. Philomena Brown."

"Speak louder so the Court can hear you, Mrs. Brown."

She narrowed her eyes at the lawyer.

"What is your religion, Mrs. Brown?"

"I am a Roman Catholic. Roman Catholic born."

"Are you presently married?"

"Yeah."

"What is your husband's name?"

"Rudolph Leroy Brown, Jr."

The old men in the second row were beginning to snicker and the Judge lowered his eyes to them. Jimmy Mulligan smiled.

"Does your husband support you?"

"Yeah. We get along all right."

"Do *you* work, Mrs. Brown?"

"Yeah. That's how I make my living."

"What do you do for a living?"

"I'm a file clerk."

"Are you working now?"

"No. I lost my job last month on account of a bad leg I got. I couldn't move outta bed."

The men in the second row were grinning and others in the audience joined them in muffled guffaws and snickerings.

"What were you doing on Beaver Avenue on the night of July twenty-eighth?"

"I was looking for a job."

Now the entire court was laughing and the Judge glared out at them from behind his bench as he paced, his arms clasped behind his back.

"Will you please tell this court, Mrs. Brown, how you intended to find a job at that hour?"

"These two guys in a car told me they knew where I could find some work."

"As a file clerk?"

"Yeah. What the hell else do you think?"

There was here a roar of laughter from the court, and when the Judge visibly twitched the corners of his usually severe mouth, Philomena Brown saw it and began to laugh too.

"Order! Order!" the Clerk shouted above the roar. But he was laughing.

Jimmy Mulligan bit his lip. "Now, Mrs. Brown, I want you to tell me the truth. Have you ever been arrested before for prostitution?"

"Hell no!" she fired back. "They had me in here a coupla time but it was all a fluke. They never got nothing on me. I was framed, right from the start."

"How old are you, Mrs. Brown?"

"Nineteen."

Now the Judge stopped pacing and stood next to his chair. His face was dubious: very close and very far away from smiling. The old men in the second row saw this and stopped laughing, awaiting a cue from him.

"That's enough of this," said the Judge. "I know you. You've been up here seven times already this year and it's still summer. I'm going to throw the book at you." He moved over to the left end of the platform and leaned down to where a husky, muscular woman Probation Officer was standing. She had very short hair and looked grim. She had not laughed with the others. "Let me see her record," said the Judge. The manly Probation Officer handed it up to him and then they talked together in whispers for a few minutes.

"All right, *Mrs. Brown,*" said the Judge, moving over to the right side of the platform near the defendant's box and pointing his finger at her. "You're still on probation from the last time you were up here. I'm tired of this."

"I don't wanna go back up there, Your Honor," the whore said. "They hate me up there."

"You're going back. That's it! You got six months on the State. Maybe while you're there you can learn how to be a file clerk so you can look for work during the day."

Now everyone laughed again.

"Plus you get a one-year suspended sentence on probation."

The woman hung her head with the gravity of this punishment.

"Maybe you can even learn a *good* profession while you're up there. Who knows? Maybe you could be a ballerina dancer."

The courtroom roared with laughter. The Judge could not control himself now.

"And another thing," he said. "When you get out, keep off the streets. You're obstructing traffic."

Such was the spontaneity of laughter from the entire courtroom after the remark that the lawyer Jimmy Mulligan had to wipe the tears from his eyes with his finger and the short-haired Probation Officer smiled, and even Philomena Brown had to laugh at this, her final moment of glory. The Judge's teeth showed through his own broad grin, and Ralph, sitting beside his Italian, a very pretty boy with clean, blue eyes, patted him on the back enthusiastically between uncontrollable bursts of laughter.

For five minutes after the smiling Probation Office led the fat whore in a miniskirt out of the courtroom, there was the sound of muffled laughter and occasional sniffles and movements in the seats. Then they settled down again and the Judge resumed his pacings and the Court Clerk, very slyly wiping his eyes with his sleeve, said in a very loud voice: "Angelico Carbone! Angelico Carbone! Come into Court!"

☆ Psychiatric Services

by Joyce Carol Oates

". . . not *depression,* then?"

"I wouldn't define it that way, no. That's listless, indifferent, isn't it, that's all-life-drained-out, like some of my own patients. . . . No, it's a confusion of all the genres, I've sifted through everything I know, I use my mind on myself but I can't come to any diagnosis. . . ."

"Whom do you fantasize killing?"

"I can't come to any diagnosis."

". . . what fantasies do you have?"

". . . I don't have time for fantasies."

"What fantasies might you have, if you had time?"

"Haha, that's a very good line. . . . Well, we all have had fantasies, haven't we, of murdering people? . . . other people? That must go back into my childhood, it must go back, oh, Jesus, twenty years . . . doesn't everyone have these fantasies?"

"I don't think everyone does, necessarily."

"Didn't *you?*"

"I'm a woman."

". . . What bothers me is the suicide fantasies, which are new."

"What means do you use?"

"Not that programmed."

"What is it, a thought, an emotion . . .? A cluster of thoughts . . .? Is it something that hasn't yet coalesced?"

"I'm sure it has, when I've been asleep, but when I wake up I

JOYCE CAROL OATES (b. 1938) is a prolific author of many works of fiction, including *Expensive People* (1968); *Them* (1969); *Wonderland* (1971); and *The Goddess and Other Women* (1974).

can't remember. . . . When I'm on duty over there I wake up and can't remember anything about myself, anything private . . . if I'm being paged I hear the name, a code name, *Saul Zimmerman,* but they could be paging anyone, they could be reading off numbers; all I know is that I respond . . . getting like a fireman: the way I suppose firemen must respond. All body."

"What means would you use?"

"Hypodermic? No. I'm too young . . . it was a rumor, Edward Aikley killed himself, did you know that? . . . must have been a hypo, if anything. No, it's something stronger . . . violent . . . *visual* somehow . . . not with pills, like the poor crazy poisoned kids they bring us. . . . No, God. Did you know of Dr. Aikley?"

"No. . . . When did you begin your residency at County General?"

". . . It isn't procedure, is it, to notify them? . . . My supervisor, uh, you're not going to notify him, are you?"

"Who is he?"

"Feucht, and he knows about some of this, I mean I've talked with him a little, he's fairly nice . . . he's interesting . . . says I'm tired."

"But you disagree with him?"

"Agree, disagree, what does it matter? You know how it is . . . who's your supervisor? . . . agree, disagree, it makes no difference whatsoever. The disturbing thing is that I'm not as tired as I should be. Everyone else is worn out, but I keep going . . . especially in the last few weeks, when I think of *it,* I mean a kind of doubleness comes over me . . . right there in the emergency ward, doing all the things, a kind of double sense, double vision . . . uh, I would define it as a mental-visual hallucination, but the word hallucination is too strong . . . hey, don't write that down! . . . No, it's too strong; there's nothing visual about it. You didn't write it down? Okay, I'll tell you: I feel very . . . I feel very powerful at those times, when I think of it, because it's, uh, the secret . . . that nobody else knows. The mess in there! . . . 900 people a day we get . . . most of them are black, of course . . . how is it over here? . . . of course, you get more students; black or white, they're better patients. But Christ, the mess. . . . So it occurs to me that I know the way out, the way they're all groping for but can't discover . . . *they don't know enough.* So in a crazy way . . . don't write that down, please, in a peculiar way, not serious, not intellectually *serious,* in a peculiar way I feel superior to them and even to the staff . . . even to my supervisor. . . . I think of *it.* The means wouldn't matter. Messes carried in here are instructional . . . I never got such specific instruction at Northwestern, where I went to medical school . . . I mean, it's so clear how and why the poor bastard blew it: some of them shoot themselves in the forehead at such an angle that the bullet ploughs up through the skull, or they try for the heart but shatter the collar bone . . . *they don't know enough.* And the ones who take poison take too much or too little. . . . So I feel very, I would say very superior . . . and I feel very masculine . . . so I don't get tired the way my friends do, which is good for my ego, I feel very masculine and I feel young again."

"How old are you?"

"Twenty-eight."

"Yeh, fine. Okay. A scrupulous detailed report, nice handwriting. But I read between the lines and am not impressed: an exhibitionist."

"But he did seem very nervous. . . . He talked rapidly, he kept making small jokes and grimaces and asides . . . he looked as if he hadn't slept for a while. I asked him if he had been taking anything and he said a little Librium, but it didn't seem to help and—"

"Who's his supervisor?"

"He didn't say."

"So? So ask him."

"I . . . he. . . . He was out in the corridor waiting with everyone else . . . dressed in old clothes, he hadn't shaved, looked sullen and frightened . . . no one would have guessed who he was, I mean that he was a resident. If they had guessed, someone else would have grabbed him, but as it was I got him. . . . I had the impression he was disappointed to draw me."

"Why, because you're a woman?"

"Yes, of course."

"Ha! The little whiner, the bastard, he wants sympathy and

someone to talk to, of course he prefers a woman . . you'll discover it to be a life-pattern in certain personalities. . . . How tall is he?"

"Medium height."

"Innocuous. All of it is innocuous."

"He's twenty-eight."

"I can see that here. . . . Okay, fine. Now who's this, what is this? *Deller?*"

"Yes, you remember, she was the—"

"I don't remember. Stop trembling."

". . . black woman, in the school system here . . . teaches fourth grade. . . ."

"Jenny, does your behavior with your patients resemble your behavior with me?"

"I. . . . I don't know."

"Do you sit there on the edge of your seat, are your lips bluish with fear? . . . do you lower your head like that just very very slightly—no, don't move!—so that you can gaze at them through your lashes? Don't be offended, Jenny, why shouldn't you show yourself to your best advantage? Have you sense enough to determine what is your best advantage, however?"

"Dr. Culloch, I . . ."

"You're an attractive woman, why shouldn't you live your life to the fullest? . . . However, there's no need to be so nervous with me; what are the rumors, eh? . . . what have you heard about me, eh?"

"I wish you wouldn't laugh at me, Dr. Culloch."

"Who's laughing? . . . this is chuckling, sighing, this is a sympathetic noise from across the desk. But you! If you're angry, go red instead of white in the face . . . much healthier. Nothing wrong with healthy anger."

"I'm not angry. . . ."

"Nothing wrong with healthy anger."

"I know, but I'm not angry, Dr. Culloch."

"Aren't you?"

"No. No."

"What is all that passion, then?—all that trembling?"

"Dr. Culloch, I wish you wouldn't do this—"

"Are you happy here?"

"Oh yes. Yes."

"We treat women better here, better than the boondocks where you interned; this is a livelier place in every way, do you agree? . . . So you're happy. So stay happy."

"Yes, Dr. Culloch."

". . . no, you're not disturbing me. . . . What time is it?"

". . . You were asleep, weren't you. I lose track of the time myself . . . it's probably around two or three . . . my watch is untrustworthy and I can't see any clocks from here. . . . I'm sorry for waking you up, did I wake you up?"

"It's all right. It doesn't matter."

". . . been wanting to call you all evening, but I didn't get a break until now. I'm on the fourteenth floor, staff lounge, do you know the layout here?"

"No."

". . . The thing is, I feel awfully shaky and embarrassed, I mean about the official nature of it. . . . You aren't going to report back to Feucht, are you?"

"Who? . . . No."

"Okay. Jesus, I'm sorry to wake you; I'll hang up now."

"No, wait—"

"And the reason I didn't show up for the second appointment, I didn't even remember it until a few hours later—a friend of mine was sick, I had to take over for him off and on—I wanted to call you and explain but so much time went by I figured what the hell, you'd forgotten. . . . I'll hang up now."

"No. How are you? Do you feel better?"

". . . I would say so, yes. Sometimes I feel very happy. That sensation of power I mentioned . . . it's rather encouraging at times. I realize this is absurd, I realize how crazy it sounds . . . God, I hope nobody's tapping this telephone! . . . I know I should hang up. . . . The reason I called you is, I feel a little strange. There's this sensation of power, of happiness, like I used to have as a boy occasionally, and when I was in high school, playing football, occasionally I'd have it also . . . a surge of joy, a pulsation of joy. . . ."

"Euphoria?"

'Euphoria. Do you know what it's like? . . . Being carried along by the pulse of it, of *it*, whatever *it* is. . . . So much excitement, so much life and death outside me, carrying me along with it, along with the flow of it. One of my patients died on me, hemorrhaged all over me, I just kept talking to him and didn't allow either of us to get excited. . . . So I thought I would call you. I've been thinking about you, but I haven't diagnosed my thinking. I'm sorry to have missed the appointment. . . . Could I come see you?"

"Now?"

"Yes."

"Of course not. No. What do you want?"

"Dr. Feucht tells me there's nothing wrong—I'm exaggerating. He says new residents always exaggerate, dramatize. Maybe that's all it is . . . maybe it's nothing real. . . . I can't come see you then?"

". . . in love with you, eh? Don't be coy!"

"Dr. Culloch, please—"

"A long nocturnal conversation—special considerations—is this what they taught you in Baltimore, Jenny? The John F. Kennedy Clinic, did they teach you such things there?"

"He missed his appointment and sounded very excited over the phone . . . I don't know how he got my number, there must be so many *Hamiltons* in the city. . . ."

"He isn't seriously disturbed; he's pleading for your special attention, your love. . . . You'll learn to recognize these symptoms and not to be flattered by them."

"I'm sorry, Dr. Culloch, but I—"

"Being professional is the acquisition of a single skill: not to let them flatter you into thinking you're—what? Eh? *God,* eh?— Or *Venus?*"

"But . . . but Dr. Zimmerman . . . Saul. . . . Why did you bring that here? Why . . . What are you going to do with that?"

"Don't be frightened!"

"Saul—"

"The last three or four days I've been awake straight through, by my own choice. I don't want to be a zombie, I want more control. . . . Don't be so alarmed, I just brought it to show you: it's rather handsome, isn't it? I'm not going to hurt you. I wouldn't hurt *you.* From where you sit, it probably looks like a toy gun, maybe; it's amazing how life-like the toy guns are, and how toy-like the real ones are . . . makes your head spin. There's a difference in price though."

"Is that a real gun?"

". . . insulting . . . castrating. . . . No, you're very nice, the first time I saw you out in the hall I thought *She's nice, any nut would have a chance with her* . . . remind me of a cousin of mine, haven't seen for years, slight little girl with freckles, pale skin. . . . It's an insult, to ask a person whether he's carrying a toy gun, don't you know that? Don't insult me. Under the circumstances I must strike you as strange enough, but not so strange that I can't give you professional advice . . . don't insult them when they're armed. . . . I'm just joking. I'm really just joking. . . . The only women at County General are the nurses. I don't think they like me."

". . . You'd better give that to me, you know. To me. You'd better . . ."

"Certainly not. Why should I give it to you?"

"I think it would be a good idea if . . . if you gave it to me."

"Why? It's my own discovery. It's my secret. I want to share it with you in a way, but I don't intend to give it to you."

"But you can't be serious! . . . Why did you bring it here, wrapped up like that—what is that, a towel?—why did you bring it here, if you don't really want to give it to me? You—you really want to give it to me—don't you? Wouldn't that be better?—You've put me in such a terrible position—I'm sure I should report you—it—you've made me an accessory to—"

"To what? I have a permit for it."

"A permit? You have . . . ?"

". . . walked into the police station down the block from the hospital, bought a permit, went to a gun store, bought the gun. . . . They're expensive but I didn't buy much ammunition. . . . You know I'm just fooling around with this, don't you? . . . just fooling around. I certainly don't intend to use it, on myself or anyone."

"That's right. That's right. . . . Obviously, you brought it here this afternoon to give to me, didn't you? . . . to give to me?"

"It's the smallest size. They have enormous ones . . . with

longer barrels so that you can take better aim . . . something so small, so the man told me, has a poor aim, the bullet is likely to veer off in any direction. I don't know anything about guns. Not even rifles. I'm from Winnetka. I didn't have a father interested in hunting. It's amazing, all the things I don't know . . . don't have experience of. Now it's too late."

"Saul, why don't you let me keep the gun for you? Please?"

"I do have a permit for it. . . . However, not for carrying it on my person; I don't have a permit to carry a concealed weapon. So maybe I'd better give it to you after all. . . . But can I have it back when I'm well?"

"You're not sick."

"Yes, but when I'm well can I have it back? . . . I can pawn it at the same place I bought it; the man might remember me."

"Yes, of course you can have it back . . . I'll keep it in my desk drawer here . . . I can lock it, this desk is assigned to me for the year . . . no one can open it except me . . . I promise . . . I promise that . . ."

". . . only afraid that if I surrender it I'll lose this feeling I have most of the time . . . it helps me get through the night shift especially. . . . With one part of my mind I realize that it's absurd, that the whole thing is absurd . . . I did my stint in psychiatrics too, and I must say I hated it . . . really hated it . . . my supervisor was a bastard, and that wasn't just my private opinion either. I realize it's absurd that I'm talking to you because you don't know anything more than I do, maybe less, you're sitting there terrified and the only advantage I have over you is that I'm not terrified . . . but if I give *it* up I might lapse into being terrified . . . and . . . I've always been so healthy, that's the goddam irony. I *am* healthy. Kids dropped out of school, blew their minds entirely, wound up in the expensive asylums along the lake, but not me, not *me,* and my father would go crazy himself if he knew I was having therapy three times a week with *you.* . . . He could do so much more for me! . . . I can hear his voice saying those words, his whining voice. . . . The one thing I'm ashamed of and must apologize for is frightening you, Dr. Hamilton."

". . . I'm not frightened. . . ."

". . . Feucht is away for a conference, Hawaii, he says it's ordinary nerves and exaggeration, I know he's right . . . but where does he get the strength from? . . . Aikley, they said he killed himself, did you hear that? . . . no, you didn't know him . . . what it is, is, something to circle around, a fixed place . . . a thought . . . the thinking of it, the possibility of *it* . . . what is it, transcendence? . . . At the same time I'm an adolescent, obnoxious bastard, to come over here and frighten a pretty young woman like you."

". . . aren't you going to give me the gun? . . . to put in the desk drawer?"

". . . maybe I only want revenge, maybe it's simplistic revenge against the usual people . . . the usual innocent people: my father, my mother. Sometimes I think that if it were possible for me to wipe out my own father, my personal father, I might get to something more primary . . . but . . . uh . . . it's difficult to talk about these things, I really don't know how to talk about them. I don't have the vocabulary. . . . must tell you, a kid in emergency hallucinating . . . shrieking and laughing and really blown . . . *very happy* . . . hadn't a good vein left in him. . . . All I want is to wipe out a few memories and start again from zero but the memories accumulate faster than I can even notice them, faster faster faster . . . all the time. But how do you wipe the memories away without blowing away the brain?"

". . . This is the drawer, see? . . . and I have the key for it, here. Here."

"Okay."

"Thank you. Thank you."

". . . sorry to be so . . ."

"Thank you very much, Saul, thank you . . . now, you see? . . . Dr. Zimmerman? . . . you see, I'm locking it up, it's your property and I can even, I can even give you a receipt for it . . . yes, I'll be happy to . . . I'll . . ."

"Are you all right? . . . not going to faint?"

"I—"

"Are you going to faint? Jesus!"

"No, I'm all right—I'm all right—"

"You sure?"

"I've never fainted in my life."

". . . sorry to be disturbing you again . . . you weren't

asleep, were you? . . . answered the phone on the first ring, you weren't asleep, were you?"

"No. What do you want, Saul?"

". . . just to apologize, I feel I've made such a fool of myself . . . and it isn't fair to involve you . . . you're younger than I am, aren't you? . . . you have lots of other patients assigned to you, God, I hope they're not as troublesome as I . . . because you know, don't you, Jenny, *you know* . . . I'm really harmless; I'm just temporarily troubled about something. It isn't uncommon."

"I understand. I'm not angry, I'm not frightened . . . well, I admit that I was a little frightened at the hospital today . . . I shouldn't have been so easily upset . . . but the gun itself, seeing it, the gun shocked me . . . it was so real."

"Yes! It was so *real*. So that struck you too?"

"Oh yes it struck me . . . it struck me too."

"Where do you live, Jenny? The operator doesn't give out that kind of information, she says . . . you're not listed in the new directory, are you, you're new to the city just like me. . . . Could I come over or is it too late?"

"It's too late, it's very late, Saul."

"What time is it?"

". . . very late. Please. Why don't you visit me at the hospital tomorrow, wouldn't that be soon enough?"

"I realize I'm disturbing you but I had the sense . . . the sensation . . . that you aren't married . . . ? I mean, there's no husband there with you, is there?"

"I'll see you tomorrow. I'll squeeze you in somehow . . . somehow . . . or . . . or, please Saul, please, we could talk in the first-floor cafeteria, at the back, I'll wait for you there at noon . . . we can talk there . . . please."

"Look: you demanded I give you the gun. And I did. I obeyed you. *Good boy* you probably thought, *good boy, look how he obeys*. Now you lose interest in me. . . . What do you care what I've been going through?"

"I care very much. . . ."

". . . I noticed a fly crawling out of some guy's nostril over here, some very old black guy in a coma for five days . . . filling up with maggots, he was, wasn't even dead, they're jammed in here and so stinking sick . . . and the pathologist making jokes about it . . . I wondered if *he* was the one I had wanted to kill and got very upset, to think I'd lost the gun. . . ."

". . . *What?*"

"What?"

"What about that man?"

". . . cardiac seizure, he wasn't that old . . . fifty-five, sixty . . it's hard to tell, they're so wrecked when they come in. . . . We're busy over here. . . What kind of a tone did you take with me? . . You sound *annoyed*."

"What about that man?—I don't believe—"

"What, are you annoyed that I woke you up? Hey look: we're in this together. I trusted you, didn't I, and you promised me, didn't you, and there's a professional bond between us . . . I'm not just another patient off the streets, off the campus, there's a professional bond between us, so don't take that tone with me. I order people around too: all the time, in fact. I order women around all the time. And they obey me. You bet they obey me! So don't you take that annoyed tone with me."

"Saul, I'm not annoyed—but I think you must be—must be imagining—must be exaggerating—"

". . . the purpose of this call was, I think it was . . . uh . . . to apologize for frightening you earlier today. And to ask you to keep it private, all right? The business about the gun. I mean, don't include it on your report, will you, you needn't tell him everything. . . . Don't be annoyed with me, please, I think I'll be through it soon . . . out the other side, soon . . . I'll be rotated to obstetrics in seventeen days which should be better news . . . unless some freaky things happen there too . . . it's a different clientele here, you know, from what I was accustomed to. . . . Hey look: don't be annoyed with me, you're my friend, don't be annoyed that I almost caused you to faint today."

"I didn't faint . . . I didn't come near to fainting."

". . . well, if . . ."

"I've never fainted in my life."

"You *what?*—Oh, you romantic girl! You baby!"

". . . What? I don't understand. Did I do something wrong, Dr. Culloch?"

"Wrong? Wrong? *Everything you have done is wrong.* Oh, it would be comic if not so alarming, that you came to us knowing so little—so meagerly trained—Had you only textbook theory, you could have handled that problem more professionally! And with the background you have, before the Baltimore clinic you were where? Nome, Alaska?—an adventuresome young woman, not a lily, a wilting fawning creature—and a year at that girls' detention home or farm or whatever in Illinois—*didn't you learn anything?* To be so manipulated by a cunning paranoid schizophrenic—to have him laughing up his sleeve at you—"

"But—"

"But! Yes, *but.* But but but.—You did exactly the wrong thing in taking that gun away from him. *Don't you know anything?*"

". . . I did the wrong thing, to take it away . . . ?"

"Absolutely. Now, you explain to *me* why it was wrong."

"It was wrong?"

". . . why it was idiotic, imbecilic."

". . . but . . . It was wrong because . . . it must have been wrong because . . . because . . . I affirmed his suicidal tendencies? Is that it, Dr. Culloch? . . . I affirmed his suicidal tendencies . . . I took him seriously . . . therefore . . ."

"Go on."

". . . therefore . . . I indicated that he didn't have rational control and responsibility for his own actions . . . yes, I see . . . I think I see now . . . it was a mistake because I showed him that in fact I didn't trust him: I took him at his word, that he would commit suicide."

"Not only that, my dear, let's have some fun with you . . . eh? Under cover of being the Virgin Mary and mothering him out of your own godliness, you in fact used it as a cover, the entire session, to act out your own willfulness and envy of men. . . . Eh? What do you say? Ah, blushing, blushing! . . . And well you might blush, eh? . . . So you turn him loose, the pathetic little bastard, a castrated young man turned loose . . . and you have the gun, eh? . . . locked up safely, eh? . . . so you gloat about it and can't wait to rush in here to let me know the latest details, eh? Fortunate for you that Max Culloch has been around a long time . . . a very very long time . . . and knows these little scenarios backwards and forwards."

"Dr. Culloch—are you joking?"

"Joking? I?"

"Sometimes you—you tease us so—"

"If you silly little geese giggle, can I help it? I have a certain reputation for my wit, I do admit it, and a reputation—wholly unearned, I tell you in all modesty—as—what?—eh?—being rather young for my age, eh?—is that what they gossip about?—but you won't gossip with them, Jenny, will you? Of this year's crop you are *very* much the outstanding resident; I tell you that frankly. . . . Only because you struck me originally as being so superior can I forgive you for this asinine blunder: affirming a paranoid schizophrenic in his suicidal delusions."

"I did wrong . . . I did wrong, then, in taking the gun from him?"

"Don't squeak at me in that little-mouse voice, you're a woman of passion and needn't make eyes at me and look through your hair . . . and don't sit like that, as if you're ashamed of your body, why be ashamed? . . . you're attractive, you know it, your physical being is most attractive and *it* senses that power whether you do or not, Dr. Hamilton . . . right? I'm decades older than you, my dear, I'm seventy-three years old and I know so much, so very much, that it's sometimes laughable even to deal with ordinary people. . . . It's become a burden to me because it obliges me to take so seriously and so politely the opinions of my ignorant colleagues . . . when I'd like simply to pull switches, shut them up, get things done as they must be done. At least you young people don't argue with me: you know better. . . . So. Let us review this fascinating lesson, Jenny. What did you do wrong?"

"I did wrong to take the gun from him and to affirm his suicidal inclinations. And . . . and he had a permit for the gun, too . . . at least to own a gun. . . . It wasn't illegal, his owning the gun. . . . And so I was exerting power over him. . . ."

"Gross maternal power, yes. The prettier and smaller you girls are, the more demonic! . . . Your secret wish right this moment, Jenny, is—is what? eh? You'd like to slap old Dr. Culloch, wouldn't you?"

"Not at all—"

"Someday we'll let you; why be so restrained? . . . But at the moment, I think it wisest for you to undo the harm you've done to that poor boy. You'd better telephone him and ask him to come over and take the gun back."

". . . ask him to take it back?"

". . . or is he your lover, and you would rather not call *him?*"

"He isn't my lover!"

". . . who is, then? Or have you many?"

"I haven't any lovers! I have my work. . . ."

"Yet you're attracted to him, aren't you? I can literally smell it—I can smell it—the bizarre forms that love-play can take—"

"I'm not attracted to him, I feel sorry for him—I—I'm not attracted to him. I have my work . . . I work very hard . . . I don't have time for . . ."

"*I* am your work."

". . . Yes."

"Yes what?"

"Yes, that's so."

"Everything is processed through me. Everything in this department. . . . Do you dream about me?"

"Yes, of course."

"And what form do I take?"

"What form? . . . The form . . . the form you have now."

"No younger?"

"I . . . I don't know. . . . Dr. Culloch, this is so upsetting to me, it's so confusing and embarrassing. . . . I never know when you're joking and when you're serious."

"I am always joking and always serious. You may quote me."

". . . I've become so mixed up during this conversation, I can't remember what . . . what we were talking about. . . ."

". . . not that I'm the Max Culloch of even eight years ago. . . . Yeh, pot-bellied, going bald, with this scratchy scraggly beard . . . but . . . *but.* You understand, eh? Many a young rival has faded out of the dreamwork entirely when old Max appears. It's nature. . . . The one thing I don't like, Jenny, is the possibility of your arranging this entire scenario with the aim of manipulating Max. . . . I wouldn't like that at all. *Did you?*"

"Did I . . . ?"

"Play with the boy, take the gun, rush into my office this morning just to tantalize me with your power? . . . force me to discipline you? . . . No, I rather doubt it; you're cunning, but not *that* cunning. No. I'm inclined to think it was a simple error, one of inexperience rather than basic ignorance, and that it shouldn't be held against you. It's only nature, that you would like to manipulate me. But you haven't a clue, my child, as to the means."

". . . I . . . I . . . Yes, that's right. You're right."

"Of course I'm right."

". . . nothing was intentional, nothing at all. When I saw the gun I followed my instincts . . . my intuition . . . I forgot to analyze the situation in terms of its consequences . . . when I saw the gun I thought *No, I don't want him to die, no, I like him, I don't want*—So I acted without thinking."

"And did you faint in his arms, my dear?"

"Of course not."

"Love-play on both sides. Totally unconscious, totally charming. Do you see it now, rationally?"

"I . . . I didn't see it at the time, but now . . . now . . . you're probably right."

"Probably?"

"You're right."

"And so?"

". . . and . . . ?"

"And so what will you do next?"

"I . . . I will telephone him and admit my error."

"And?"

". . . tell him I misjudged him . . . that he can pick the gun up any time he wants it . . . I'll tell him that my supervisor has . . ."

"No, no. No sloughing off of authority!"

". . . tell him . . . tell him that I trust him . . . and . . . it was an emotional error on my side . . . inexperience . . . fear. . . . I trust him and . . . and I know he'll be safe with the gun. . . ."

"Go on, go on! You'll have to speak to him more convincingly than that. And smile—yes, a little—yes, not too much—try to avoid that bright manic grin, Jenny, it looks grotesque on a woman with your small facial features. . . . The boy is an idealist like everyone, and like everyone he must learn . . . as I learned and you will, eh? . . . or will you? . . . he's an idealist and stupid that way but not so stupid that he wouldn't be able to see through that ghastly smile of yours. I have the impression,

Jenny, that you don't believe me: that you're resisting me. Are you trying to antagonize me?"

"No, of course not! I'm . . . I'm just very nervous. I didn't sleep at all last night. I'm very nervous and . . ."

"Chatter, chatter! . . . So you've given your young friend his gun back . . . you've made things right between you again . . . yeh, fine, fine. Now what?"

"Now . . . ?"

"Now what do you say? Will you say anything further?"

". . . I will say that . . . that he'll be rotated out of the service he's in, and he'll be eventually out of the hospital . . . maybe he'll have a private practice in the area . . . his home-town is north of here, along the lake . . . and . . . and . . . and he'll escape, he'll forget. . . . I can't remember what I was saying."

"What a goose! . . . At any rate, what do you think *he* will say? When you give him his masculinity back?"

"He'll say. . . ."

"Think hard!"

"He'll say . . . probably . . . He'll probably say *Thank you.*"

"*Thank you?*"

". . . *Thank you.*"

☆☆☆ A&P

by John Updike

In walks these three girls in nothing but bathing suits. I'm in the third checkout slot, with my back to the door, so I don't see them until they're over by the bread. The one that caught my eye first was the one in the plaid green two-piece. She was a chunky kid, with a good tan and a sweet broad soft-looking can with those two crescents of white just under it, where the sun never seems to hit, at the top of the backs of her legs. I stood there with my hand on a box of HiHo crackers trying to remember if I rang it up or not. I ring it up again and the customer starts giving me hell. She's one of these cash-register-watchers, a witch about fifty with rouge on her cheekbones and no eyebrows, and I know it made her day to trip me up. She'd been watching cash registers for fifty years and probably never seen a mistake before.

By the time I got her feathers smoothed and her goodies into a bag—she gives me a little snort in passing, if she'd been born at the right time they would have burned her over in Salem—by the time I get her on her way the girls had circled around the bread and were coming back, without a pushcart, back my way along the counters, in the aisle between the checkouts and the Special bins. They didn't even have shoes on. There was this chunky one, with the two-piece—it was bright green and the seams on the bra were still sharp and her belly was still pretty pale so I guessed she just got it (the suit)—there was this one, with one of those chubby berry-faces, the lips all bunched together under her nose, this one, and a tall one, with black hair that hadn't quite frizzed

JOHN UPDIKE (b. 1932) is the author of eight novels, including *Rabbit Run* (1960) and *Rabbit Redux* (1971), and four short-story collections, the most recent being *Museums and Women* (1972).

right, and one of these sunburns right across under the eyes, and
a chin that was too long—you know, the kind of girl other girls
think is very "striking" and "attractive" but never quite makes it,
as they very well know, which is why they like her so much—and
then the third one, that wasn't quite so tall. She was the queen.
She kind of led them, the other two peeking around and making
their shoulders round. She didn't look around, not this queen, she
just walked straight on slowly, on these long white prima-donna
legs. She came down a little hard on her heels, as if she didn't
walk in her bare feet that much, putting down her heels and then
letting the weight move along to her toes as if she was testing the
floor with every step, putting a little deliberate extra action into
it. You never know for sure how girls' minds work (do you really
think it's a mind in there or just a little buzz like a bee in a glass
jar?) but you got the idea she had talked the other two into
coming in here with her, and now she was showing them how to
do it, walk slow and hold yourself straight.

She had on a kind of dirty-pink—beige maybe, I don't know—
bathing suit with a little nubble all over it and, what got me, the
straps were down. They were off her shoulders looped loose
around the cool tops of her arms, and I guess as a result the suit
had slipped a little on her, so all around the top of the cloth there
was this shining rim. If it hadn't been there you wouldn't have
known there could have been anything whiter than those shoulders. With the straps pushed off, there was nothing between the
top of the suit and the top of her head except just *her,* this clean
bare plane of the top of her chest down from the shoulder bones
like a dented sheet of metal tilted in the light. I mean, it was
more than pretty.

She had sort of oaky hair that the sun and salt had bleached,
done up in a bun that was unravelling, and a kind of prim face.
Walking into the A&P with your straps down, I suppose it's the
only kind of face you *can* have. She held her head so high her
neck, coming up out of those white shoulders, looked kind of
stretched, but I didn't mind. The longer her neck was, the more
of her there was.

She must have felt in the corner of her eye me and over my
shoulder Stokesie in the second slot watching, but she didn't tip.
Not this queen. She kept her eyes moving across the racks, and
stopped, and turned so slow it made my stomach rub the inside of

my apron, and buzzed to the other two, who kind of huddled against her for relief, and then they all three of them went up the cat-and-dog-food-breakfast-cereal-macaroni-rice-raisins-sea-sonings-spreads-spaghetti-soft-drinks-crackers-and-cookies aisle. From the third slot I look straight up this aisle to the meat counter, and I watched them all the way. The fat one with the tan sort of fumbled with the cookies, but on second thought she put the package back. The sheep pushing their carts down the aisle— the girls were walking against the usual traffic (not that we have one-way signs or anything)—were pretty hilarious. You could see them, when Queenie's white shoulders dawned on them, kind of jerk, or hop, or hiccup, but their eyes snapped back to their own baskets and on they pushed. I bet you could set off dynamite in an A&P and the people would by and large keep reaching and checking oatmeal off their lists and muttering "Let me see, there was a third thing, began with A, asparagus, no, ah, yes, apple-sauce!" or whatever it is they do mutter. But there was no doubt, this jiggled them. A few houseslaves in pin curlers even looked around after pushing their carts past to make sure what they had seen was correct.

You know, it's one thing to have a girl in a bathing suit down on the beach, where what with the glare nobody can look at each other much anyway, and another thing in the cool of the A&P, under the fluorescent lights, against all those stacked packages, with her feet paddling along naked over our checkerboard green-and-cream rubber-tile floor.

"Oh Daddy," Stokesie said beside me. "I feel so faint."

"Darling," I said. "Hold me tight." Stokesie's married, with two babies chalked up on his fuselage already, but as far as I can tell that's the only difference. He's twenty-two, and I was nine-teen this April.

"Is it done?" he asks, the responsible married man finding his voice. I forgot to say he thinks he's going to be manager some sunny day, maybe in 1990 when it's called the Great Alexandrov and Petrooshki Tea Company or something.

What he meant was, our town is five miles from a beach, with a big summer colony out on the Point, but we're right in the middle of town, and the women generally put on a shirt or shorts or something before they get out of the car into the street. And anyway these are usually women with six children and varicose veins mapping their legs and nobody, including them, could care less. As I say, we're right in the middle of town, and if you stand at our front doors you can see two banks and the Congregational church and the newspaper store and three real-estate offices and about twenty-seven old freeloaders tearing up Central Street because the sewer broke again. It's not as if we're on the Cape; we're north of Boston and there's people in this town haven't seen the ocean for twenty years.

The girls had reached the meat counter and were asking McMahon something. He pointed, they pointed, and they shuffled out of sight behind a pyramid of Diet Delight peaches. All that was left for us to see was old McMahon patting his mouth and looking after them sizing up their joints. Poor kids, I began to feel sorry for them, they couldn't help it.

Now here comes the sad part of the story, at least my family says it's sad, but I don't think it's so sad myself. The store's pretty empty, it being Thursday afternoon, so there was nothing much to do except lean on the register and wait for the girls to show up again. The whole store was like a pinball machine and I didn't know which tunnel they'd come out of. After a while they come around out of the far aisle, around the light bulbs, records at discount of the Caribbean Six or Tony Martin Sings or some such gunk you wonder they waste the wax on, sixpacks of candy bars, and plastic toys done up in cellophane that fall apart when a kid looks at them anyway. Around they come, Queenie still leading the way, and holding a little gray jar in her hand. Slots Three through Seven are unmanned and I could see her wondering between Stokes and me, but Stokesie with his usual luck draws an old party in baggy gray pants who stumbles up with four giant cans of pineapple juice (what do these bums *do* with all that pineapple juice? I've often asked myself) so the girls come to me. Queenie puts down the jar and I take it into my fingers icy cold. Kingfish Fancy Herring Snacks in Pure Sour Cream: 49¢. Now her hands are empty, not a ring or a bracelet, bare as God made them, and I wonder where the money's coming from. Still with that prim look she lifts a folded dollar bill out of the hollow at the center of her nubbied pink top. The jar went heavy in my hand. Really, I thought that was so cute.

Then everybody's luck begins to run out. Lengel comes in from haggling with a truck full of cabbages on the lot and is about to scuttle into that door marked MANAGER behind which he hides all day when the girls touch his eye. Lengel's pretty dreary, teaches Sunday school and the rest, but he doesn't miss that much. He comes over and says, "Girls, this isn't the beach."

Queenie blushes, though maybe it's just a brush of sunburn I was noticing for the first time, now that she was so close. "My mother asked me to pick up a jar of herring snacks." Her voice kind of startled me, the way voices do when you see the people first, coming out so flat and dumb yet kind of tony, too, the way it ticked over "pick up" and "snacks." All of a sudden I slid right down her voice into her living room. Her father and the other men were standing around in ice-cream coats and bow ties and the women were in sandals picking up herring snacks on toothpicks off a big glass plate and they were all holding drinks the color of water with olives and sprigs of mint in them. When my parents have somebody over they get lemonade and if it's a real racy affair Schlitz in tall glasses with "They'll Do It Every Time" cartoons stencilled on.

"That's all right," Lengel said. "But this isn't the beach." His repeating this struck me as funny, as if it had just occurred to him, and he had been thinking all these years the A&P was a great big dune and he was the head lifeguard. He didn't like my smiling—as I say he doesn't miss much—but he concentrates on giving the girls that sad Sunday-school-superintendent stare.

Queenie's blush is no sunburn now, and the plump one in plaid, that I liked better from the back—a really sweet can—pipes up, "We weren't doing any shopping. We just came in for the one thing."

"That makes no difference," Lengel tells her, and I could see from the way his eyes went that he hadn't noticed she was wearing a two-piece before. "We want you decently dressed when you come in here."

"We *are* decent," Queenie says suddenly, her lower lip pushing, getting sore now that she remembers her place, a place from which the crowd that runs the A&P must look pretty crummy. Fancy Herring Snacks flashed in her very blue eyes.

"Girls, I don't want to argue with you. After this come in here with your shoulders covered. It's our policy." He turns his back. That's policy for you. Policy is what the kingpins want. What the others want is juvenile delinquency.

All this while, the customers had been showing up with their carts but, you know, sheep, seeing a scene, they had all bunched up on Stokesie, who shook open a paper bag as gently as peeling a peach, not wanting to miss a word. I could feel in the silence everybody getting nervous, most of all Lengel, who asks me, "Sammy, have you rung up their purchase?"

I thought and said "No" but it wasn't about that I was thinking. I go through the punches, 4, 9, GROC, TOT—it's more complicated than you think, and after you do it often enough, it begins to make a little song, that you hear words to, in my case "Hello (*bing*) there, you (*gung*) hap-py pee-pul (*splat*)!"—the *splat* being the drawer flying out. I uncrease the bill, tenderly as you may imagine, it just having come from between the two smoothest scoops of vanilla I had ever known were there, and pass a half and a penny into her narrow pink palm, and nestle the herrings in a bag and twist its neck and hand it over, all the time thinking.

The girls, and who'd blame them, are in a hurry to get out, so I say "I quit" to Lengel quick enough for them to hear, hoping they'll stop and watch me, their unsuspected hero. They keep right on going, into the electric eye; the door flies open and they flicker across the lot to their car, Queenie and Plaid and Big Tall Goony-Goony (not that as raw material she was so bad), leaving me with Lengel and a kink in his eyebrow.

"Did you say something, Sammy?"

"I said I quit."

"I thought you did."

"You didn't have to embarrass them."

"It was they who were embarrassing us."

I started to say something that came out "Fiddle-de-doo." It's a saying of my grandmother's, and I know she would have been pleased.

"I don't think you know what you're saying," Lengel said.

"I know you don't," I said. "But I do." I pull the bow at the back of my apron and start shrugging it off my shoulders. A couple customers that had been heading for my slot begin to knock against each other, like scared pigs in a chute.

Lengel sighs and begins to look very patient and old and gray. He's been a friend of my parents for years. "Sammy, you don't want to do this to your Mom and Dad," he tells me. It's true, I

don't. But it seems to me that once you begin a gesture it's fatal
not to go through with it. I fold the apron, "Sammy" stitched in
red on the pocket, and put it on the counter, and drop the bow tie
on top of it. The bow tie is theirs, if you've ever wondered.
"You'll feel this for the rest of your life," Lengel says, and I
know that's true, too, but remembering how he made that pretty
girl blush makes me so scrunchy inside I punch the No Sale tab
and the machine whirs "pee-pul" and the drawer splats out. One
advantage to this scene taking place in summer, I can follow this
up with a clean exit, there's no fumbling around getting your coat
and galoshes, I just saunter into the electric eye in my white shirt
that my mother ironed the night before, and the door heaves itself
open, and outside the sunshine is skating around on the asphalt.

I look around for my girls, but they're gone, of course. There
wasn't anybody but some young married screaming with her
children about some candy they didn't get by the door of a
powder-blue Falcon station wagon. Looking back in the big
windows, over the bags of peat moss and aluminum lawn furniture stacked on the pavement, I could see Lengel in my place in
the slot, checking the sheep through. His face was dark gray and
his back stiff, as if he'd just had an injection of iron, and my
stomach kind of fell as I felt how hard the world was going to be
to me hereafter.

☆ ☆
☆ ☆
A Man at the Top
of His Trade

by Ward Just

He told them to hold all calls, except any that might come from her. There was no reason for her to call, but that was no guarantee that she wouldn't. She often called. Once several weeks ago she'd called and insisted on being put through, and there'd been an awkward five minutes while he muttered into the telephone and the others sat silently looking at their fingernails or otherwise pretending that they weren't listening. Of course, they couldn't hear what he was saying; he normally spoke into the phone in a guttural, a tone so soft that it couldn't be heard more than a foot away. That night when he asked her about it she'd laughed and said her only demand on him was instant access. When she was blue and wanted to talk, he'd have to listen. That was his half of the bargain.

His colleagues were due now, five of them. He'd had the chairs arranged just so, in a semicircle in front of his desk. Ashtrays within easy reach. Pads and pencils on the chairs. There was a conference room across the hall, but Stone didn't like it. The conference room was formal, and this discussion did not need formality. At exactly ten thirty they had a radio hookup with Browne.

Stone lit a cigarette, thinking about Browne. He'd be preparing his notes now in the tank in the basement of the embassy, the lead-lined color-coordinated "module" sunk like a squash court below the foundations of the building. It was a completely secure room; Stone had helped with the design. Data banks lined one

WARD JUST (b. 1935) is the author of *To What End: Report from Vietnam* (1968); *A Soldier of the Revolution* (1970); *Military Men* (1970); *The Congressmen Who Loved Flaubert* (1973); and *Stringer* (1974).

wall; the technology was phenomenal: computers scrambled the voice at one end and unscrambled it at the other, a fresh matrix for each transmission. That had been the true breakthrough. The number of available matrices was virtually infinite, encoding and decoding accomplished in two and a half seconds. Stone had made a hundred transmissions from that same office, before they'd made him an inside man. In his mind's eye he saw Browne sitting in the swivel chair, checking the control panel. He smiled; thirty minutes in the tank could seem a brief life.

Browne felt the same way. Their careers and personalities were similar in many ways; perhaps there was a pattern to their trade. They worked well together, always had; it was on Stone's strong recommendation that Brown had succeeded him as chief of station in C—. And he'd been excellent, though the station had declined in importance. However, that was no fault of Browne's: it was a reflection of changing times and attitudes and priorities. Now Browne was out too: this was his last operation. He could not see Browne as an inside man any more than he had seen himself as an inside man, two years ago. But Browne would adapt. He would be very good as an inside man, though he worried about the girl. Chris. When Browne left C— Chris would go with him. Well, he was a professional. Stone and Browne were both professionals.

The buzzer sounded, and Stone picked up the telephone. The five of them were in the outer office, waiting.

They would have thirty minutes of discussion before the transmission. The split was two to two, with Otto on the fence as usual. All of them understood that the decision was Stone's, but if the disagreement was profound, they'd be obliged to file a dissent. They knew that Stone would want to avoid that. Stone did not like what he called "pieces of paper" circulating around the building. Stone had a passion for unanimity.

Stone opened the discussion. "The position is this. Browne has to have a definite go or no-go by 11 A.M. It's short notice, but it can't be helped. Everything in the way of transport is laid on. If the decision is go, Browne meets his man"—Stone looked over the tops of his eyeglasses, smiling—"under the clock at the Biltmore . . ." This was the customary euphemism; there was no need for these men to know where the meeting was taking place; that was an operational detail strictly under Stone's control. ". . . at noon. Browne and his man get in the car. There's a second car and a third car. Classic procedure, and we anticipate no difficulties. We've got an airplane that will have him in Brussels in three hours and at Andrews by tomorrow morning." He looked at his watch. "Comment?"

"You have no doubts about his authenticity?"

"Browne is completely confident," Stone said.

Otto asked, "And you?"

"I have doubts about everything. I always have doubts; that's one reason I'm here. But I've satisfied myself that he's genuine."

"What makes Browne so sure?"

Stone hesitated a moment before replying. "Instinct."

"The approach came out of the blue, is that right?"

Stone nodded. "Over the transom."

"A week ago?"

"No, three days. And he wanted to do it now. Right now."

Jason McAlvin looked at Otto, then at Stone. "The procedure seems sound, and I agree that he's probably genuine. In the past we've gone on a lot less. But I think the main question is, What does he have? What can he give us? And the answer to that is, military intelligence. Right?" McAlvin looked at the men grouped around the desk. "Well, we're quite up to date on that. I have a sufficiency of information. I believe that what we'll get from this man is corroboration. Useful but not decisive. I don't think he'll be able to give us much that is new. Perhaps a scrap here and there. But hell's bells, when you think of the effort that's going to go into it. *His* care and feeding for the next year, maybe two years. That's a lot of coin for small beer. What is he, anyway?" McAlvin shrugged his shoulders and lit a cigarette. "A colonel? We could no doubt get some cute details from him. Personalities, procedures. It's interesting reading, but in this case I don't think it's worth it. Worth the time, the effort, and the money. I recommend no-go."

"Browne thinks it's worth it." Stone said. "Very much."

"This is his last run, isn't it?"

Stone looked at McAlvin, a restless, fluid man; his wiry body seemed almost boneless. He'd never been an operator in the field. He was strictly an inside man. Stone said, "Yes."

"It would be a nice coup for him," McAlvin said.

Stone turned to Bricker and Stein, sitting impassively, listening to the discussion. Bricker spoke first. "It doesn't sound high-risk to me. My reaction is, why not? Even if we got just one nugget, it would be worth it."

Stein was doubtful. "Normally, in cases of this kind, I like to go with the man in the field. So long as everything else holds up. However, in this case . . ."

"What's different about this case?" Stone asked quickly.

"It's always a temptation . . . this is Browne's last operation. It's always a temptation to ride out on a big success. There hasn't been much happening in his area lately. Isn't that right? This is the first good news we've had from Browne in a long time. And what the hell, it's Jason's section. If Jason says he has all he needs . . ."

McAlvin interrupted with a wave of his hand. "You never have all you need. I merely meant to indicate there are limits."

"Well, either way. In fact, this operation sounds quite high-risk to me. High-risk versus a possible no-gain. Or no, not *no*-gain; minimum-gain. I'm a persuadable, but on the evidence so far I'm inclined to counsel no-go."

Stone turned to Carmichael, who had said nothing. Carmichael was the youngest man in the room by ten years, an economist by training; he was the director's man. "Bill?"

Carmichael said, "I'd like to hear what Browne says on the radio."

Stone had been aware of the white light blinking on his telephone. He picked up the receiver and tucked it into his chin, his mouth a quarter of an inch from the perforated black plastic. He heard her low laugh and then his name with a question mark. He said nothing. "I love you," she said at last and hung up. He waited a few moments before replacing the phone. In ten minutes Browne would come on circuit.

She turned away from the bedside table and walked downstairs to the kitchen to make another cup of coffee. That evil secretary of his; it had taken her five minutes to get by the secretary. "Is Mr. Stone in?" "Who is calling, please?" "Miss Morris." "He's in a meeting right now, Miss Morris." "Oh, my. A meeting." "I'm sorry." "I just wanted a very quick word with him." Silence. "It wouldn't take more than half a minute." "He'll be out of the meeting at noon." "But it is important." Silence. "Very." "One moment please," the secretary said, and put her on hold. Finally the connection was made, and she heard him breathing. She'd watched him talk on the telephone a thousand times and could see him now, his eyes focused elsewhere as he listened. He didn't say *anything,* that was typical. She'd asked him about that once and he'd apologized and explained that it was part of his telephone technique; he hated telephones, and when he used them, he thought of the old down-east expression. Better to close your mouth and be thought a fool than open it and remove all doubt. She did not understand how that pertained to her, *them;* but she'd let it go. He was very attentive in other ways. If he did not choose to be attentive on the telephone, that was all right. Still, a word now and again; a word wouldn't have hurt. She prepared a cup of instant and turned on the FM. Bach, they were playing Bach. The rhythmic logic of Bach enchanted her. She smiled to herself, then laughed out loud.

Browne's voice came from the receiver evenly and naturally. It was as if they were in the same room. He spoke for only five minutes, a complete report, concise and informative, no wasted words.

Stone looked around the room, satisfied. "Comment?"

Otto asked, "No doubts about authenticity?"

Browne's voice sounded a trifle bored. "None."

"And everything is laid on?"

"To a 'T,' " Browne said.

They were all silent a moment, watching each other. It was apparent that Browne had covered all the bases. Then Jason McAlvin cleared his throat. "One question. I didn't understand from your . . . presentation. How did he come to you?"

"He approached us. It was strictly over the transom, out of the blue. No cleverness on our part," he said disarmingly.

McAlvin said, "I know that. I know that, it was in the preliminary report. I mean exactly *how*. How the approach was made. And to whom."

"To a girl who works here in the embassy."

"Ah," McAlvin said. He paused, waiting for Browne to continue. But the radio was silent. McAlvin smiled. "Well, if it isn't demanding too much. One wouldn't want to pry," he said archly. "But where. When. And how."

Browne said, "Three days ago. In a café. A note. It's all quite genuine."

"And what is the girl's name?"

"She works for me," Browne said. Then he was silent again.

"Is that generally known? That she works for you?"

"I suppose the other side knows it," Browne said.

"The plot thickens," McAlvin said. He was doodling on his yellow pad, a series of connected boxes. He was carefully inking in each box.

Stone thought it was time to cut this off. McAlvin was making mischief, as usual. Stone switched off the receiver so the six of them could talk among themselves. "In what way does the plot thicken, Jason?"

"Well, these are facts I hadn't known. I thought our man had made a normal approach to one of the embassy officers. I hadn't known it was made to Browne's . . . secretary. Or whoever she is, Browne wasn't exactly precise. That changes the bidding, don't you think? He knew who she was, obviously he knows who Browne is."

"Be a damned poor intelligence man if he didn't," Stone said irritably. "He's a colonel of intelligence. That's the sort of information he'd have as a matter of course, for Christ's sake."

"Well, yes . . ."

"He made an approach to his opposite number. Not to Browne directly; he knows that Browne's watched. That would have been obvious and dangerous. So he goes to his secretary."

"Yes, indeed," McAlvin said. "That's slightly less dangerous than going to Browne himself."

Stone switched on the receiver and turned to McAlvin. "Put the question to Browne."

"We were talking here," McAlvin said suavely. "Why do you suppose the approach was made to your secretary? Isn't that a bit dangerous? Or stupid?"

Browne said, "It all seems quite straightforward to me. A classic approach, no surprises. It seems to me"—his voice showed signs of impatience. Stone thought—"that the authenticity can easily be established by you people there. Once we have the bird in hand. My assignment is to pick him up and get him out of the country. Which I am prepared to do. And give you my evaluation of his worth, which I am also prepared to do; have done, in fact. Let me go over the salient points again . . ."

"With all the details of the approach, please," said McAlvin.

The radio was silent; Stone knew that Browne was waiting for some sign or signal. Perhaps some sign of support. Stone said, "Proceed."

"The approach was made on the fifth of May. The girl, whose name is Chris DuPage, has a coffee in the same café every morning at nine . . ."

Stone was listening carefully; there was something new in Browne's voice. It was something irregular. He could hear it even through the scrambling and the metallic quality of radio transmission. There was a tone and timbre he couldn't identify. Browne was being too casual. Stone knew the approach had been made through the girl; it was not unusual, though it was risky. This was Browne's girl, the one he intended to bring back with him. She was a very solid girl; Stone had known her for years. He listened to Browne talk, and suddenly something else forced its way into Stone's mind. It was a hunch from nowhere, one question, just one, and when Browne had finished, Stone asked it. "Had they ever met before?"

"Not to my knowledge," Browne said slowly.

Stone was silent a moment, along with the others. He knew what that meant. It was lawyers' talk, and not responsive. Stone looked at the radio speaker, his expression betraying nothing. He said, "We'll get back to you." Browne started to protest, but Stone didn't wait for him to finish. He switched off the radio. The operation was dead. "We'll get back to you" meant no-go.

"What happened today?" She asked the question playfully, not expecting an answer. To questions about his work he seldom answered her in any responsive way. Of course, she knew what he did but had no idea whatever how he did it or what was involved. She had no idea of the details of his professional life. But this time he surprised her.

"I had to kill one of Browne's operations."

"Brownie? But I thought he was on his way back."

"He is; this was his last job."

"What was it?"

"A defector. He'd picked up a defector."

She was astonished; he'd never disclosed so much before. Living with Stone was a continual surprise. More as a lark than anything else she decided to press him. "Why did you have to kill it?"

He shrugged and sipped his drink. "Brownie trimmed on me; he'd never done that before. There was no alternative, none at all. The thing began to smell. All you need is a whiff in an operation like that. One whiff, and you kill it."

"You caught a whiff," she said. "How?"

"Instinct." He lit a cigarette.

She looked at him. "Instinct?"

"Besides, this was just a marginal operation. It wasn't as if we were about to snatch Castro. This was just a"—he hesitated, smiling slightly—"third-level character. A bureaucrat. Useful to have, but far from necessary. Not necessary at all."

"Well," she said. She leaned toward him and plucked his cigarette from the ashtray and took a long drag. "Well, why did it smell?"

He said, "That's complicated."

She laughed, knowing he'd fall silent now. She had all she was going to get. From now on he'd turn every question with a joke, and finally change the conversation altogether. That was his habit. She said, "All the better. I like complicated stories."

"Well, it turns out that the contact was Chris. I knew that, but this morning I found out that she'd known him before. Known the defector. God knows how, or in what capacity. I *didn't* know that, and I should've known. Brownie should have told me. He didn't, and there was a reason behind that. The reason doesn't matter. It was enough that he withheld the information. That was enough to kill the operation."

She was fascinated and wanted to respond in such a way as to keep him talking. "But . . . it might have been innocent."

"I'm sure it was," Stone said.

"But if it was innocent . . . ?"

"He withheld, that was reason enough. Innocent or sinister, it makes no difference."

"You didn't *ask* him?" She was incredulous. He and Brownie

had been friends for ten years. On the job and off it. They were as close as brothers.

"No. No point to that."

They were sitting on the back porch of Stone's house. He refilled their glasses with ice and tonic and stood looking into the garden. The roses were doing very nicely. They covered the board fence and drooped down to the flat bricks. He cultivated three varieties of roses, and one of the varieties was always blooming in the spring and summer.

She looked at him a moment, puzzled, not speaking. Then, "You really didn't ask him what it was about?"

"No, of course not. He'll be back here next month. I can ask him then."

"But the operation . . ."

"That's dead in any case."

She thought, what a strange world he lived in. A whiff of trouble. An "operation" abruptly "dead." No reconsideration. "In any case." He seemed to give no more thought to it than to the gin and tonic he was drinking. "Instinct," she said. "You said it was instinct. Is that all it is?"

"Informed by experience," he said dryly.

"And the experience . . ."

He said, "Informed by instinct."

She laughed, moving closer to him. "Oh, that's very helpful. May I quote that, Mr. Stone?" She looked at him a moment, wondering whether to pursue. No, that was useless. She was amazed that he'd told her as much as he had. On the other hand, she knew them both. Browne and the girl. She and Stone had seen a lot of them in the old days. The girl, Chris, had been particularly kind. "Was Chris trying to pull . . . something funny?"

"I don't know. I doubt it. You know her better than I do. What do you think?"

"I can't imagine," she said. "Chris was always careful in her work. Devoted to Brownie. I can't imagine her . . ." She let the sentence hang. "It'll be nice having them back here, won't it?"

"Yes," Stone said.

"Well," she said. "Thanks for telling me."

He said, "Thanks for the phone call."

"You didn't say anything."

"I was in a meeting."

"Well, you could've said, 'Thanks,' Or, 'Me, too.' Or just anything."

"I should've, you're right."

She said, "I feel lonely in the mornings. After you've gone to work. It's nice to hear your voice, I like it . . ." She told him then about the day she'd had, cleaning the house, talking to a friend on the telephone; two invitations for dinner, a doctor's appointment. Then in the afternoon she lay down for a nap and had a bad dream. She almost never dreamed in the afternoon, and that upset her. It was her old dream about walking up a ramp to an airplane, the ramp becoming longer and longer in front of her eyes. The stewardess beckoning. She shook her head and reached for his cigarette; it was a very scary dream. She had tried to call him again, but he was out of his office. The dream frightened her, and she had stayed in her room until he'd come home. She had a headache . . .

He looked at her, nodding sympathetically. He thought. What was there about him that attracted unhappy women?

About the Editor

WILLIAM O'ROURKE, thirty-one, was born in Chicago, Illinois, and educated at the University of Missouri and Columbia University. He is the author of *The Harrisburg 7 and the New Catholic Left,* selected by *The New York Times* as one of the best books of its year, and a novel, *The Meekness of Isaac,* which won a New York State Council on the Arts CAPS award. He is currently an assistant professor in the Department of English of Rutgers University in Newark, New Jersey.

VINTAGE FICTION, POETRY, AND PLAYS

VINTAGE CRITICISM: LITERATURE, MUSIC, AND ART